WITHDRAWN

OTHER PEOPLE

by JOFF WINTERHART

DAYS OF THE BAGNOLD SUMMER
& DRIVING SHORT DISTANCES

WITHDRAWN

GALLERY 13

NEW YORK   LONDON   TORONTO   SYDNEY   NEW DELHI

GALLERY 13
AN IMPRINT OF SIMON & SCHUSTER, INC.
1230 AVENUE OF THE AMERICAS
NEW YORK, NY 10020

FIRST GALLERY 13 HARDCOVER EDITION SEPTEMBER 2018

GALLERY 13 AND COLOPHON ARE TRADEMARKS OF SIMON & SCHUSTER, INC.

FOR INFORMATION ABOUT SPECIAL DISCOUNTS FOR BULK PURCHASES, PLEASE CONTACT SIMON & SCHUSTER SPECIAL SALES AT 1-866-506-1949 OR BUSINESS@SIMONANDSCHUSTER.COM.

THE SIMON & SCHUSTER SPEAKERS BUREAU CAN BRING AUTHORS TO YOUR LIVE EVENT. FOR MORE INFORMATION OR TO BOOK AN EVENT CONTACT THE SIMON & SCHUSTER SPEAKERS BUREAU AT 1-866-248-3049 OR VISIT OUR WEBSITE AT WWW.SIMONSPEAKERS.COM.

MANUFACTURED IN THE UNITED STATES OF AMERICA

2 4 6 8 10 9 7 5 3 1

LIBRARY OF CONGRESS CATALOGING-IN-PUBLICATION DATA IS AVAILABLE.

ISBN 978-1-5011-9174-9
ISBN 978-1-5011-9175-6 (EBOOK)

DAYS OF THE BAGNOLD SUMMER

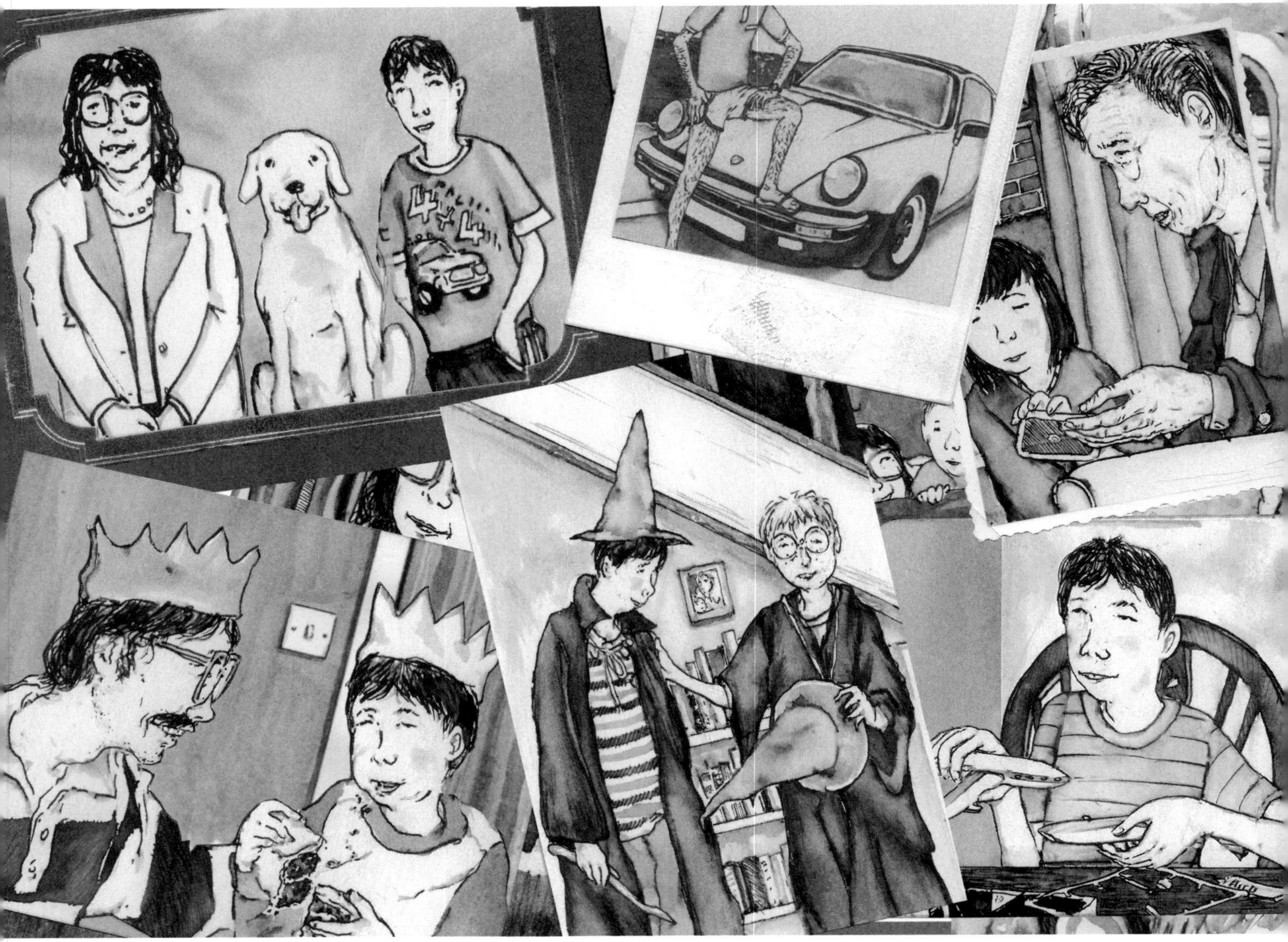

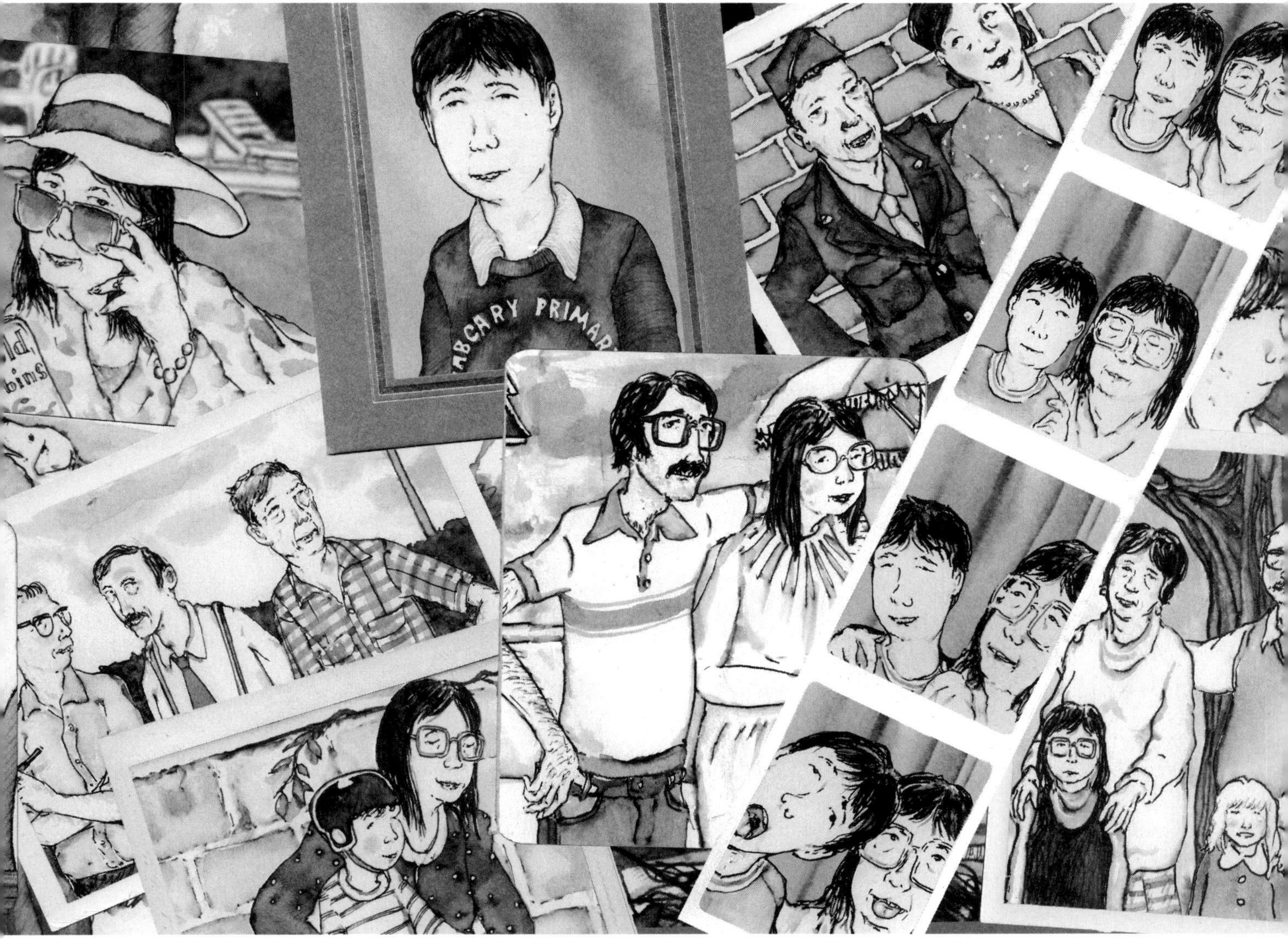

BAGNOLD

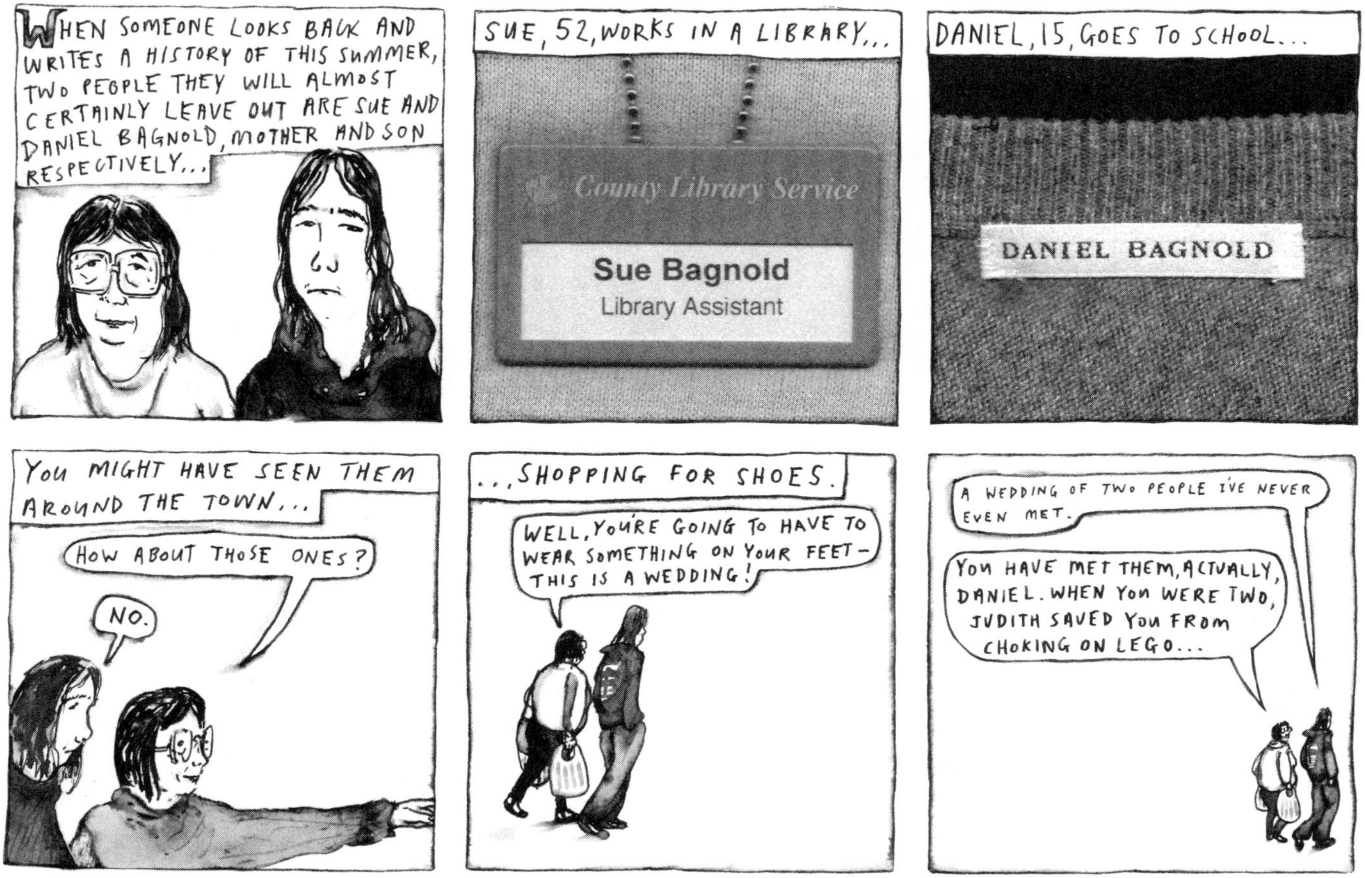
WHEN SOMEONE LOOKS BACK AND WRITES A HISTORY OF THIS SUMMER, TWO PEOPLE THEY WILL ALMOST CERTAINLY LEAVE OUT ARE SUE AND DANIEL BAGNOLD, MOTHER AND SON RESPECTIVELY...
SUE, 52, WORKS IN A LIBRARY...
County Library Service
Sue Bagnold
Library Assistant
DANIEL, 15, GOES TO SCHOOL...
DANIEL BAGNOLD
YOU MIGHT HAVE SEEN THEM AROUND THE TOWN...
HOW ABOUT THOSE ONES?
NO.
...SHOPPING FOR SHOES.
WELL, YOU'RE GOING TO HAVE TO WEAR SOMETHING ON YOUR FEET – THIS IS A WEDDING!
A WEDDING OF TWO PEOPLE I'VE NEVER EVEN MET.
YOU HAVE MET THEM, ACTUALLY, DANIEL. WHEN YOU WERE TWO, JUDITH SAVED YOU FROM CHOKING ON LEGO...

FIRST WEEK

SORRY

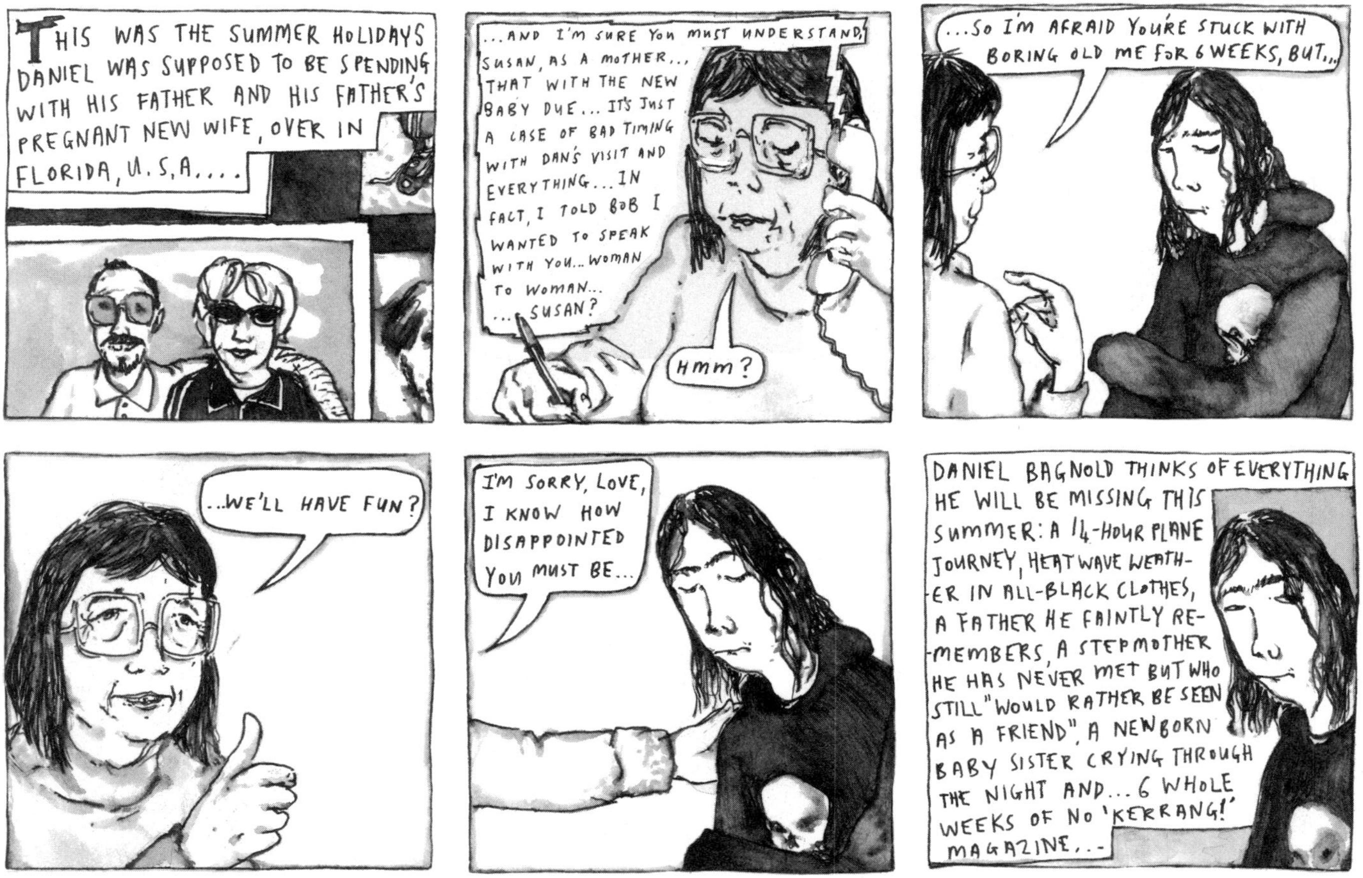
THIS WAS THE SUMMER HOLIDAYS DANIEL WAS SUPPOSED TO BE SPENDING WITH HIS FATHER AND HIS FATHER'S PREGNANT NEW WIFE, OVER IN FLORIDA, U.S.A. . . .
...AND I'M SURE YOU MUST UNDERSTAND, SUSAN, AS A MOTHER... THAT WITH THE NEW BABY DUE... IT'S JUST A CASE OF BAD TIMING WITH DAN'S VISIT AND EVERYTHING... IN FACT, I TOLD BOB I WANTED TO SPEAK WITH YOU... WOMAN TO WOMAN... ...SUSAN?
HMM?
...SO I'M AFRAID YOU'RE STUCK WITH BORING OLD ME FOR 6 WEEKS, BUT...
...WE'LL HAVE FUN?
I'M SORRY, LOVE, I KNOW HOW DISAPPOINTED YOU MUST BE...
DANIEL BAGNOLD THINKS OF EVERYTHING HE WILL BE MISSING THIS SUMMER: A 14-HOUR PLANE JOURNEY, HEATWAVE WEATH-ER IN ALL-BLACK CLOTHES, A FATHER HE FAINTLY RE-MEMBERS, A STEPMOTHER HE HAS NEVER MET BUT WHO STILL "WOULD RATHER BE SEEN AS A FRIEND", A NEWBORN BABY SISTER CRYING THROUGH THE NIGHT AND... 6 WHOLE WEEKS OF NO 'KERRANG!' MAGAZINE...

SKULL

As SUE WASHES UP...

SHE THINKS OF HOW EVERY MAN IN HER LIFE HAS LEFT HER FOR THE UNITED STATES...

HER FATHER, THE AMERICAN G I WHO MARRIED HER MOTHER DURING THE WAR, BUT LEFT TO GO BACK TO AMERICA WHEN SUE WAS SEVEN...

...AND HER EX-HUSBAND, BOB, WHO WENT AWAY TO FLORIDA "ON BUSINESS" AND NEVER CAME BACK...

UPSTAIRS, DANIEL IS IN THE BATH. HE IS THINKING OF THE BADGER SKULL HE HAS DRAWN FOR HIS GCSE ART COURSEWORK...

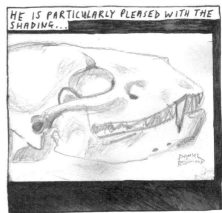

HE IS PARTICULARLY PLEASED WITH THE SHADING...

NAMES

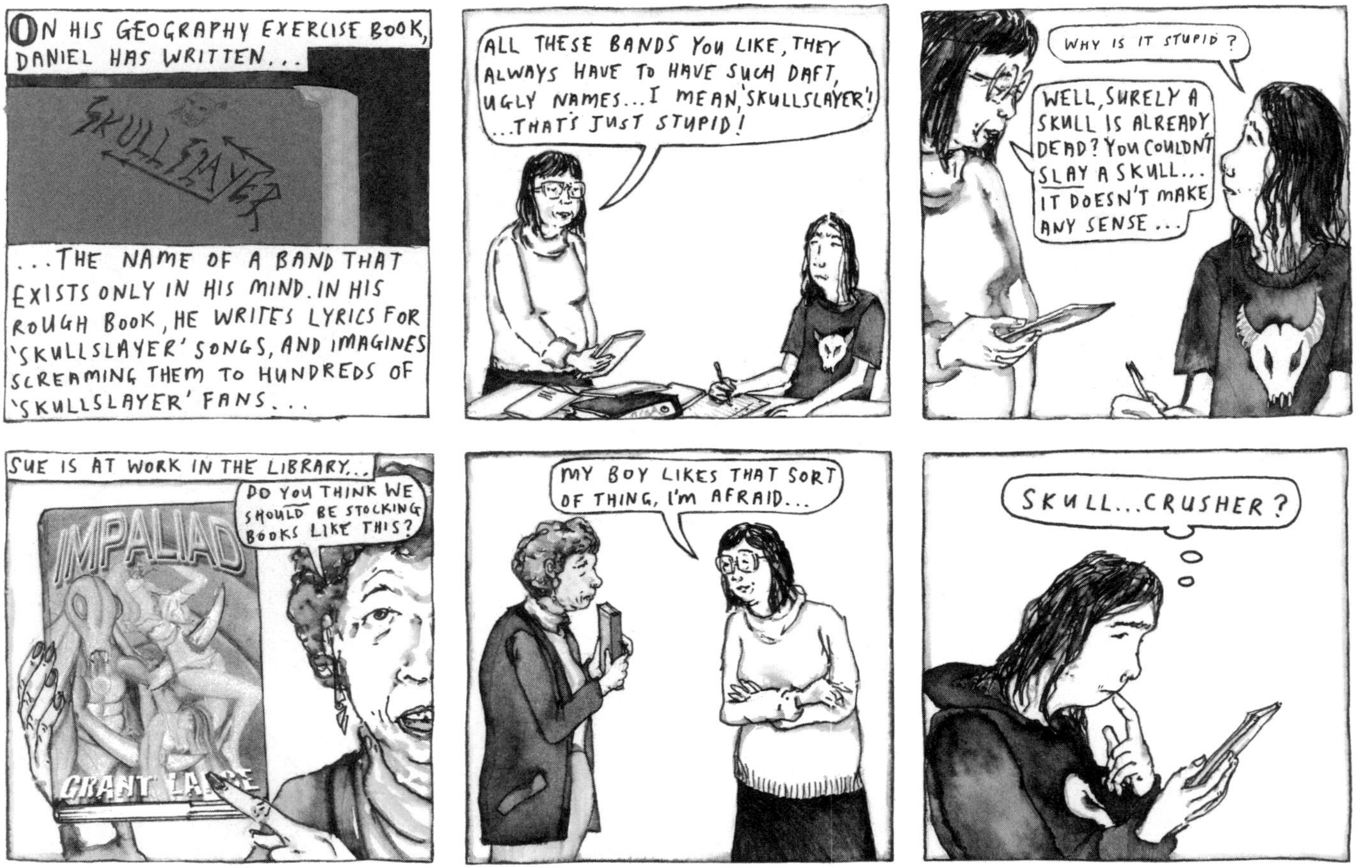

ON HIS GEOGRAPHY EXERCISE BOOK, DANIEL HAS WRITTEN...
SKULLSLAYER
...THE NAME OF A BAND THAT EXISTS ONLY IN HIS MIND. IN HIS ROUGH BOOK, HE WRITES LYRICS FOR 'SKULLSLAYER' SONGS, AND IMAGINES SCREAMING THEM TO HUNDREDS OF 'SKULLSLAYER' FANS...
ALL THESE BANDS YOU LIKE, THEY ALWAYS HAVE TO HAVE SUCH DAFT, UGLY NAMES... I MEAN, 'SKULLSLAYER'! ...THAT'S JUST STUPID!
WHY IS IT STUPID?
WELL, SURELY A SKULL IS ALREADY DEAD? YOU COULDN'T SLAY A SKULL... IT DOESN'T MAKE ANY SENSE...
SUE IS AT WORK IN THE LIBRARY...
DO YOU THINK WE SHOULD BE STOCKING BOOKS LIKE THIS?
IMPALIAD
MY BOY LIKES THAT SORT OF THING, I'M AFRAID...
SKULL...CRUSHER?

HAIR

SUE HAS TOLD DANIEL TO LOOK FOR A SUMMER JOB ON THE NOTICEBOARD IN COSTCUTTER...

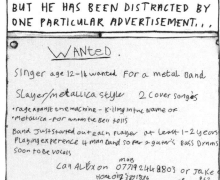

BUT HE HAS BEEN DISTRACTED BY ONE PARTICULAR ADVERTISEMENT...

WANTED.

SINger age 12-14 wanted For a metal Band

Slayer/metallica style   2 cover songs
• rage against the machine - Killing in the name of
• metallica - For whom the Bell tolls
Band Just started out each player at least 1-2 years
Playing experience 4 man Band so far 2 guitars Bass Drums
soon to be vocals
Call ALEX on 07719 244 8803 or Jake
Home 0117 3271886
Ho 0117 4362 92

DANIEL IS AMAZED BY THE FACT THAT PEOPLE HIS AGE, IN HIS TOWN, LIKING THE SAME BANDS AS HIM, ARE IN A BAND. HIS FRIEND KY LIKES THE SAME BANDS AS HIM, BUT HE IS THE SORT OF PER-SON WHO WEARS A HAT LIKE THIS IN PUBLIC...

...AND HE CAN'T PLAY ANY INSTRUMENTS.

SUE'S SISTER, CAROL, A HAIRDRESSER IS VISITING...

DO YOU REMEMBER? I SAID TO YOU... I SAID TO HIM, IF YOU GROW YOUR HAIR, IT WILL GO WRONG! I WARNED YOU, YOU JUST DON'T HAVE THE RIGHT TYPE OF HAIR FOR LONG HAIR...IT'S BAGNOLD HAIR, I'M AFRAID. YOUR DAD HAS THE SAME HAIR, IT'S QUITE THIN AND...CRINKLY.

NOW DON'T GET ME WRONG, I LIKE LONG HAIR ON MEN...

JAMES TAYLOR HAD LONG HAIR!

AND BON JOVI, GORGEOUS!

NORMALLY, THIS SORT OF CONVERSATION WOULD MAKE DANIEL GO UP TO HIS ROOM FOR THE WHOLE AFTERNOON, BUT HE IS THINKING...

SINger age 12-14 wanted For a metal Band

RECORDS

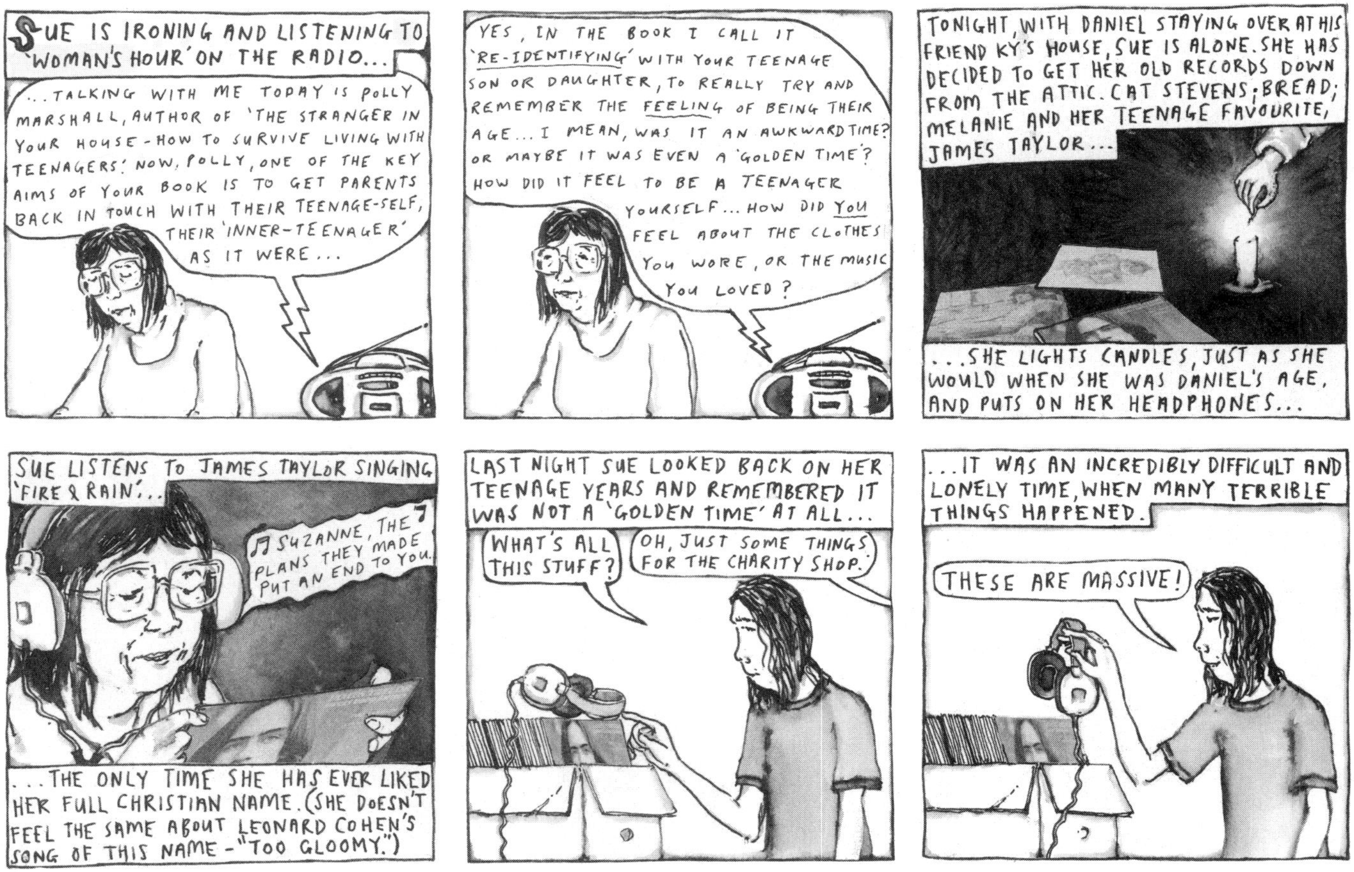
SUE IS IRONING AND LISTENING TO 'WOMAN'S HOUR' ON THE RADIO...
...TALKING WITH ME TODAY IS POLLY MARSHALL, AUTHOR OF 'THE STRANGER IN YOUR HOUSE - HOW TO SURVIVE LIVING WITH TEENAGERS.' NOW, POLLY, ONE OF THE KEY AIMS OF YOUR BOOK IS TO GET PARENTS BACK IN TOUCH WITH THEIR TEENAGE-SELF, THEIR 'INNER-TEENAGER' AS IT WERE...
YES, IN THE BOOK I CALL IT 'RE-IDENTIFYING' WITH YOUR TEENAGE SON OR DAUGHTER, TO REALLY TRY AND REMEMBER THE FEELING OF BEING THEIR AGE... I MEAN, WAS IT AN AWKWARD TIME? OR MAYBE IT WAS EVEN A 'GOLDEN TIME'? HOW DID IT FEEL TO BE A TEENAGER YOURSELF... HOW DID YOU FEEL ABOUT THE CLOTHES YOU WORE, OR THE MUSIC YOU LOVED?
TONIGHT, WITH DANIEL STAYING OVER AT HIS FRIEND KY'S HOUSE, SUE IS ALONE. SHE HAS DECIDED TO GET HER OLD RECORDS DOWN FROM THE ATTIC. CAT STEVENS; BREAD; MELANIE AND HER TEENAGE FAVOURITE, JAMES TAYLOR...
...SHE LIGHTS CANDLES, JUST AS SHE WOULD WHEN SHE WAS DANIEL'S AGE, AND PUTS ON HER HEADPHONES...
SUE LISTENS TO JAMES TAYLOR SINGING 'FIRE & RAIN'...
♫ SUZANNE, THE PLANS THEY MADE PUT AN END TO YOU.
...THE ONLY TIME SHE HAS EVER LIKED HER FULL CHRISTIAN NAME. (SHE DOESN'T FEEL THE SAME ABOUT LEONARD COHEN'S SONG OF THIS NAME - "TOO GLOOMY.")
LAST NIGHT SUE LOOKED BACK ON HER TEENAGE YEARS AND REMEMBERED IT WAS NOT A 'GOLDEN TIME' AT ALL...
WHAT'S ALL THIS STUFF?
OH, JUST SOME THINGS FOR THE CHARITY SHOP.
...IT WAS AN INCREDIBLY DIFFICULT AND LONELY TIME, WHEN MANY TERRIBLE THINGS HAPPENED.
THESE ARE MASSIVE!

SELF-EXPRESSION

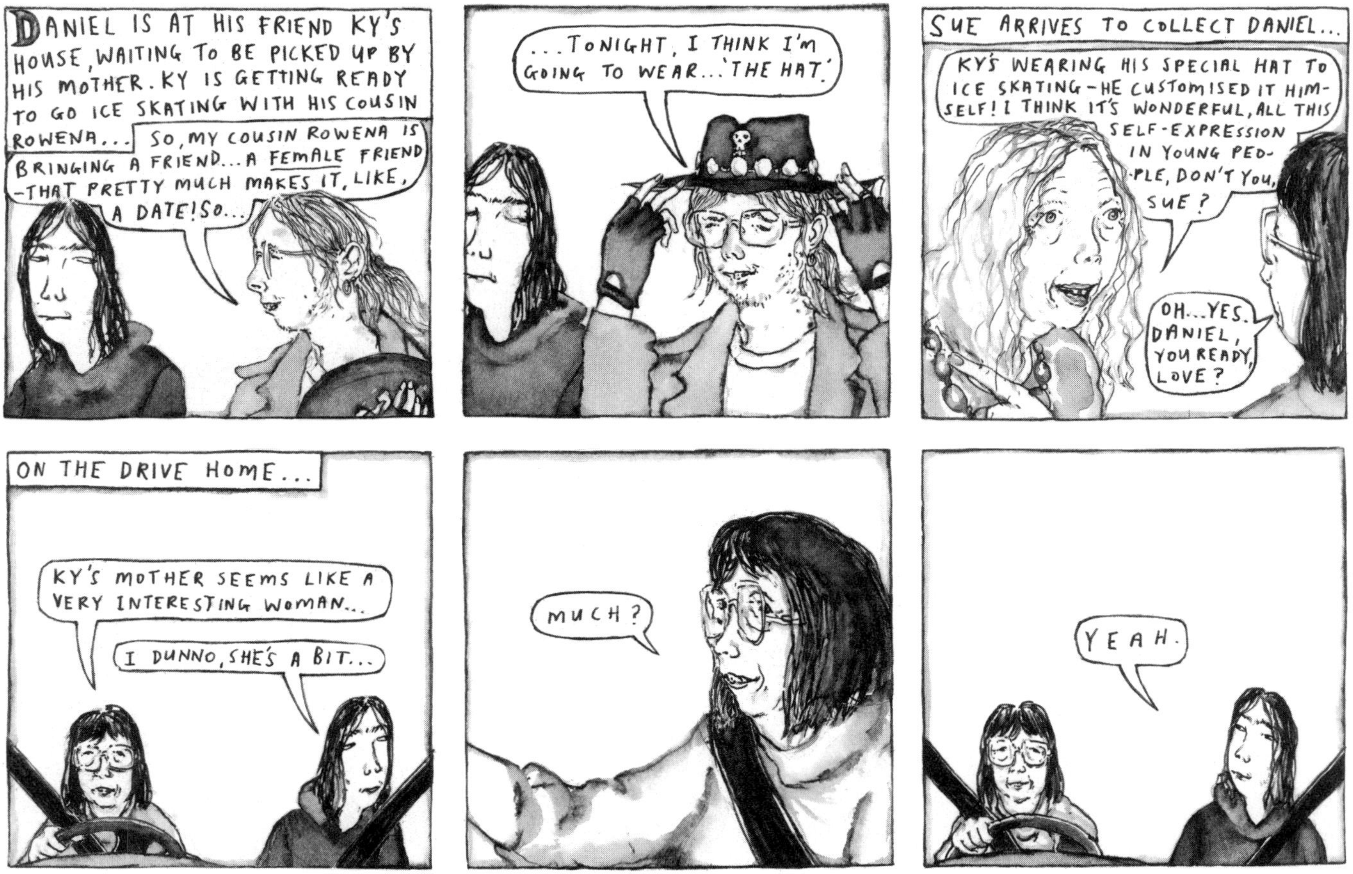

DANIEL IS AT HIS FRIEND KY'S HOUSE, WAITING TO BE PICKED UP BY HIS MOTHER. KY IS GETTING READY TO GO ICE SKATING WITH HIS COUSIN ROWENA...
SO, MY COUSIN ROWENA IS BRINGING A FRIEND... A FEMALE FRIEND -THAT PRETTY MUCH MAKES IT, LIKE, A DATE! SO...
...TONIGHT, I THINK I'M GOING TO WEAR...'THE HAT.'
SUE ARRIVES TO COLLECT DANIEL...
KY'S WEARING HIS SPECIAL HAT TO ICE SKATING - HE CUSTOMISED IT HIMSELF! I THINK IT'S WONDERFUL, ALL THIS SELF-EXPRESSION IN YOUNG PEOPLE, DON'T YOU, SUE?
OH... YES. DANIEL, YOU READY, LOVE?
ON THE DRIVE HOME...
KY'S MOTHER SEEMS LIKE A VERY INTERESTING WOMAN...
I DUNNO, SHE'S A BIT...
MUCH?
YEAH.

NUMBER

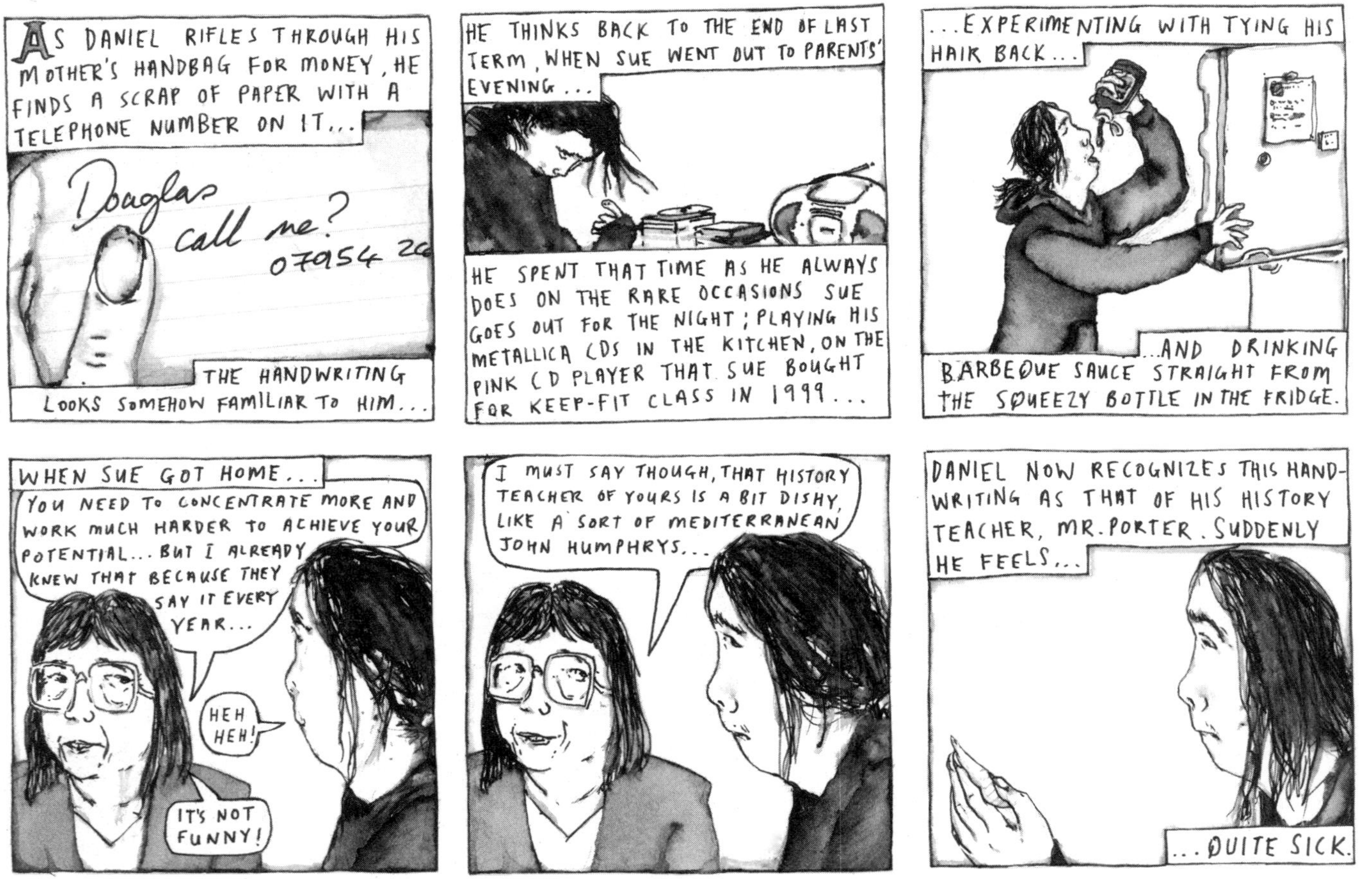
AS DANIEL RIFLES THROUGH HIS MOTHER'S HANDBAG FOR MONEY, HE FINDS A SCRAP OF PAPER WITH A TELEPHONE NUMBER ON IT...
Douglas call me? 07954 20
THE HANDWRITING LOOKS SOMEHOW FAMILIAR TO HIM...
HE THINKS BACK TO THE END OF LAST TERM, WHEN SUE WENT OUT TO PARENTS' EVENING...
HE SPENT THAT TIME AS HE ALWAYS DOES ON THE RARE OCCASIONS SUE GOES OUT FOR THE NIGHT; PLAYING HIS METALLICA CDS IN THE KITCHEN, ON THE PINK CD PLAYER THAT SUE BOUGHT FOR KEEP-FIT CLASS IN 1999...
...EXPERIMENTING WITH TYING HIS HAIR BACK...
...AND DRINKING BARBEQUE SAUCE STRAIGHT FROM THE SQUEEZY BOTTLE IN THE FRIDGE.
WHEN SUE GOT HOME...
YOU NEED TO CONCENTRATE MORE AND WORK MUCH HARDER TO ACHIEVE YOUR POTENTIAL... BUT I ALREADY KNEW THAT BECAUSE THEY SAY IT EVERY YEAR...
HEH HEH!
IT'S NOT FUNNY!
I MUST SAY THOUGH, THAT HISTORY TEACHER OF YOURS IS A BIT DISHY, LIKE A SORT OF MEDITERRANEAN JOHN HUMPHRYS...
DANIEL NOW RECOGNIZES THIS HAND-WRITING AS THAT OF HIS HISTORY TEACHER, MR. PORTER. SUDDENLY HE FEELS...
...QUITE SICK.

D O G

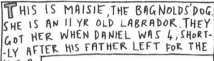

THIS IS MAISIE, THE BAGNOLDS' DOG. SHE IS AN 11 YR OLD LABRADOR. THEY GOT HER WHEN DANIEL WAS 4, SHORT-LY AFTER HIS FATHER LEFT FOR THE U.S.A.

FOR A LONG TIME, DANIEL AND MAISIE WERE DEVOTED TO EACH OTHER, INSEPARABLE...

...EVEN TO THE EXTENT SUE HAD TO FIND A 'PET-FRIENDLY' PHOTOGRAPHER BECAUSE DANIEL INSISTED ON MAISIE BEING IN-CLUDED IN THEIR FAMILY PORTRAIT...

FOR THE LAST FEW YEARS THOUGH, MAISIE HAS BEEN INCREASINGLY IG-NORED BY DANIEL...

URRGH MAISIE!

...UNLESS SHE IS PARTICULARLY FLATULENT.

NOWADAYS IT IS SUE WHO WILL WALK MAISIE; JUST HOW OFTEN DEPENDS ON A WAVERING COMMITMENT TO HER KEEP-FIT REGIME...

DOES MAISIE NOTICE THOSE TIMES DANIEL AND SUE YELL AT EACH OTHER AND SLAM DOORS? WHEN DANIEL'S FACE GOES RED AND HIS VOICE BE-COMES HOARSE FROM SHOUTING, AND SUE WILL END UP CRYING...

...OR HOW AFTER ONE OF THESE ROWS, SUE WILL ALWAYS FEED HER MORE TREATS THAN USUAL?..

...HENCE HER EVER-WIDENING GIRTH.

REALISE

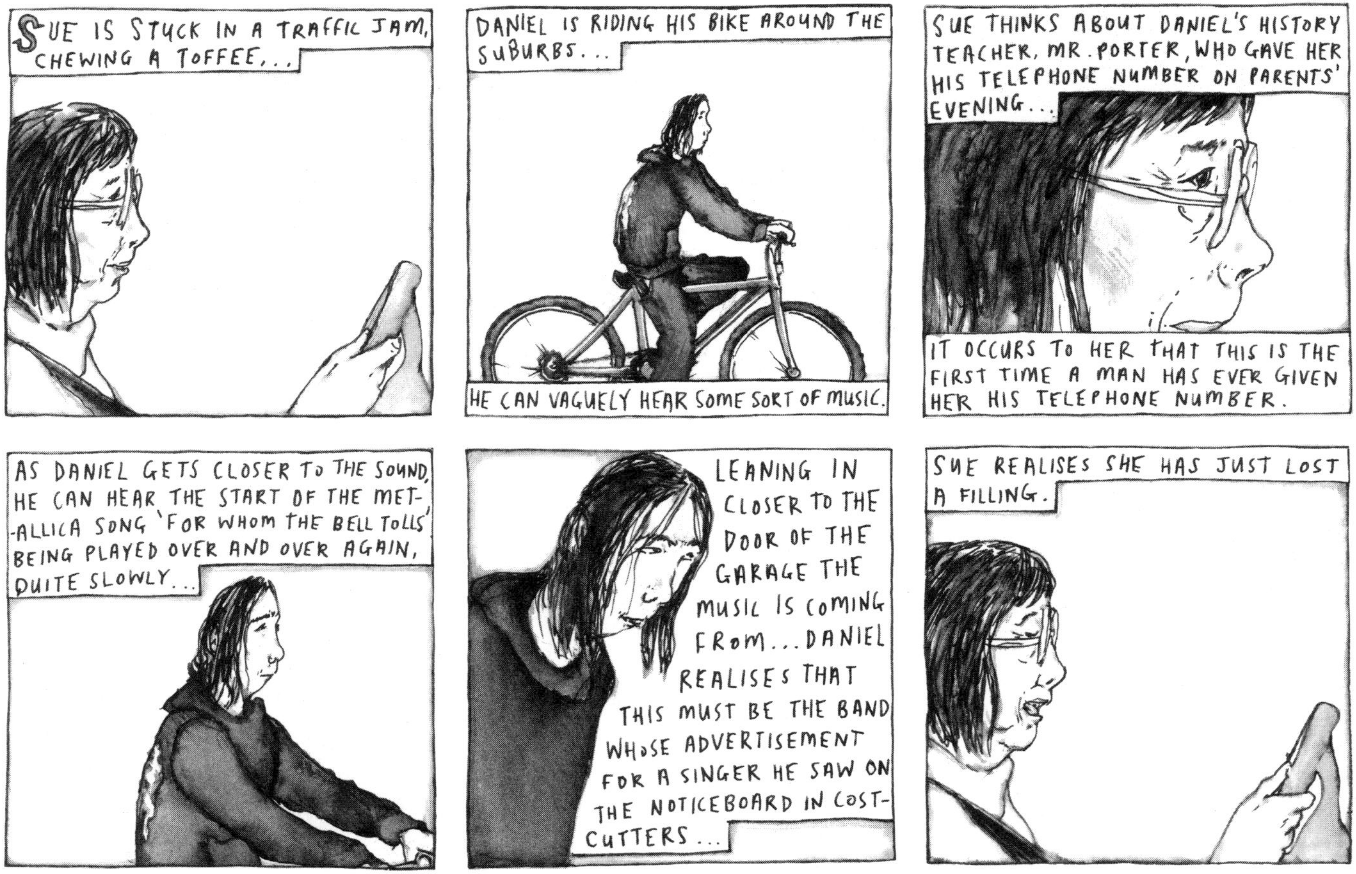
SUE IS STUCK IN A TRAFFIC JAM, CHEWING A TOFFEE, . .
DANIEL IS RIDING HIS BIKE AROUND THE SUBURBS. . .
HE CAN VAGUELY HEAR SOME SORT OF MUSIC.
SUE THINKS ABOUT DANIEL'S HISTORY TEACHER, MR. PORTER, WHO GAVE HER HIS TELEPHONE NUMBER ON PARENTS' EVENING. . .
IT OCCURS TO HER THAT THIS IS THE FIRST TIME A MAN HAS EVER GIVEN HER HIS TELEPHONE NUMBER.
AS DANIEL GETS CLOSER TO THE SOUND, HE CAN HEAR THE START OF THE MET- -ALLICA SONG 'FOR WHOM THE BELL TOLLS' BEING PLAYED OVER AND OVER AGAIN, QUITE SLOWLY. . .
LEANING IN CLOSER TO THE DOOR OF THE GARAGE THE MUSIC IS COMING FROM. . . DANIEL REALISES THAT THIS MUST BE THE BAND WHOSE ADVERTISEMENT FOR A SINGER HE SAW ON THE NOTICEBOARD IN COST- CUTTERS . . .
SUE REALISES SHE HAS JUST LOST A FILLING.

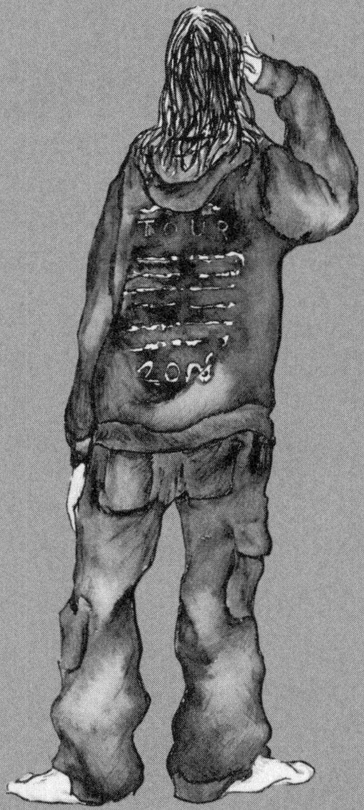
TOUR

SECOND WEEK

OPPOSITE

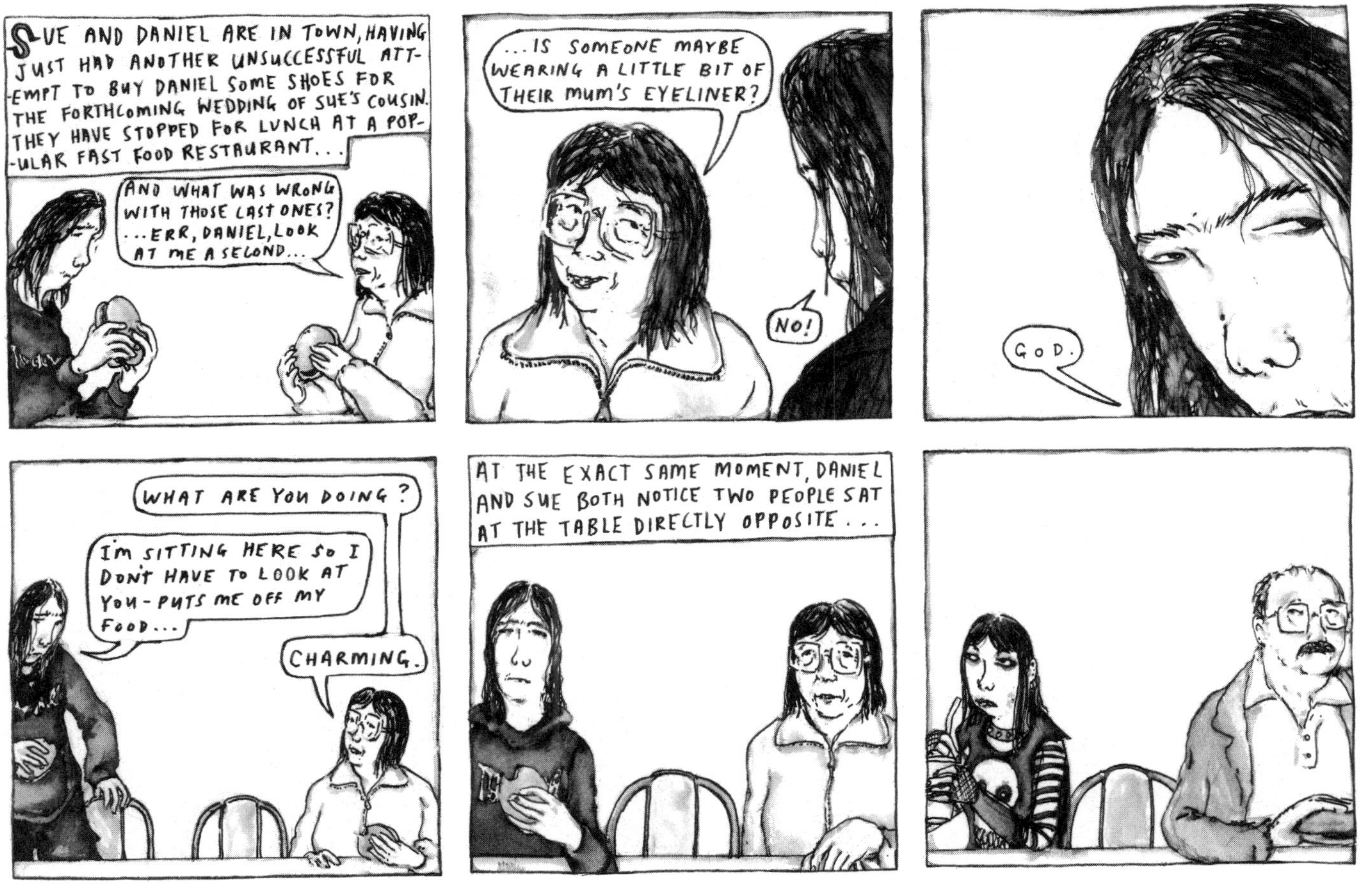
SUE AND DANIEL ARE IN TOWN, HAVING JUST HAD ANOTHER UNSUCCESSFUL ATT-EMPT TO BUY DANIEL SOME SHOES FOR THE FORTHCOMING WEDDING OF SUE'S COUSIN. THEY HAVE STOPPED FOR LUNCH AT A POP-ULAR FAST FOOD RESTAURANT...
AND WHAT WAS WRONG WITH THOSE LAST ONES? ...ERR, DANIEL, LOOK AT ME A SECOND...
...IS SOMEONE MAYBE WEARING A LITTLE BIT OF THEIR MUM'S EYELINER?
NO!
GOD.
WHAT ARE YOU DOING?
I'M SITTING HERE SO I DON'T HAVE TO LOOK AT YOU - PUTS ME OFF MY FOOD...
CHARMING.
AT THE EXACT SAME MOMENT, DANIEL AND SUE BOTH NOTICE TWO PEOPLE SAT AT THE TABLE DIRECTLY OPPOSITE...

SOLO

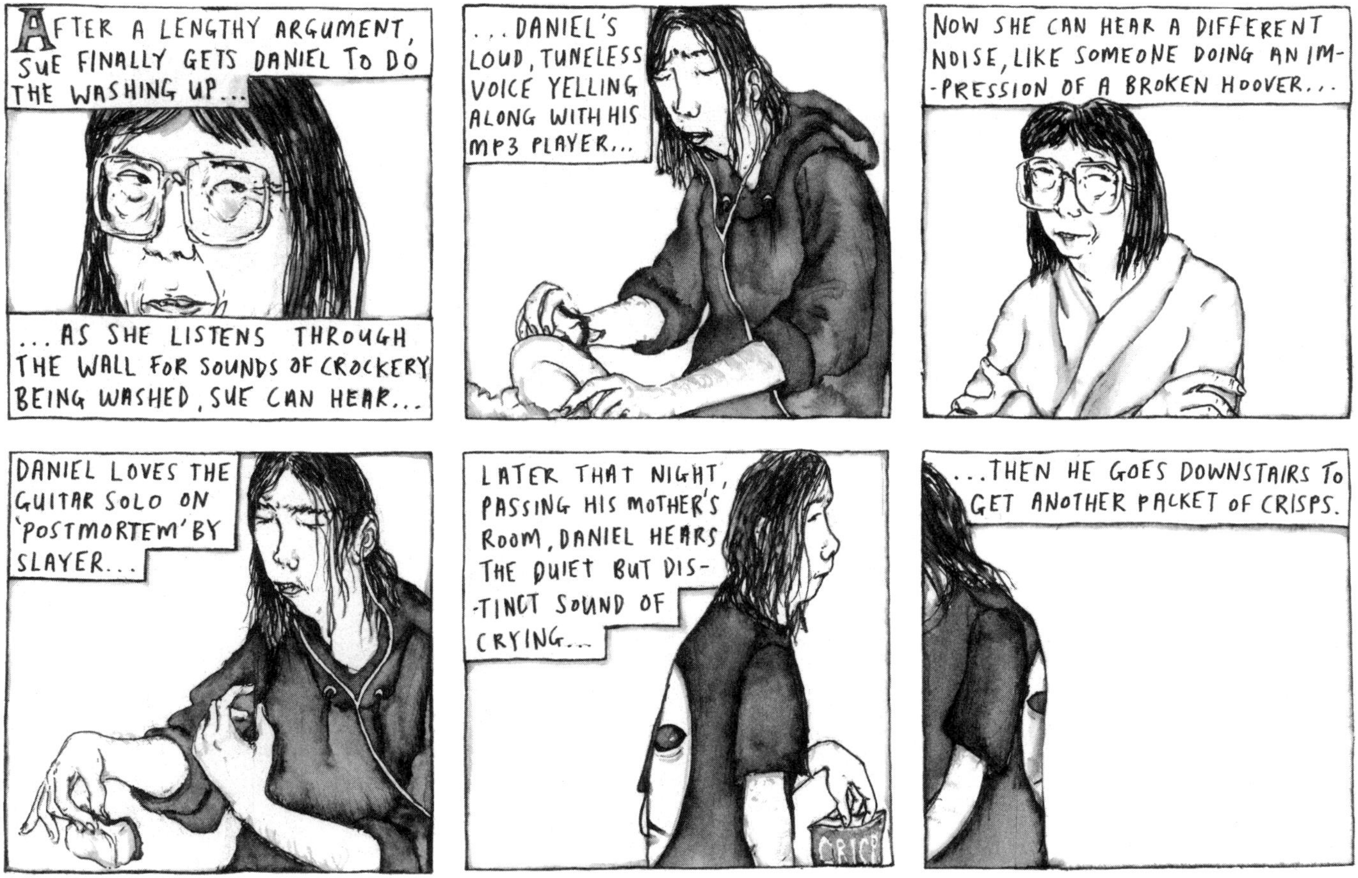
AFTER A LENGTHY ARGUMENT, SUE FINALLY GETS DANIEL TO DO THE WASHING UP...
...AS SHE LISTENS THROUGH THE WALL FOR SOUNDS OF CROCKERY BEING WASHED, SUE CAN HEAR...
...DANIEL'S LOUD, TUNELESS VOICE YELLING ALONG WITH HIS MP3 PLAYER...
NOW SHE CAN HEAR A DIFFERENT NOISE, LIKE SOMEONE DOING AN IM-PRESSION OF A BROKEN HOOVER...
DANIEL LOVES THE GUITAR SOLO ON 'POSTMORTEM' BY SLAYER...
LATER THAT NIGHT, PASSING HIS MOTHER'S ROOM, DANIEL HEARS THE QUIET BUT DIS-TINCT SOUND OF CRYING...
...THEN HE GOES DOWNSTAIRS TO GET ANOTHER PACKET OF CRISPS.

HABIT

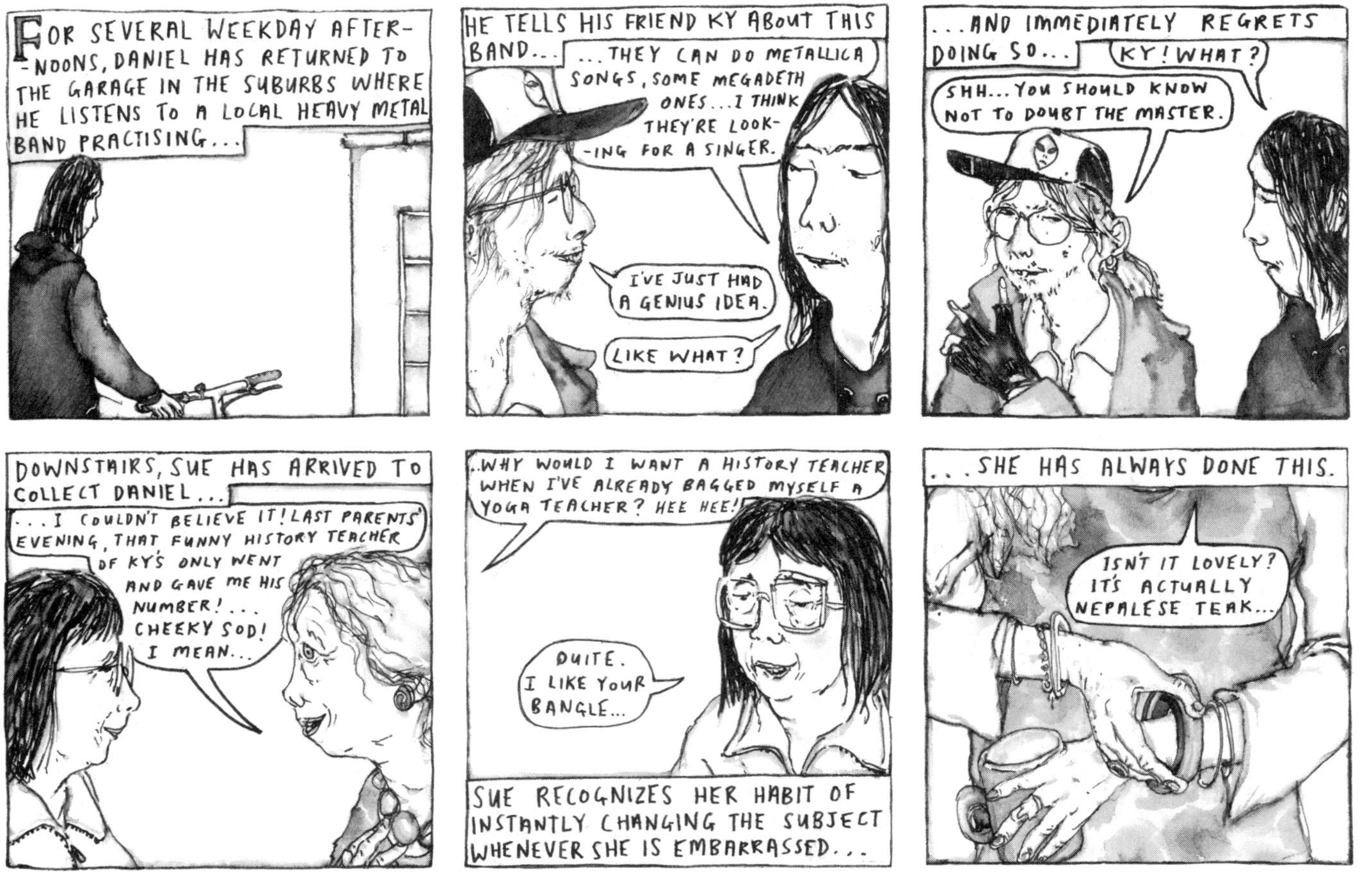
FOR SEVERAL WEEKDAY AFTER-NOONS, DANIEL HAS RETURNED TO THE GARAGE IN THE SUBURBS WHERE HE LISTENS TO A LOCAL HEAVY METAL BAND PRACTISING...
HE TELLS HIS FRIEND KY ABOUT THIS BAND...
...THEY CAN DO METALLICA SONGS, SOME MEGADETH ONES... I THINK THEY'RE LOOK-ING FOR A SINGER.
I'VE JUST HAD A GENIUS IDEA.
LIKE WHAT?
...AND IMMEDIATELY REGRETS DOING SO...
KY! WHAT?
SHH... YOU SHOULD KNOW NOT TO DOUBT THE MASTER.
DOWNSTAIRS, SUE HAS ARRIVED TO COLLECT DANIEL...
...I COULDN'T BELIEVE IT! LAST PARENTS' EVENING, THAT FUNNY HISTORY TEACHER OF KY'S ONLY WENT AND GAVE ME HIS NUMBER!... CHEEKY SOD! I MEAN...
..WHY WOULD I WANT A HISTORY TEACHER WHEN I'VE ALREADY BAGGED MYSELF A YOGA TEACHER? HEE HEE!
QUITE. I LIKE YOUR BANGLE...
SUE RECOGNIZES HER HABIT OF INSTANTLY CHANGING THE SUBJECT WHENEVER SHE IS EMBARRASSED...
...SHE HAS ALWAYS DONE THIS.
ISN'T IT LOVELY? IT'S ACTUALLY NEPALESE TEAK...

HOUSE

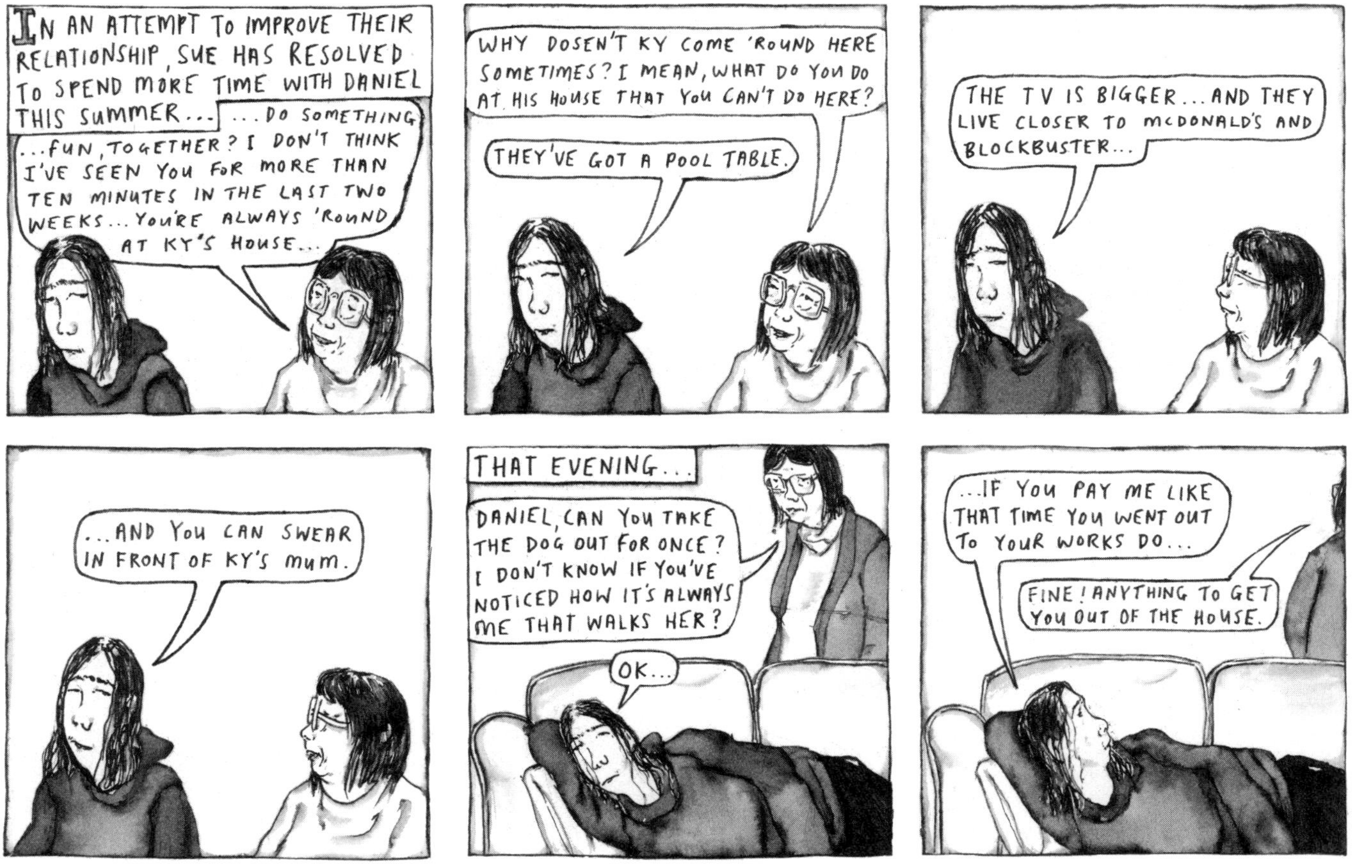

IN AN ATTEMPT TO IMPROVE THEIR RELATIONSHIP, SUE HAS RESOLVED TO SPEND MORE TIME WITH DANIEL THIS SUMMER...
...DO SOMETHING ...FUN, TOGETHER? I DON'T THINK I'VE SEEN YOU FOR MORE THAN TEN MINUTES IN THE LAST TWO WEEKS... YOU'RE ALWAYS 'ROUND AT KY'S HOUSE...
WHY DOSEN'T KY COME 'ROUND HERE SOMETIMES? I MEAN, WHAT DO YOU DO AT HIS HOUSE THAT YOU CAN'T DO HERE?
THEY'VE GOT A POOL TABLE.
THE TV IS BIGGER... AND THEY LIVE CLOSER TO McDONALD'S AND BLOCKBUSTER...
...AND YOU CAN SWEAR IN FRONT OF KY'S MUM.
THAT EVENING...
DANIEL, CAN YOU TAKE THE DOG OUT FOR ONCE? I DON'T KNOW IF YOU'VE NOTICED HOW IT'S ALWAYS ME THAT WALKS HER?
OK...
...IF YOU PAY ME LIKE THAT TIME YOU WENT OUT TO YOUR WORKS DO...
FINE! ANYTHING TO GET YOU OUT OF THE HOUSE.

BOYS

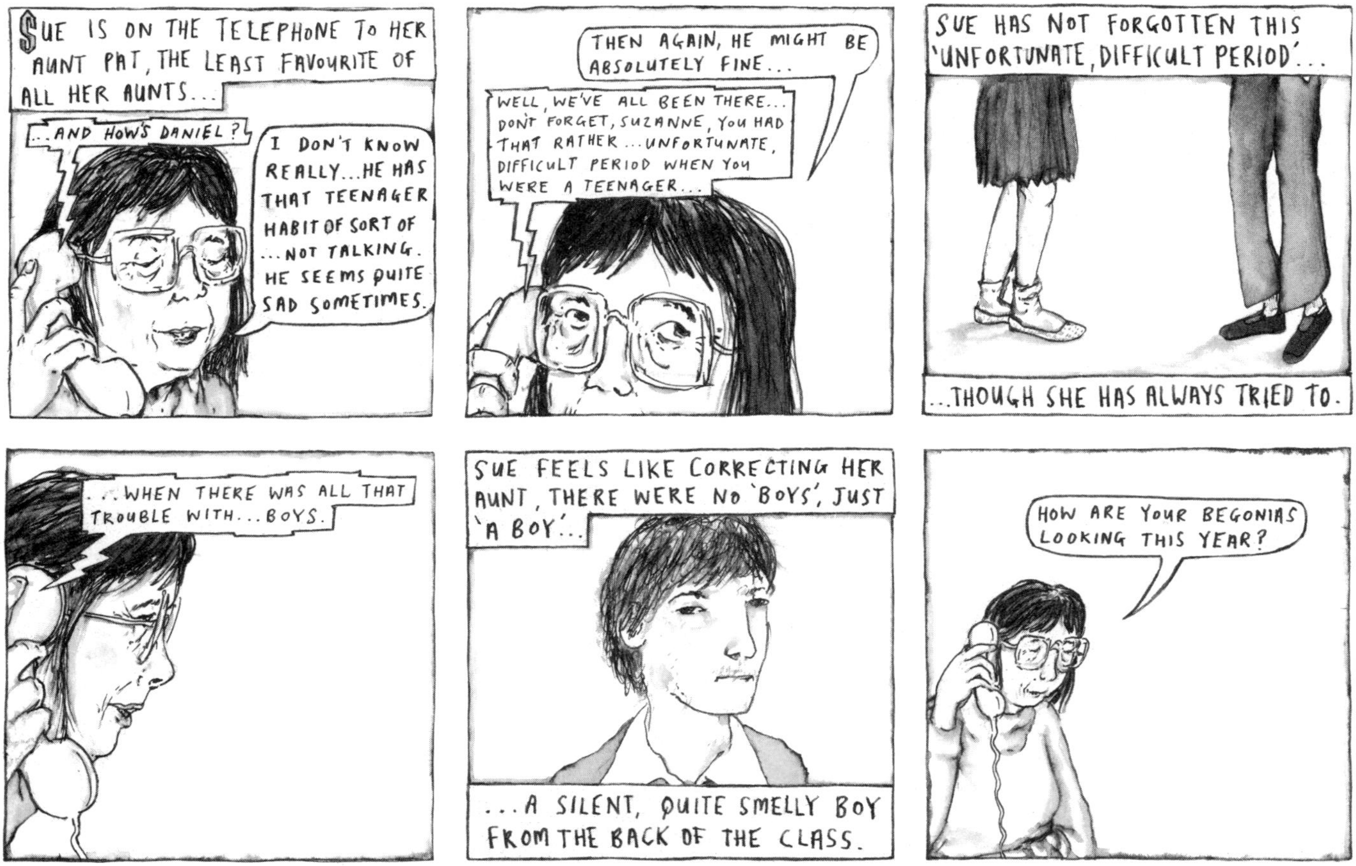

SUE IS ON THE TELEPHONE TO HER AUNT PAT, THE LEAST FAVOURITE OF ALL HER AUNTS...
...AND HOW'S DANIEL?
I DON'T KNOW REALLY...HE HAS THAT TEENAGER HABIT OF SORT OF ...NOT TALKING. HE SEEMS QUITE SAD SOMETIMES.
THEN AGAIN, HE MIGHT BE ABSOLUTELY FINE...
WELL, WE'VE ALL BEEN THERE... DON'T FORGET, SUZANNE, YOU HAD THAT RATHER ...UNFORTUNATE, DIFFICULT PERIOD WHEN YOU WERE A TEENAGER...
SUE HAS NOT FORGOTTEN THIS 'UNFORTUNATE, DIFFICULT PERIOD'...
...THOUGH SHE HAS ALWAYS TRIED TO.
...WHEN THERE WAS ALL THAT TROUBLE WITH...BOYS.
SUE FEELS LIKE CORRECTING HER AUNT, THERE WERE NO 'BOYS', JUST 'A BOY'...
...A SILENT, QUITE SMELLY BOY FROM THE BACK OF THE CLASS.
HOW ARE YOUR BEGONIAS LOOKING THIS YEAR?

TWELVE

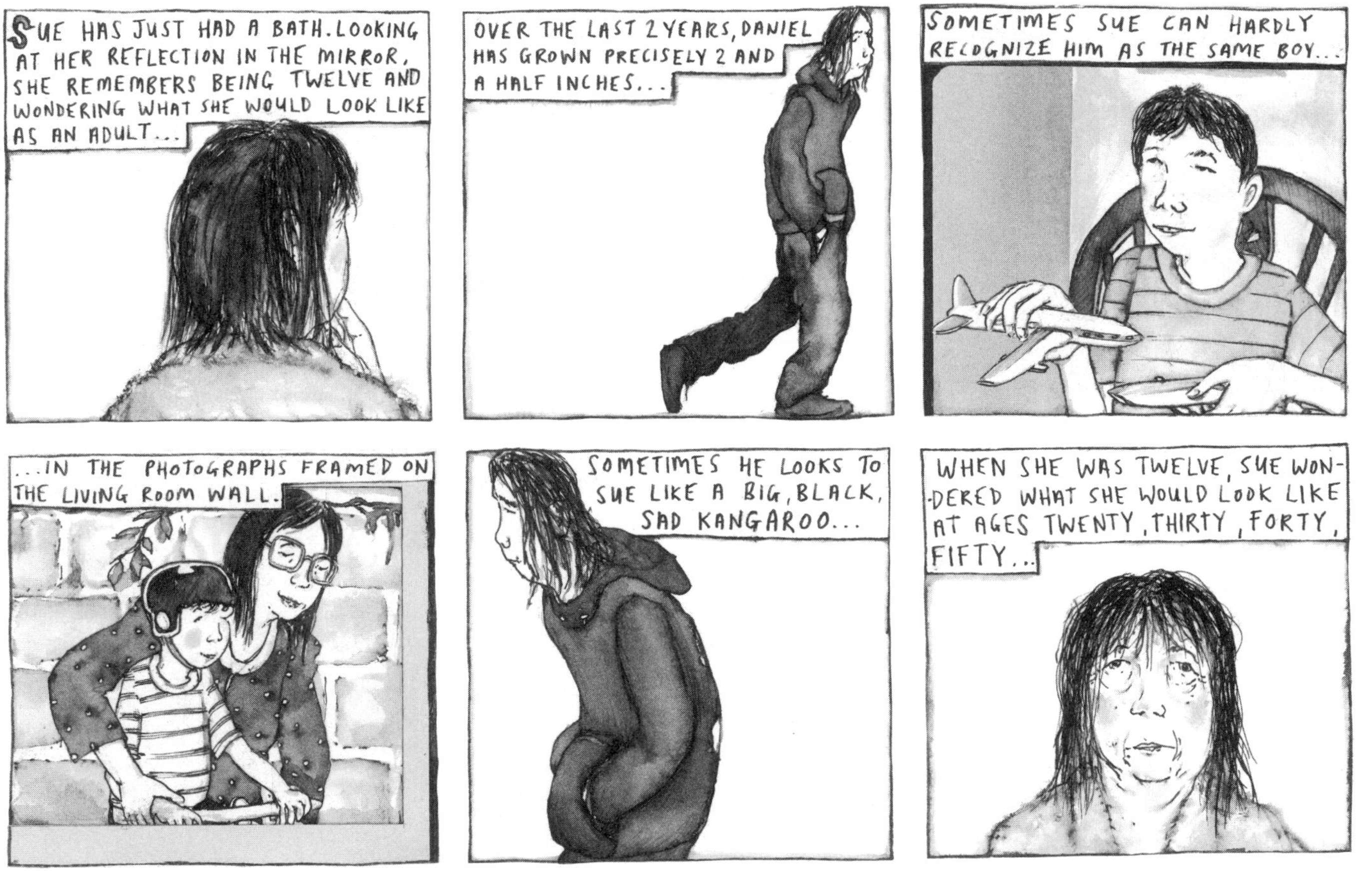
SUE HAS JUST HAD A BATH. LOOKING AT HER REFLECTION IN THE MIRROR, SHE REMEMBERS BEING TWELVE AND WONDERING WHAT SHE WOULD LOOK LIKE AS AN ADULT...
OVER THE LAST 2 YEARS, DANIEL HAS GROWN PRECISELY 2 AND A HALF INCHES...
SOMETIMES SUE CAN HARDLY RECOGNIZE HIM AS THE SAME BOY...
...IN THE PHOTOGRAPHS FRAMED ON THE LIVING ROOM WALL.
SOMETIMES HE LOOKS TO SUE LIKE A BIG, BLACK, SAD KANGAROO...
WHEN SHE WAS TWELVE, SUE WON-DERED WHAT SHE WOULD LOOK LIKE AT AGES TWENTY, THIRTY, FORTY, FIFTY...

BIRTHDAY

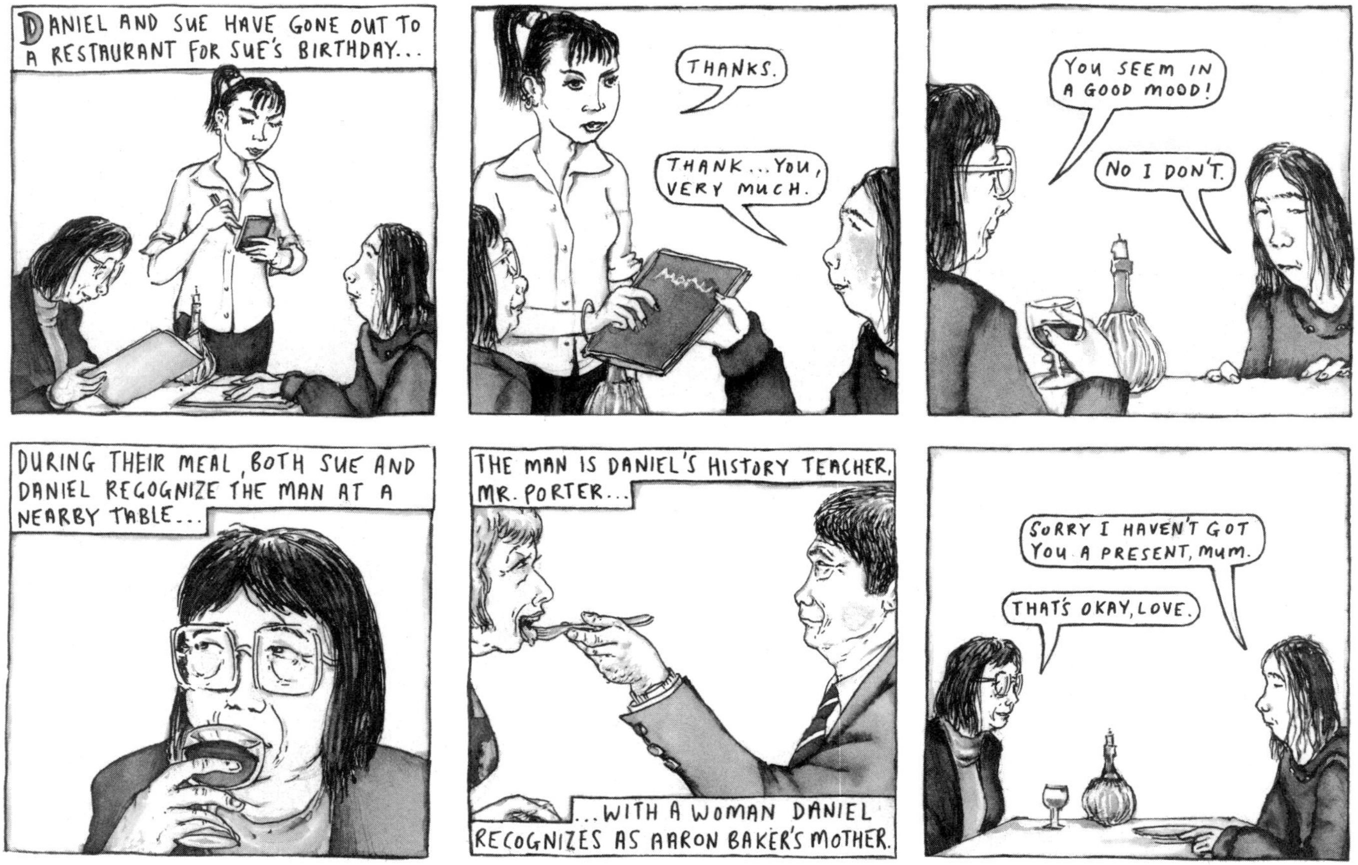
DANIEL AND SUE HAVE GONE OUT TO A RESTAURANT FOR SUE'S BIRTHDAY...
THANKS.
THANK...YOU, VERY MUCH.
MENU
YOU SEEM IN A GOOD MOOD!
NO I DON'T.
DURING THEIR MEAL, BOTH SUE AND DANIEL RECOGNIZE THE MAN AT A NEARBY TABLE...
THE MAN IS DANIEL'S HISTORY TEACHER, MR. PORTER...
...WITH A WOMAN DANIEL RECOGNIZES AS AARON BAKER'S MOTHER.
SORRY I HAVEN'T GOT YOU A PRESENT, MUM.
THAT'S OKAY, LOVE.

LYRICS

IN THE FADING SUMMER EVENING, DANIEL ONCE AGAIN RIDES HIS BIKE TO THE GARAGE IN THE SUBURBS WHERE A LOCAL HEAVY METAL BAND ARE PRACTISING...

...AS HE LISTENS OUTSIDE, DANIEL QUIETLY TRIES SINGING OVER THE BAND SOME LYRICS HE HAS WRITTEN FOR HIS OWN IMAGINED HEAVY METAL BAND, 'SKULLSLAYER'.

IT'S HARD TO MAKE THEM SCAN.

SHE HAS FOUND A SHEET OF PAPER WITH DANIEL'S HANDWRITING ON IT...

THAT EVENING...

THAT POEM YOU WROTE...IT'S NOT REALLY MY SORT OF THING, BUT... IT WAS VERY...VIVID, AND I WAS WON-DERING IF YOU REALLY FEEL... THAT WAY?

DANIEL DOES NOT CLAIM THESE WORDS AS HIS OWN, OR CHOOSE TO EXPLAIN THEY ARE IN FACT THE LYRICS TO 'DYERS EVE' BY METALLICA, WHICH HE HAS COPIED OUT FOR INSPIRATION.

Dear Mother, Dear Father
What is this hell you have put me through
Believer, Deciever
Day in day out live my life through you
pushed onto me Whats wrong or right
Hidden from this thing that they call life
Dear mother, Dear father
Every thought I'd think you disapprove
Curator, Dicktator
Always censoring my every move
Children are seen but are not heard

SIGNING

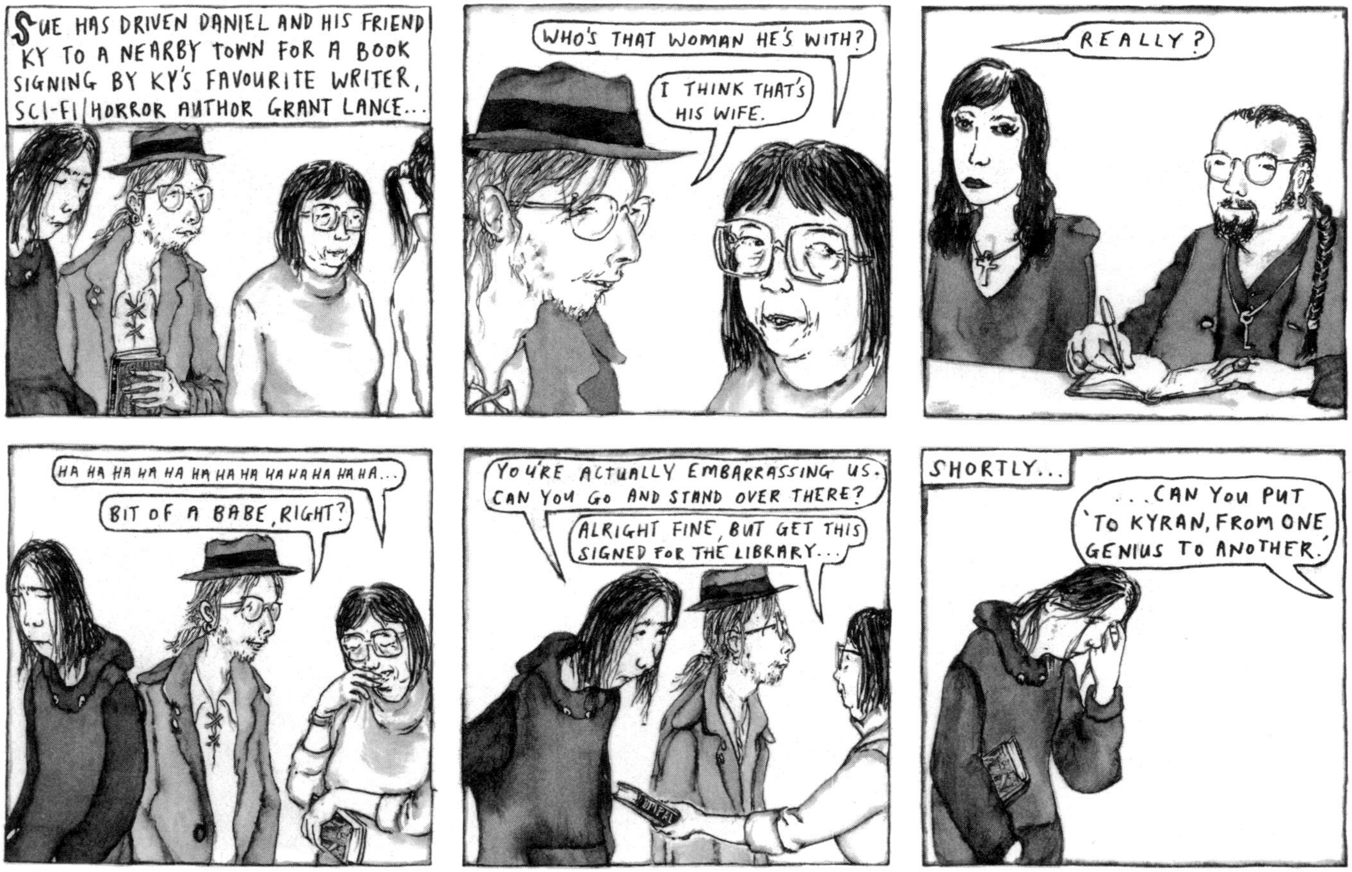
SUE HAS DRIVEN DANIEL AND HIS FRIEND KY TO A NEARBY TOWN FOR A BOOK SIGNING BY KY'S FAVOURITE WRITER, SCI-FI/HORROR AUTHOR GRANT LANCE...
WHO'S THAT WOMAN HE'S WITH?
I THINK THAT'S HIS WIFE.
REALLY?
HA HA HA HA HA HA HA HA HA HA HA HA HA HA...
BIT OF A BABE, RIGHT?
YOU'RE ACTUALLY EMBARRASSING US. CAN YOU GO AND STAND OVER THERE?
ALRIGHT FINE, BUT GET THIS SIGNED FOR THE LIBRARY...
SHORTLY...
...CAN YOU PUT 'TO KYRAN, FROM ONE GENIUS TO ANOTHER.'

RESEMBLANCE

SOMETIMES SUE FINDS HERSELF LOOKING AT DANIEL FOR SOME RE--SEMBLANCE TO HER FATHER...

AS SHE WAS SEVEN THE LAST TIME SHE SAW HIM, SUE WONDERS IF THE MEMORIES OF HER FATHER'S FACE...

...ARE BASED PURELY ON THE THREE PHOTOGRAPHS SHE HAS OF HIM...

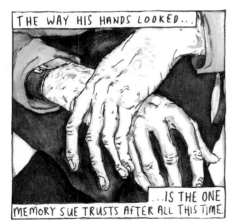

THE WAY HIS HANDS LOOKED...

...IS THE ONE MEMORY SUE TRUSTS AFTER ALL THIS TIME.

OKAY, STOP LOOKING AT ME NOW.

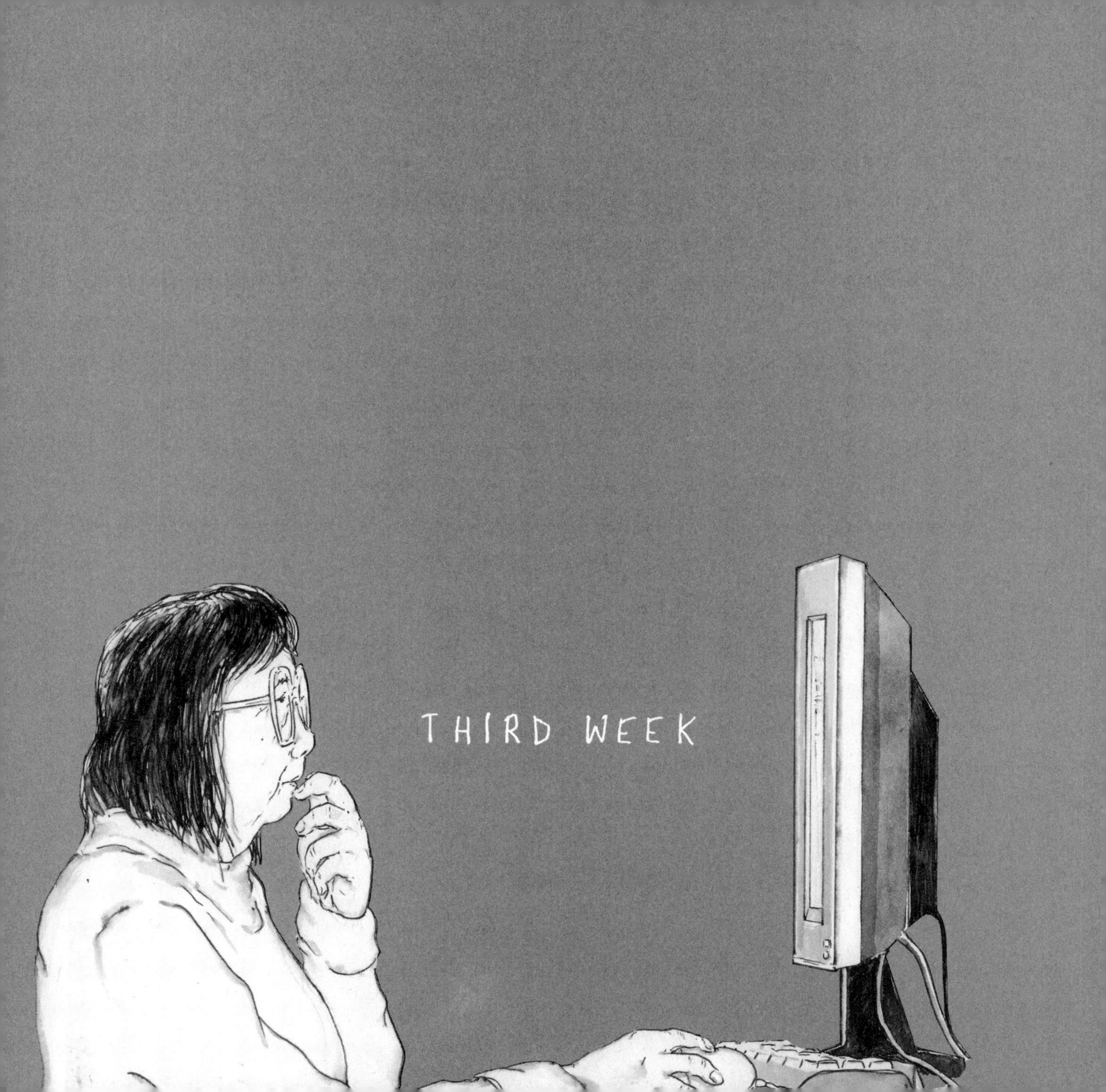
THIRD WEEK

STEREO

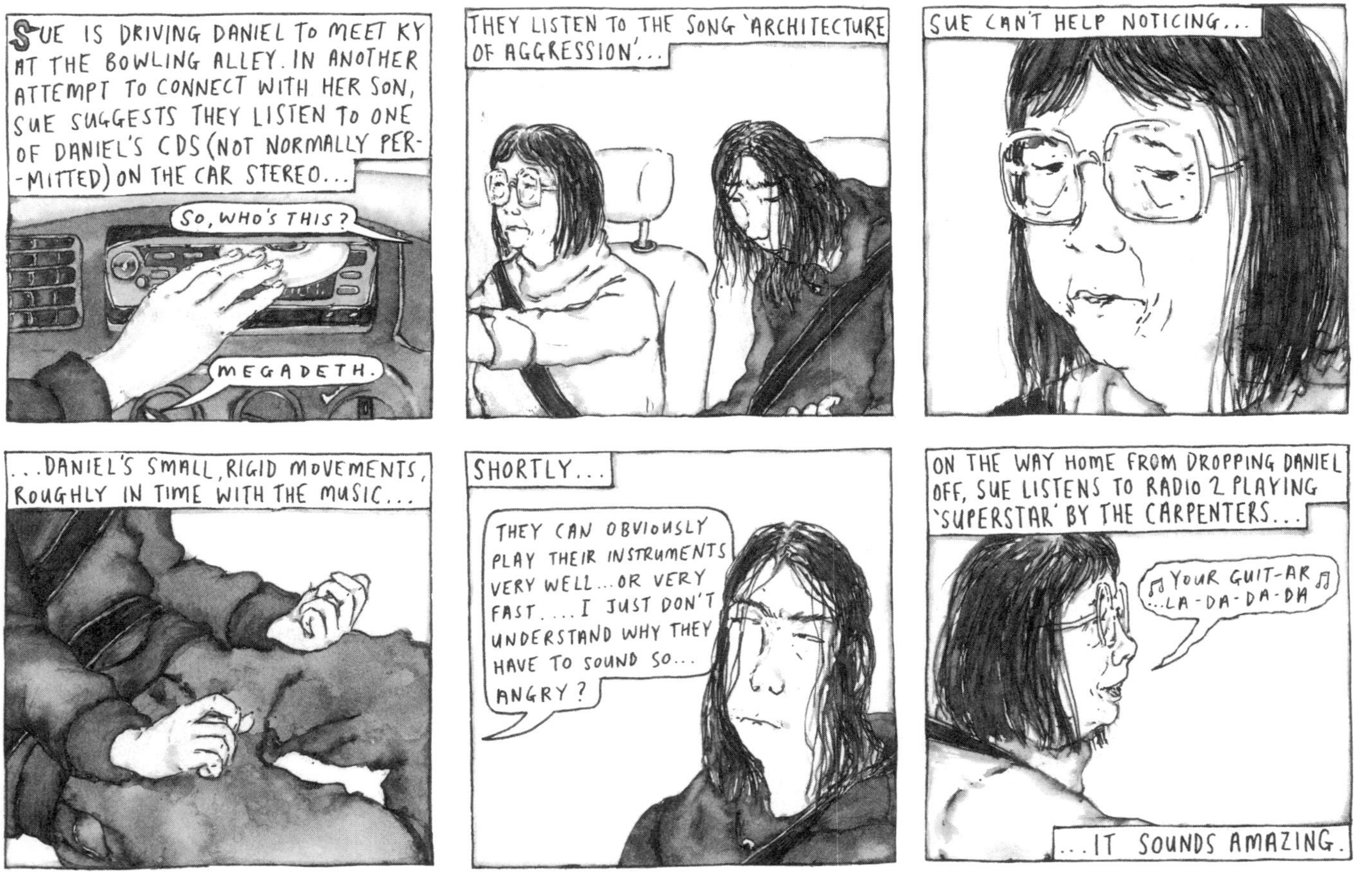
SUE IS DRIVING DANIEL TO MEET KY AT THE BOWLING ALLEY. IN ANOTHER ATTEMPT TO CONNECT WITH HER SON, SUE SUGGESTS THEY LISTEN TO ONE OF DANIEL'S CDS (NOT NORMALLY PER-MITTED) ON THE CAR STEREO...
SO, WHO'S THIS?
MEGADETH.
THEY LISTEN TO THE SONG 'ARCHITECTURE OF AGGRESSION'...
SUE CAN'T HELP NOTICING...
...DANIEL'S SMALL, RIGID MOVEMENTS, ROUGHLY IN TIME WITH THE MUSIC...
SHORTLY...
THEY CAN OBVIOUSLY PLAY THEIR INSTRUMENTS VERY WELL... OR VERY FAST.... I JUST DON'T UNDERSTAND WHY THEY HAVE TO SOUND SO... ANGRY?
ON THE WAY HOME FROM DROPPING DANIEL OFF, SUE LISTENS TO RADIO 2 PLAYING 'SUPERSTAR' BY THE CARPENTERS...
♫ YOUR GUIT-AR ♫ ...LA-DA-DA-DA
...IT SOUNDS AMAZING.

TABLE

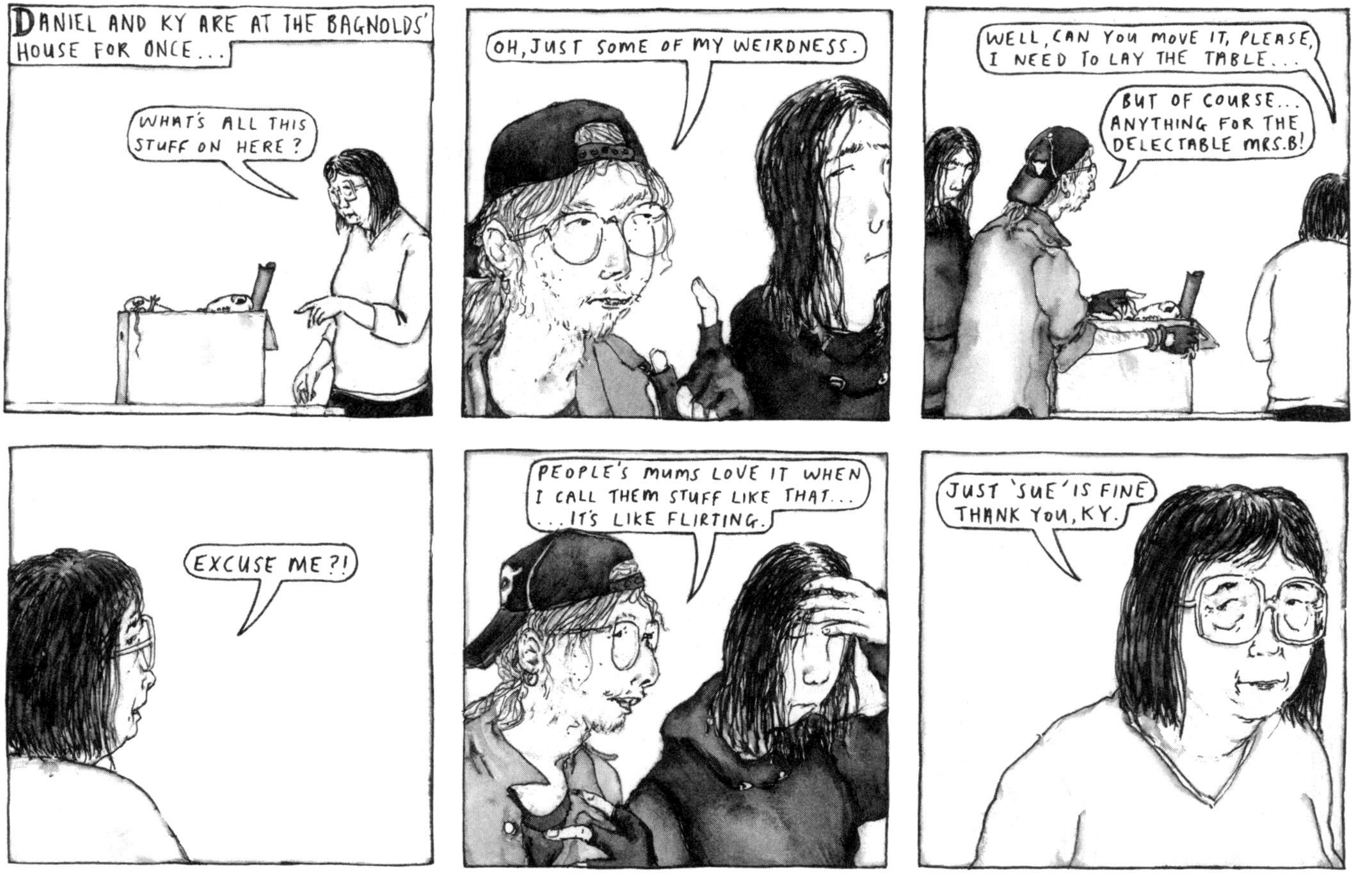
DANIEL AND KY ARE AT THE BAGNOLDS' HOUSE FOR ONCE...
WHAT'S ALL THIS STUFF ON HERE?
OH, JUST SOME OF MY WEIRDNESS.
WELL, CAN YOU MOVE IT, PLEASE, I NEED TO LAY THE TABLE...
BUT OF COURSE... ANYTHING FOR THE DELECTABLE MRS. B!
EXCUSE ME?!
PEOPLE'S MUMS LOVE IT WHEN I CALL THEM STUFF LIKE THAT... ...IT'S LIKE FLIRTING.
JUST 'SUE' IS FINE THANK YOU, KY.

GUITAR

As she attempts to tidy Daniel's room, Sue notices the electric guitar he borrowed from KY several months ago... ...She has never seen or heard him try to play it.

She thinks of that first (and only) term in halls of residence at Wolverhampton Polytechnic, where she somehow told a boy named Barnaby that she too played the guitar...

...IF YOU MISS PLAYING YOURS.

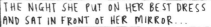

The night she put on her best dress and sat in front of her mirror...

...In a variety of poses with the guitar...

She returned it the next day.

YOU CAN BORROW IT FOR LONGER IF YOU LIKE... GOT A NICE ACTION, HASN'T IT?

YES, NICE. DO YOU STILL WANT TO BORROW THAT BREAD LP?

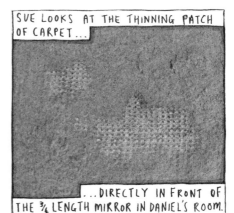

Sue looks at the thinning patch of carpet...

...Directly in front of the 3/4 length mirror in Daniel's room.

FAMILY

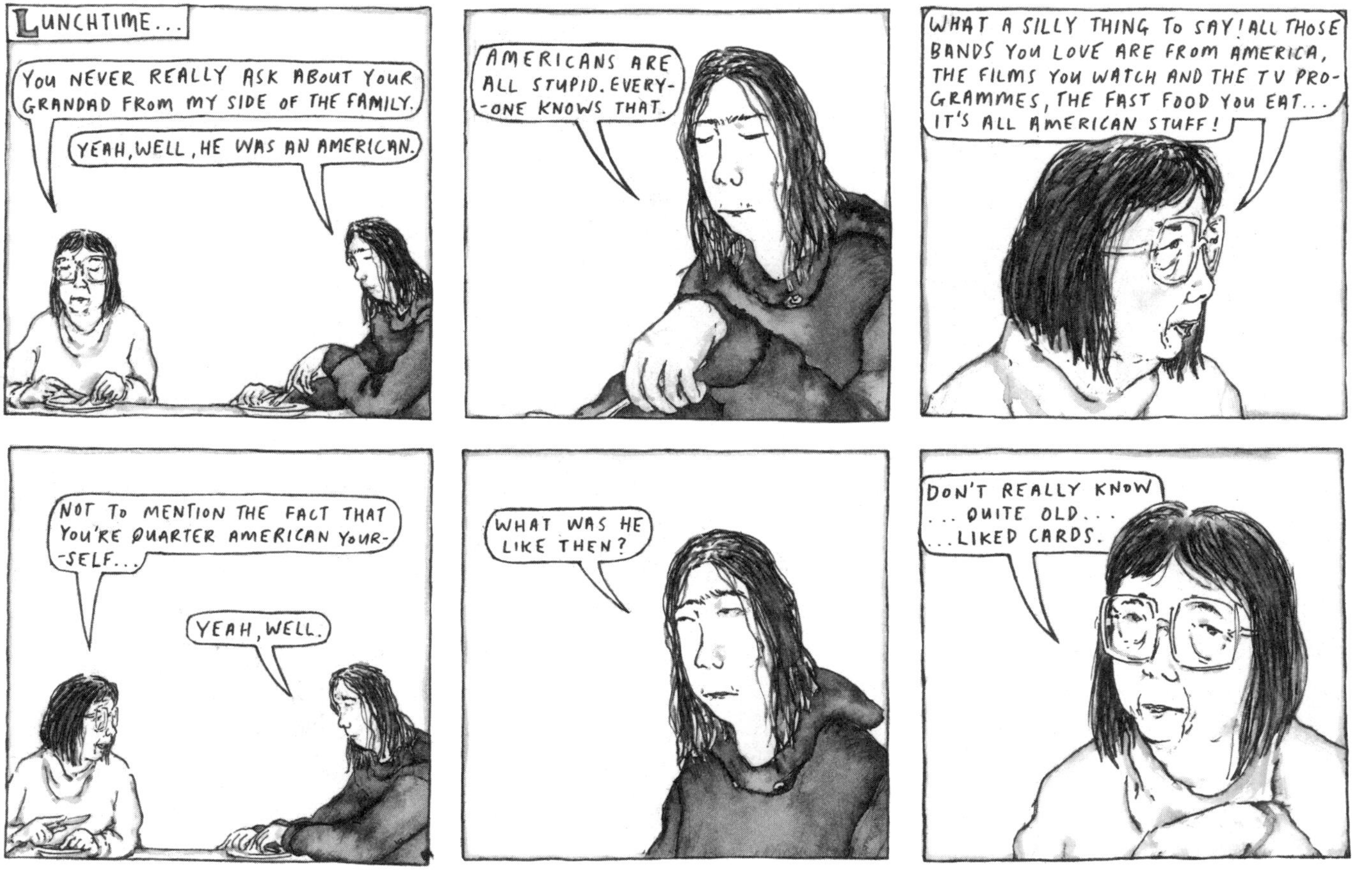
LUNCHTIME...
YOU NEVER REALLY ASK ABOUT YOUR GRANDAD FROM MY SIDE OF THE FAMILY.
YEAH, WELL, HE WAS AN AMERICAN.
AMERICANS ARE ALL STUPID. EVERY-ONE KNOWS THAT.
WHAT A SILLY THING TO SAY! ALL THOSE BANDS YOU LOVE ARE FROM AMERICA, THE FILMS YOU WATCH AND THE TV PRO-GRAMMES, THE FAST FOOD YOU EAT... IT'S ALL AMERICAN STUFF!
NOT TO MENTION THE FACT THAT YOU'RE QUARTER AMERICAN YOUR-SELF...
YEAH, WELL.
WHAT WAS HE LIKE THEN?
DON'T REALLY KNOW ...QUITE OLD... ...LIKED CARDS.

SIGNATURE

SUE RECEIVES ONE OF THE CHEQUES SHE (INFREQUENTLY) GETS SENT BY HER EX-HUSBAND, BOB...

MR R BAGNOLD

SHE IS WELL AWARE THAT, AS A SUCCESS--FUL INTERNATIONAL BUSINESS MAN, HE COULD AFFORD TO SEND FAR MORE.

IT AMUSES SUE TO THINK OF ALL THOSE EARLY DATES...

OH.

...WHEN SHE WOULD ALWAYS PAY.

OF COURSE, HE ALWAYS WAS AMBITIOUS...

CAN YOU TAKE A PHOTO OF ME WITH THAT PORSCHE...

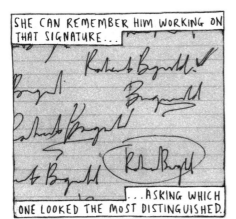

SHE CAN REMEMBER HIM WORKING ON THAT SIGNATURE...

...ASKING WHICH ONE LOOKED THE MOST DISTINGUISHED.

SOMETIMES SUE THINKS ABOUT REVERT--ING TO HER MAIDEN NAME...

...BUT SHE HAS ALWAYS MAINTAINED THAT SHE GOT TWO THINGS FROM HER MARRIAGE; DANIEL, AND AN IMPROVEMENT ON THE SURNAME SHE ALWAYS HATED...

...SNEED.

ART

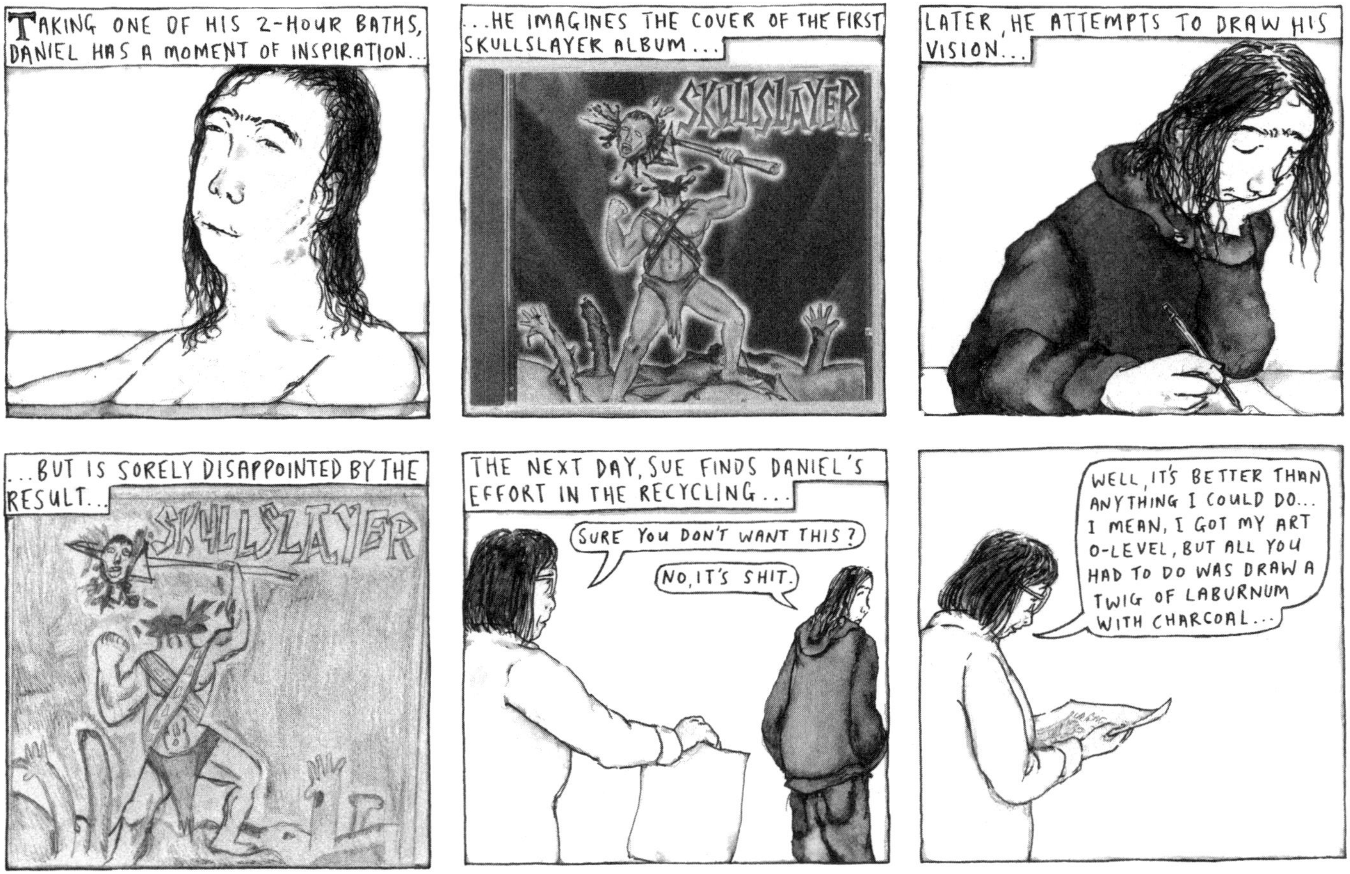
TAKING ONE OF HIS 2-HOUR BATHS, DANIEL HAS A MOMENT OF INSPIRATION...
...HE IMAGINES THE COVER OF THE FIRST SKULLSLAYER ALBUM...
SKULLSLAYER
LATER, HE ATTEMPTS TO DRAW HIS VISION...
...BUT IS SORELY DISAPPOINTED BY THE RESULT...
SKULLSLAYER
THE NEXT DAY, SUE FINDS DANIEL'S EFFORT IN THE RECYCLING...
SURE YOU DON'T WANT THIS?
NO, IT'S SHIT.
WELL, IT'S BETTER THAN ANYTHING I COULD DO... I MEAN, I GOT MY ART O-LEVEL, BUT ALL YOU HAD TO DO WAS DRAW A TWIG OF LABURNUM WITH CHARCOAL...

BABY

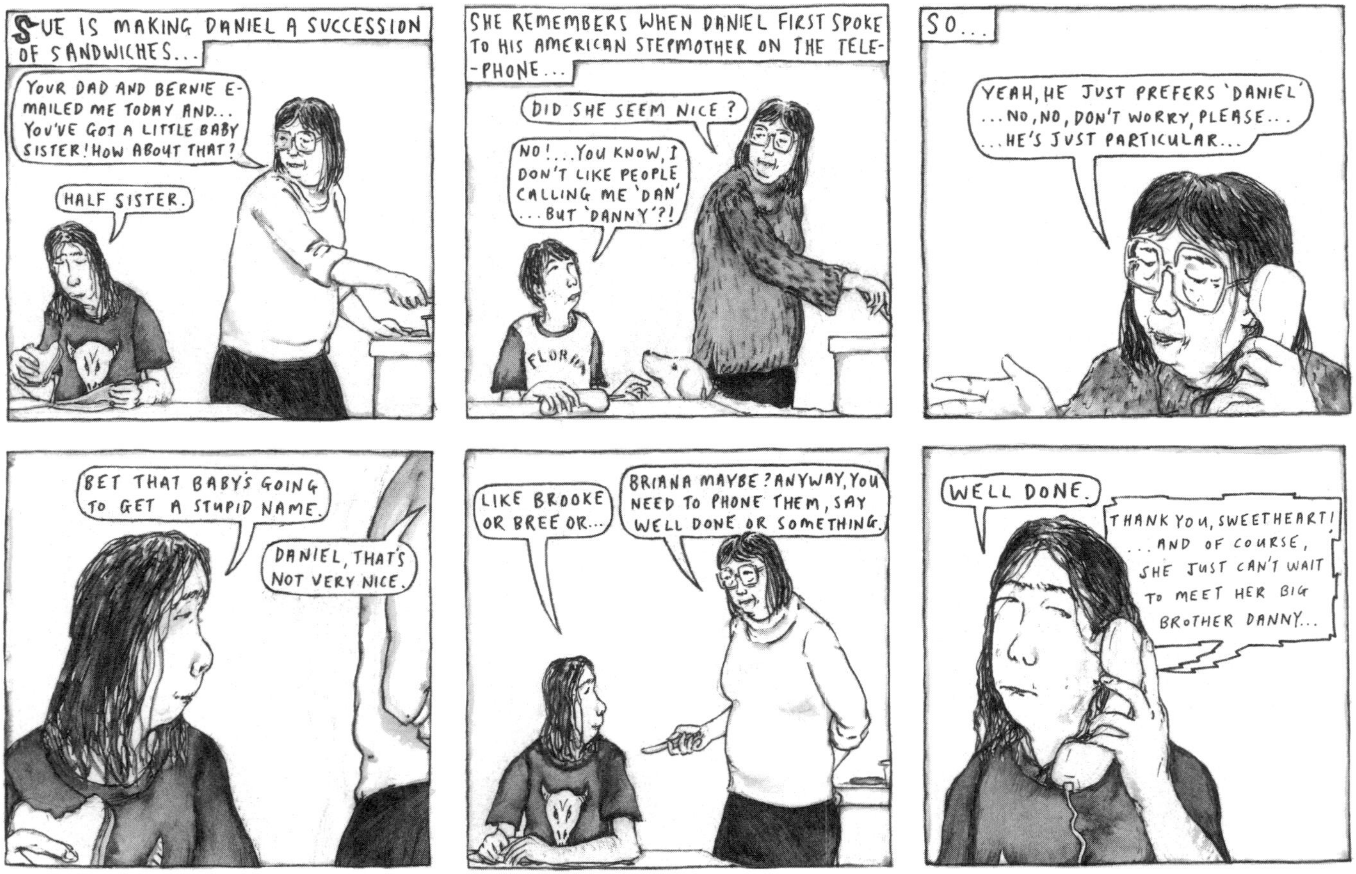
SUE IS MAKING DANIEL A SUCCESSION OF SANDWICHES...
YOUR DAD AND BERNIE E-MAILED ME TODAY AND... YOU'VE GOT A LITTLE BABY SISTER! HOW ABOUT THAT?
HALF SISTER.
SHE REMEMBERS WHEN DANIEL FIRST SPOKE TO HIS AMERICAN STEPMOTHER ON THE TELE-PHONE...
DID SHE SEEM NICE?
NO!...YOU KNOW, I DON'T LIKE PEOPLE CALLING ME 'DAN' ...BUT 'DANNY'?!
FLORIDA
SO...
YEAH, HE JUST PREFERS 'DANIEL' ...NO, NO, DON'T WORRY, PLEASE... ...HE'S JUST PARTICULAR...
BET THAT BABY'S GOING TO GET A STUPID NAME.
DANIEL, THAT'S NOT VERY NICE.
LIKE BROOKE OR BREE OR...
BRIANA MAYBE? ANYWAY, YOU NEED TO PHONE THEM, SAY WELL DONE OR SOMETHING.
WELL DONE.
THANK YOU, SWEETHEART! ...AND OF COURSE, SHE JUST CAN'T WAIT TO MEET HER BIG BROTHER DANNY...

ALCOHOL

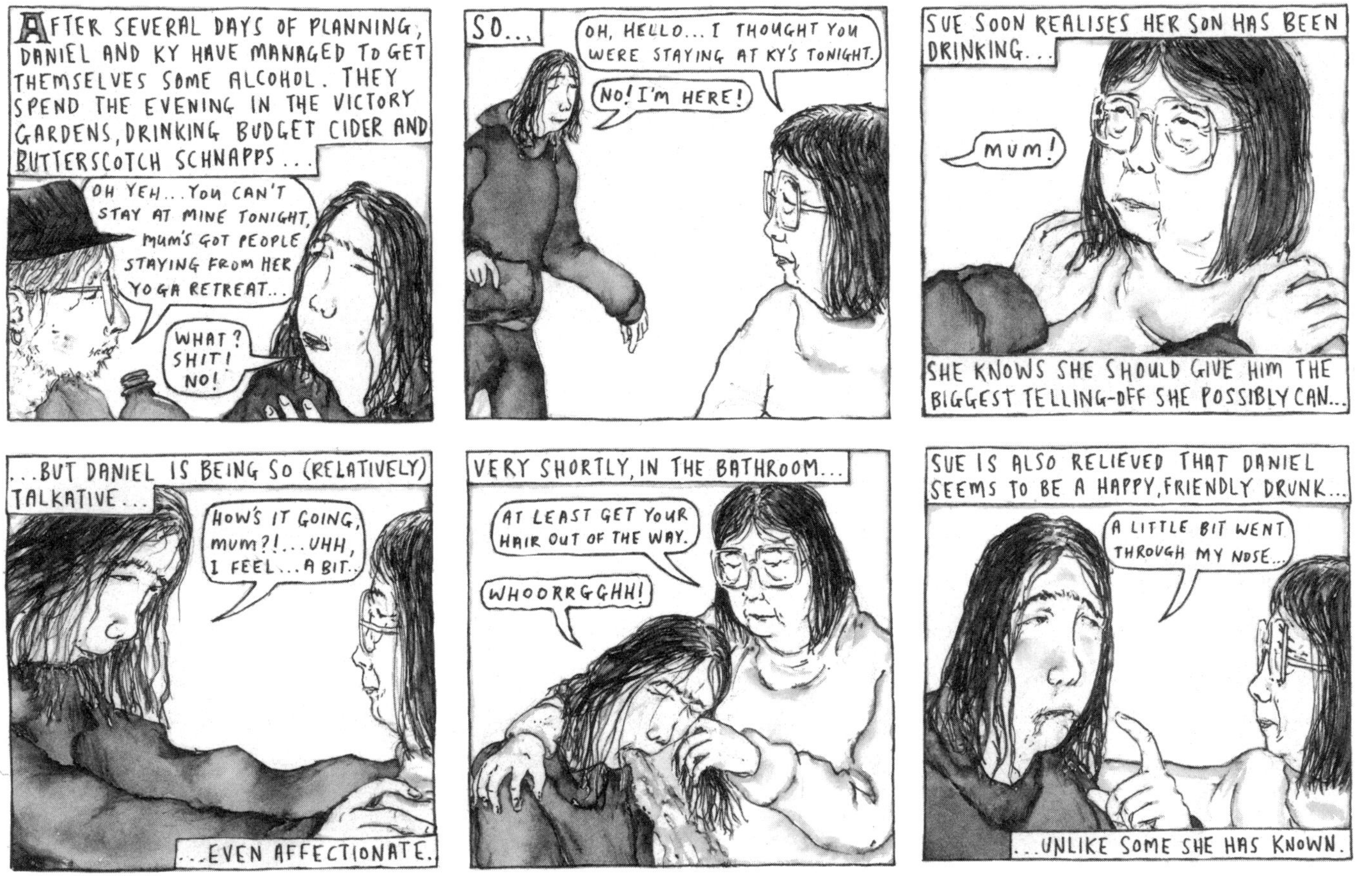
AFTER SEVERAL DAYS OF PLANNING, DANIEL AND KY HAVE MANAGED TO GET THEMSELVES SOME ALCOHOL. THEY SPEND THE EVENING IN THE VICTORY GARDENS, DRINKING BUDGET CIDER AND BUTTERSCOTCH SCHNAPPS...
OH YEH... YOU CAN'T STAY AT MINE TONIGHT, MUM'S GOT PEOPLE STAYING FROM HER YOGA RETREAT...
WHAT? SHIT! NO!
SO...
OH, HELLO... I THOUGHT YOU WERE STAYING AT KY'S TONIGHT.
NO! I'M HERE!
SUE SOON REALISES HER SON HAS BEEN DRINKING...
MUM!
SHE KNOWS SHE SHOULD GIVE HIM THE BIGGEST TELLING-OFF SHE POSSIBLY CAN...
...BUT DANIEL IS BEING SO (RELATIVELY) TALKATIVE...
HOW'S IT GOING, MUM?!... UHH, I FEEL... A BIT..
...EVEN AFFECTIONATE.
VERY SHORTLY, IN THE BATHROOM...
AT LEAST GET YOUR HAIR OUT OF THE WAY.
WHOORRGGHH!
SUE IS ALSO RELIEVED THAT DANIEL SEEMS TO BE A HAPPY, FRIENDLY DRUNK...
A LITTLE BIT WENT THROUGH MY NOSE...
...UNLIKE SOME SHE HAS KNOWN.

GIRLS

Sue is taking her lunch break on the green outside the library...

Watching a group of black-clad teenagers...,

...she gets the feeling Daniel doesn't really hang around in big groups like this...

...with girls.

He just seems to spend all his time alone or with KY...

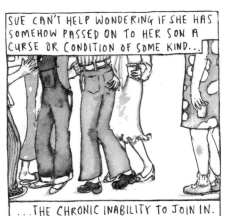

Sue can't help wondering if she has somehow passed on to her son a curse or condition of some kind...

...the chronic inability to join in.

Suddenly, the granary bread reminds Sue of her missing filling...

T-SHIRT

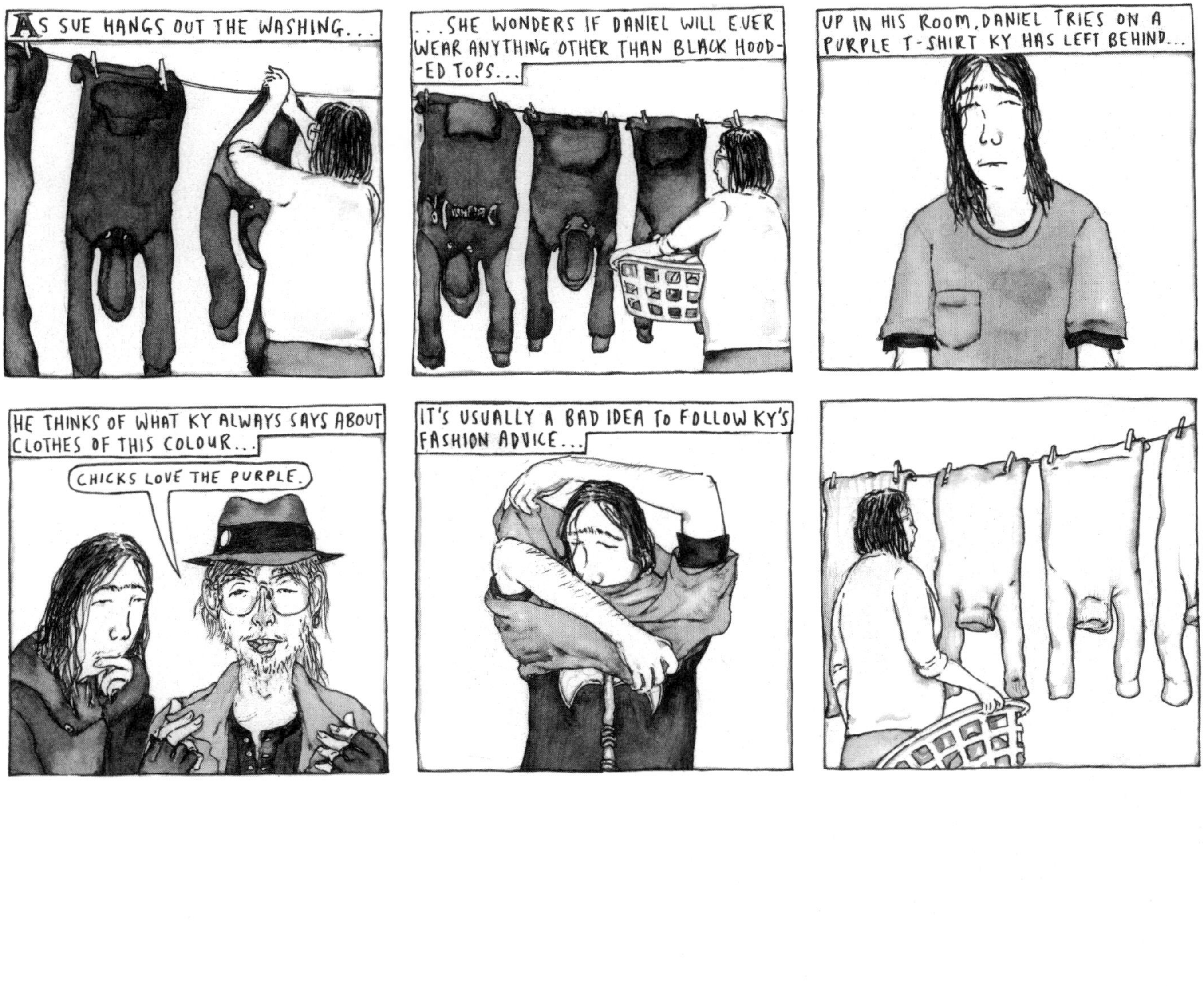

AS SUE HANGS OUT THE WASHING...
...SHE WONDERS IF DANIEL WILL EVER WEAR ANYTHING OTHER THAN BLACK HOOD-ED TOPS...
UP IN HIS ROOM, DANIEL TRIES ON A PURPLE T-SHIRT KY HAS LEFT BEHIND...
HE THINKS OF WHAT KY ALWAYS SAYS ABOUT CLOTHES OF THIS COLOUR...
CHICKS LOVE THE PURPLE.
IT'S USUALLY A BAD IDEA TO FOLLOW KY'S FASHION ADVICE...

FOURTH WEEK

TREES

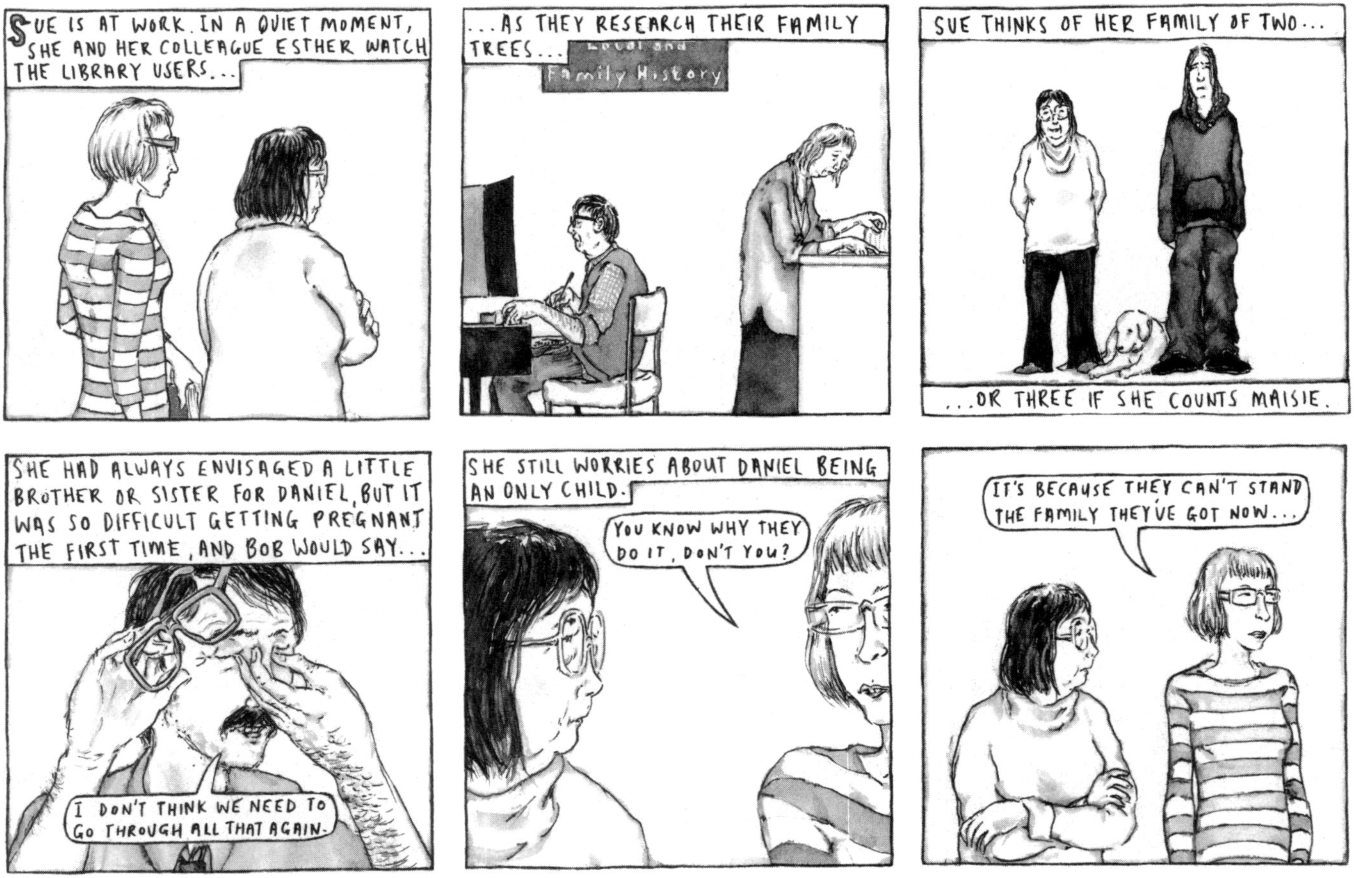
SUE IS AT WORK. IN A QUIET MOMENT, SHE AND HER COLLEAGUE ESTHER WATCH THE LIBRARY USERS...
...AS THEY RESEARCH THEIR FAMILY TREES...
Family History
SUE THINKS OF HER FAMILY OF TWO...
...OR THREE IF SHE COUNTS MAISIE.
SHE HAD ALWAYS ENVISAGED A LITTLE BROTHER OR SISTER FOR DANIEL, BUT IT WAS SO DIFFICULT GETTING PREGNANT THE FIRST TIME, AND BOB WOULD SAY...
I DON'T THINK WE NEED TO GO THROUGH ALL THAT AGAIN.
SHE STILL WORRIES ABOUT DANIEL BEING AN ONLY CHILD.
YOU KNOW WHY THEY DO IT, DON'T YOU?
IT'S BECAUSE THEY CAN'T STAND THE FAMILY THEY'VE GOT NOW...

MESS

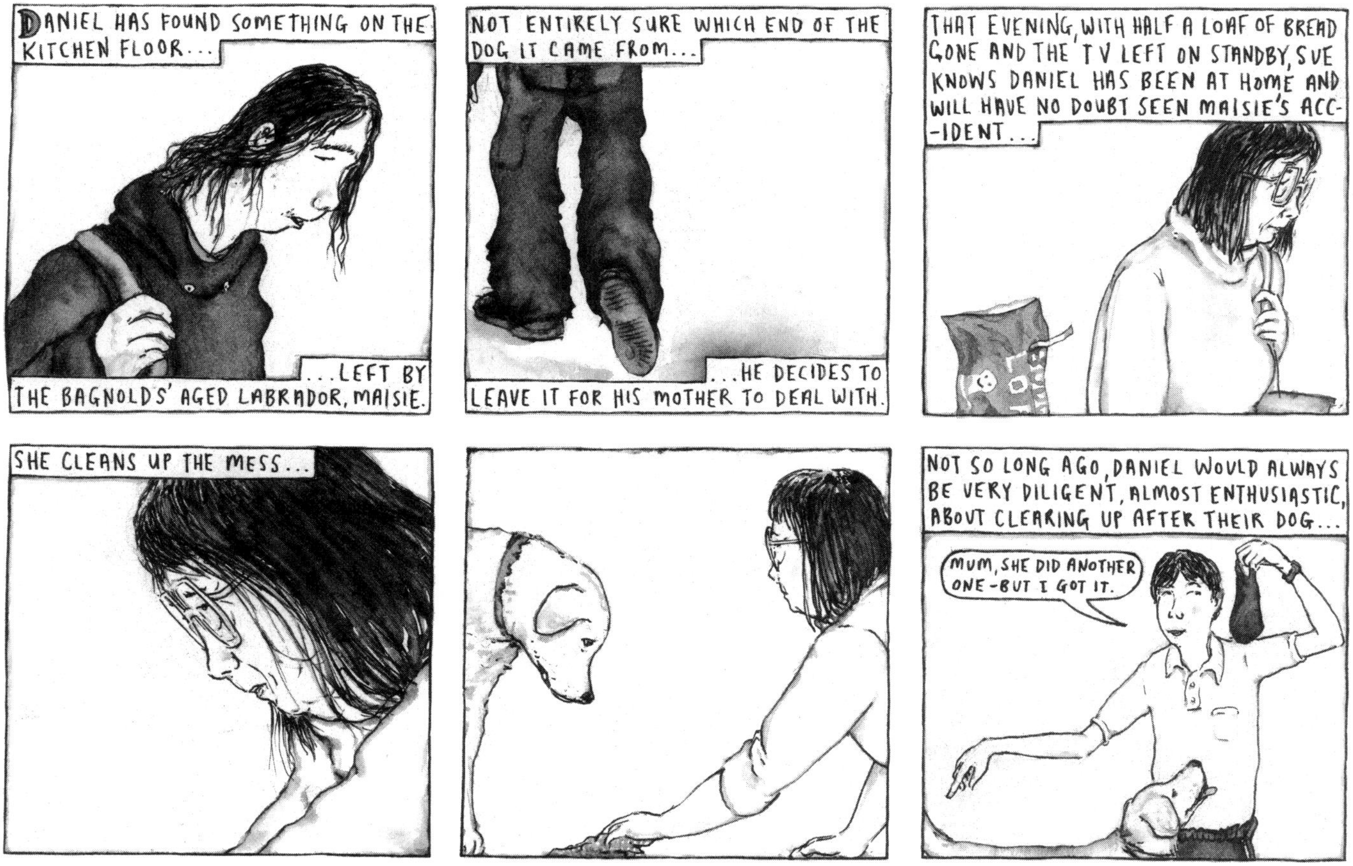
DANIEL HAS FOUND SOMETHING ON THE KITCHEN FLOOR...
...LEFT BY THE BAGNOLD'S' AGED LABRADOR, MAISIE.
NOT ENTIRELY SURE WHICH END OF THE DOG IT CAME FROM...
...HE DECIDES TO LEAVE IT FOR HIS MOTHER TO DEAL WITH.
THAT EVENING, WITH HALF A LOAF OF BREAD GONE AND THE TV LEFT ON STANDBY, SUE KNOWS DANIEL HAS BEEN AT HOME AND WILL HAVE NO DOUBT SEEN MAISIE'S ACC-IDENT...
SHE CLEANS UP THE MESS...
NOT SO LONG AGO, DANIEL WOULD ALWAYS BE VERY DILIGENT, ALMOST ENTHUSIASTIC, ABOUT CLEARING UP AFTER THEIR DOG...
MUM, SHE DID ANOTHER ONE - BUT I GOT IT.

LONG

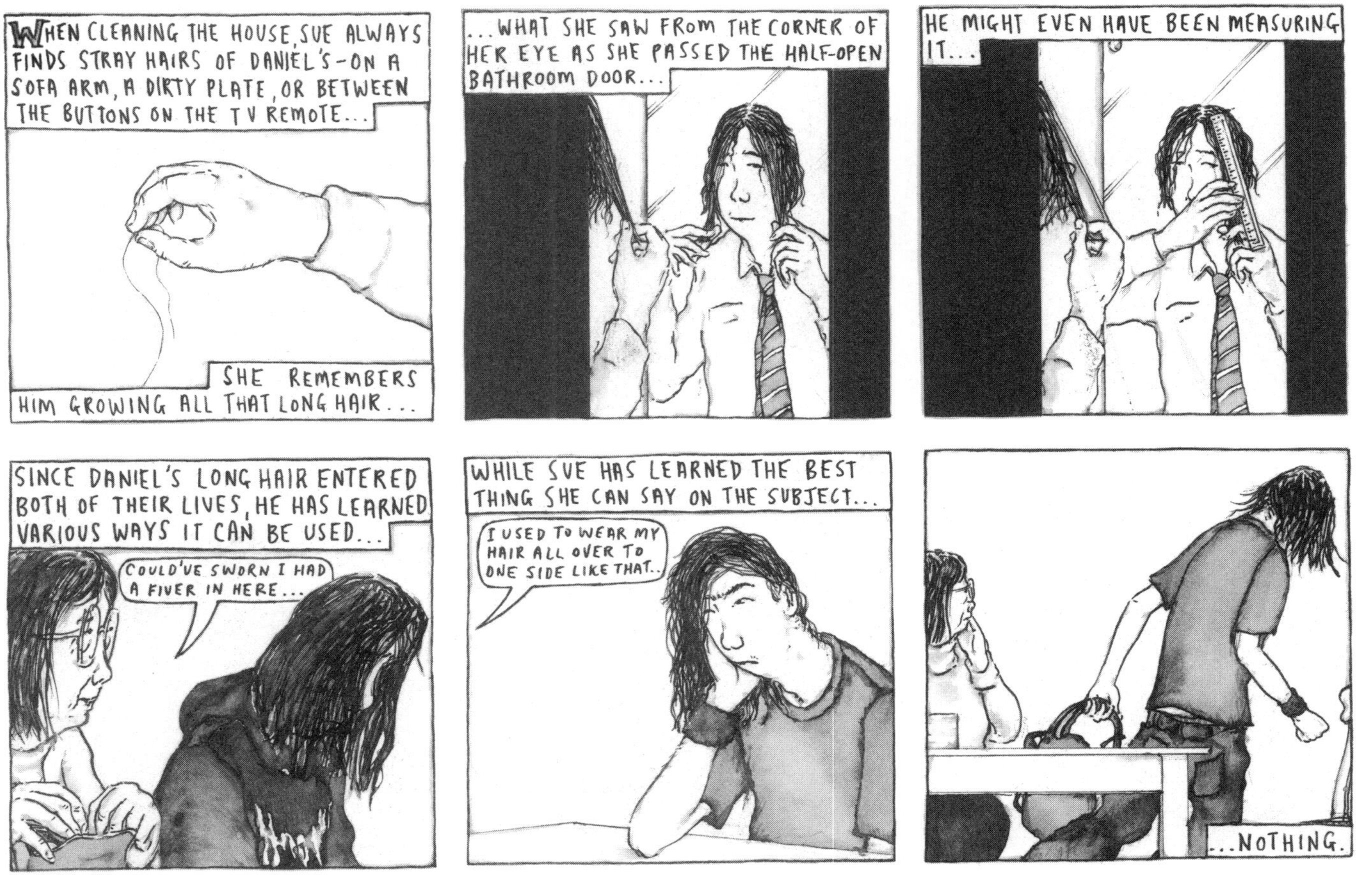
WHEN CLEANING THE HOUSE, SUE ALWAYS FINDS STRAY HAIRS OF DANIEL'S – ON A SOFA ARM, A DIRTY PLATE, OR BETWEEN THE BUTTONS ON THE TV REMOTE...
SHE REMEMBERS HIM GROWING ALL THAT LONG HAIR...
...WHAT SHE SAW FROM THE CORNER OF HER EYE AS SHE PASSED THE HALF-OPEN BATHROOM DOOR...
HE MIGHT EVEN HAVE BEEN MEASURING IT...
SINCE DANIEL'S LONG HAIR ENTERED BOTH OF THEIR LIVES, HE HAS LEARNED VARIOUS WAYS IT CAN BE USED...
COULD'VE SWORN I HAD A FIVER IN HERE...
WHILE SUE HAS LEARNED THE BEST THING SHE CAN SAY ON THE SUBJECT...
I USED TO WEAR MY HAIR ALL OVER TO ONE SIDE LIKE THAT...
...NOTHING.

HOT

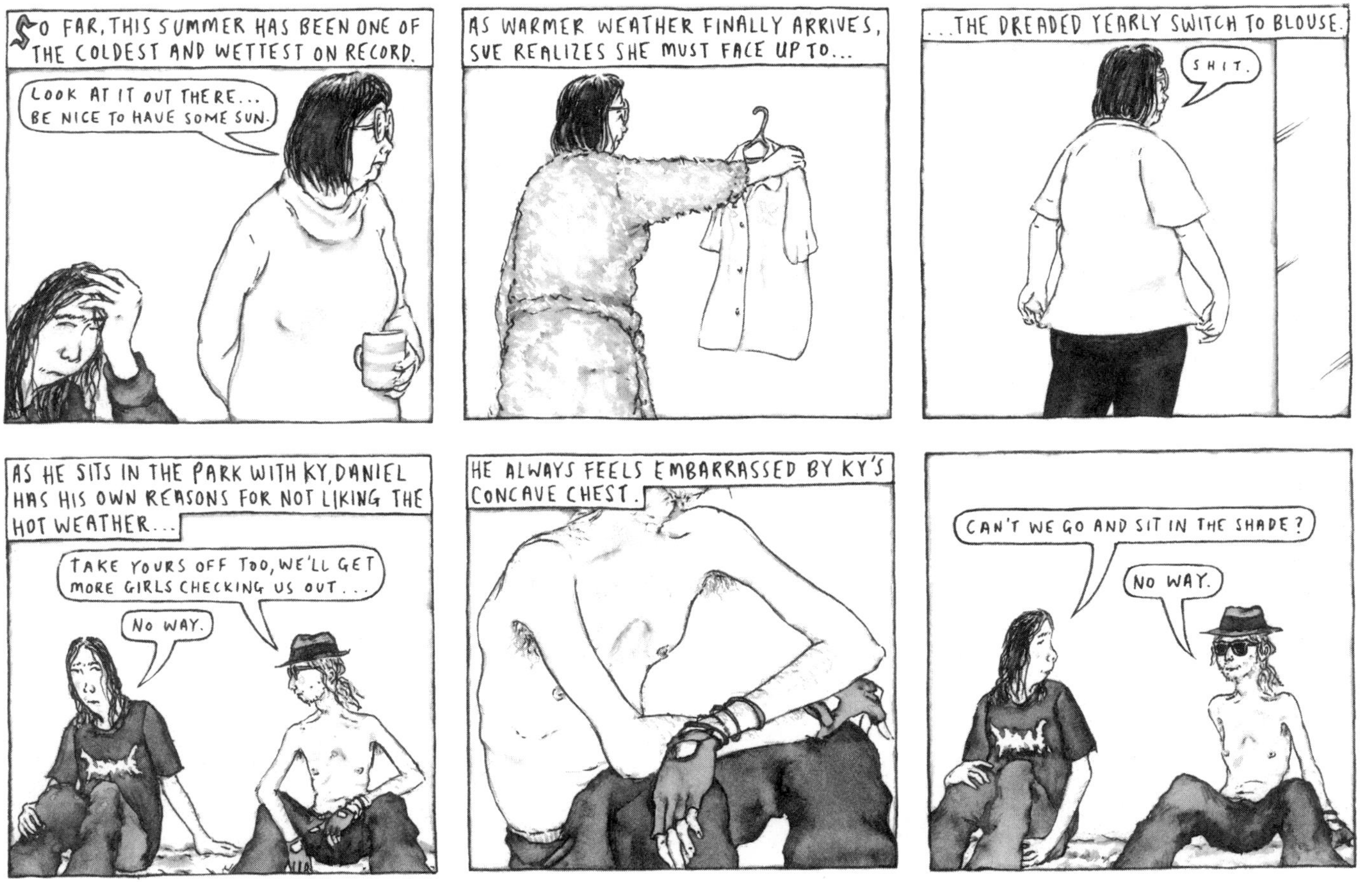
SO FAR, THIS SUMMER HAS BEEN ONE OF THE COLDEST AND WETTEST ON RECORD.
LOOK AT IT OUT THERE... BE NICE TO HAVE SOME SUN.
AS WARMER WEATHER FINALLY ARRIVES, SUE REALIZES SHE MUST FACE UP TO...
...THE DREADED YEARLY SWITCH TO BLOUSE.
SHIT.
AS HE SITS IN THE PARK WITH KY, DANIEL HAS HIS OWN REASONS FOR NOT LIKING THE HOT WEATHER...
TAKE YOURS OFF TOO, WE'LL GET MORE GIRLS CHECKING US OUT...
NO WAY.
HE ALWAYS FEELS EMBARRASSED BY KY'S CONCAVE CHEST.
CAN'T WE GO AND SIT IN THE SHADE?
NO WAY.

NIGHT

IT IS 3.45 AM ON THE HOTTEST NIGHT OF THE YEAR SO FAR AND DANIEL CANNOT SLEEP...

IN THE NEXT DOOR ROOM, SUE IS ALSO AWAKE. SHE IS WORRYING ABOUT DANIEL, WHO SEEMS TO BE IN A WORSE MOOD THAN USUAL WITH THE HOT WEATHER.

DANIEL GOES DOWNSTAIRS TO THE KITCHEN. UNABLE TO FIND ANYTHING TO EAT IN THE FRIDGE, HE DRINKS AN ENTIRE 2 LITRE BOTTLE OF ECONOMY COLA...

SOMETIME AROUND 5 AM, SUE FINALLY GETS BACK TO SLEEP...

SHE HAS A DREAM ABOUT DRIVING HER FIAT PUNTO AND BEING OVERTAKEN BY JEREMY PAXMAN ON A LARGE WHITE HORSE.

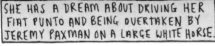

BURP

GAME

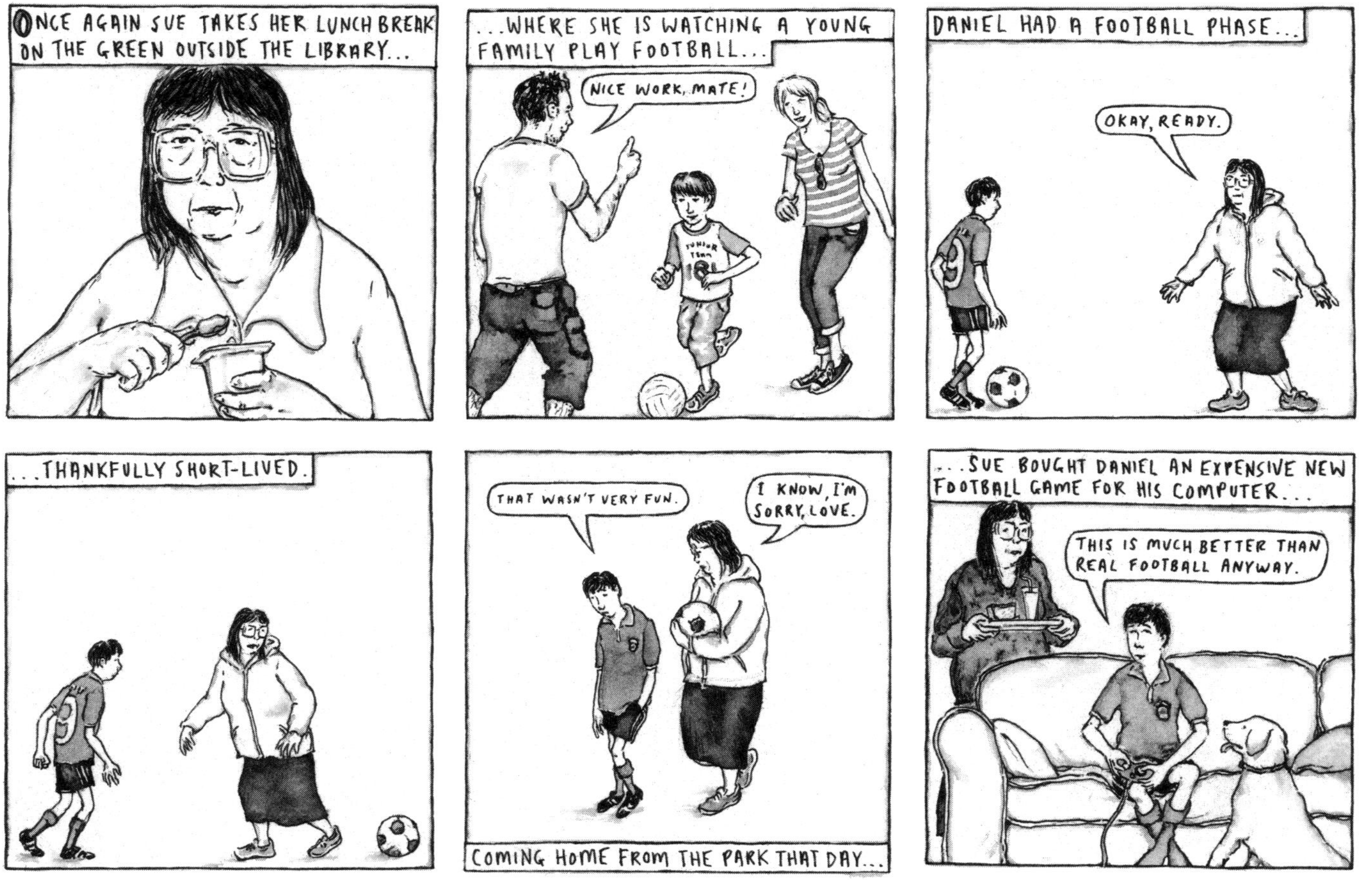
ONCE AGAIN SUE TAKES HER LUNCH BREAK ON THE GREEN OUTSIDE THE LIBRARY...
...WHERE SHE IS WATCHING A YOUNG FAMILY PLAY FOOTBALL...
NICE WORK, MATE!
JUNIOR TEAM
DANIEL HAD A FOOTBALL PHASE...
OKAY, READY.
...THANKFULLY SHORT-LIVED.
THAT WASN'T VERY FUN.
I KNOW, I'M SORRY, LOVE.
COMING HOME FROM THE PARK THAT DAY...
...SUE BOUGHT DANIEL AN EXPENSIVE NEW FOOTBALL GAME FOR HIS COMPUTER...
THIS IS MUCH BETTER THAN REAL FOOTBALL ANYWAY.

WINNING

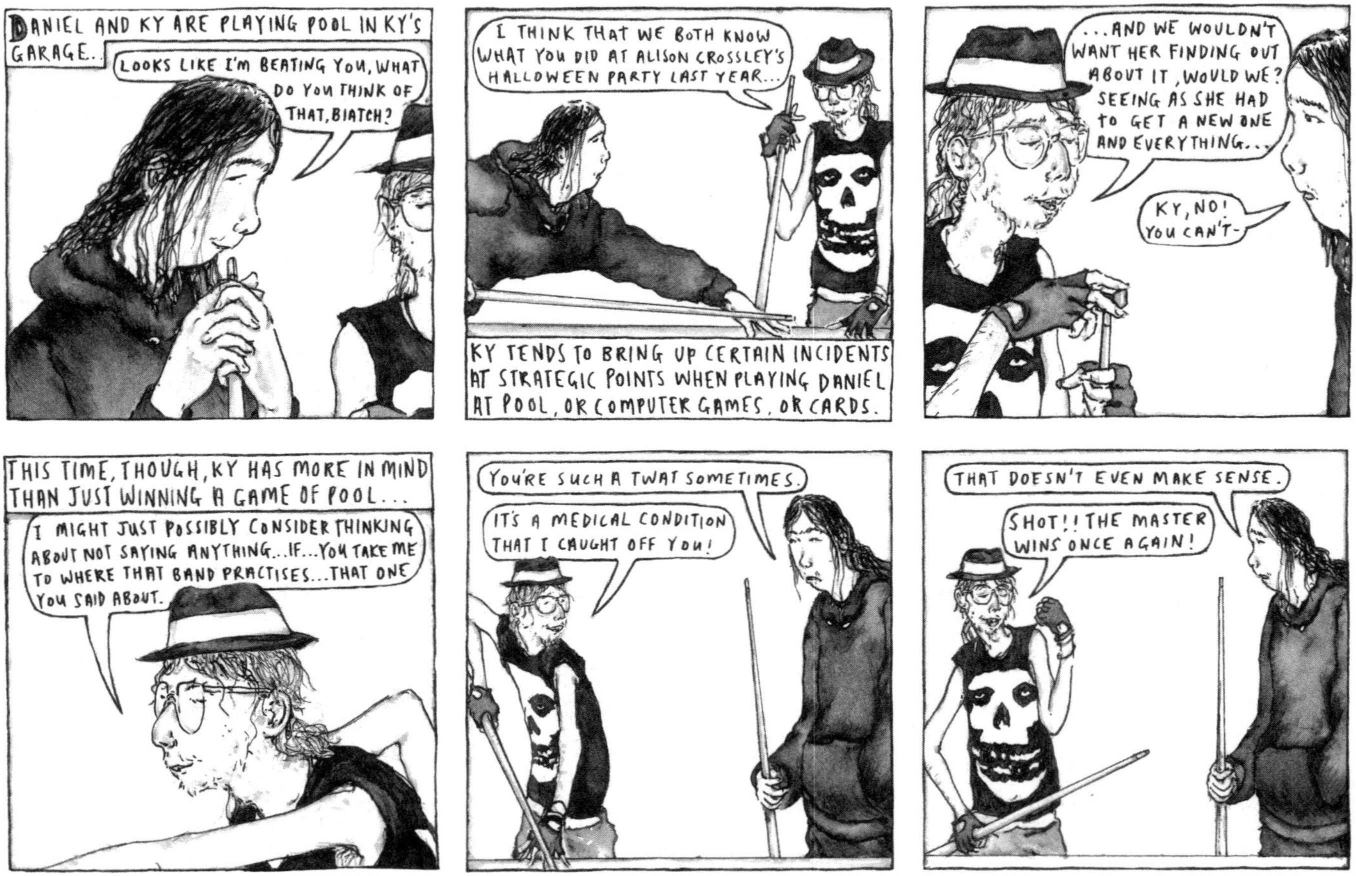
DANIEL AND KY ARE PLAYING POOL IN KY'S GARAGE..
LOOKS LIKE I'M BEATING YOU, WHAT DO YOU THINK OF THAT, BIATCH?
I THINK THAT WE BOTH KNOW WHAT YOU DID AT ALISON CROSSLEY'S HALLOWEEN PARTY LAST YEAR...
KY TENDS TO BRING UP CERTAIN INCIDENTS AT STRATEGIC POINTS WHEN PLAYING DANIEL AT POOL, OR COMPUTER GAMES, OR CARDS.
...AND WE WOULDN'T WANT HER FINDING OUT ABOUT IT, WOULD WE? SEEING AS SHE HAD TO GET A NEW ONE AND EVERYTHING...
KY, NO! YOU CAN'T-
THIS TIME, THOUGH, KY HAS MORE IN MIND THAN JUST WINNING A GAME OF POOL...
I MIGHT JUST POSSIBLY CONSIDER THINKING ABOUT NOT SAYING ANYTHING...IF...YOU TAKE ME TO WHERE THAT BAND PRACTISES...THAT ONE YOU SAID ABOUT.
YOU'RE SUCH A TWAT SOMETIMES.
IT'S A MEDICAL CONDITION THAT I CAUGHT OFF YOU!
THAT DOESN'T EVEN MAKE SENSE.
SHOT!! THE MASTER WINS ONCE AGAIN!

FRIEND

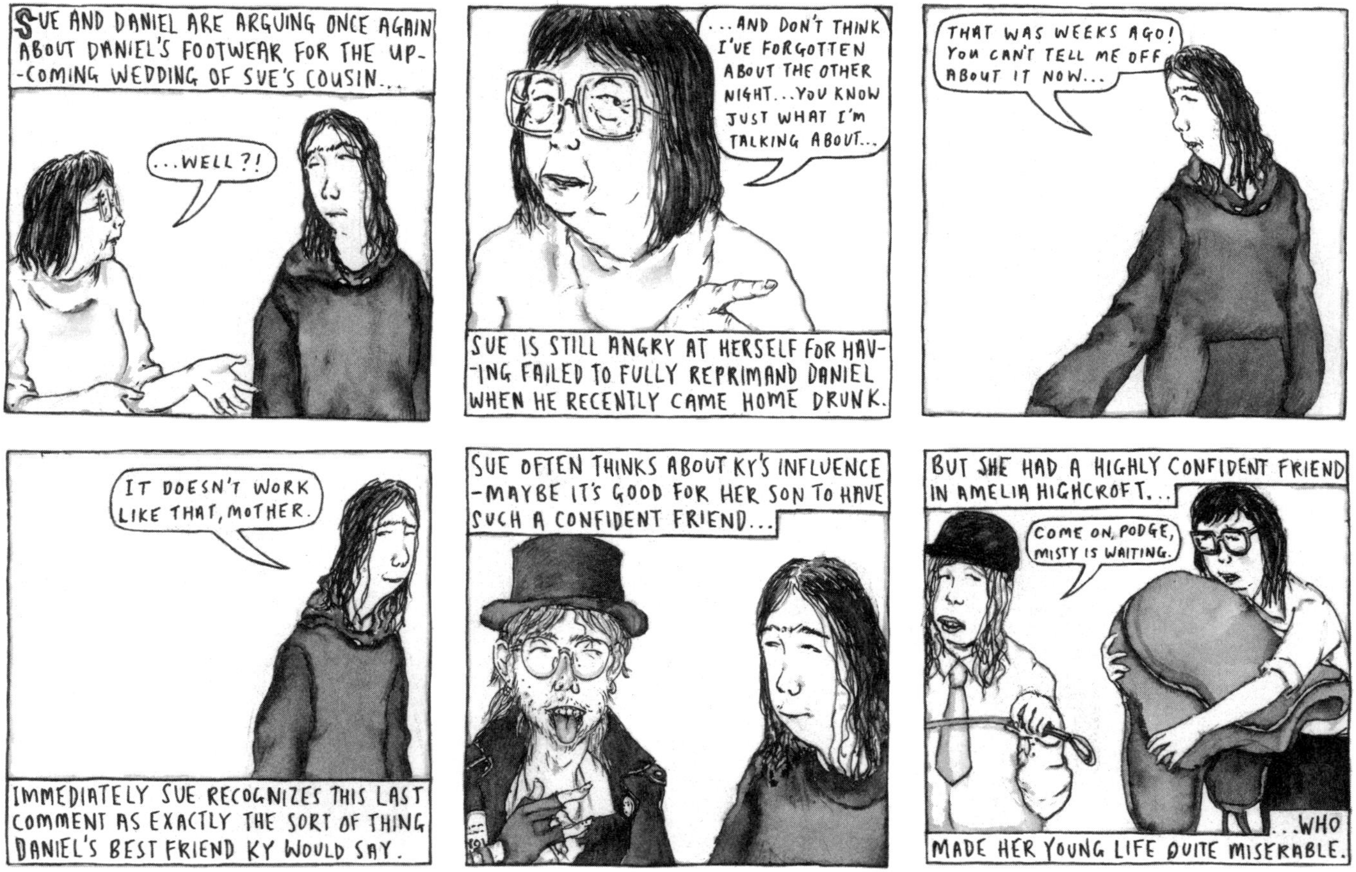
SUE AND DANIEL ARE ARGUING ONCE AGAIN ABOUT DANIEL'S FOOTWEAR FOR THE UP-COMING WEDDING OF SUE'S COUSIN...
...WELL?!
...AND DON'T THINK I'VE FORGOTTEN ABOUT THE OTHER NIGHT...YOU KNOW JUST WHAT I'M TALKING ABOUT...
SUE IS STILL ANGRY AT HERSELF FOR HAV-ING FAILED TO FULLY REPRIMAND DANIEL WHEN HE RECENTLY CAME HOME DRUNK.
THAT WAS WEEKS AGO! YOU CAN'T TELL ME OFF ABOUT IT NOW...
IT DOESN'T WORK LIKE THAT, MOTHER.
IMMEDIATELY SUE RECOGNIZES THIS LAST COMMENT AS EXACTLY THE SORT OF THING DANIEL'S BEST FRIEND KY WOULD SAY.
SUE OFTEN THINKS ABOUT KY'S INFLUENCE -MAYBE IT'S GOOD FOR HER SON TO HAVE SUCH A CONFIDENT FRIEND...
BUT SHE HAD A HIGHLY CONFIDENT FRIEND IN AMELIA HIGHCROFT...
COME ON, PODGE, MISTY IS WAITING.
...WHO MADE HER YOUNG LIFE QUITE MISERABLE.

PACKAGE

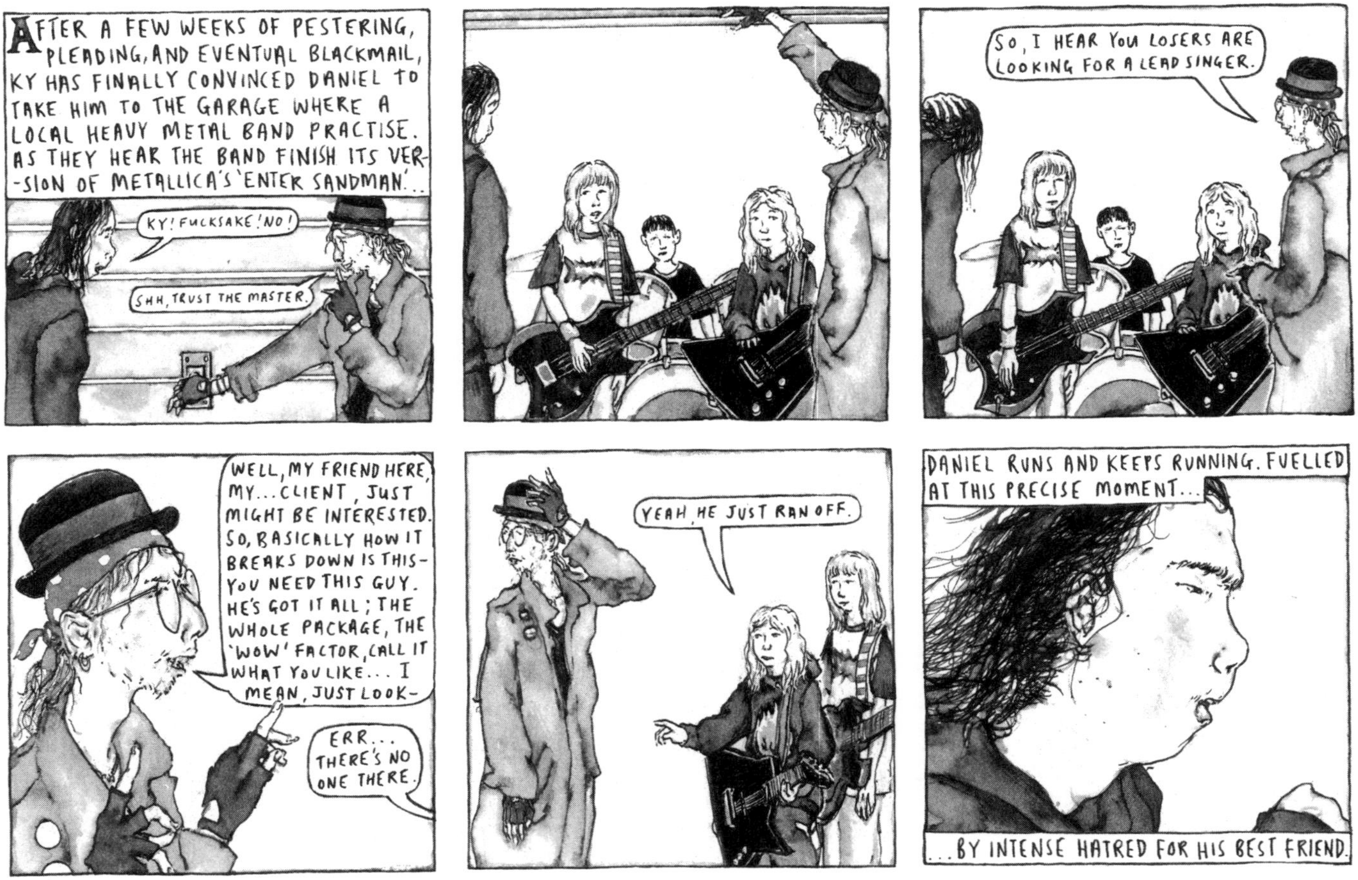
AFTER A FEW WEEKS OF PESTERING, PLEADING, AND EVENTUAL BLACKMAIL, KY HAS FINALLY CONVINCED DANIEL TO TAKE HIM TO THE GARAGE WHERE A LOCAL HEAVY METAL BAND PRACTISE. AS THEY HEAR THE BAND FINISH ITS VER-SION OF METALLICA'S 'ENTER SANDMAN'...
KY! FUCKSAKE! NO!
SHH, TRUST THE MASTER.
SO, I HEAR YOU LOSERS ARE LOOKING FOR A LEAD SINGER.
WELL, MY FRIEND HERE, MY... CLIENT, JUST MIGHT BE INTERESTED. SO, BASICALLY HOW IT BREAKS DOWN IS THIS- YOU NEED THIS GUY. HE'S GOT IT ALL; THE WHOLE PACKAGE, THE 'WOW' FACTOR, CALL IT WHAT YOU LIKE... I MEAN, JUST LOOK-
ERR... THERE'S NO ONE THERE.
YEAH, HE JUST RAN OFF.
DANIEL RUNS AND KEEPS RUNNING. FUELLED AT THIS PRECISE MOMENT...
...BY INTENSE HATRED FOR HIS BEST FRIEND.

FIFTH WEEK

TELLING

OVER THE LAST FEW DAYS, SUE HAS NOTICED DANIEL AROUND THE HOUSE A LOT.

NOT THAT SHE HAS ACTUALLY SEEN HIM ANY MORE THAN USUAL, BUT THERE ARE OTHER WAYS OF TELLING THAT HE'S IN...

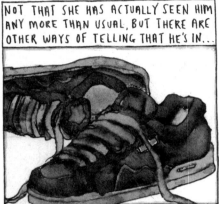

THE BASS RUMBLE OF FOOTSTEPS AND MUSIC COMING THROUGH THE KITCHEN CEILING...

THE TRAIL OF BLACK HOODED TOPS LEFT THROUGHOUT THE HOUSE...

THE FREQUENTLY EMPTY FRIDGE...

WITH THE OCCASIONAL GRUNTED EXCHANGE ON THE LANDING...

IN AGAIN TONIGHT, LOVE?

MMFFH.

TATTOO

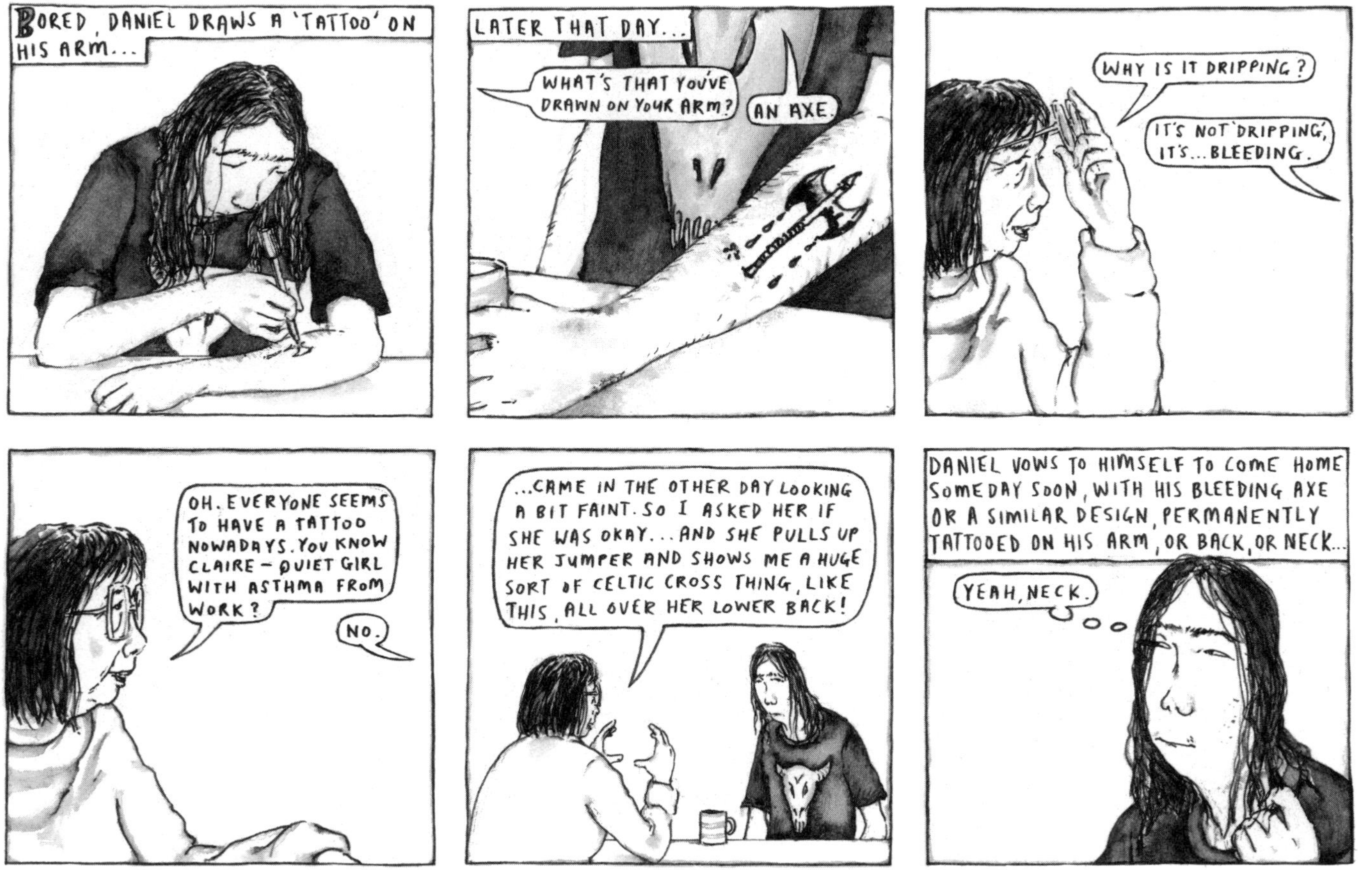

BORED, DANIEL DRAWS A 'TATTOO' ON HIS ARM...
LATER THAT DAY...
WHAT'S THAT YOU'VE DRAWN ON YOUR ARM?
AN AXE.
WHY IS IT DRIPPING?
IT'S NOT 'DRIPPING', IT'S... BLEEDING.
OH. EVERYONE SEEMS TO HAVE A TATTOO NOWADAYS. YOU KNOW CLAIRE – QUIET GIRL WITH ASTHMA FROM WORK?
NO.
...CAME IN THE OTHER DAY LOOKING A BIT FAINT. SO I ASKED HER IF SHE WAS OKAY... AND SHE PULLS UP HER JUMPER AND SHOWS ME A HUGE SORT OF CELTIC CROSS THING, LIKE THIS, ALL OVER HER LOWER BACK!
DANIEL VOWS TO HIMSELF TO COME HOME SOMEDAY SOON, WITH HIS BLEEDING AXE OR A SIMILAR DESIGN, PERMANENTLY TATTOOED ON HIS ARM, OR BACK, OR NECK...
YEAH, NECK.

SHOPPING

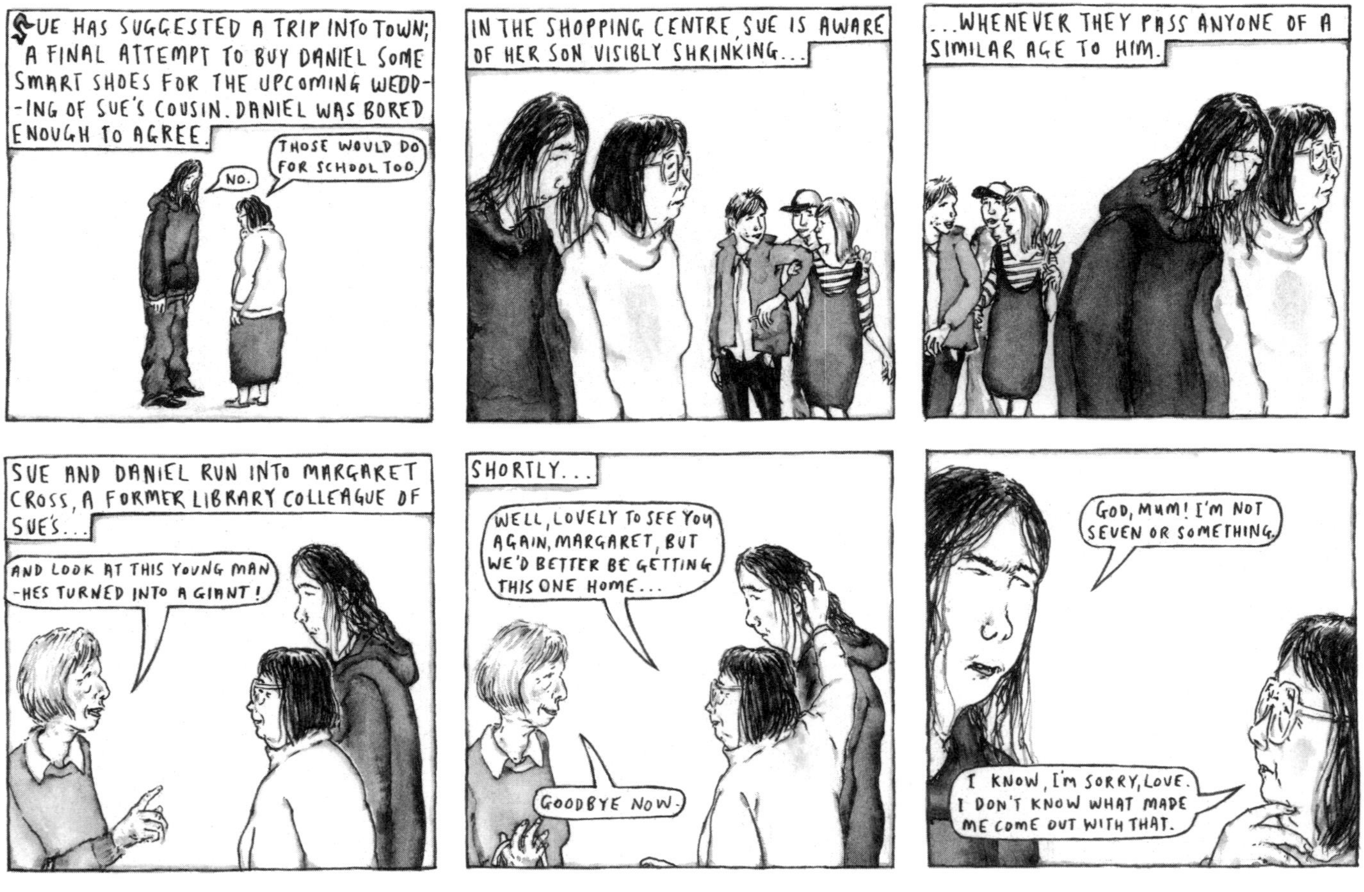

SUE HAS SUGGESTED A TRIP INTO TOWN; A FINAL ATTEMPT TO BUY DANIEL SOME SMART SHOES FOR THE UPCOMING WEDD-ING OF SUE'S COUSIN. DANIEL WAS BORED ENOUGH TO AGREE.
THOSE WOULD DO FOR SCHOOL TOO.
NO.
IN THE SHOPPING CENTRE, SUE IS AWARE OF HER SON VISIBLY SHRINKING...
...WHENEVER THEY PASS ANYONE OF A SIMILAR AGE TO HIM.
SUE AND DANIEL RUN INTO MARGARET CROSS, A FORMER LIBRARY COLLEAGUE OF SUE'S...
AND LOOK AT THIS YOUNG MAN -HES TURNED INTO A GIANT!
SHORTLY...
WELL, LOVELY TO SEE YOU AGAIN, MARGARET, BUT WE'D BETTER BE GETTING THIS ONE HOME...
GOODBYE NOW.
GOD, MUM! I'M NOT SEVEN OR SOMETHING.
I KNOW, I'M SORRY, LOVE. I DON'T KNOW WHAT MADE ME COME OUT WITH THAT.

MAKEOVER

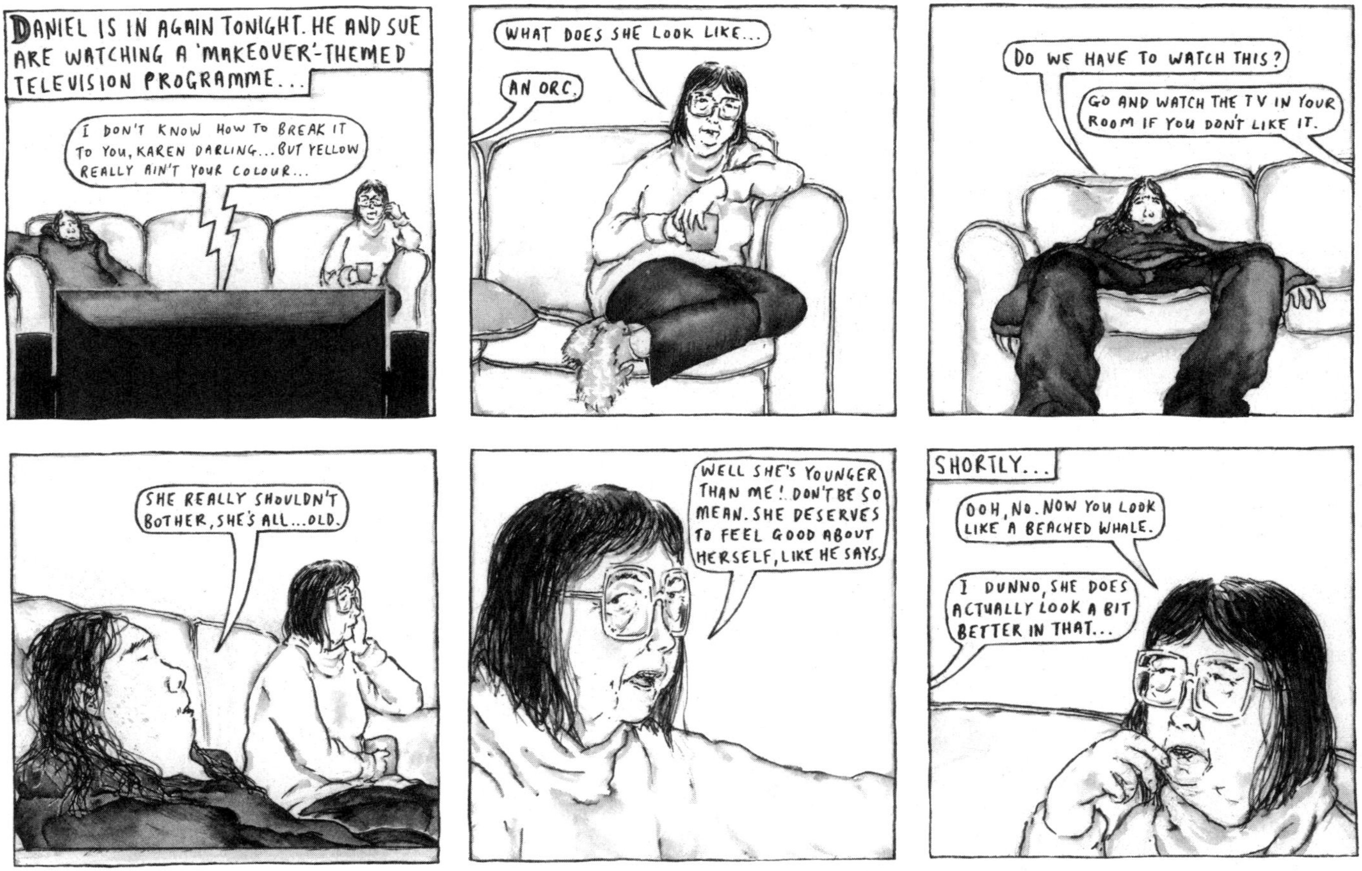
DANIEL IS IN AGAIN TONIGHT. HE AND SUE ARE WATCHING A 'MAKEOVER'-THEMED TELEVISION PROGRAMME...
I DON'T KNOW HOW TO BREAK IT TO YOU, KAREN DARLING... BUT YELLOW REALLY AIN'T YOUR COLOUR...
WHAT DOES SHE LOOK LIKE...
AN ORC.
DO WE HAVE TO WATCH THIS?
GO AND WATCH THE TV IN YOUR ROOM IF YOU DON'T LIKE IT.
SHE REALLY SHOULDN'T BOTHER, SHE'S ALL...OLD.
WELL SHE'S YOUNGER THAN ME! DON'T BE SO MEAN. SHE DESERVES TO FEEL GOOD ABOUT HERSELF, LIKE HE SAYS.
SHORTLY...
OOH, NO. NOW YOU LOOK LIKE A BEACHED WHALE.
I DUNNO, SHE DOES ACTUALLY LOOK A BIT BETTER IN THAT...

CHIPS

DANIEL AND SUE ARE WAITING FOR FISH AND CHIPS...

HE HATES BEING SEEN IN PUBLIC WITH HIS MOTHER, MOST OF ALL WHEN THERE'S A CHANCE OF SEEING SOMEONE FROM SCHOOL.

...LIKE THE TWO BOYS HE RECOGNIZES FROM THE YEAR BELOW, CURRENTLY STARING AT HIM FROM THE QUEUE...

DANIEL DOES HIS BEST TO BECOME LESS VISIBLE...

...WITHOUT SUCCESS.

COD AND CHIPS TWICE, SALT AND VINEGAR?

THAT'S £8.50 PLEASE.

THANKS.

DANIEL, WOULD YOU MIND WAITING FOR ME PLEASE?

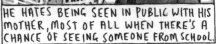

SOFA

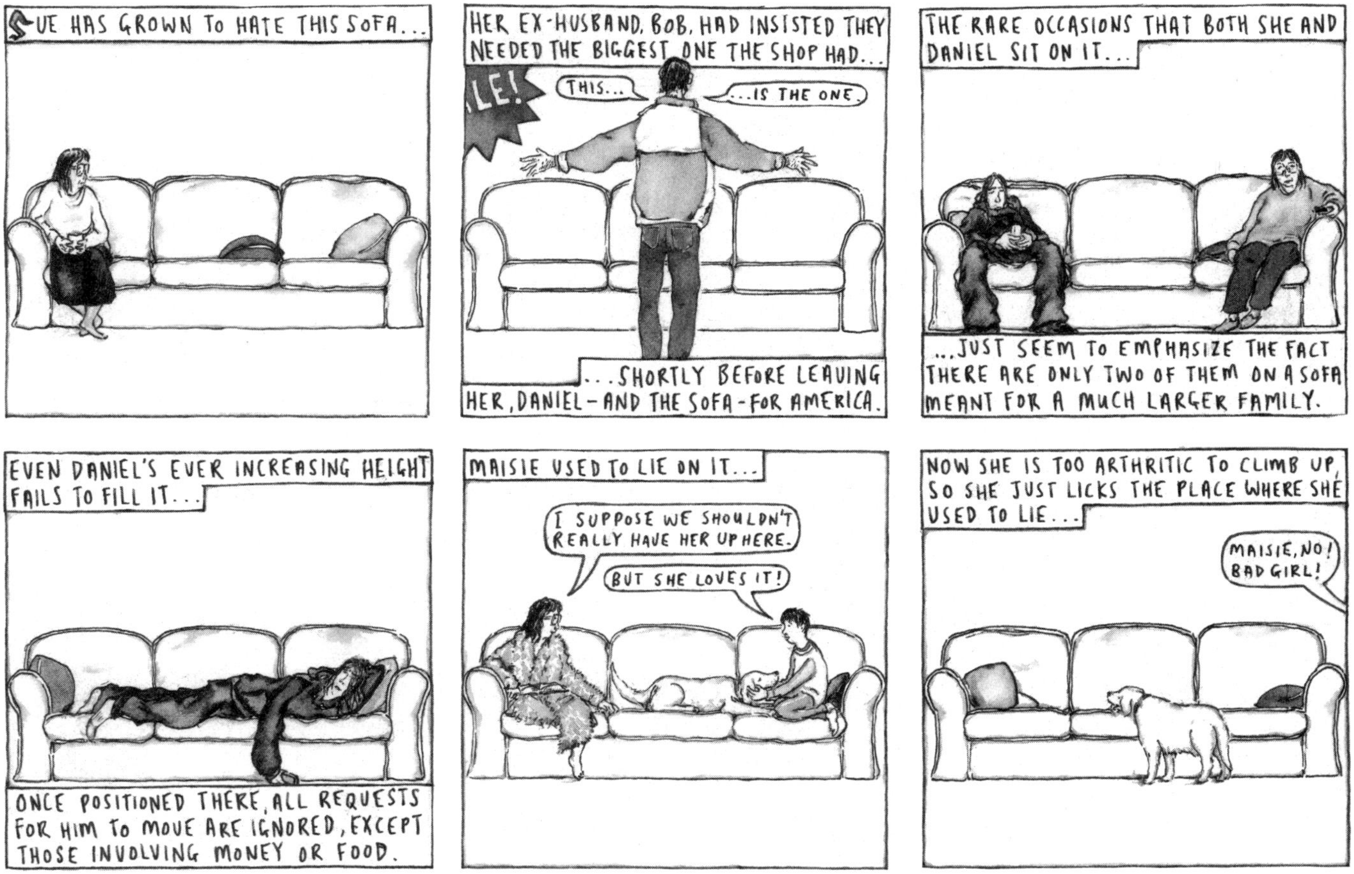
SUE HAS GROWN TO HATE THIS SOFA...
HER EX-HUSBAND, BOB, HAD INSISTED THEY NEEDED THE BIGGEST ONE THE SHOP HAD...
LE!
THIS...
...IS THE ONE.
...SHORTLY BEFORE LEAVING HER, DANIEL - AND THE SOFA - FOR AMERICA.
THE RARE OCCASIONS THAT BOTH SHE AND DANIEL SIT ON IT...
...JUST SEEM TO EMPHASIZE THE FACT THERE ARE ONLY TWO OF THEM ON A SOFA MEANT FOR A MUCH LARGER FAMILY.
EVEN DANIEL'S EVER INCREASING HEIGHT FAILS TO FILL IT...
ONCE POSITIONED THERE, ALL REQUESTS FOR HIM TO MOVE ARE IGNORED, EXCEPT THOSE INVOLVING MONEY OR FOOD.
MAISIE USED TO LIE ON IT...
I SUPPOSE WE SHOULDN'T REALLY HAVE HER UP HERE.
BUT SHE LOVES IT!
NOW SHE IS TOO ARTHRITIC TO CLIMB UP, SO SHE JUST LICKS THE PLACE WHERE SHE USED TO LIE...
MAISIE, NO! BAD GIRL!

TAXIDERMY

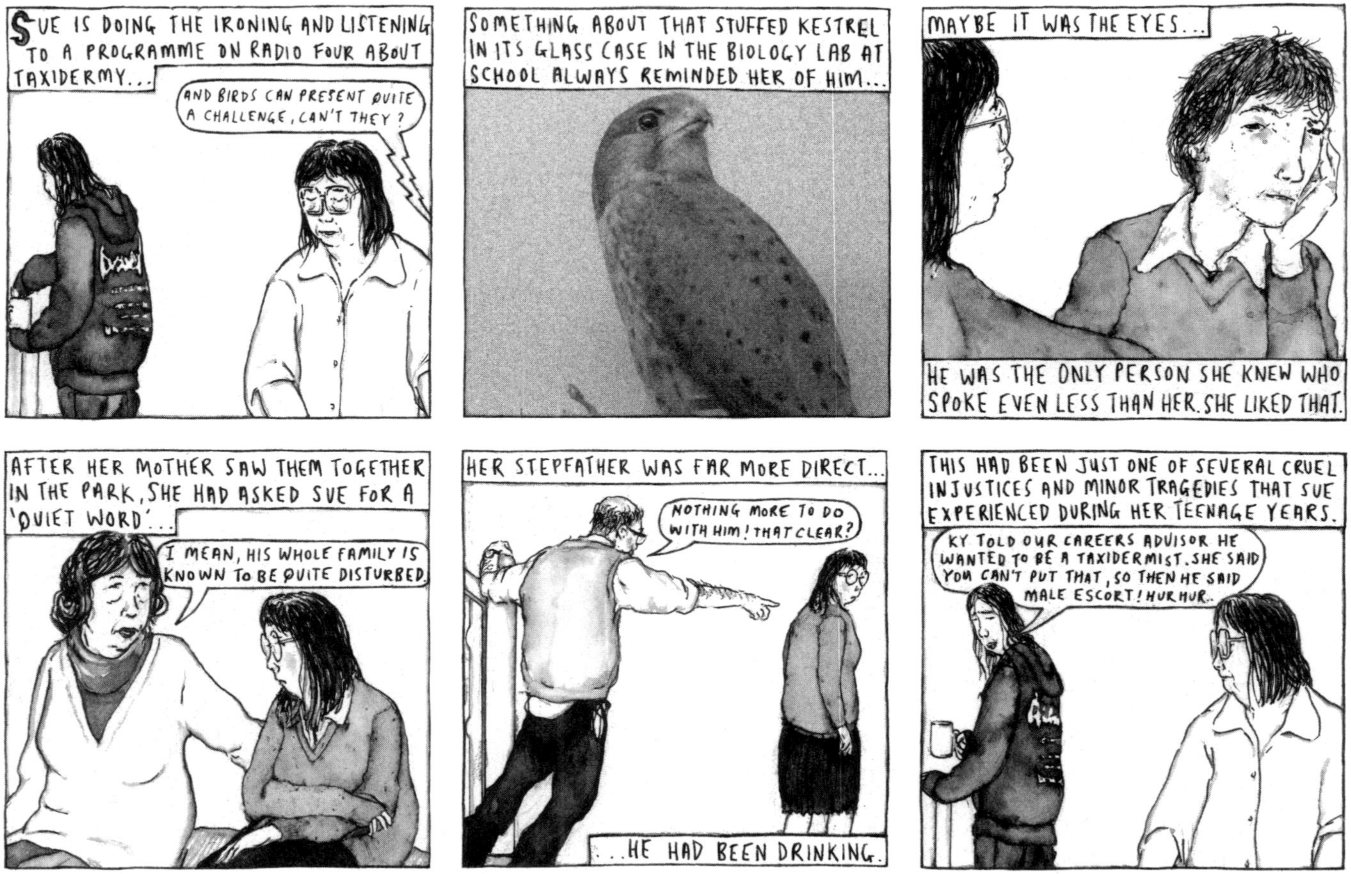
SUE IS DOING THE IRONING AND LISTENING TO A PROGRAMME ON RADIO FOUR ABOUT TAXIDERMY...
AND BIRDS CAN PRESENT QUITE A CHALLENGE, CAN'T THEY?
SOMETHING ABOUT THAT STUFFED KESTREL IN ITS GLASS CASE IN THE BIOLOGY LAB AT SCHOOL ALWAYS REMINDED HER OF HIM...
MAYBE IT WAS THE EYES...
HE WAS THE ONLY PERSON SHE KNEW WHO SPOKE EVEN LESS THAN HER. SHE LIKED THAT.
AFTER HER MOTHER SAW THEM TOGETHER IN THE PARK, SHE HAD ASKED SUE FOR A 'QUIET WORD'...
I MEAN, HIS WHOLE FAMILY IS KNOWN TO BE QUITE DISTURBED.
HER STEPFATHER WAS FAR MORE DIRECT...
NOTHING MORE TO DO WITH HIM! THAT CLEAR?
...HE HAD BEEN DRINKING.
THIS HAD BEEN JUST ONE OF SEVERAL CRUEL INJUSTICES AND MINOR TRAGEDIES THAT SUE EXPERIENCED DURING HER TEENAGE YEARS.
KY TOLD OUR CAREERS ADVISOR HE WANTED TO BE A TAXIDERMIST. SHE SAID YOU CAN'T PUT THAT, SO THEN HE SAID MALE ESCORT! HUR HUR..

SOMEONE

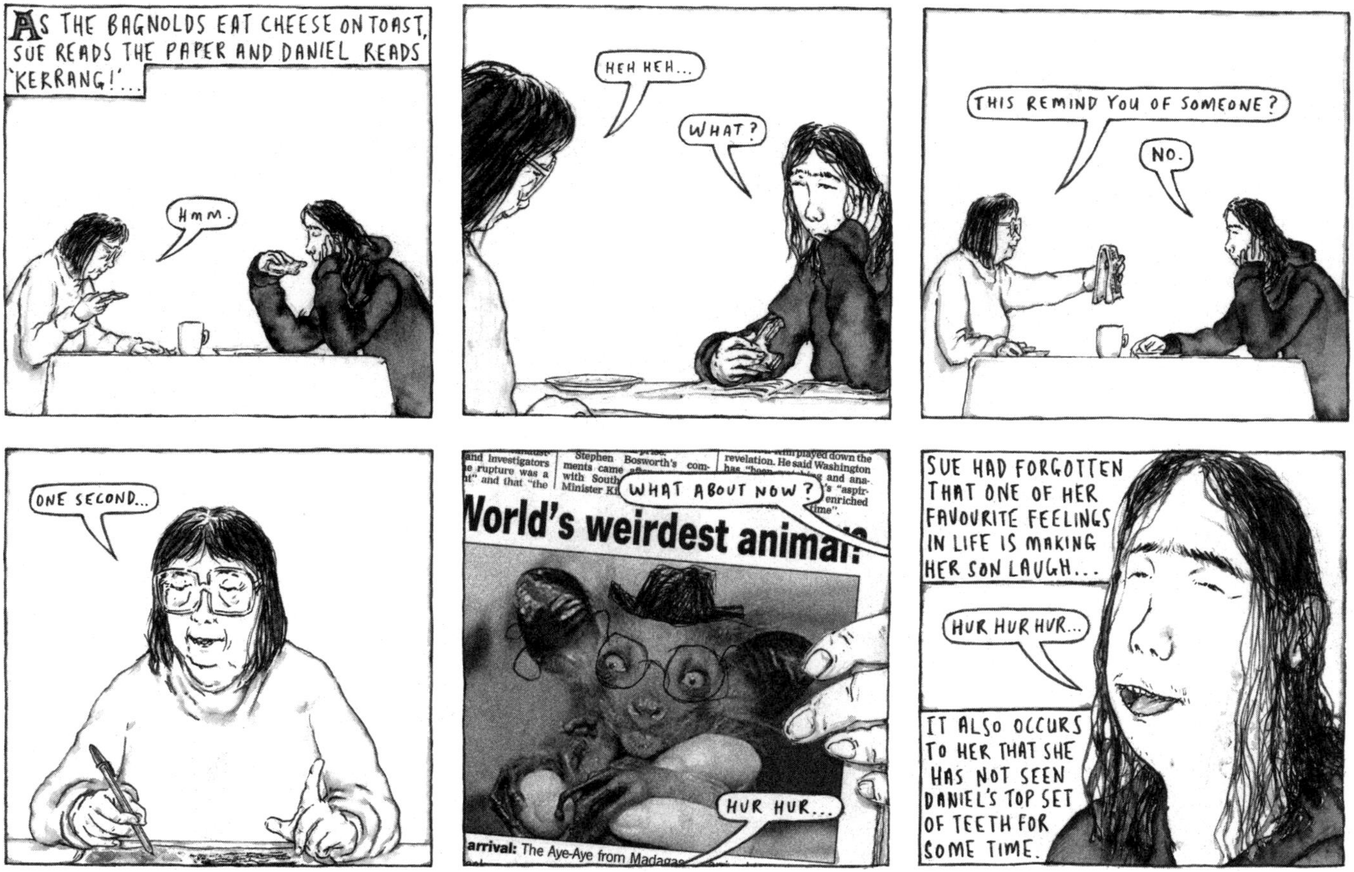
AS THE BAGNOLDS EAT CHEESE ON TOAST, SUE READS THE PAPER AND DANIEL READS 'KERRANG!'...
HMM.
HEH HEH...
WHAT?
THIS REMIND YOU OF SOMEONE?
NO.
ONE SECOND...
World's weirdest animal
WHAT ABOUT NOW?
HUR HUR...
arrival: The Aye-Aye from Madagas
SUE HAD FORGOTTEN THAT ONE OF HER FAVOURITE FEELINGS IN LIFE IS MAKING HER SON LAUGH...
HUR HUR HUR...
IT ALSO OCCURS TO HER THAT SHE HAS NOT SEEN DANIEL'S TOP SET OF TEETH FOR SOME TIME.

STUCK

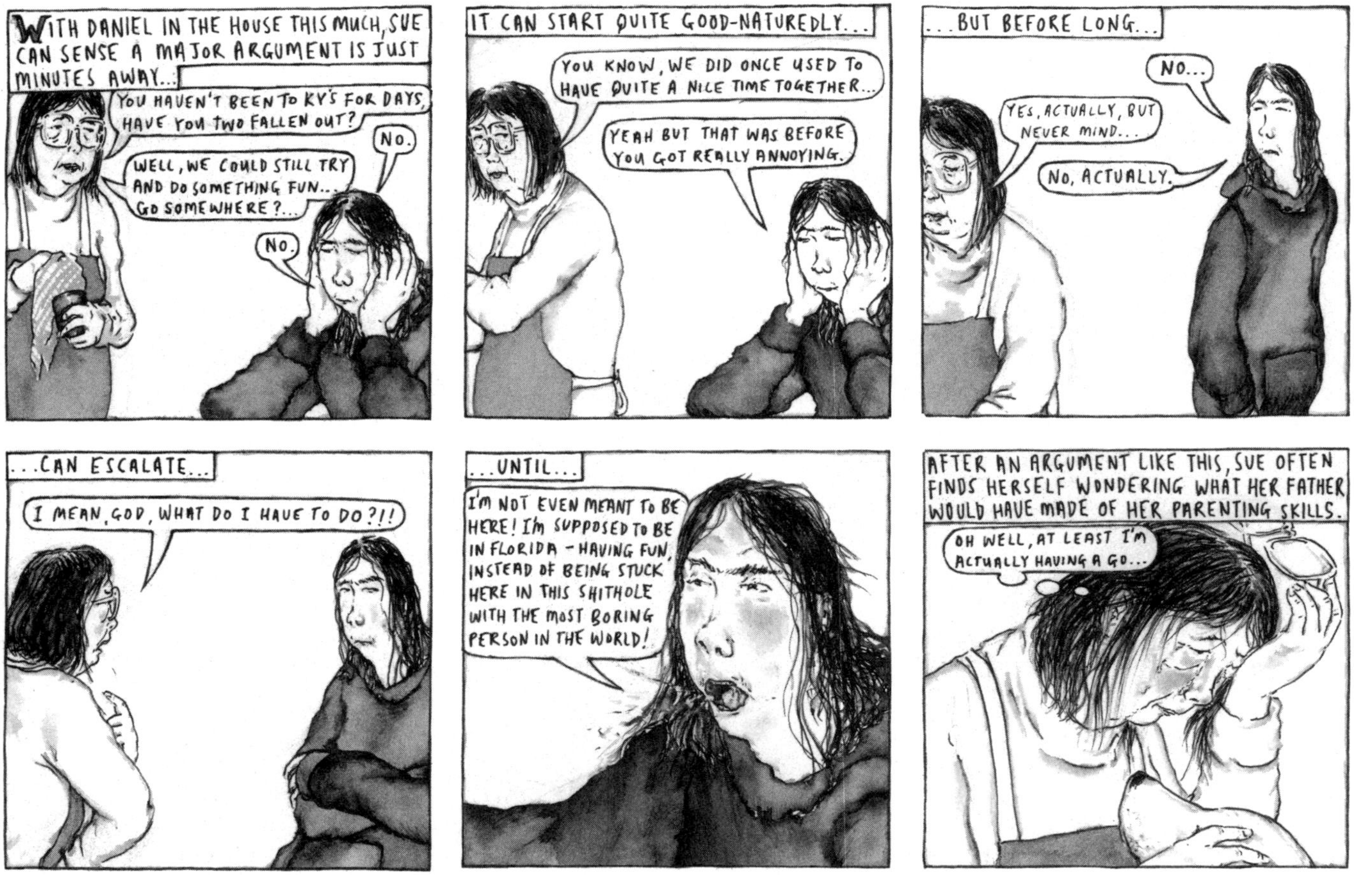
WITH DANIEL IN THE HOUSE THIS MUCH, SUE CAN SENSE A MAJOR ARGUMENT IS JUST MINUTES AWAY...
YOU HAVEN'T BEEN TO KY'S FOR DAYS, HAVE YOU TWO FALLEN OUT?
NO.
WELL, WE COULD STILL TRY AND DO SOMETHING FUN... GO SOMEWHERE?...
NO.
IT CAN START QUITE GOOD-NATUREDLY...
YOU KNOW, WE DID ONCE USED TO HAVE QUITE A NICE TIME TOGETHER...
YEAH BUT THAT WAS BEFORE YOU GOT REALLY ANNOYING.
...BUT BEFORE LONG...
NO...
YES, ACTUALLY, BUT NEVER MIND...
NO, ACTUALLY.
...CAN ESCALATE...
I MEAN, GOD, WHAT DO I HAVE TO DO?!!
...UNTIL...
I'M NOT EVEN MEANT TO BE HERE! I'M SUPPOSED TO BE IN FLORIDA - HAVING FUN, INSTEAD OF BEING STUCK HERE IN THIS SHITHOLE WITH THE MOST BORING PERSON IN THE WORLD!
AFTER AN ARGUMENT LIKE THIS, SUE OFTEN FINDS HERSELF WONDERING WHAT HER FATHER WOULD HAVE MADE OF HER PARENTING SKILLS.
OH WELL, AT LEAST I'M ACTUALLY HAVING A GO...

HOURS

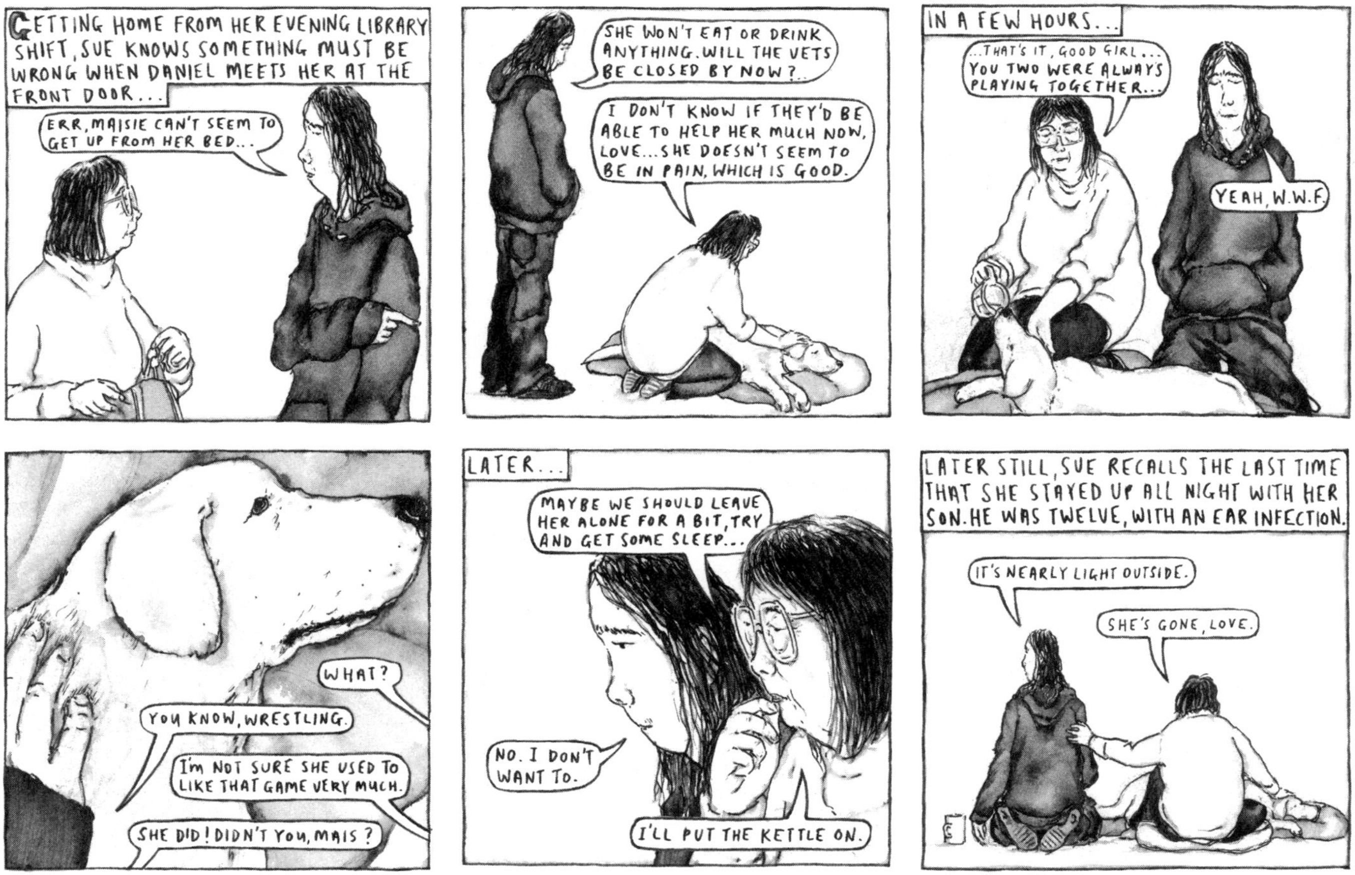

GETTING HOME FROM HER EVENING LIBRARY SHIFT, SUE KNOWS SOMETHING MUST BE WRONG WHEN DANIEL MEETS HER AT THE FRONT DOOR...
ERR, MAISIE CAN'T SEEM TO GET UP FROM HER BED...
SHE WON'T EAT OR DRINK ANYTHING. WILL THE VETS BE CLOSED BY NOW?..
I DON'T KNOW IF THEY'D BE ABLE TO HELP HER MUCH NOW, LOVE... SHE DOESN'T SEEM TO BE IN PAIN, WHICH IS GOOD.
IN A FEW HOURS...
...THAT'S IT, GOOD GIRL... YOU TWO WERE ALWAYS PLAYING TOGETHER...
YEAH, W.W.F.
WHAT?
YOU KNOW, WRESTLING.
I'M NOT SURE SHE USED TO LIKE THAT GAME VERY MUCH.
SHE DID! DIDN'T YOU, MAIS?
LATER...
MAYBE WE SHOULD LEAVE HER ALONE FOR A BIT, TRY AND GET SOME SLEEP...
NO. I DON'T WANT TO.
I'LL PUT THE KETTLE ON.
LATER STILL, SUE RECALLS THE LAST TIME THAT SHE STAYED UP ALL NIGHT WITH HER SON. HE WAS TWELVE, WITH AN EAR INFECTION.
IT'S NEARLY LIGHT OUTSIDE.
SHE'S GONE, LOVE.

APART

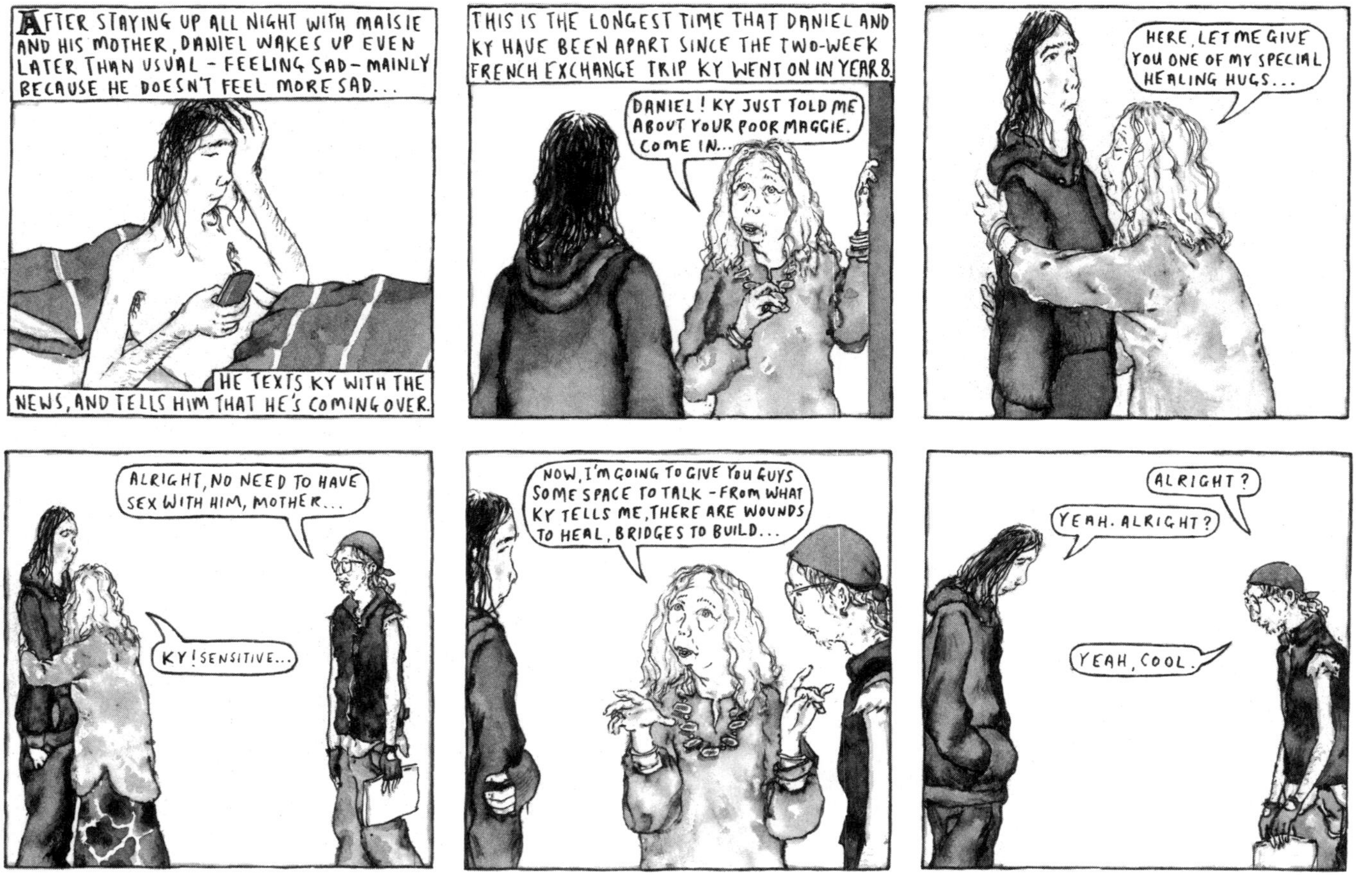

AFTER STAYING UP ALL NIGHT WITH MAISIE AND HIS MOTHER, DANIEL WAKES UP EVEN LATER THAN USUAL - FEELING SAD - MAINLY BECAUSE HE DOESN'T FEEL MORE SAD...
HE TEXTS KY WITH THE NEWS, AND TELLS HIM THAT HE'S COMING OVER.
THIS IS THE LONGEST TIME THAT DANIEL AND KY HAVE BEEN APART SINCE THE TWO-WEEK FRENCH EXCHANGE TRIP KY WENT ON IN YEAR 8.
DANIEL! KY JUST TOLD ME ABOUT YOUR POOR MAGGIE. COME IN...
HERE, LET ME GIVE YOU ONE OF MY SPECIAL HEALING HUGS...
ALRIGHT, NO NEED TO HAVE SEX WITH HIM, MOTHER...
KY! SENSITIVE...
NOW, I'M GOING TO GIVE YOU GUYS SOME SPACE TO TALK - FROM WHAT KY TELLS ME, THERE ARE WOUNDS TO HEAL, BRIDGES TO BUILD...
ALRIGHT?
YEAH. ALRIGHT?
YEAH, COOL.

SIXTH WEEK

DATE

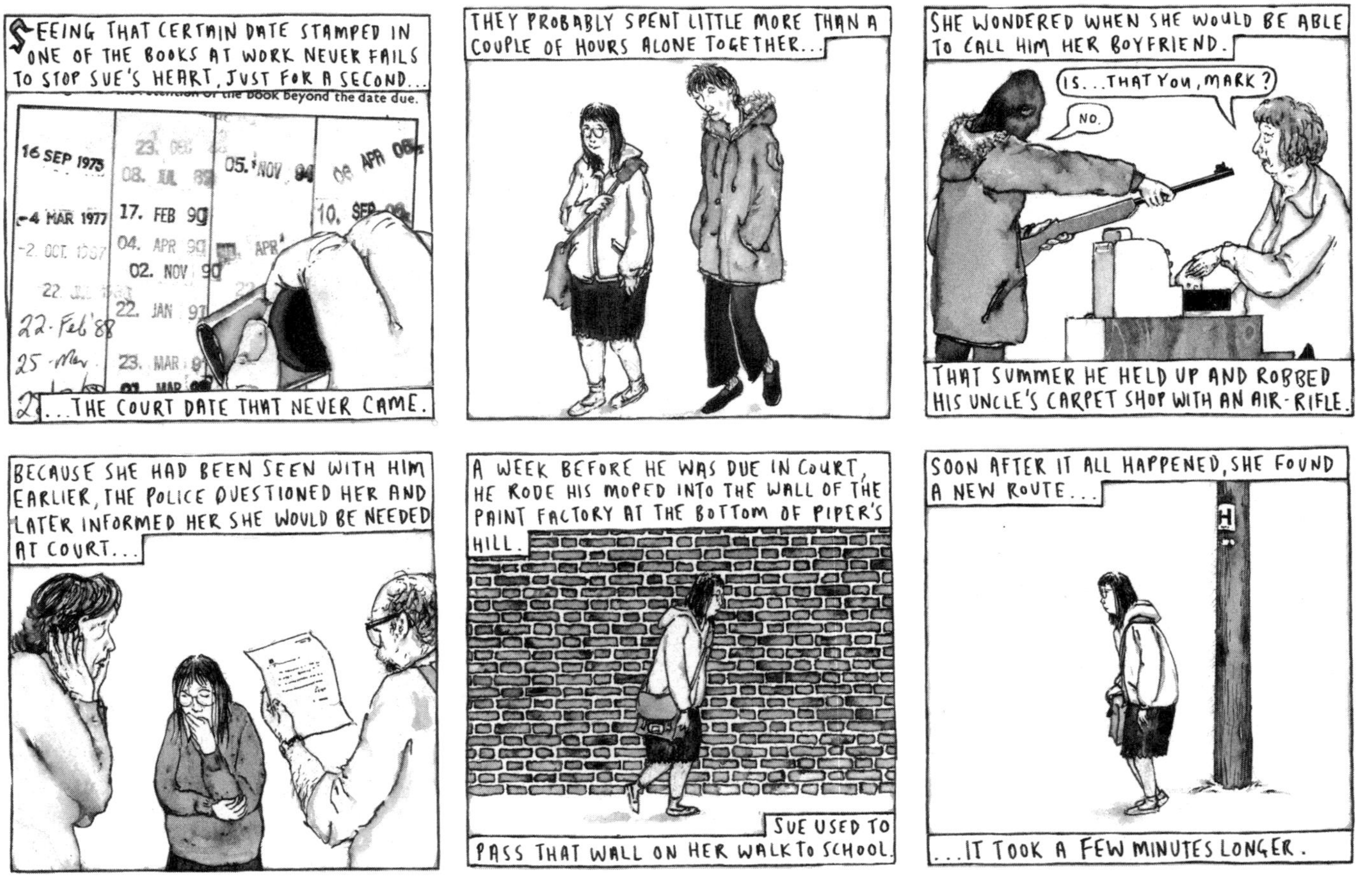
SEEING THAT CERTAIN DATE STAMPED IN ONE OF THE BOOKS AT WORK NEVER FAILS TO STOP SUE'S HEART, JUST FOR A SECOND...
16 SEP 1975
4 MAR 1977
17. FEB 90
04. APR 90
02. NOV 90
22. JAN 91
22·Feb'88
...THE COURT DATE THAT NEVER CAME.
THEY PROBABLY SPENT LITTLE MORE THAN A COUPLE OF HOURS ALONE TOGETHER...
SHE WONDERED WHEN SHE WOULD BE ABLE TO CALL HIM HER BOYFRIEND.
IS...THAT YOU, MARK?
NO.
THAT SUMMER HE HELD UP AND ROBBED HIS UNCLE'S CARPET SHOP WITH AN AIR-RIFLE.
BECAUSE SHE HAD BEEN SEEN WITH HIM EARLIER, THE POLICE QUESTIONED HER AND LATER INFORMED HER SHE WOULD BE NEEDED AT COURT...
A WEEK BEFORE HE WAS DUE IN COURT, HE RODE HIS MOPED INTO THE WALL OF THE PAINT FACTORY AT THE BOTTOM OF PIPER'S HILL.
SUE USED TO PASS THAT WALL ON HER WALK TO SCHOOL.
SOON AFTER IT ALL HAPPENED, SHE FOUND A NEW ROUTE...
...IT TOOK A FEW MINUTES LONGER.

HARD

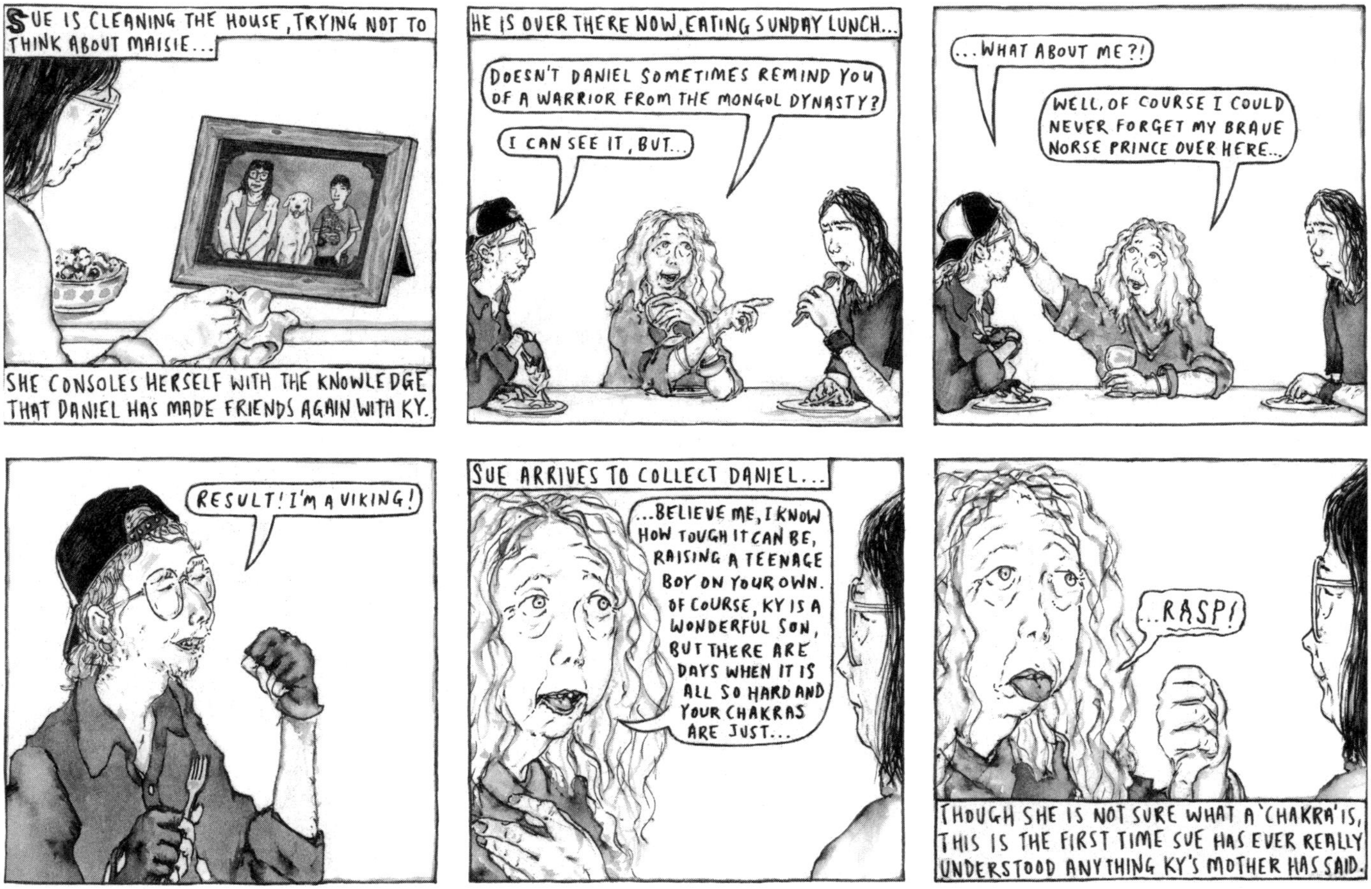
SUE IS CLEANING THE HOUSE, TRYING NOT TO THINK ABOUT MAISIE...
SHE CONSOLES HERSELF WITH THE KNOWLEDGE THAT DANIEL HAS MADE FRIENDS AGAIN WITH KY.
HE IS OVER THERE NOW, EATING SUNDAY LUNCH...
DOESN'T DANIEL SOMETIMES REMIND YOU OF A WARRIOR FROM THE MONGOL DYNASTY?
I CAN SEE IT, BUT...
...WHAT ABOUT ME?!
WELL, OF COURSE I COULD NEVER FORGET MY BRAVE NORSE PRINCE OVER HERE...
RESULT! I'M A VIKING!
SUE ARRIVES TO COLLECT DANIEL...
...BELIEVE ME, I KNOW HOW TOUGH IT CAN BE, RAISING A TEENAGE BOY ON YOUR OWN. OF COURSE, KY IS A WONDERFUL SON, BUT THERE ARE DAYS WHEN IT IS ALL SO HARD AND YOUR CHAKRAS ARE JUST...
...RASP!
THOUGH SHE IS NOT SURE WHAT A 'CHAKRA' IS, THIS IS THE FIRST TIME SUE HAS EVER REALLY UNDERSTOOD ANYTHING KY'S MOTHER HAS SAID.

LOOKING

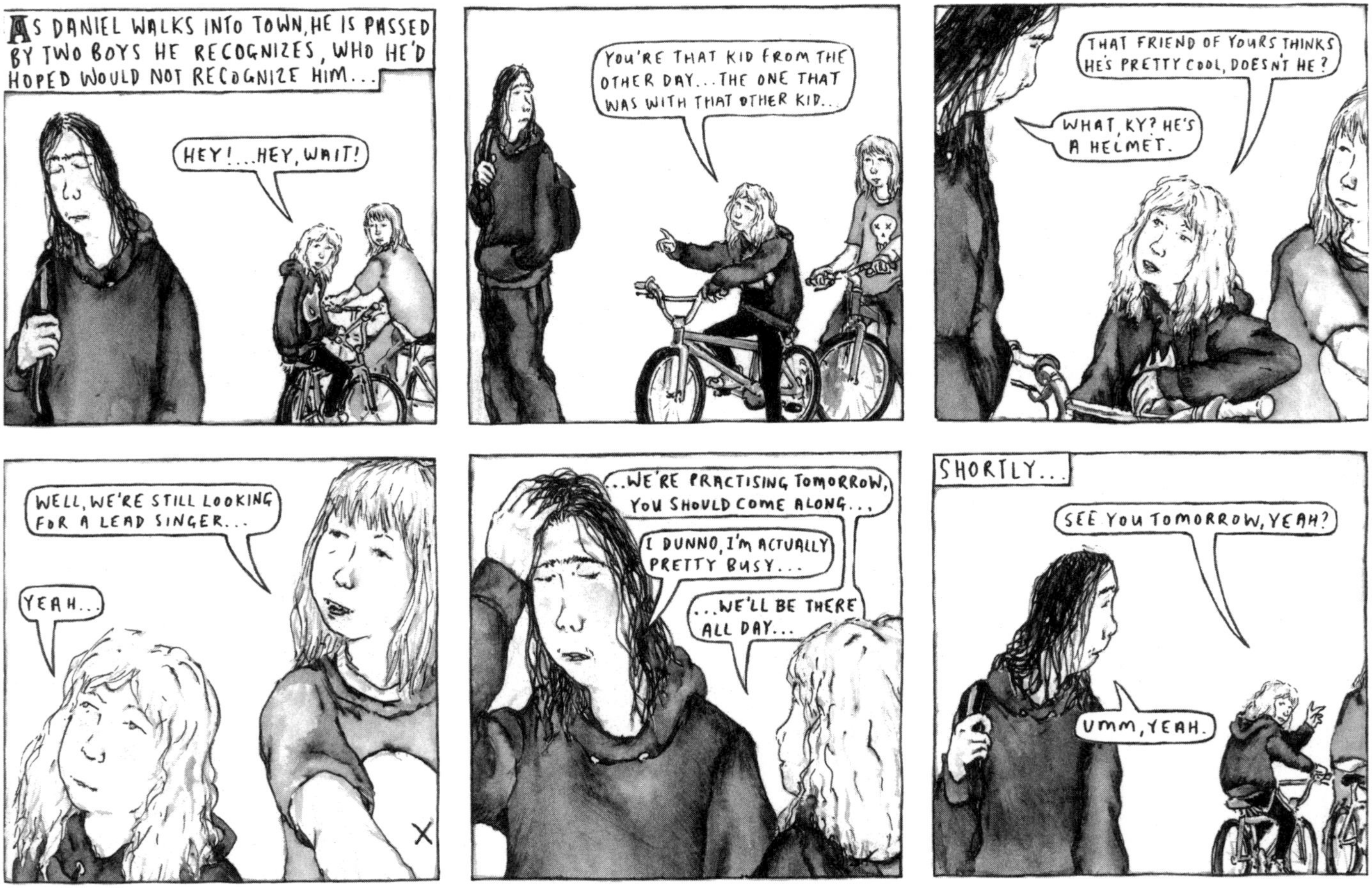
AS DANIEL WALKS INTO TOWN, HE IS PASSED BY TWO BOYS HE RECOGNIZES, WHO HE'D HOPED WOULD NOT RECOGNIZE HIM...
HEY!...HEY, WAIT!
YOU'RE THAT KID FROM THE OTHER DAY... THE ONE THAT WAS WITH THAT OTHER KID...
THAT FRIEND OF YOURS THINKS HE'S PRETTY COOL, DOESN'T HE?
WHAT, KY? HE'S A HELMET.
WELL, WE'RE STILL LOOKING FOR A LEAD SINGER...
YEAH...
...WE'RE PRACTISING TOMORROW, YOU SHOULD COME ALONG...
I DUNNO, I'M ACTUALLY PRETTY BUSY...
...WE'LL BE THERE ALL DAY...
SHORTLY...
SEE YOU TOMORROW, YEAH?
UMM, YEAH.

HAIRCUT

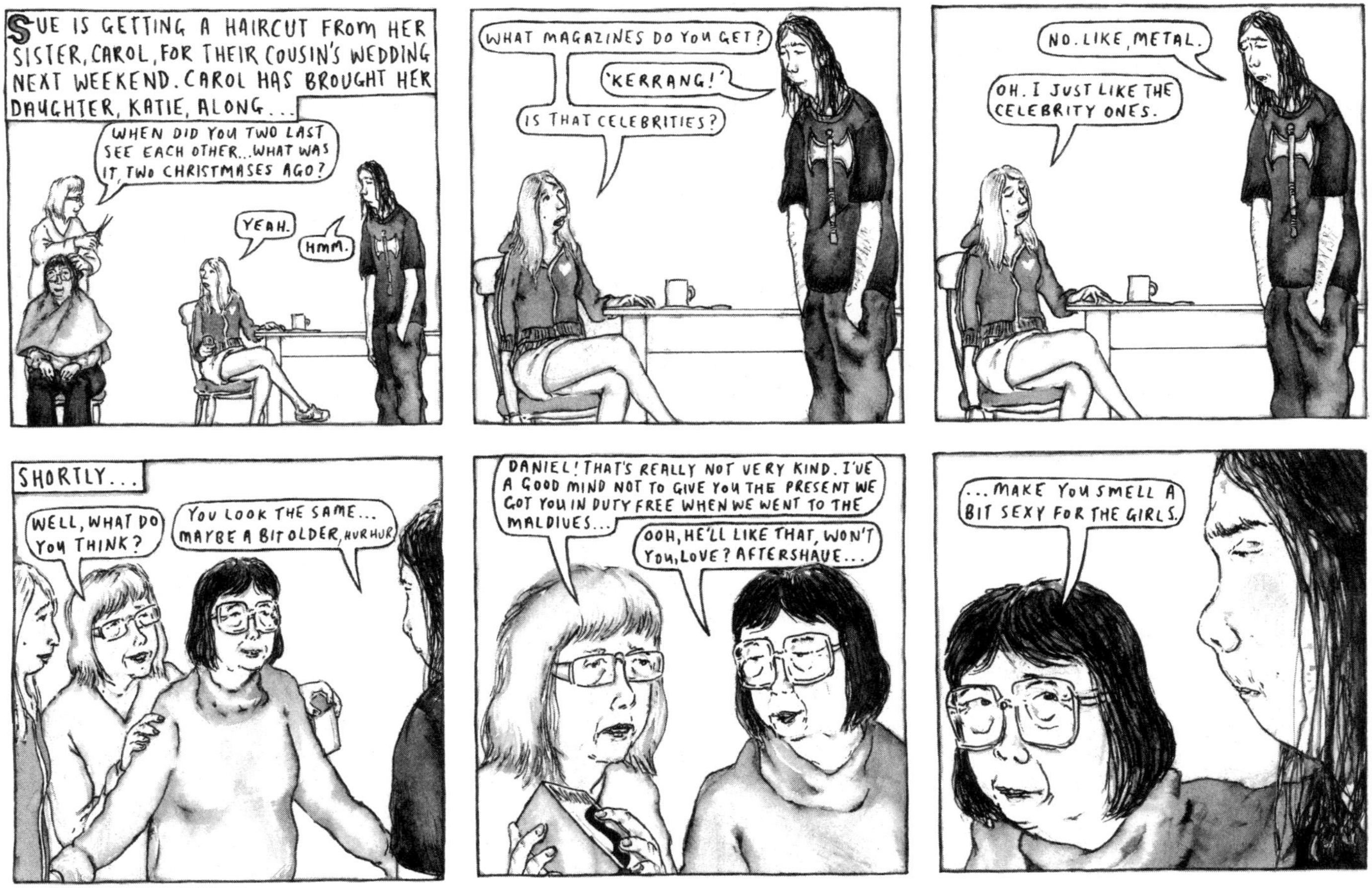
SUE IS GETTING A HAIRCUT FROM HER SISTER, CAROL, FOR THEIR COUSIN'S WEDDING NEXT WEEKEND. CAROL HAS BROUGHT HER DAUGHTER, KATIE, ALONG...
WHEN DID YOU TWO LAST SEE EACH OTHER...WHAT WAS IT, TWO CHRISTMASES AGO?
YEAH.
HMM.
WHAT MAGAZINES DO YOU GET?
'KERRANG!'
IS THAT CELEBRITIES?
NO. LIKE, METAL.
OH. I JUST LIKE THE CELEBRITY ONES.
SHORTLY...
WELL, WHAT DO YOU THINK?
YOU LOOK THE SAME... MAYBE A BIT OLDER, HUR HUR
DANIEL! THAT'S REALLY NOT VERY KIND. I'VE A GOOD MIND NOT TO GIVE YOU THE PRESENT WE GOT YOU IN DUTY FREE WHEN WE WENT TO THE MALDIVES...
OOH, HE'LL LIKE THAT, WON'T YOU, LOVE? AFTERSHAVE...
...MAKE YOU SMELL A BIT SEXY FOR THE GIRLS.

SICK

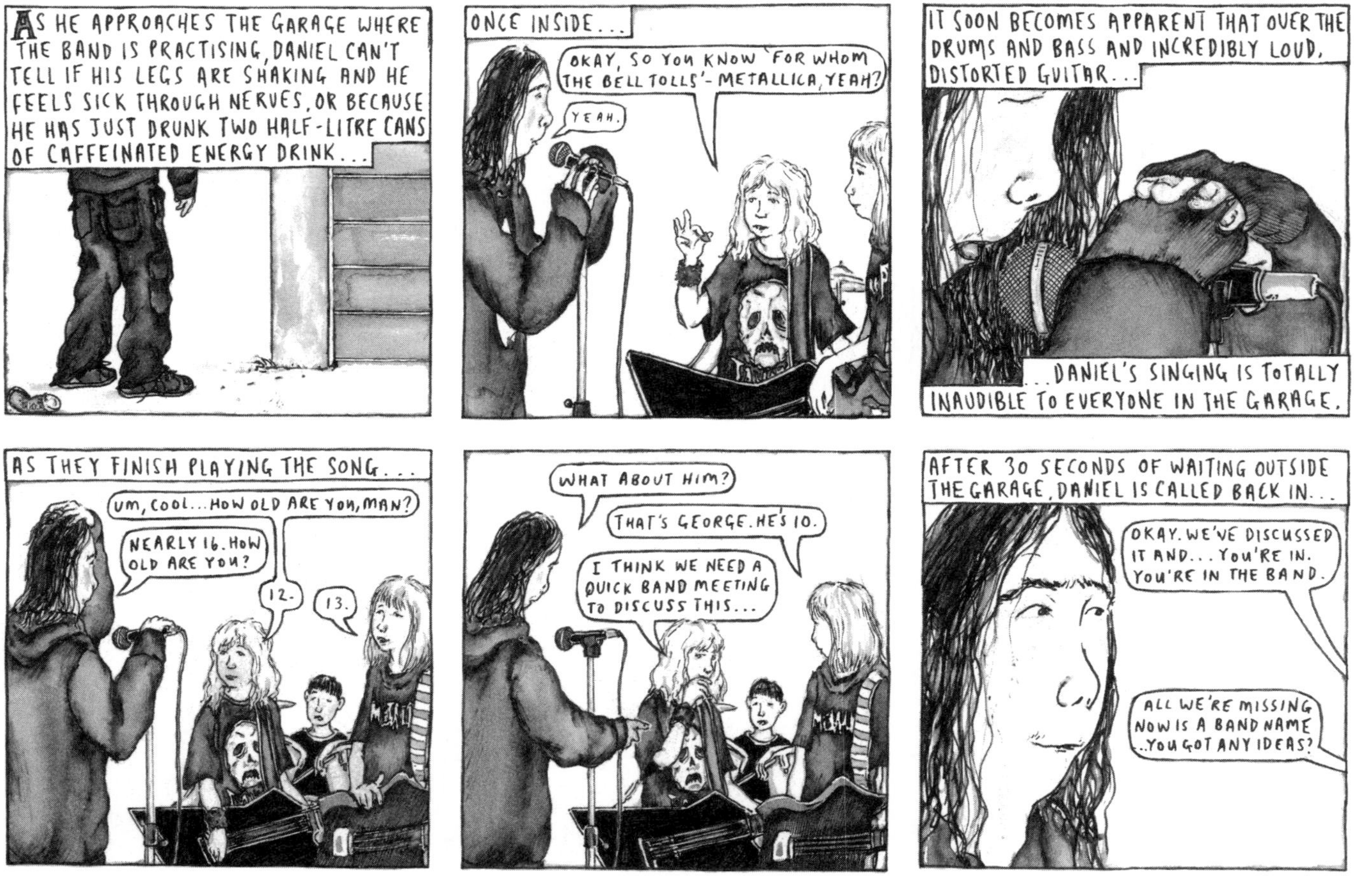
AS HE APPROACHES THE GARAGE WHERE THE BAND IS PRACTISING, DANIEL CAN'T TELL IF HIS LEGS ARE SHAKING AND HE FEELS SICK THROUGH NERVES, OR BECAUSE HE HAS JUST DRUNK TWO HALF-LITRE CANS OF CAFFEINATED ENERGY DRINK...
ONCE INSIDE...
OKAY, SO YOU KNOW 'FOR WHOM THE BELL TOLLS'- METALLICA, YEAH?
YEAH.
IT SOON BECOMES APPARENT THAT OVER THE DRUMS AND BASS AND INCREDIBLY LOUD, DISTORTED GUITAR...
...DANIEL'S SINGING IS TOTALLY INAUDIBLE TO EVERYONE IN THE GARAGE.
AS THEY FINISH PLAYING THE SONG...
UM, COOL... HOW OLD ARE YOU, MAN?
NEARLY 16. HOW OLD ARE YOU?
12.
13.
WHAT ABOUT HIM?
THAT'S GEORGE. HE'S 10.
I THINK WE NEED A QUICK BAND MEETING TO DISCUSS THIS...
AFTER 30 SECONDS OF WAITING OUTSIDE THE GARAGE, DANIEL IS CALLED BACK IN...
OKAY. WE'VE DISCUSSED IT AND... YOU'RE IN. YOU'RE IN THE BAND.
ALL WE'RE MISSING NOW IS A BAND NAME ..YOU GOT ANY IDEAS?

MASSAGE

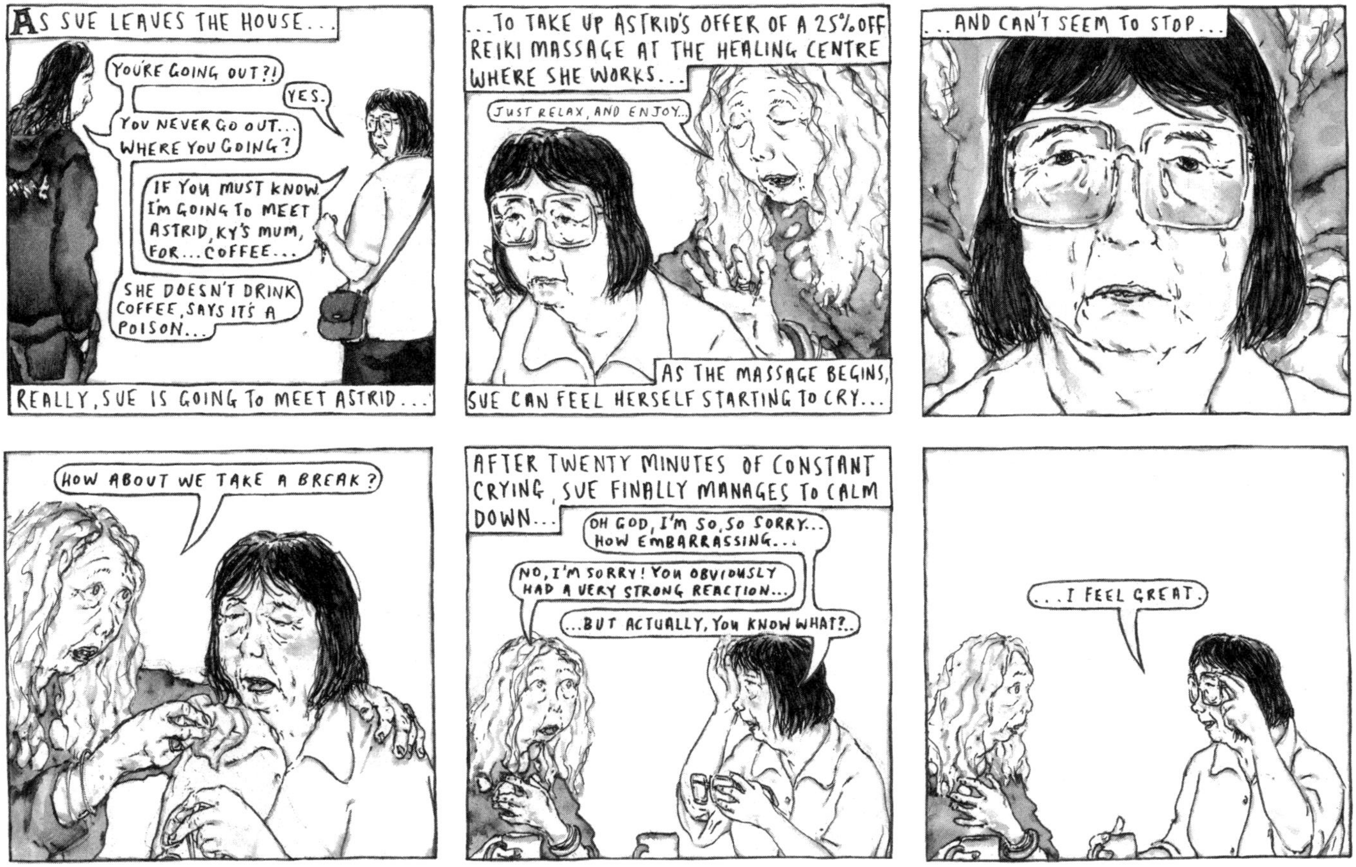
AS SUE LEAVES THE HOUSE...
YOU'RE GOING OUT?!
YES.
YOU NEVER GO OUT... WHERE YOU GOING?
IF YOU MUST KNOW I'M GOING TO MEET ASTRID, KY'S MUM, FOR... COFFEE...
SHE DOESN'T DRINK COFFEE, SAYS IT'S A POISON...
REALLY, SUE IS GOING TO MEET ASTRID...
...TO TAKE UP ASTRID'S OFFER OF A 25% OFF REIKI MASSAGE AT THE HEALING CENTRE WHERE SHE WORKS...
JUST RELAX, AND ENJOY...
AS THE MASSAGE BEGINS, SUE CAN FEEL HERSELF STARTING TO CRY...
...AND CAN'T SEEM TO STOP...
HOW ABOUT WE TAKE A BREAK?
AFTER TWENTY MINUTES OF CONSTANT CRYING, SUE FINALLY MANAGES TO CALM DOWN...
OH GOD, I'M SO, SO SORRY... HOW EMBARRASSING...
NO, I'M SORRY! YOU OBVIOUSLY HAD A VERY STRONG REACTION...
...BUT ACTUALLY, YOU KNOW WHAT?...
...I FEEL GREAT.

WORD

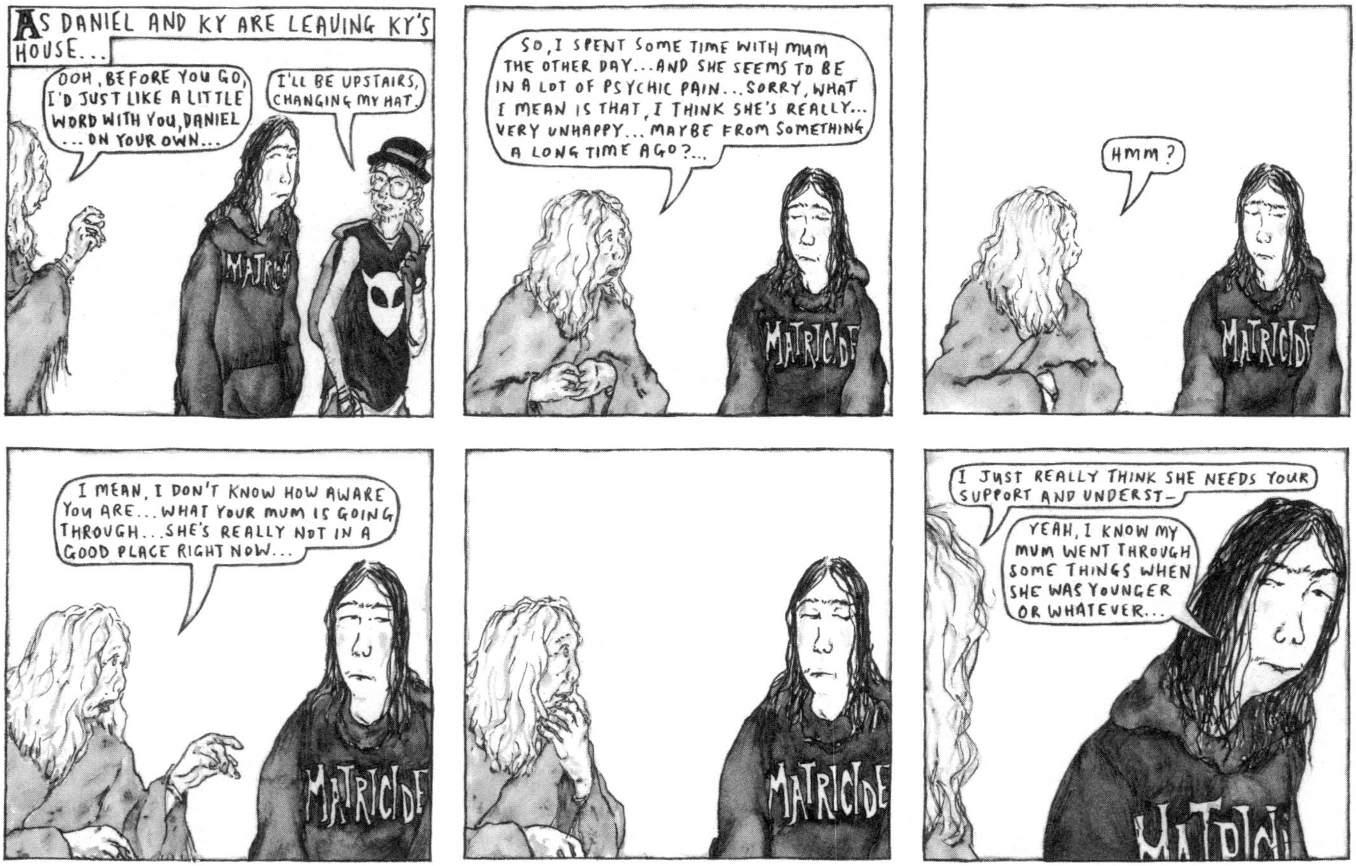

AS DANIEL AND KY ARE LEAVING KY'S HOUSE...
OOH, BEFORE YOU GO, I'D JUST LIKE A LITTLE WORD WITH YOU, DANIEL ...ON YOUR OWN...
I'LL BE UPSTAIRS, CHANGING MY HAT.
SO, I SPENT SOME TIME WITH MUM THE OTHER DAY...AND SHE SEEMS TO BE IN A LOT OF PSYCHIC PAIN...SORRY, WHAT I MEAN IS THAT, I THINK SHE'S REALLY... VERY UNHAPPY... MAYBE FROM SOMETHING A LONG TIME AGO?...
HMM?
I MEAN, I DON'T KNOW HOW AWARE YOU ARE...WHAT YOUR MUM IS GOING THROUGH...SHE'S REALLY NOT IN A GOOD PLACE RIGHT NOW...
I JUST REALLY THINK SHE NEEDS YOUR SUPPORT AND UNDERST–
YEAH, I KNOW MY MUM WENT THROUGH SOME THINGS WHEN SHE WAS YOUNGER OR WHATEVER...

STRATEGY

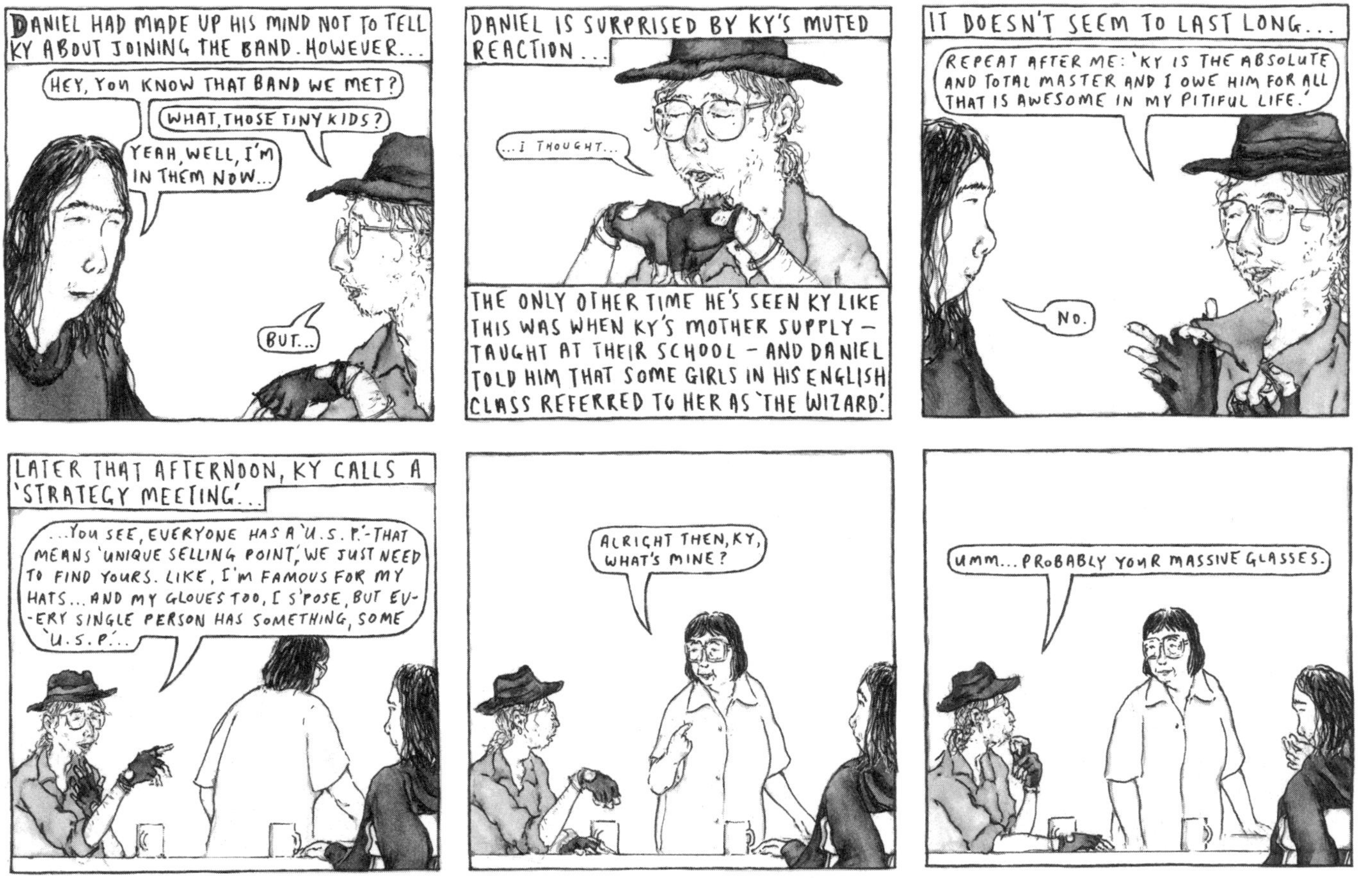

DANIEL HAD MADE UP HIS MIND NOT TO TELL KY ABOUT JOINING THE BAND. HOWEVER...
HEY, YOU KNOW THAT BAND WE MET?
WHAT, THOSE TINY KIDS?
YEAH, WELL, I'M IN THEM NOW...
BUT...
DANIEL IS SURPRISED BY KY'S MUTED REACTION...
...I THOUGHT...
THE ONLY OTHER TIME HE'S SEEN KY LIKE THIS WAS WHEN KY'S MOTHER SUPPLY-TAUGHT AT THEIR SCHOOL - AND DANIEL TOLD HIM THAT SOME GIRLS IN HIS ENGLISH CLASS REFERRED TO HER AS 'THE WIZARD'.
IT DOESN'T SEEM TO LAST LONG...
REPEAT AFTER ME: 'KY IS THE ABSOLUTE AND TOTAL MASTER AND I OWE HIM FOR ALL THAT IS AWESOME IN MY PITIFUL LIFE.'
NO.
LATER THAT AFTERNOON, KY CALLS A 'STRATEGY MEETING'...
...YOU SEE, EVERYONE HAS A 'U.S.P.' - THAT MEANS 'UNIQUE SELLING POINT', WE JUST NEED TO FIND YOURS. LIKE, I'M FAMOUS FOR MY HATS... AND MY GLOVES TOO, I S'POSE, BUT EV-ERY SINGLE PERSON HAS SOMETHING, SOME 'U.S.P.'...
ALRIGHT THEN, KY, WHAT'S MINE?
UMM... PROBABLY YOUR MASSIVE GLASSES.

PLAYING

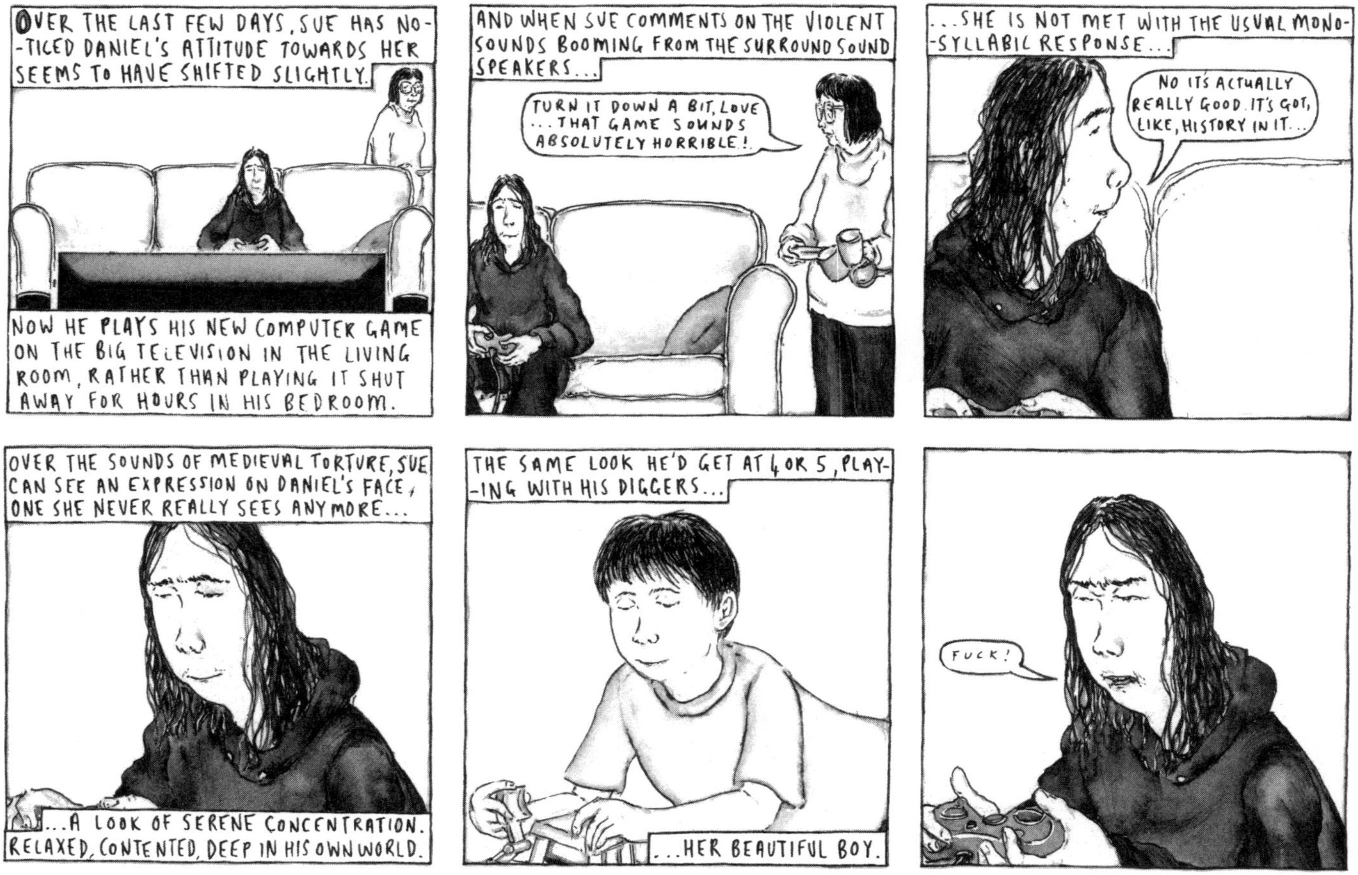
OVER THE LAST FEW DAYS, SUE HAS NOTICED DANIEL'S ATTITUDE TOWARDS HER SEEMS TO HAVE SHIFTED SLIGHTLY.
NOW HE PLAYS HIS NEW COMPUTER GAME ON THE BIG TELEVISION IN THE LIVING ROOM, RATHER THAN PLAYING IT SHUT AWAY FOR HOURS IN HIS BEDROOM.
AND WHEN SUE COMMENTS ON THE VIOLENT SOUNDS BOOMING FROM THE SURROUND SOUND SPEAKERS...
TURN IT DOWN A BIT, LOVE ... THAT GAME SOUNDS ABSOLUTELY HORRIBLE!
...SHE IS NOT MET WITH THE USUAL MONOSYLLABIC RESPONSE...
NO IT'S ACTUALLY REALLY GOOD. IT'S GOT, LIKE, HISTORY IN IT...
OVER THE SOUNDS OF MEDIEVAL TORTURE, SUE CAN SEE AN EXPRESSION ON DANIEL'S FACE, ONE SHE NEVER REALLY SEES ANYMORE...
...A LOOK OF SERENE CONCENTRATION. RELAXED, CONTENTED, DEEP IN HIS OWN WORLD.
THE SAME LOOK HE'D GET AT 4 OR 5, PLAYING WITH HIS DIGGERS...
...HER BEAUTIFUL BOY.
FUCK!

WEDDING

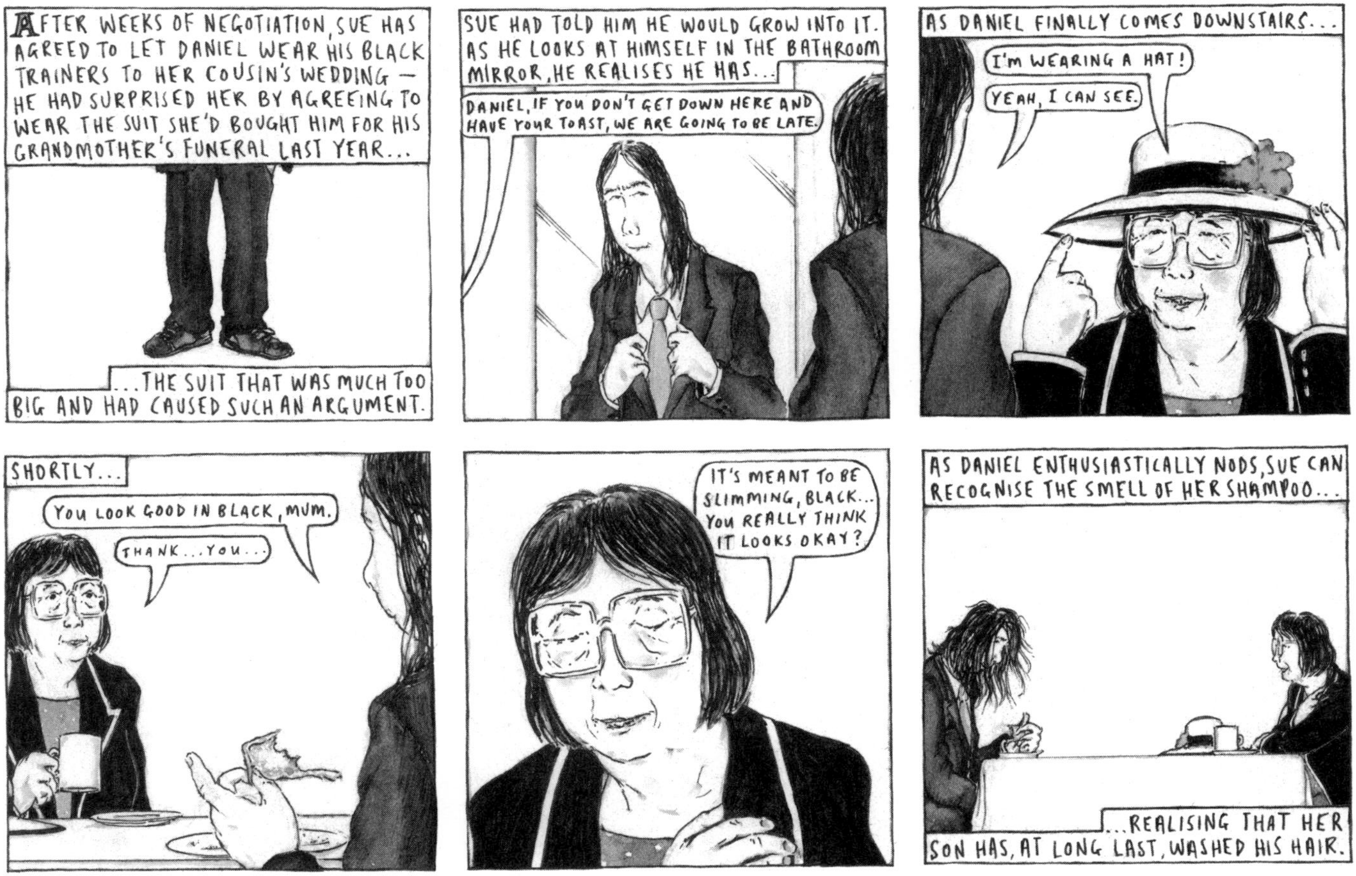
AFTER WEEKS OF NEGOTIATION, SUE HAS AGREED TO LET DANIEL WEAR HIS BLACK TRAINERS TO HER COUSIN'S WEDDING — HE HAD SURPRISED HER BY AGREEING TO WEAR THE SUIT SHE'D BOUGHT HIM FOR HIS GRANDMOTHER'S FUNERAL LAST YEAR...
...THE SUIT THAT WAS MUCH TOO BIG AND HAD CAUSED SUCH AN ARGUMENT.
SUE HAD TOLD HIM HE WOULD GROW INTO IT. AS HE LOOKS AT HIMSELF IN THE BATHROOM MIRROR, HE REALISES HE HAS...
DANIEL, IF YOU DON'T GET DOWN HERE AND HAVE YOUR TOAST, WE ARE GOING TO BE LATE.
AS DANIEL FINALLY COMES DOWNSTAIRS...
I'M WEARING A HAT!
YEAH, I CAN SEE.
SHORTLY...
YOU LOOK GOOD IN BLACK, MUM.
THANK... YOU...
IT'S MEANT TO BE SLIMMING, BLACK... YOU REALLY THINK IT LOOKS OKAY?
AS DANIEL ENTHUSIASTICALLY NODS, SUE CAN RECOGNISE THE SMELL OF HER SHAMPOO...
...REALISING THAT HER SON HAS, AT LONG LAST, WASHED HIS HAIR.

DAYS

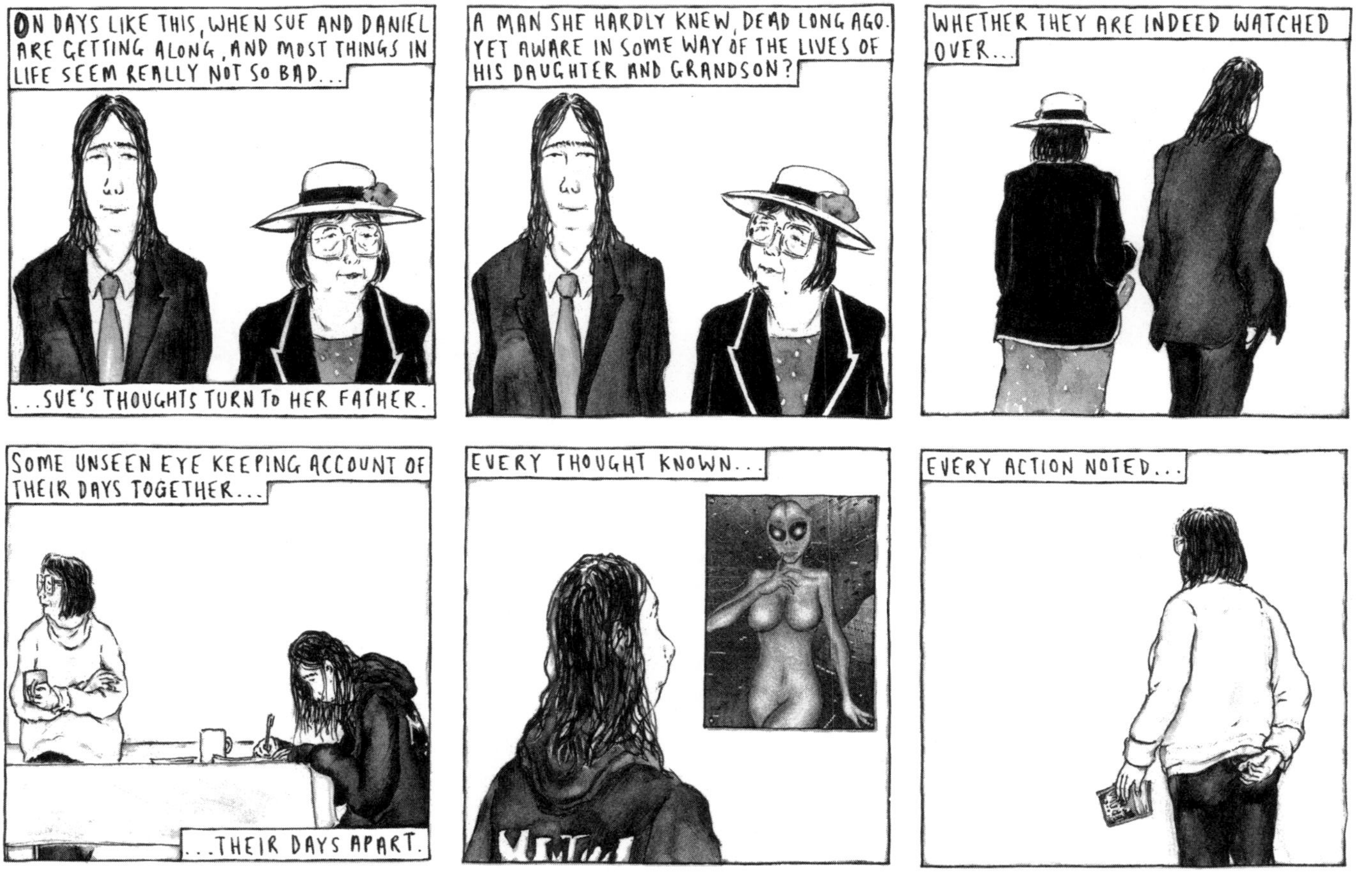
ON DAYS LIKE THIS, WHEN SUE AND DANIEL ARE GETTING ALONG, AND MOST THINGS IN LIFE SEEM REALLY NOT SO BAD...
...SUE'S THOUGHTS TURN TO HER FATHER.
A MAN SHE HARDLY KNEW, DEAD LONG AGO. YET AWARE IN SOME WAY OF THE LIVES OF HIS DAUGHTER AND GRANDSON?
WHETHER THEY ARE INDEED WATCHED OVER...
SOME UNSEEN EYE KEEPING ACCOUNT OF THEIR DAYS TOGETHER...
...THEIR DAYS APART.
EVERY THOUGHT KNOWN...
EVERY ACTION NOTED...

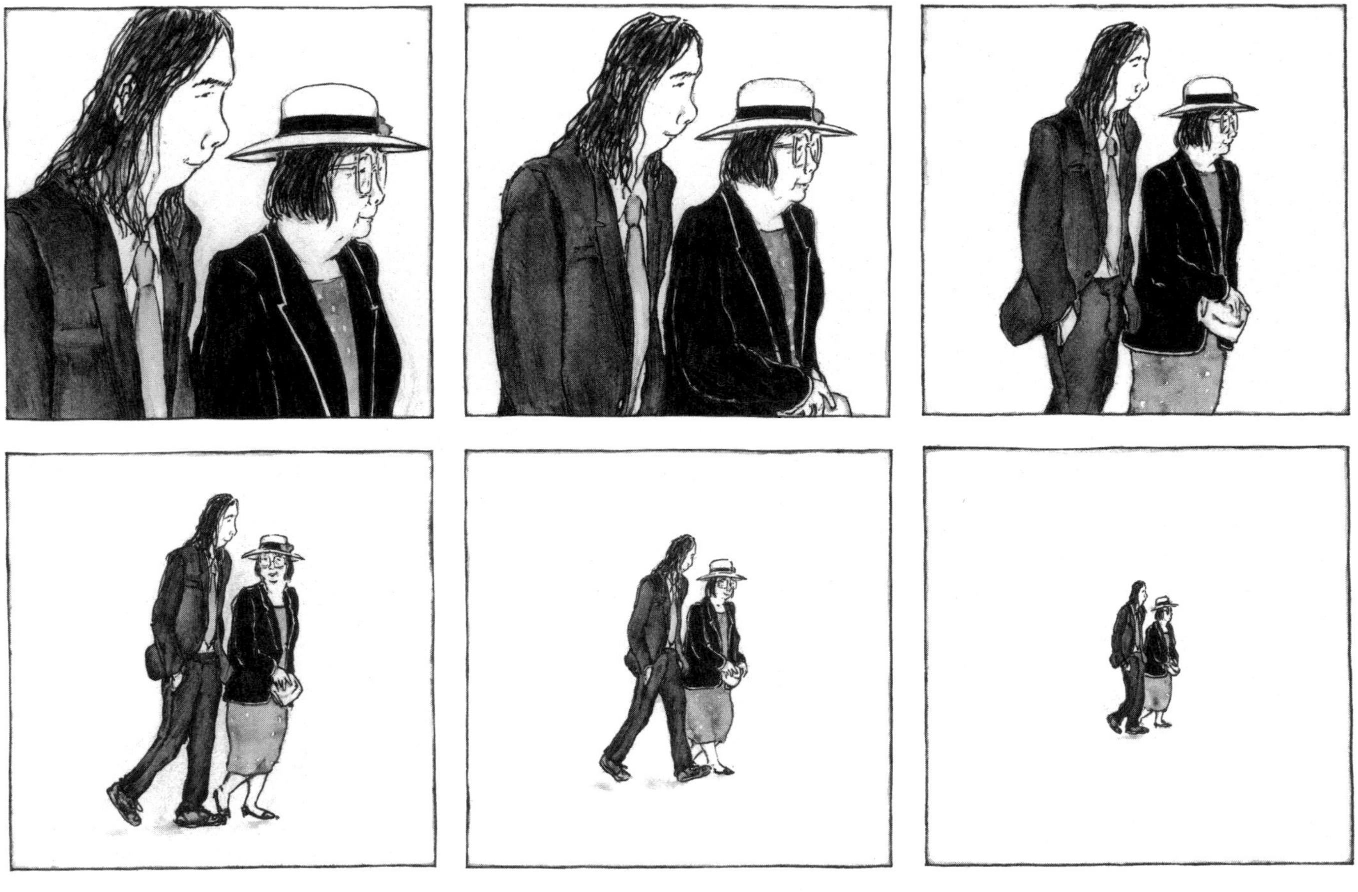

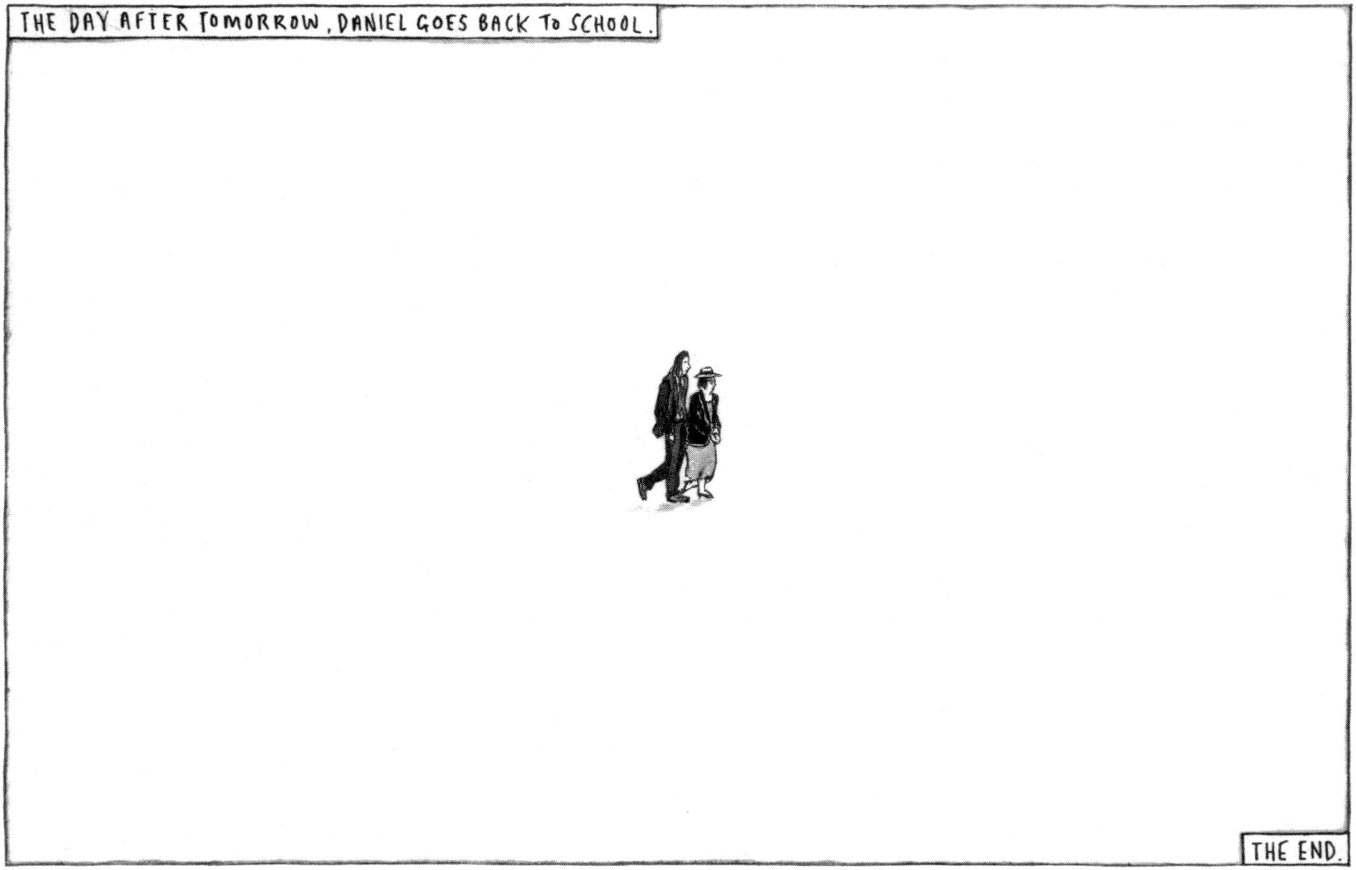
THE DAY AFTER TOMORROW, DANIEL GOES BACK TO SCHOOL.
THE END.

THANKYOU!

FOR ADVICE, HELP AND SUPPORT...

DAN FRANKLIN AND ALL AT JONATHAN CAPE, SUE PALMER, SIMON ROBERTS, LUCY ROBERTS, KRISTEN GRAYEWSKI, HOLLY ABNEY, TOM STUBBS, DAVID WILLIAMS, DR. HANNAH CONDRY, CHARLIE GRAY, JOEL WILSON, ANNA KNOWLES, ANNE HEALEY, ROB ASH, ALISON CROSS, PAOLO DAVANZO, LISA MARR, BEN O'LEARY & THE HERE SHOP, PAUL WINTERHART, NICOLE FROBUSCH, SOMERSET LIBRARY SERVICE, PHILL PAYNE, POSY SIMMONDS, CHRIS STAROS, MY MUM, ALL THE PEOPLE WHO MADE ALL THE (MOSTLY SAD-SOUNDING) MUSIC I CONSTANTLY LISTENED TO WHILE DRAWING, AND MOST OF ALL TO MY DAD FOR WORDS HELP; AND TO TOM COPS AND NAT BAIRD — WITHOUT WHOM THIS BOOK WOULDN'T EXIST!

DRIVING SHORT DISTANCES

FOR THE **MUCH MISSED;**
MY MUM **JENNY,**
MY DOG **PEEP-PEEP.**

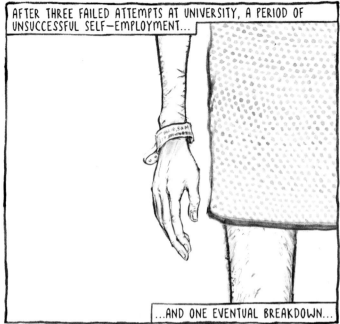

AFTER THREE FAILED ATTEMPTS AT UNIVERSITY, A PERIOD OF UNSUCCESSFUL SELF—EMPLOYMENT...

...AND ONE EVENTUAL BREAKDOWN...

I WAS STARTING AGAIN...AGAIN.

NOW EVERYTHING I OWNED FITTED INTO A PADDED ENVELOPE.

I MOVED BACK TO MY MUM'S, TO THE HOUSE WHERE I GREW UP...

THINGS WERE BETTER NOW, THOUGH I STILL WASN'T SLEEPING...

ONE THING I HAD LEARNED FROM ALL OF THIS: ANY ATTEMPT AT MAKING MONEY DOING SOMETHING I CARED ABOUT OR ENJOYED HAD ENDED IN DISASTER...

SO, TO GET A SIMPLE JOB, JUST TO EARN MONEY, DOING SOMETHING I KNEW NOTHING ABOUT AND WAS GENERALLY UNINTERESTED IN. THAT WAS THE PLAN.

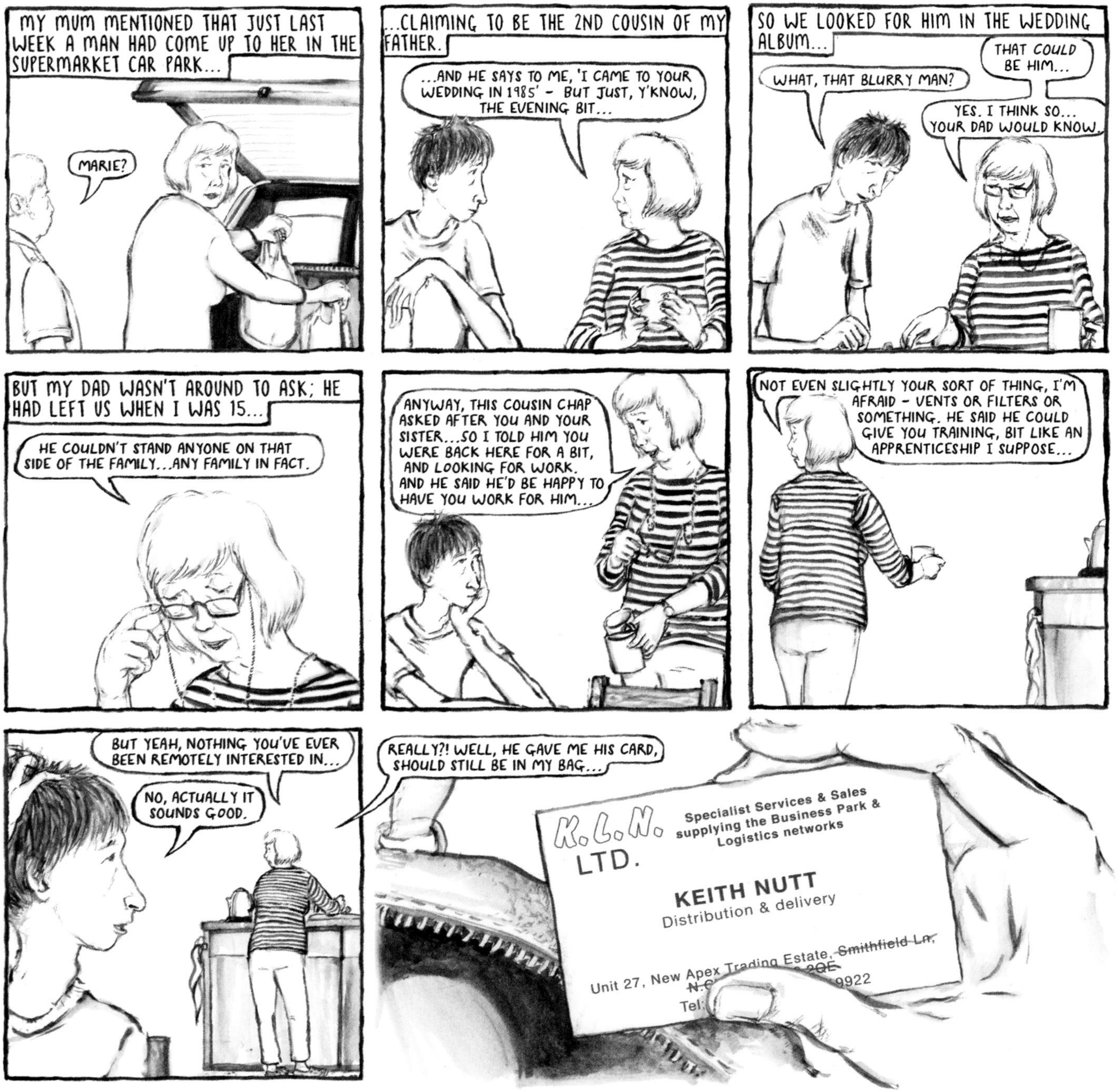
MY MUM MENTIONED THAT JUST LAST WEEK A MAN HAD COME UP TO HER IN THE SUPERMARKET CAR PARK...
MARIE?
...CLAIMING TO BE THE 2ND COUSIN OF MY FATHER.
...AND HE SAYS TO ME, 'I CAME TO YOUR WEDDING IN 1985' - BUT JUST, Y'KNOW, THE EVENING BIT...
SO WE LOOKED FOR HIM IN THE WEDDING ALBUM...
WHAT, THAT BLURRY MAN?
THAT COULD BE HIM...
YES. I THINK SO... YOUR DAD WOULD KNOW.
BUT MY DAD WASN'T AROUND TO ASK; HE HAD LEFT US WHEN I WAS 15...
HE COULDN'T STAND ANYONE ON THAT SIDE OF THE FAMILY...ANY FAMILY IN FACT.
ANYWAY, THIS COUSIN CHAP ASKED AFTER YOU AND YOUR SISTER...SO I TOLD HIM YOU WERE BACK HERE FOR A BIT, AND LOOKING FOR WORK. AND HE SAID HE'D BE HAPPY TO HAVE YOU WORK FOR HIM...
NOT EVEN SLIGHTLY YOUR SORT OF THING, I'M AFRAID - VENTS OR FILTERS OR SOMETHING. HE SAID HE COULD GIVE YOU TRAINING, BIT LIKE AN APPRENTICESHIP I SUPPOSE...
BUT YEAH, NOTHING YOU'VE EVER BEEN REMOTELY INTERESTED IN...
NO, ACTUALLY IT SOUNDS GOOD.
REALLY?! WELL, HE GAVE ME HIS CARD, SHOULD STILL BE IN MY BAG...
K.L.N. LTD.
Specialist Services & Sales supplying the Business Park & Logistics networks
KEITH NUTT
Distribution & delivery
Unit 27, New Apex Trading Estate, ~~Smithfield Ln,~~
Tel:

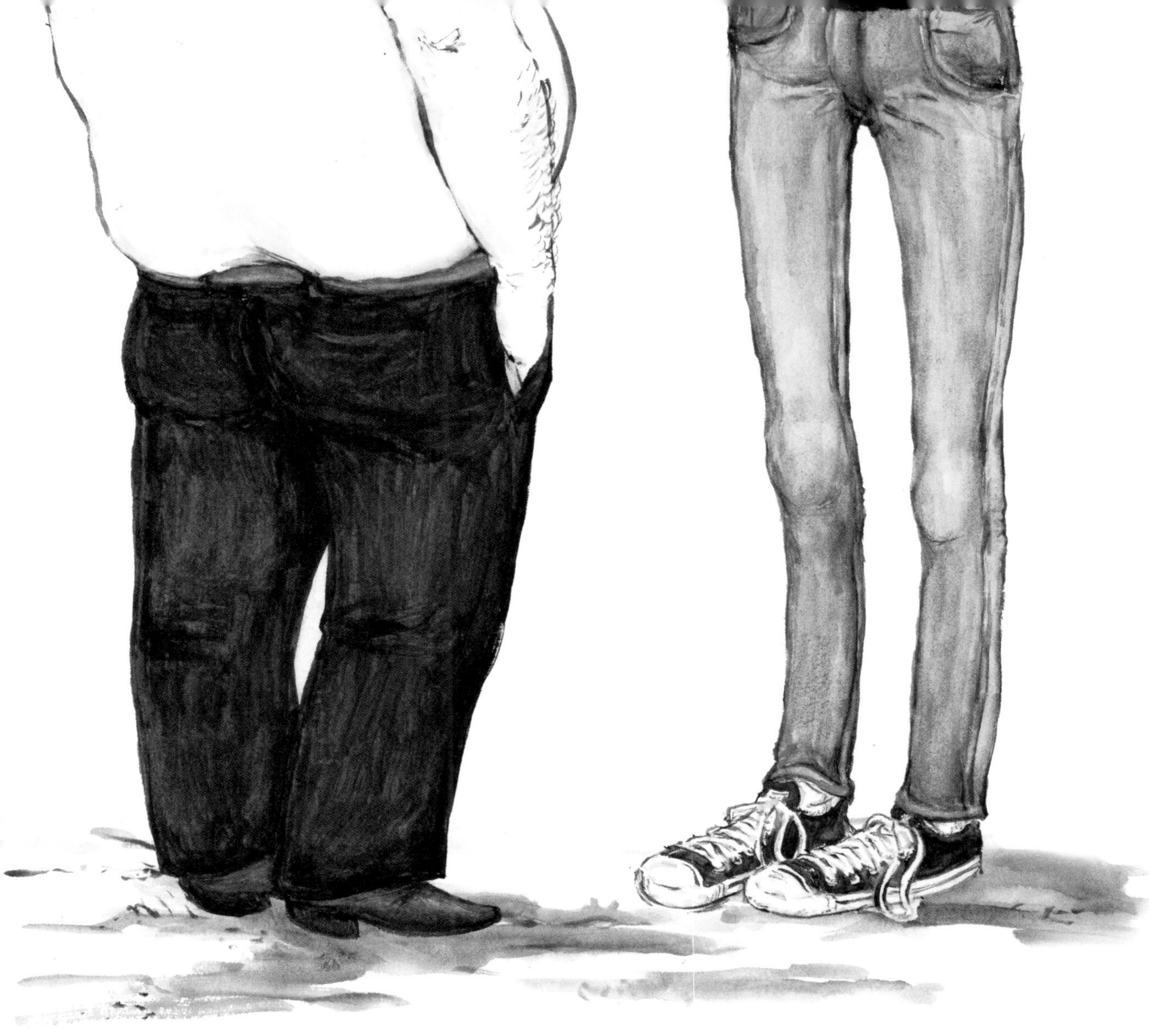

THE FIRST TIME I MEET HIM...

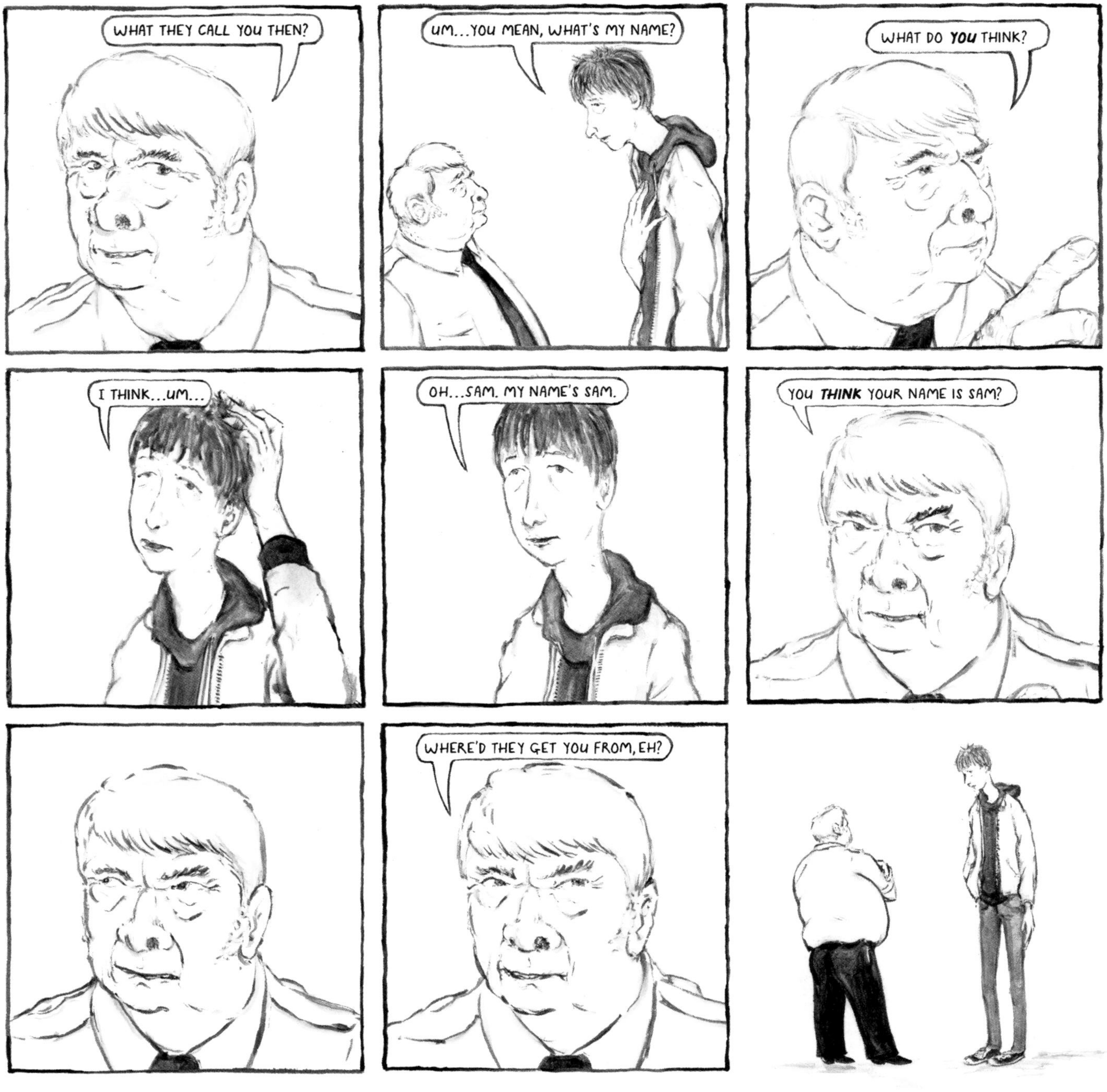
WHAT THEY CALL YOU THEN?
UM...YOU MEAN, WHAT'S MY NAME?
WHAT DO **YOU** THINK?
I THINK...UM...
OH...SAM. MY NAME'S SAM.
YOU **THINK** YOUR NAME IS SAM?
WHERE'D THEY GET YOU FROM, EH?

AS WE SIT IN HIS CAR, KEITH BEGINS TO EXPLAIN HIS JOB TO ME...

FIRSTLY...

HE DRAWS COMPLEX DIAGRAMS IN THE AIR...

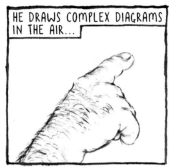

ALREADY I AM A BIT LOST.

THEN HE STARTS TO TELL ME WHAT MY JOB WILL BE. HE TALKS ABOUT A B38 FORM AND A B388 FORM...

...THEN OF COURSE, THERE'S THE C422...

HE TALKS ABOUT GOING TO THE CENTRAL DEPOT, DELIVERY BAYS, AND THE TRADING ESTATE NETWORKS...

...THESE HI-FLYERS TODAY CALL THEM BUSINESS PARKS.

AND I START TO GET THAT FEELING FROM SCHOOL — THE ONES FROM MATHS, PHYSICS AND CHEMISTRY LESSONS...

IT'S LIKE LISTENING TO WELSH RADIO...

YOU CAN JUST MAKE OUT THE ODD WORD...

I TRY TO LOOK LIKE I AM LISTENING...

... FOR EXAMPLE, ...

CONCENTRATING...

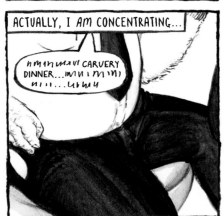

ACTUALLY, I AM CONCENTRATING...

... CARVERY DINNER... ...

JUST NOT ON THE RIGHT THING.

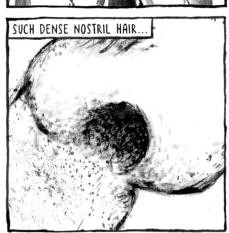

SUCH DENSE NOSTRIL HAIR...

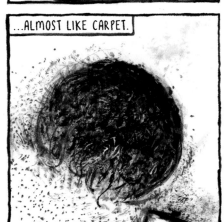

...ALMOST LIKE CARPET.

... LISTEN WELL, PAY CLOSE ATTENTION, AND YOU'LL DO ME PROUD, LAD.

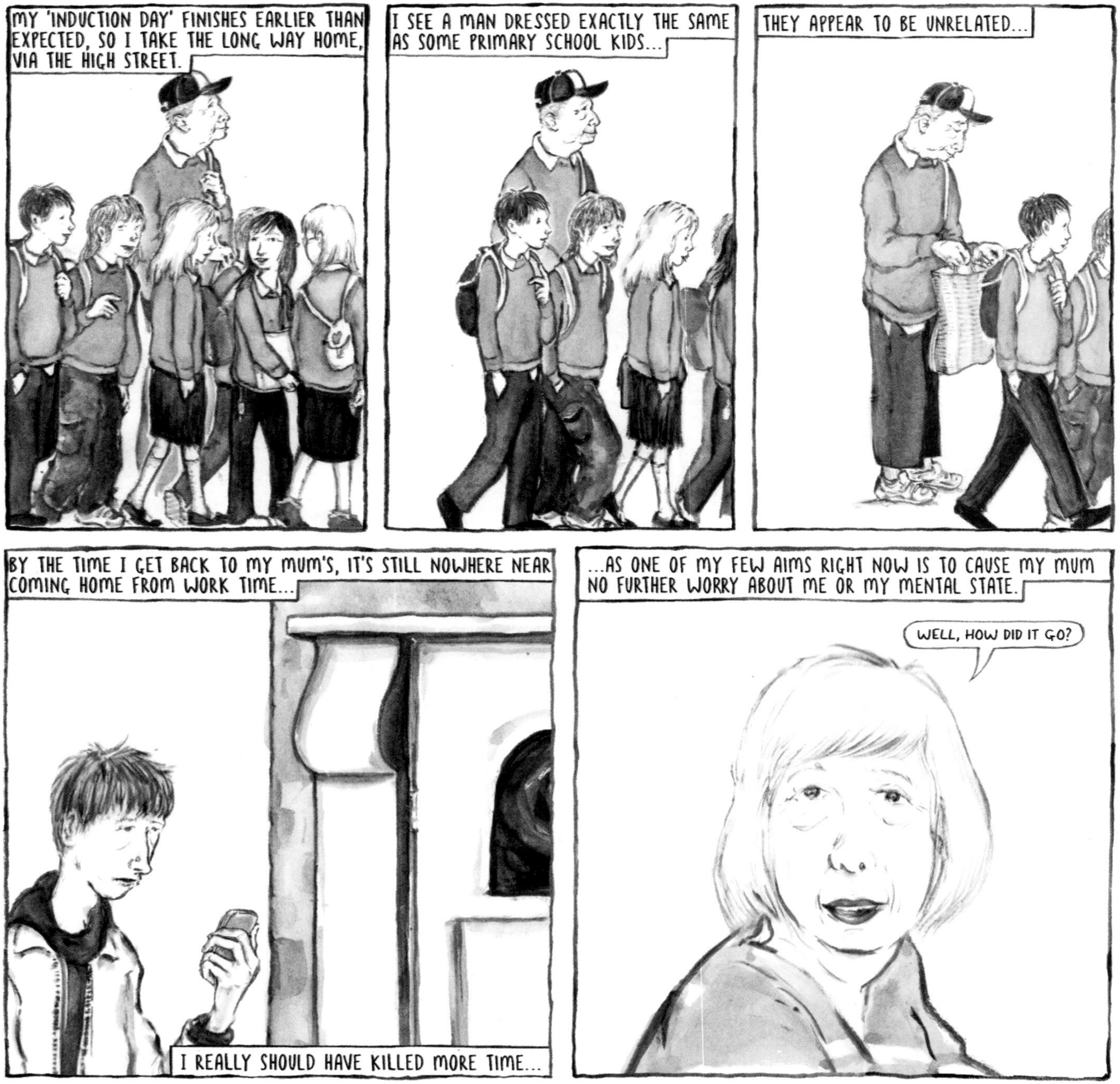
MY 'INDUCTION DAY' FINISHES EARLIER THAN EXPECTED, SO I TAKE THE LONG WAY HOME, VIA THE HIGH STREET.
I SEE A MAN DRESSED EXACTLY THE SAME AS SOME PRIMARY SCHOOL KIDS...
THEY APPEAR TO BE UNRELATED...
BY THE TIME I GET BACK TO MY MUM'S, IT'S STILL NOWHERE NEAR COMING HOME FROM WORK TIME...
I REALLY SHOULD HAVE KILLED MORE TIME...
...AS ONE OF MY FEW AIMS RIGHT NOW IS TO CAUSE MY MUM NO FURTHER WORRY ABOUT ME OR MY MENTAL STATE.
WELL, HOW DID IT GO?

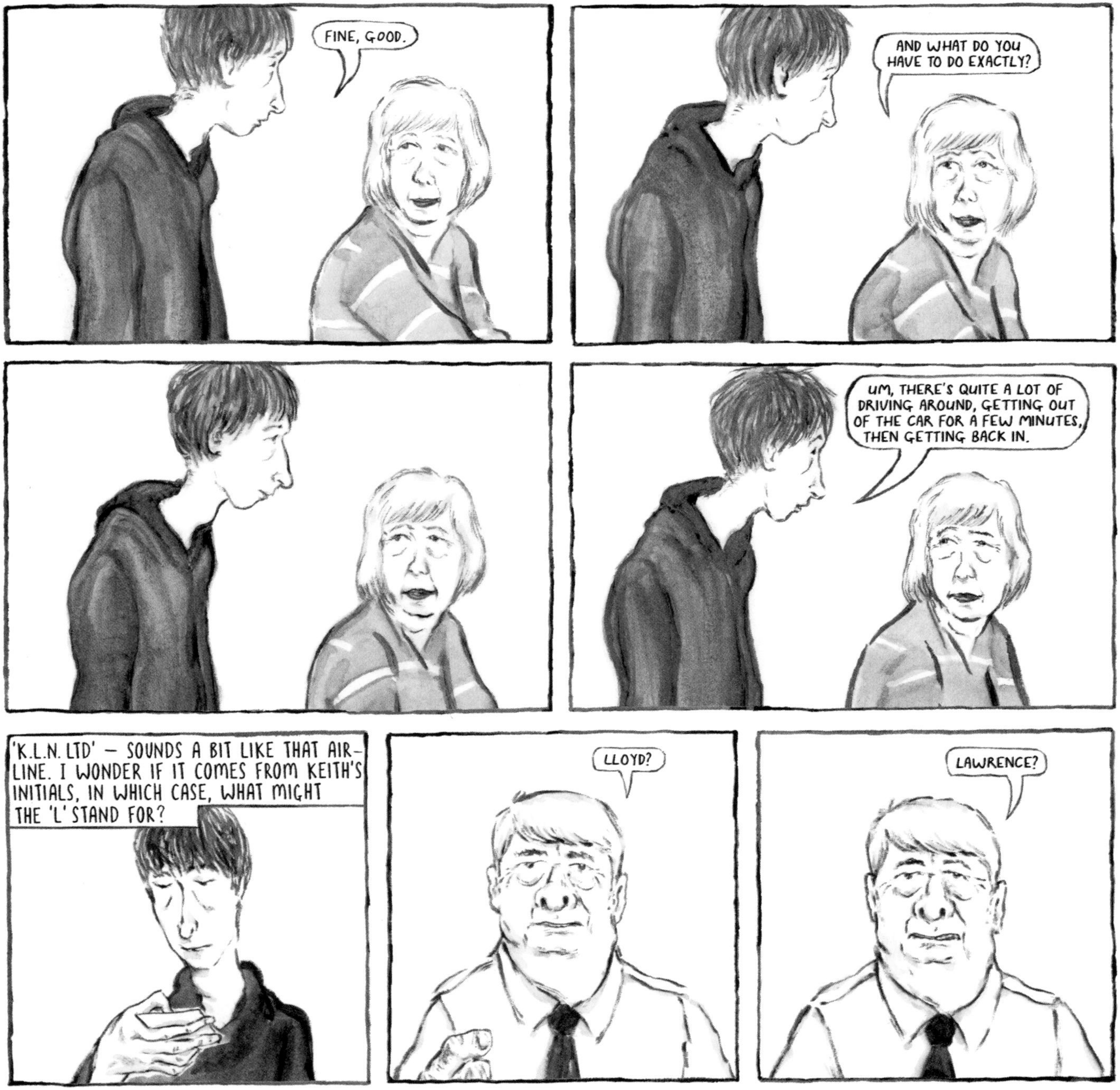
FINE, GOOD.
AND WHAT DO YOU HAVE TO DO EXACTLY?
UM, THERE'S QUITE A LOT OF DRIVING AROUND, GETTING OUT OF THE CAR FOR A FEW MINUTES, THEN GETTING BACK IN.
'K.L.N. LTD' – SOUNDS A BIT LIKE THAT AIR-LINE. I WONDER IF IT COMES FROM KEITH'S INITIALS, IN WHICH CASE, WHAT MIGHT THE 'L' STAND FOR?
LLOYD?
LAWRENCE?

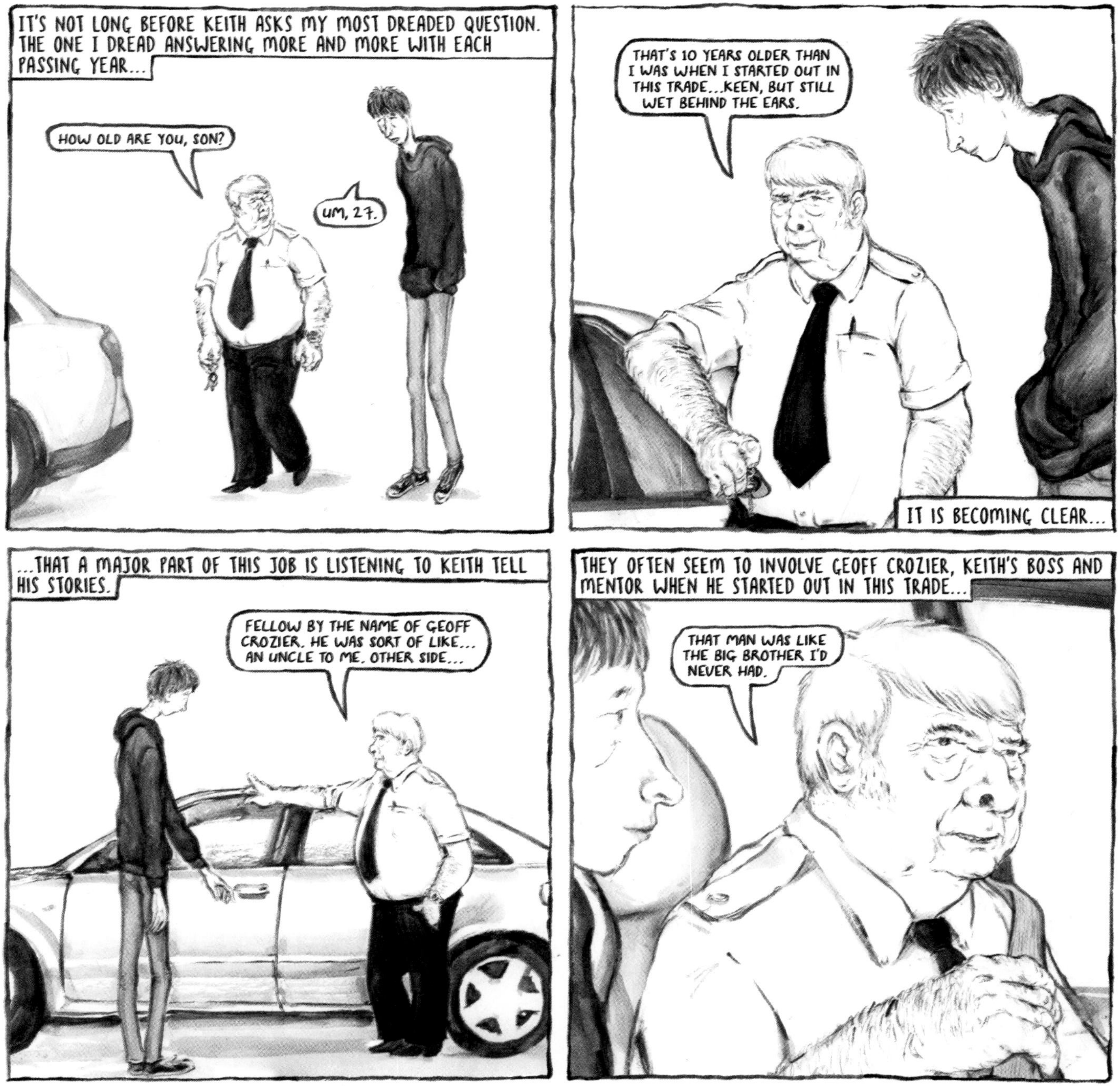
IT'S NOT LONG BEFORE KEITH ASKS MY MOST DREADED QUESTION. THE ONE I DREAD ANSWERING MORE AND MORE WITH EACH PASSING YEAR...
HOW OLD ARE YOU, SON?
UM, 27.
THAT'S 10 YEARS OLDER THAN I WAS WHEN I STARTED OUT IN THIS TRADE...KEEN, BUT STILL WET BEHIND THE EARS.
IT IS BECOMING CLEAR...
...THAT A MAJOR PART OF THIS JOB IS LISTENING TO KEITH TELL HIS STORIES.
FELLOW BY THE NAME OF GEOFF CROZIER. HE WAS SORT OF LIKE... AN UNCLE TO ME. OTHER SIDE...
THEY OFTEN SEEM TO INVOLVE GEOFF CROZIER, KEITH'S BOSS AND MENTOR WHEN HE STARTED OUT IN THIS TRADE...
THAT MAN WAS LIKE THE BIG BROTHER I'D NEVER HAD.

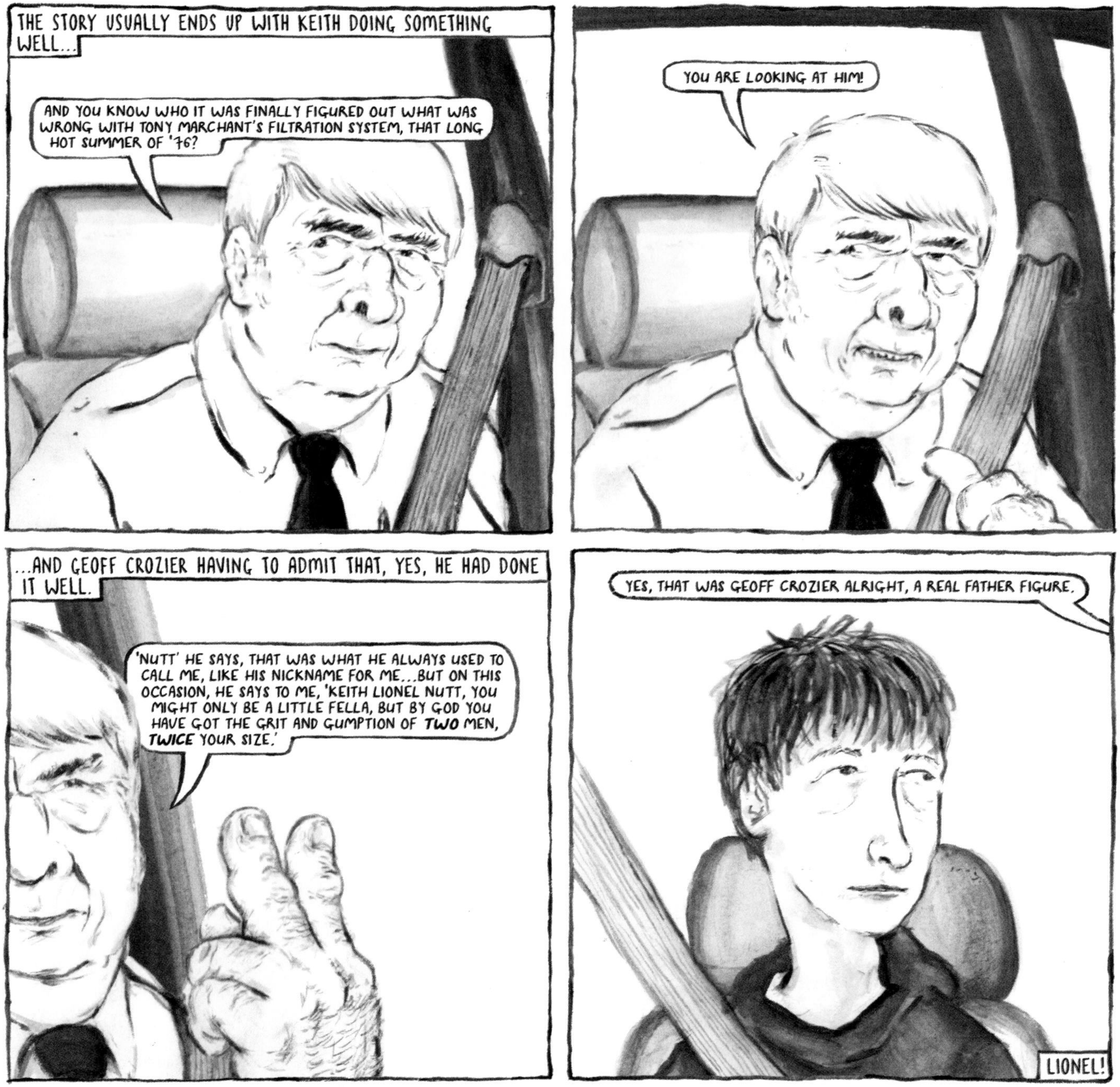
THE STORY USUALLY ENDS UP WITH KEITH DOING SOMETHING WELL...
AND YOU KNOW WHO IT WAS FINALLY FIGURED OUT WHAT WAS WRONG WITH TONY MARCHANT'S FILTRATION SYSTEM, THAT LONG HOT SUMMER OF '76?
YOU ARE LOOKING AT HIM!
...AND GEOFF CROZIER HAVING TO ADMIT THAT, YES, HE HAD DONE IT WELL.
'NUTT' HE SAYS, THAT WAS WHAT HE ALWAYS USED TO CALL ME, LIKE HIS NICKNAME FOR ME...BUT ON THIS OCCASION, HE SAYS TO ME, 'KEITH LIONEL NUTT, YOU MIGHT ONLY BE A LITTLE FELLA, BUT BY GOD YOU HAVE GOT THE GRIT AND GUMPTION OF **TWO** MEN, **TWICE** YOUR SIZE.'
YES, THAT WAS GEOFF CROZIER ALRIGHT, A REAL FATHER FIGURE.
LIONEL!

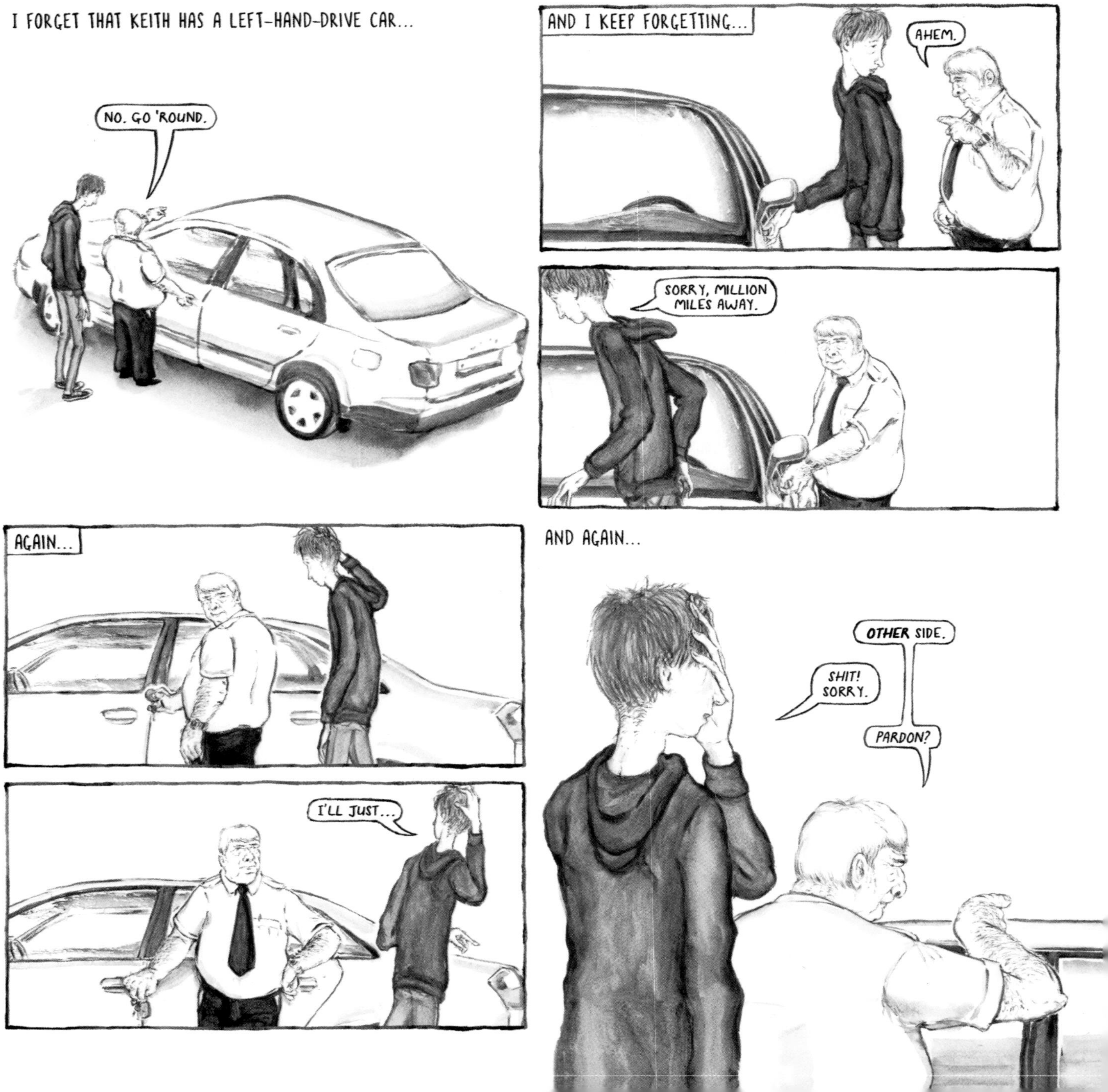

I FORGET THAT KEITH HAS A LEFT-HAND-DRIVE CAR...
NO. GO 'ROUND.
AND I KEEP FORGETTING...
AHEM.
SORRY, MILLION MILES AWAY.
AGAIN...
I'LL JUST...
AND AGAIN...
OTHER SIDE.
SHIT! SORRY.
PARDON?

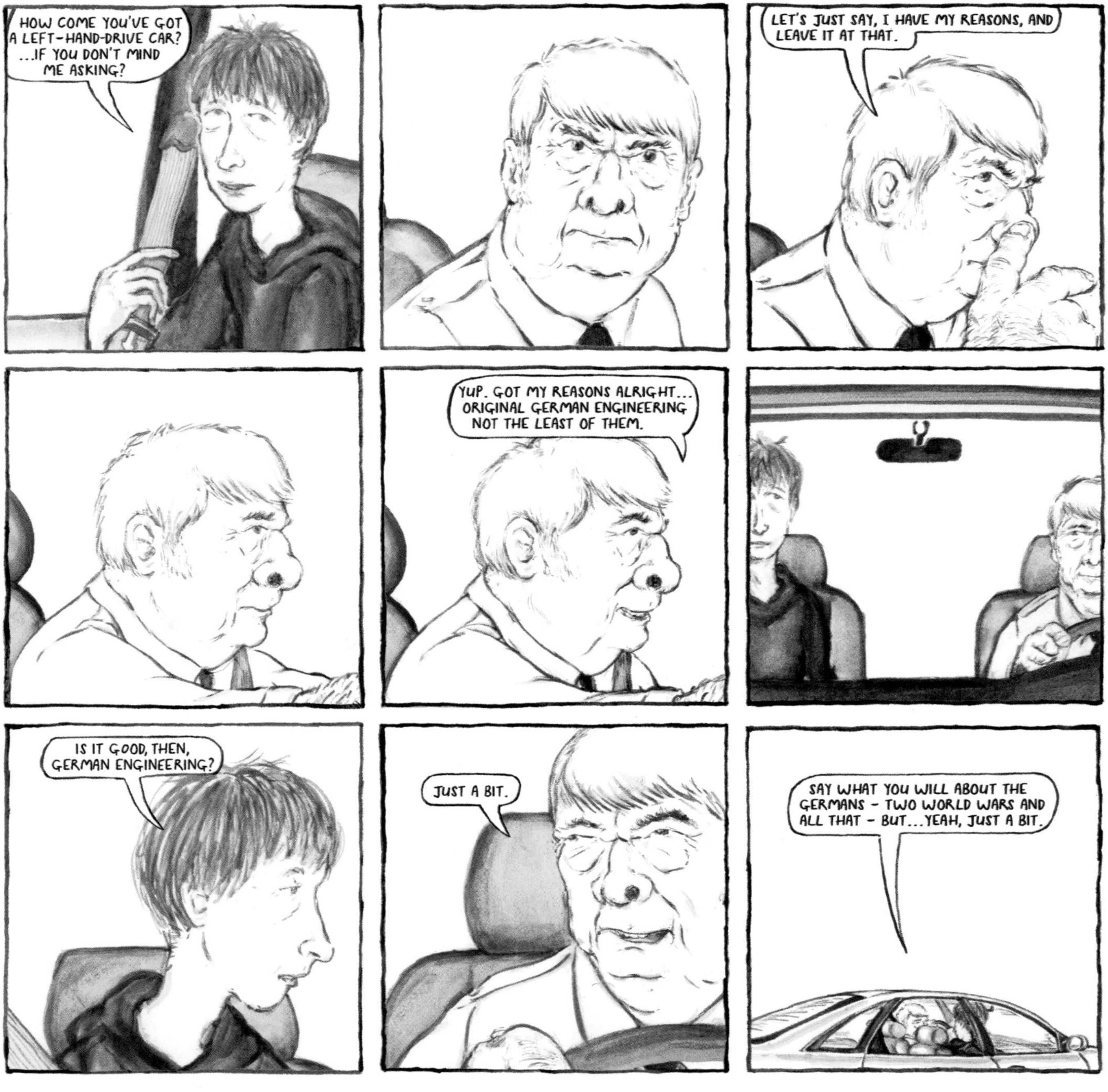
HOW COME YOU'VE GOT A LEFT-HAND-DRIVE CAR? ...IF YOU DON'T MIND ME ASKING?
LET'S JUST SAY, I HAVE MY REASONS, AND LEAVE IT AT THAT.
YUP. GOT MY REASONS ALRIGHT... ORIGINAL GERMAN ENGINEERING NOT THE LEAST OF THEM.
IS IT GOOD, THEN, GERMAN ENGINEERING?
JUST A BIT.
SAY WHAT YOU WILL ABOUT THE GERMANS - TWO WORLD WARS AND ALL THAT - BUT... YEAH, JUST A BIT.

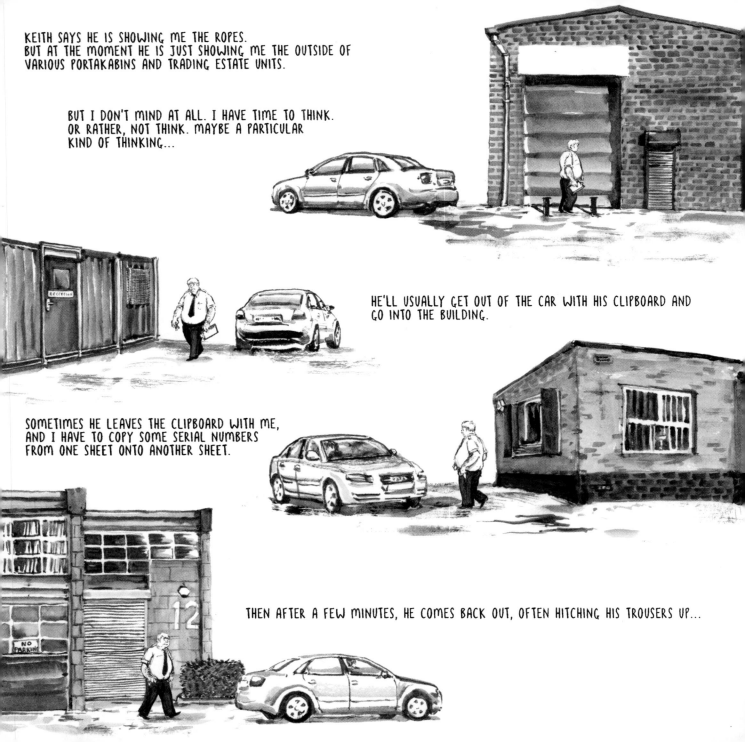

KEITH SAYS HE IS SHOWING ME THE ROPES. BUT AT THE MOMENT HE IS JUST SHOWING ME THE OUTSIDE OF VARIOUS PORTAKABINS AND TRADING ESTATE UNITS.

BUT I DON'T MIND AT ALL. I HAVE TIME TO THINK. OR RATHER, NOT THINK. MAYBE A PARTICULAR KIND OF THINKING...

HE'LL USUALLY GET OUT OF THE CAR WITH HIS CLIPBOARD AND GO INTO THE BUILDING.

SOMETIMES HE LEAVES THE CLIPBOARD WITH ME, AND I HAVE TO COPY SOME SERIAL NUMBERS FROM ONE SHEET ONTO ANOTHER SHEET.

THEN AFTER A FEW MINUTES, HE COMES BACK OUT, OFTEN HITCHING HIS TROUSERS UP...

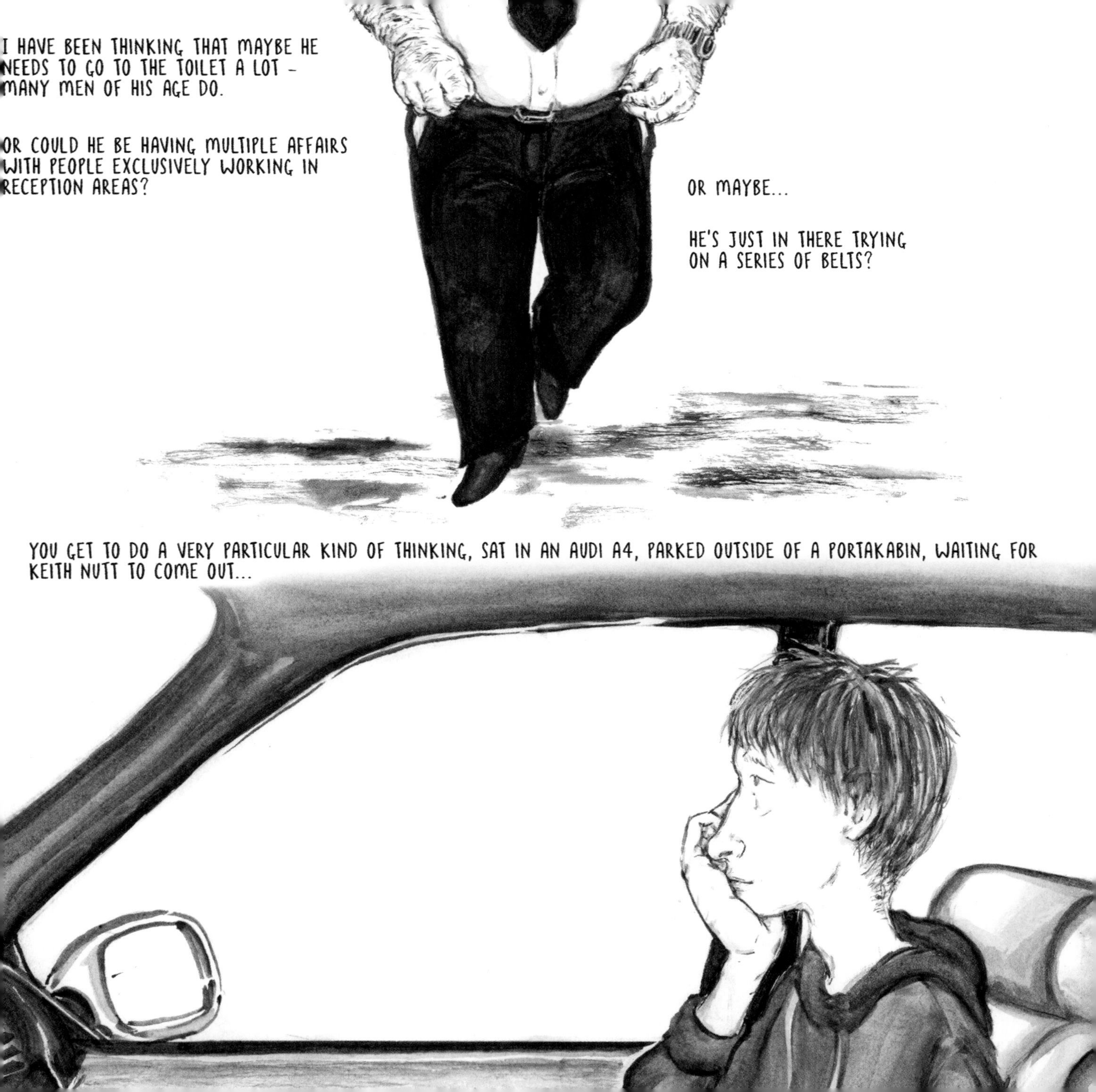
I HAVE BEEN THINKING THAT MAYBE HE NEEDS TO GO TO THE TOILET A LOT – MANY MEN OF HIS AGE DO.
OR COULD HE BE HAVING MULTIPLE AFFAIRS WITH PEOPLE EXCLUSIVELY WORKING IN RECEPTION AREAS?
OR MAYBE...
HE'S JUST IN THERE TRYING ON A SERIES OF BELTS?
YOU GET TO DO A VERY PARTICULAR KIND OF THINKING, SAT IN AN AUDI A4, PARKED OUTSIDE OF A PORTAKABIN, WAITING FOR KEITH NUTT TO COME OUT...

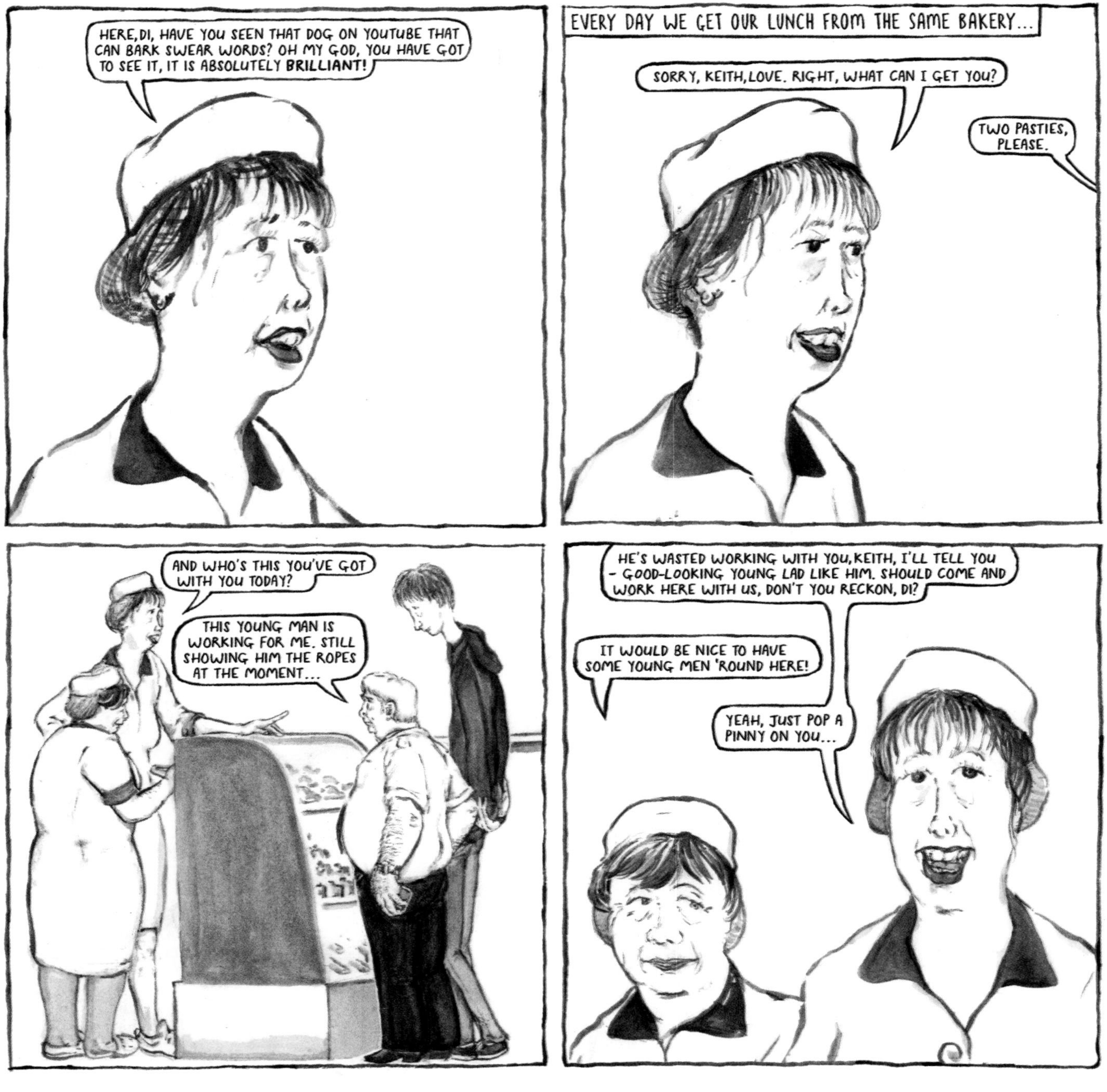
HERE, DI, HAVE YOU SEEN THAT DOG ON YOUTUBE THAT CAN BARK SWEAR WORDS? OH MY GOD, YOU HAVE GOT TO SEE IT, IT IS ABSOLUTELY **BRILLIANT!**
EVERY DAY WE GET OUR LUNCH FROM THE SAME BAKERY...
SORRY, KEITH, LOVE. RIGHT, WHAT CAN I GET YOU?
TWO PASTIES, PLEASE.
AND WHO'S THIS YOU'VE GOT WITH YOU TODAY?
THIS YOUNG MAN IS WORKING FOR ME. STILL SHOWING HIM THE ROPES AT THE MOMENT...
HE'S WASTED WORKING WITH YOU, KEITH, I'LL TELL YOU - GOOD-LOOKING YOUNG LAD LIKE HIM. SHOULD COME AND WORK HERE WITH US, DON'T YOU RECKON, DI?
IT WOULD BE NICE TO HAVE SOME YOUNG MEN 'ROUND HERE!
YEAH, JUST POP A PINNY ON YOU...

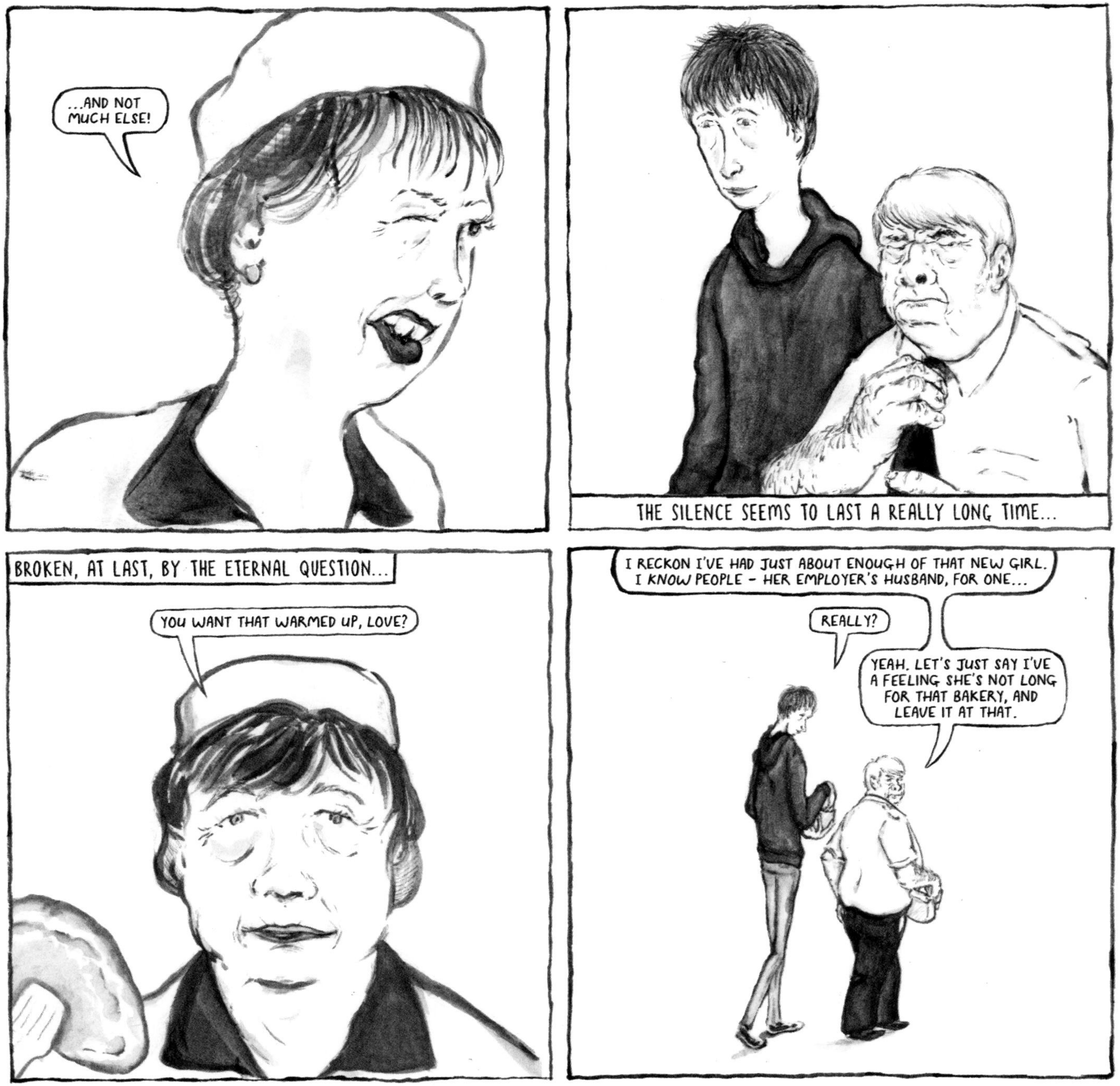
...AND NOT MUCH ELSE!
THE SILENCE SEEMS TO LAST A REALLY LONG TIME...
BROKEN, AT LAST, BY THE ETERNAL QUESTION...
YOU WANT THAT WARMED UP, LOVE?
I RECKON I'VE HAD JUST ABOUT ENOUGH OF THAT NEW GIRL. I KNOW PEOPLE - HER EMPLOYER'S HUSBAND, FOR ONE...
REALLY?
YEAH. LET'S JUST SAY I'VE A FEELING SHE'S NOT LONG FOR THAT BAKERY, AND LEAVE IT AT THAT.

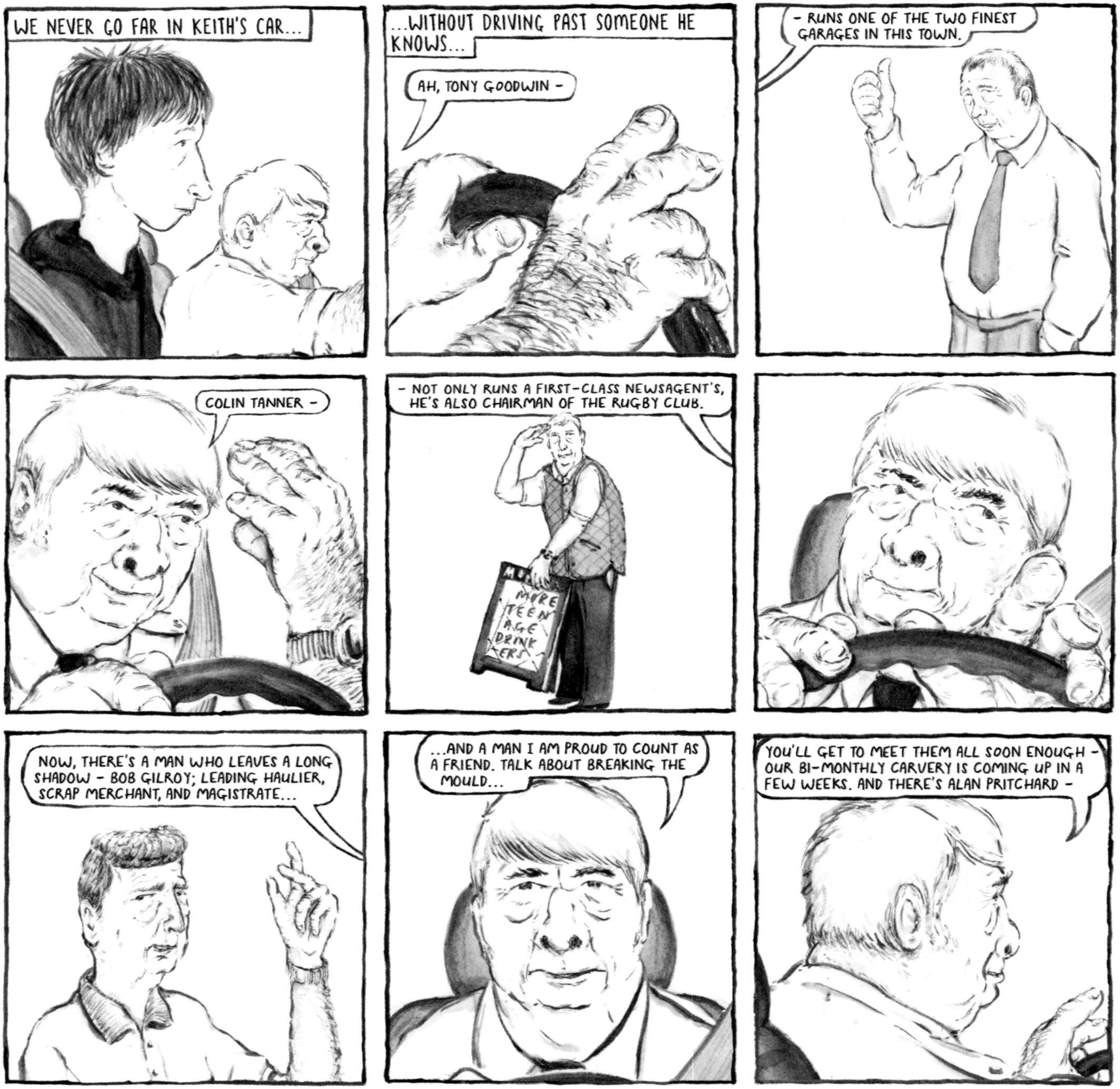
WE NEVER GO FAR IN KEITH'S CAR...
...WITHOUT DRIVING PAST SOMEONE HE KNOWS...
AH, TONY GOODWIN -
- RUNS ONE OF THE TWO FINEST GARAGES IN THIS TOWN.
COLIN TANNER -
- NOT ONLY RUNS A FIRST-CLASS NEWSAGENT'S, HE'S ALSO CHAIRMAN OF THE RUGBY CLUB.
MORE TEEN AGE DRINK ERS
NOW, THERE'S A MAN WHO LEAVES A LONG SHADOW - BOB GILROY; LEADING HAULIER, SCRAP MERCHANT, AND MAGISTRATE...
...AND A MAN I AM PROUD TO COUNT AS A FRIEND. TALK ABOUT BREAKING THE MOULD...
YOU'LL GET TO MEET THEM ALL SOON ENOUGH - OUR BI-MONTHLY CARVERY IS COMING UP IN A FEW WEEKS. AND THERE'S ALAN PRITCHARD -

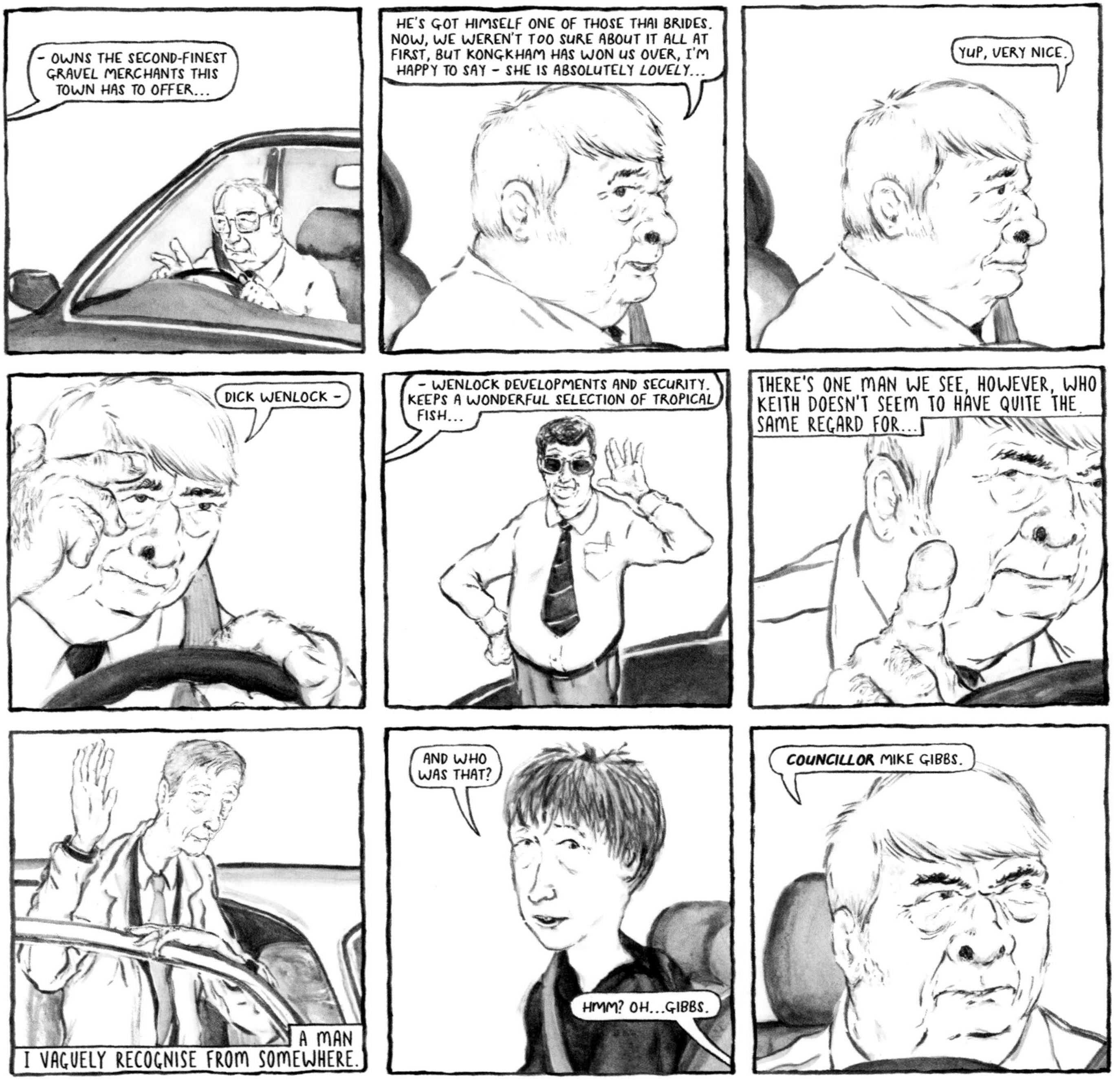
- OWNS THE SECOND-FINEST GRAVEL MERCHANTS THIS TOWN HAS TO OFFER...
HE'S GOT HIMSELF ONE OF THOSE THAI BRIDES. NOW, WE WEREN'T TOO SURE ABOUT IT ALL AT FIRST, BUT KONGKHAM HAS WON US OVER, I'M HAPPY TO SAY - SHE IS ABSOLUTELY *LOVELY*...
YUP, VERY NICE.
DICK WENLOCK -
- WENLOCK DEVELOPMENTS AND SECURITY. KEEPS A WONDERFUL SELECTION OF TROPICAL FISH...
THERE'S ONE MAN WE SEE, HOWEVER, WHO KEITH DOESN'T SEEM TO HAVE QUITE THE SAME REGARD FOR...
A MAN I VAGUELY RECOGNISE FROM SOMEWHERE.
AND WHO WAS THAT?
HMM? OH...GIBBS.
COUNCILLOR MIKE GIBBS.

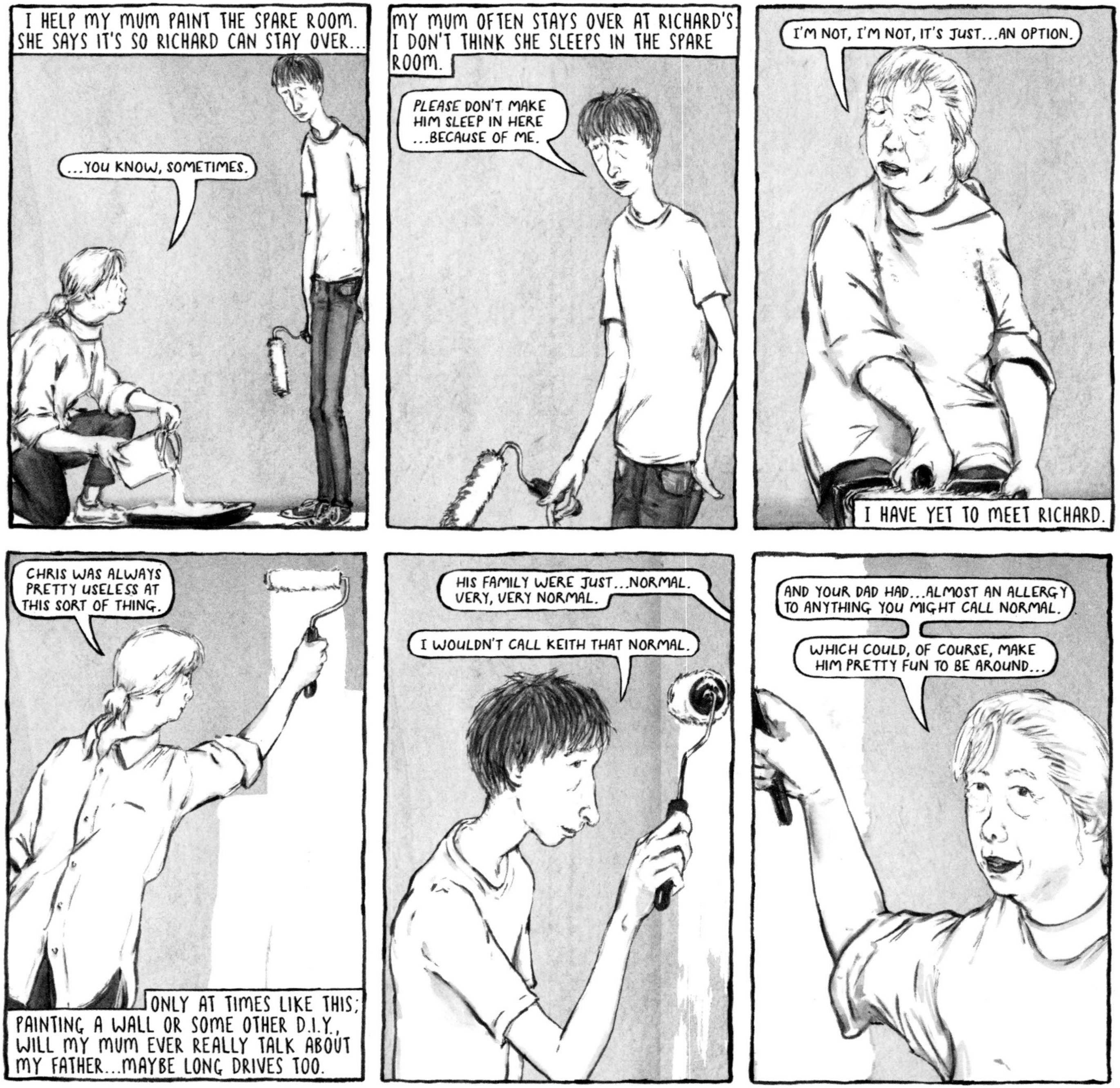
I HELP MY MUM PAINT THE SPARE ROOM. SHE SAYS IT'S SO RICHARD CAN STAY OVER...
...YOU KNOW, SOMETIMES.
MY MUM OFTEN STAYS OVER AT RICHARD'S. I DON'T THINK SHE SLEEPS IN THE SPARE ROOM.
PLEASE DON'T MAKE HIM SLEEP IN HERE ...BECAUSE OF ME.
I'M NOT, I'M NOT, IT'S JUST...AN OPTION.
I HAVE YET TO MEET RICHARD.
CHRIS WAS ALWAYS PRETTY USELESS AT THIS SORT OF THING.
ONLY AT TIMES LIKE THIS; PAINTING A WALL OR SOME OTHER D.I.Y., WILL MY MUM EVER REALLY TALK ABOUT MY FATHER...MAYBE LONG DRIVES TOO.
HIS FAMILY WERE JUST...NORMAL. VERY, VERY NORMAL.
I WOULDN'T CALL KEITH THAT NORMAL.
AND YOUR DAD HAD...ALMOST AN ALLERGY TO ANYTHING YOU MIGHT CALL NORMAL.
WHICH COULD, OF COURSE, MAKE HIM PRETTY FUN TO BE AROUND...

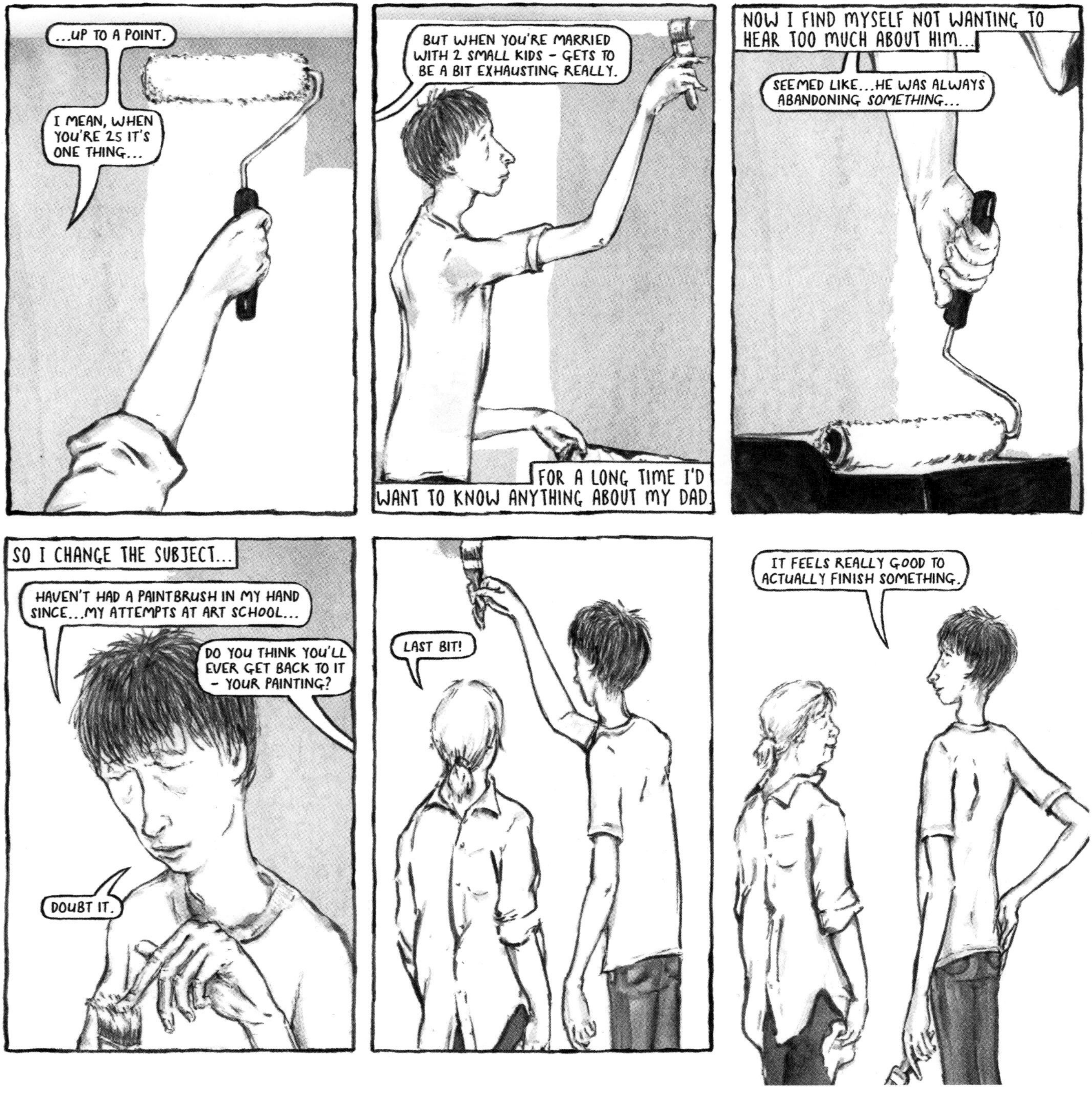
...UP TO A POINT.
I MEAN, WHEN YOU'RE 25 IT'S ONE THING...
BUT WHEN YOU'RE MARRIED WITH 2 SMALL KIDS - GETS TO BE A BIT EXHAUSTING REALLY.
FOR A LONG TIME I'D WANT TO KNOW ANYTHING ABOUT MY DAD.
NOW I FIND MYSELF NOT WANTING TO HEAR TOO MUCH ABOUT HIM...
SEEMED LIKE...HE WAS ALWAYS ABANDONING SOMETHING...
SO I CHANGE THE SUBJECT...
HAVEN'T HAD A PAINTBRUSH IN MY HAND SINCE...MY ATTEMPTS AT ART SCHOOL...
DO YOU THINK YOU'LL EVER GET BACK TO IT - YOUR PAINTING?
DOUBT IT.
LAST BIT!
IT FEELS REALLY GOOD TO ACTUALLY FINISH SOMETHING.

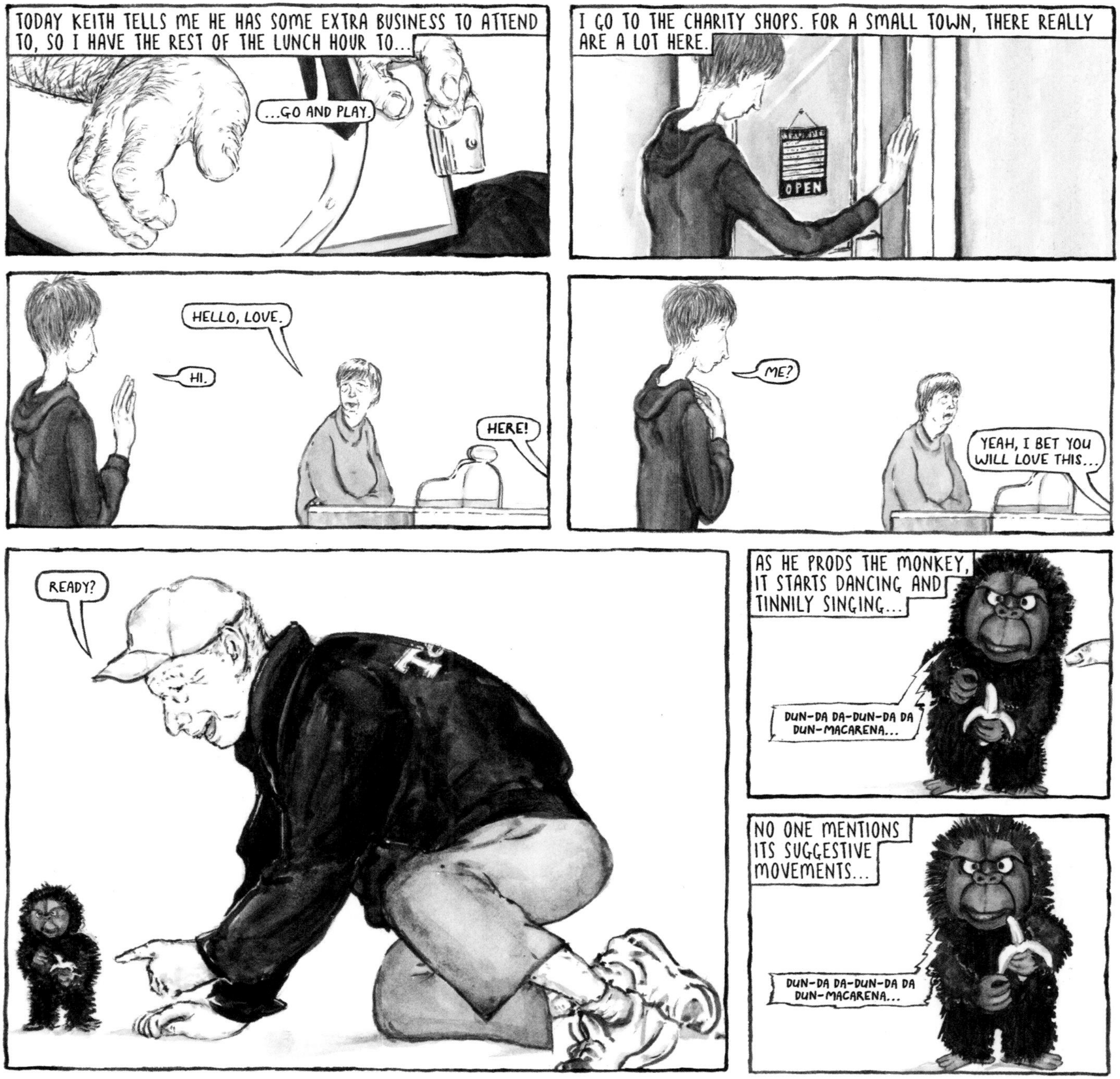
TODAY KEITH TELLS ME HE HAS SOME EXTRA BUSINESS TO ATTEND TO, SO I HAVE THE REST OF THE LUNCH HOUR TO...
...GO AND PLAY.
I GO TO THE CHARITY SHOPS. FOR A SMALL TOWN, THERE REALLY ARE A LOT HERE.
OPEN
HELLO, LOVE.
HI.
HERE!
ME?
YEAH, I BET YOU WILL LOVE THIS...
READY?
AS HE PRODS THE MONKEY, IT STARTS DANCING AND TINNILY SINGING...
DUN-DA DA-DUN-DA DA DUN-MACARENA...
NO ONE MENTIONS ITS SUGGESTIVE MOVEMENTS...
DUN-DA DA-DUN-DA DA DUN-MACARENA...

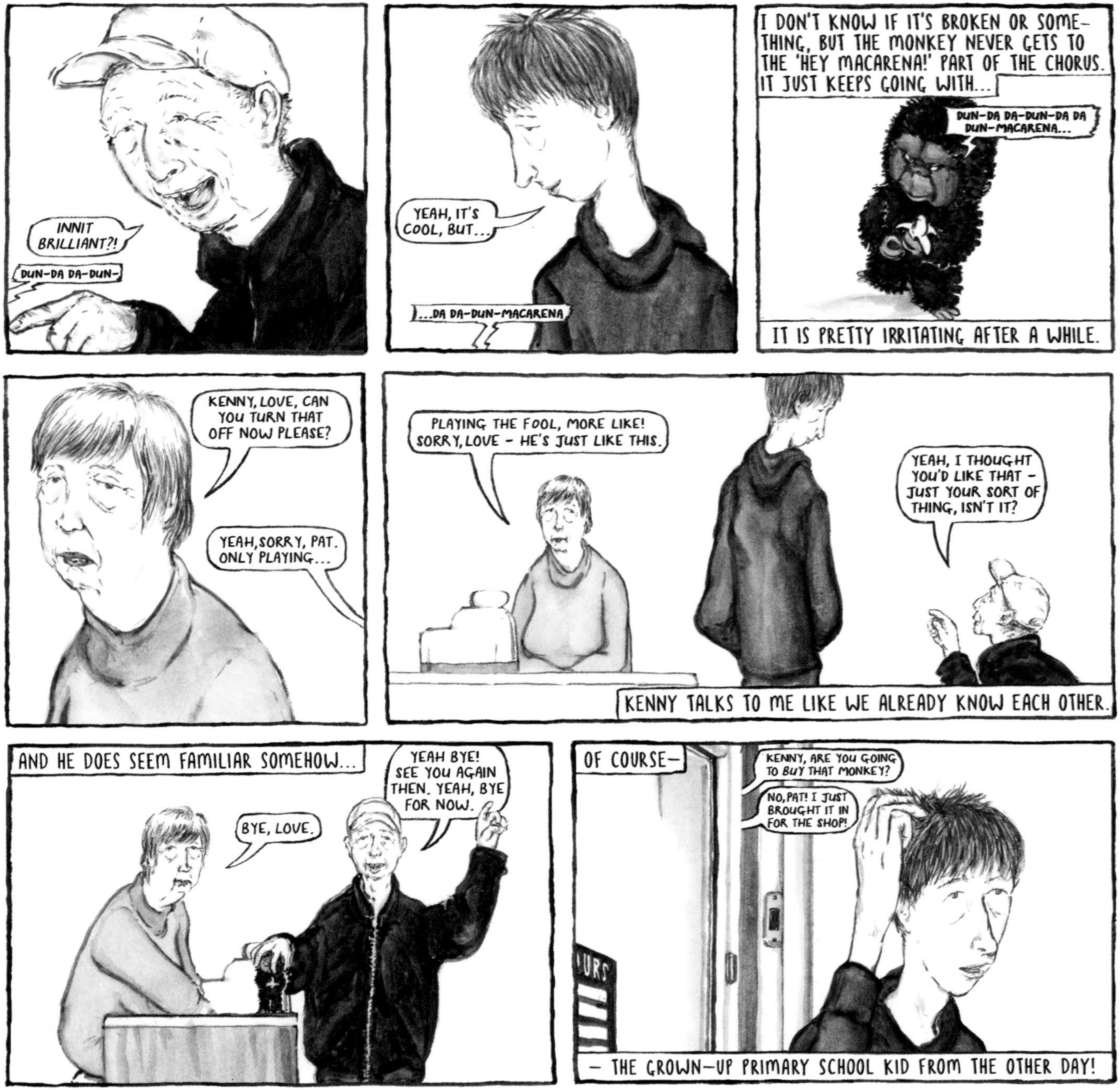

INNIT BRILLIANT?!
DUN-DA DA-DUN-
YEAH, IT'S COOL, BUT...
...DA DA-DUN-MACARENA
I DON'T KNOW IF IT'S BROKEN OR SOMETHING, BUT THE MONKEY NEVER GETS TO THE 'HEY MACARENA!' PART OF THE CHORUS. IT JUST KEEPS GOING WITH...
DUN-DA DA-DUN-DA DA DUN-MACARENA...
IT IS PRETTY IRRITATING AFTER A WHILE.
KENNY, LOVE, CAN YOU TURN THAT OFF NOW PLEASE?
YEAH, SORRY, PAT. ONLY PLAYING...
PLAYING THE FOOL, MORE LIKE! SORRY, LOVE - HE'S JUST LIKE THIS.
YEAH, I THOUGHT YOU'D LIKE THAT - JUST YOUR SORT OF THING, ISN'T IT?
KENNY TALKS TO ME LIKE WE ALREADY KNOW EACH OTHER.
AND HE DOES SEEM FAMILIAR SOMEHOW...
BYE, LOVE.
YEAH BYE! SEE YOU AGAIN THEN. YEAH, BYE FOR NOW.
OF COURSE-
KENNY, ARE YOU GOING TO BUY THAT MONKEY?
NO, PAT! I JUST BROUGHT IT IN FOR THE SHOP!
- THE GROWN-UP PRIMARY SCHOOL KID FROM THE OTHER DAY!

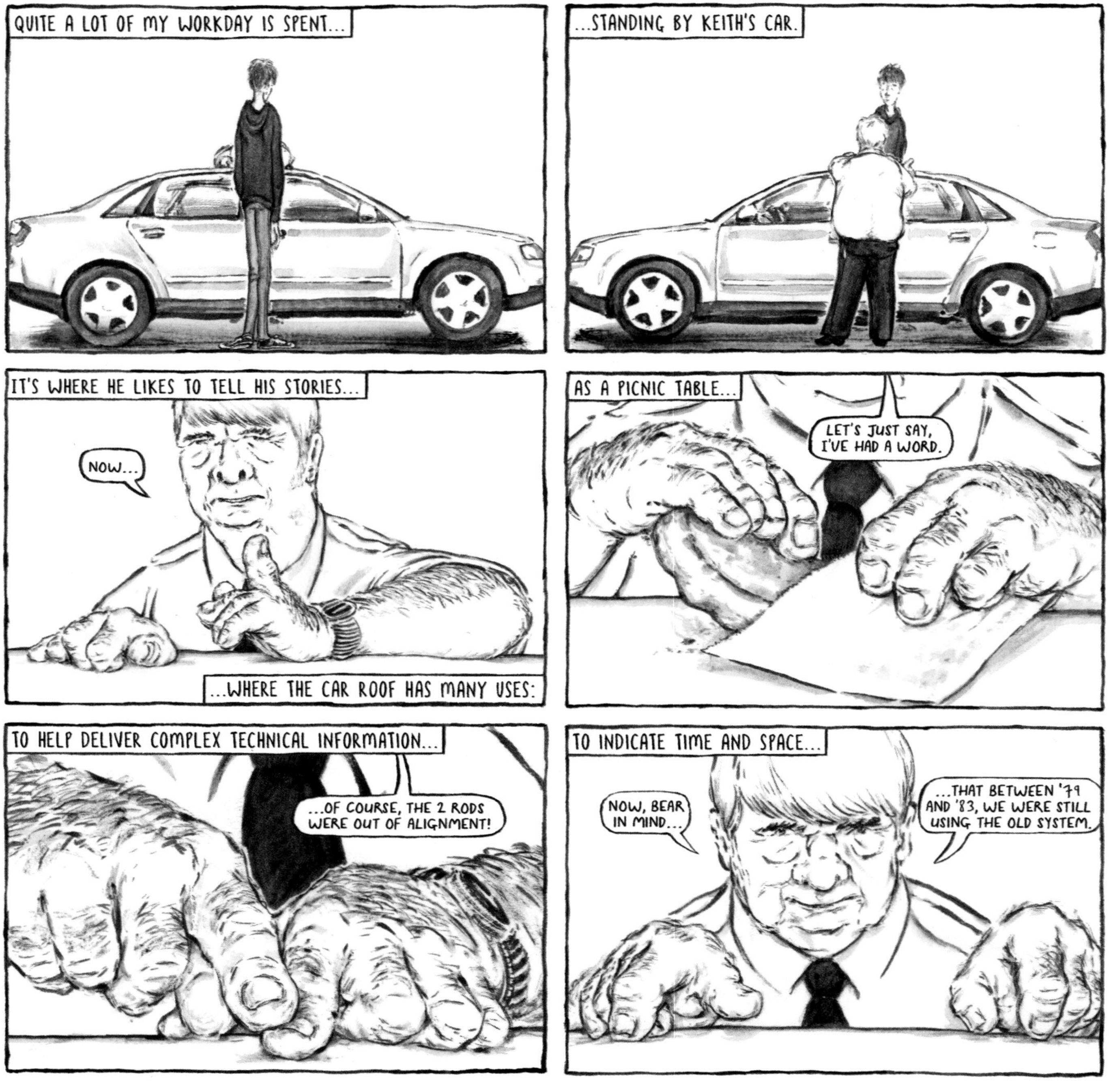
QUITE A LOT OF MY WORKDAY IS SPENT...
...STANDING BY KEITH'S CAR.
IT'S WHERE HE LIKES TO TELL HIS STORIES...
NOW...
...WHERE THE CAR ROOF HAS MANY USES:
AS A PICNIC TABLE...
LET'S JUST SAY, I'VE HAD A WORD.
TO HELP DELIVER COMPLEX TECHNICAL INFORMATION...
...OF COURSE, THE 2 RODS WERE OUT OF ALIGNMENT!
TO INDICATE TIME AND SPACE...
NOW, BEAR IN MIND...
...THAT BETWEEN '79 AND '83, WE WERE STILL USING THE OLD SYSTEM.

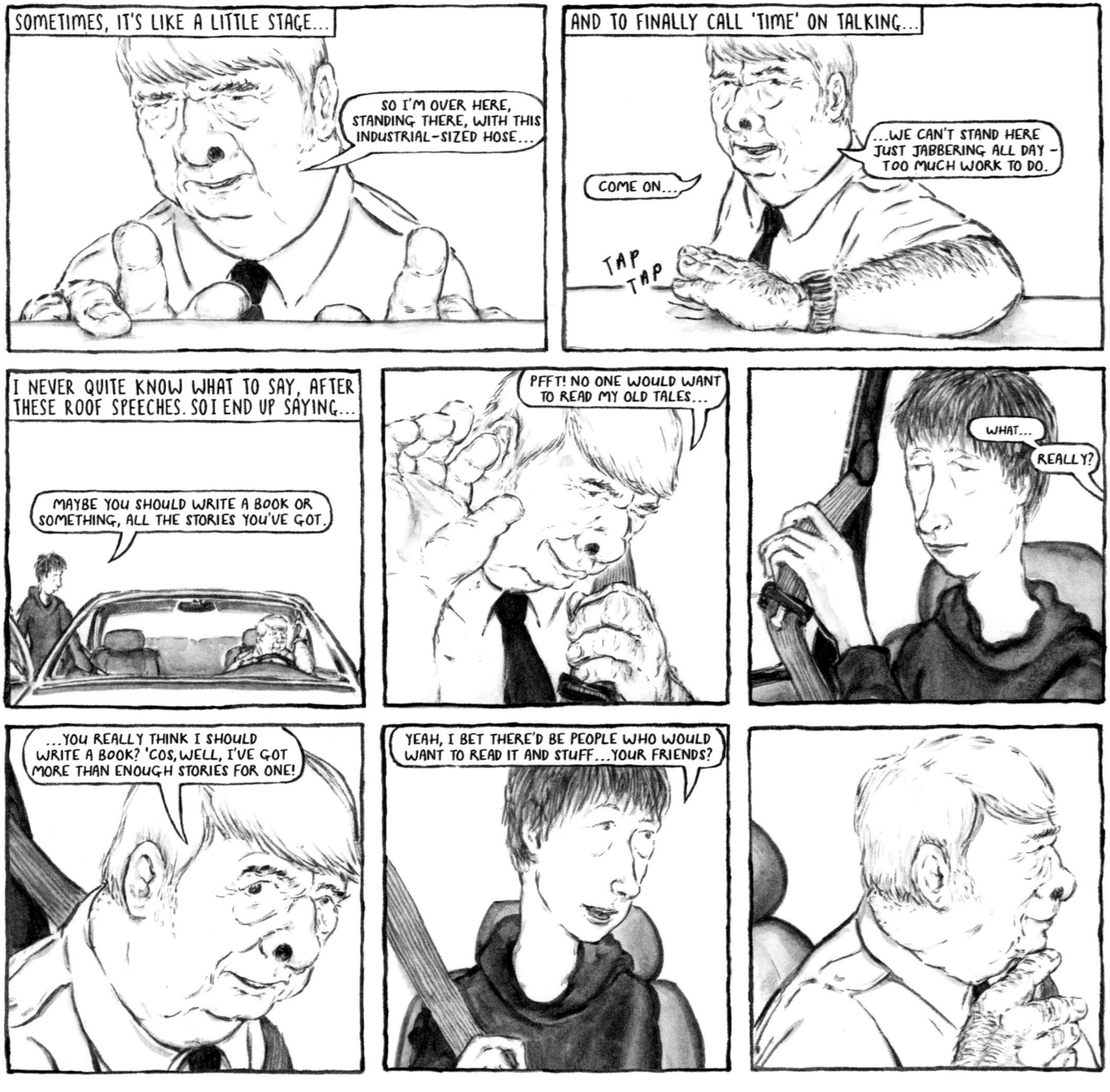
SOMETIMES, IT'S LIKE A LITTLE STAGE...
SO I'M OVER HERE, STANDING THERE, WITH THIS INDUSTRIAL-SIZED HOSE...
AND TO FINALLY CALL 'TIME' ON TALKING...
...WE CAN'T STAND HERE JUST JABBERING ALL DAY - TOO MUCH WORK TO DO.
COME ON...
TAP TAP
I NEVER QUITE KNOW WHAT TO SAY, AFTER THESE ROOF SPEECHES. SO I END UP SAYING...
MAYBE YOU SHOULD WRITE A BOOK OR SOMETHING, ALL THE STORIES YOU'VE GOT.
PFFT! NO ONE WOULD WANT TO READ MY OLD TALES...
WHAT...
REALLY?
...YOU REALLY THINK I SHOULD WRITE A BOOK? 'COS, WELL, I'VE GOT MORE THAN ENOUGH STORIES FOR ONE!
YEAH, I BET THERE'D BE PEOPLE WHO WOULD WANT TO READ IT AND STUFF...YOUR FRIENDS?

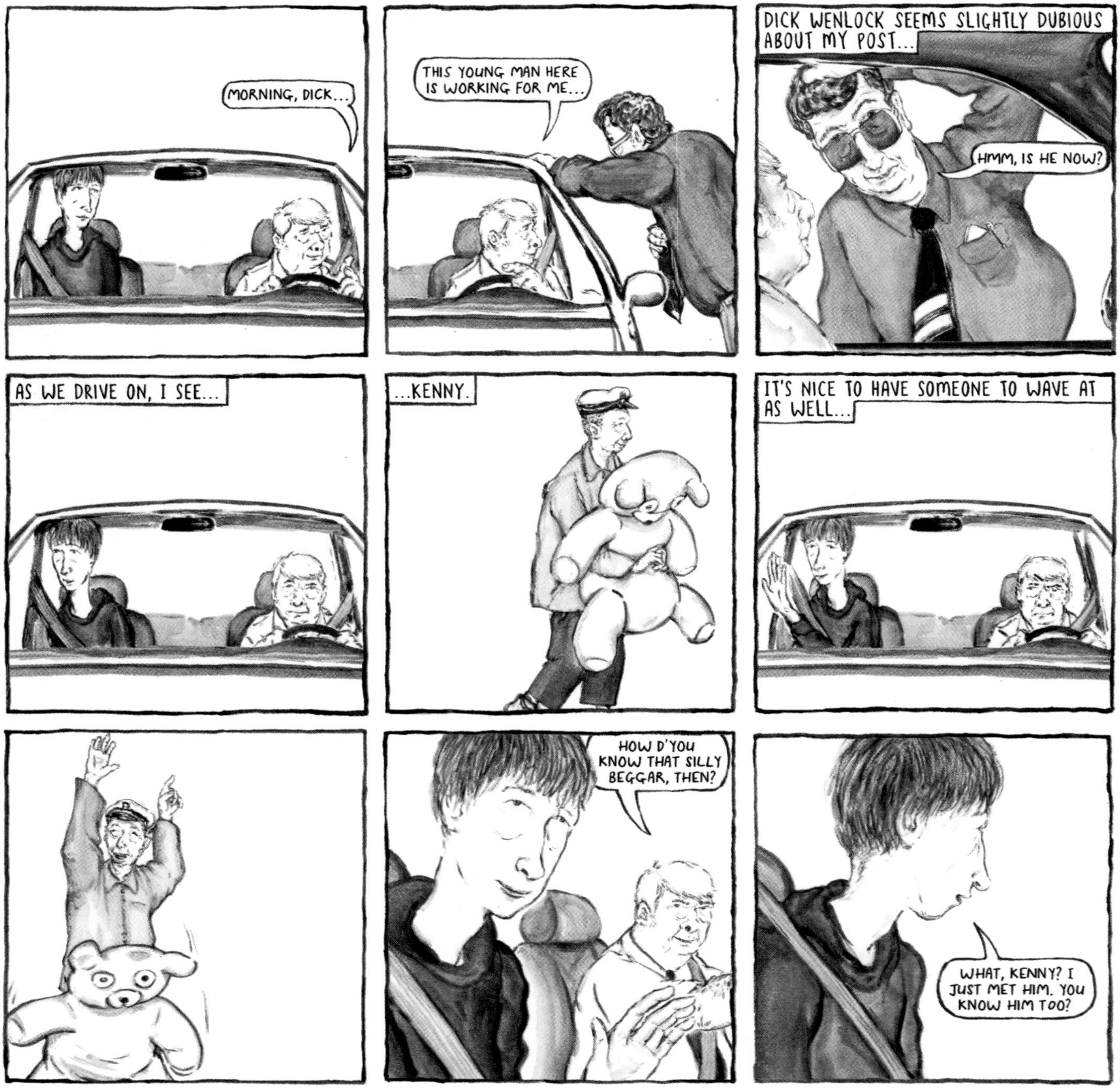
MORNING, DICK...
THIS YOUNG MAN HERE IS WORKING FOR ME...
DICK WENLOCK SEEMS SLIGHTLY DUBIOUS ABOUT MY POST...
HMM, IS HE NOW?
AS WE DRIVE ON, I SEE...
...KENNY.
IT'S NICE TO HAVE SOMEONE TO WAVE AT AS WELL...
HOW D'YOU KNOW THAT SILLY BEGGAR, THEN?
WHAT, KENNY? I JUST MET HIM. YOU KNOW HIM TOO?

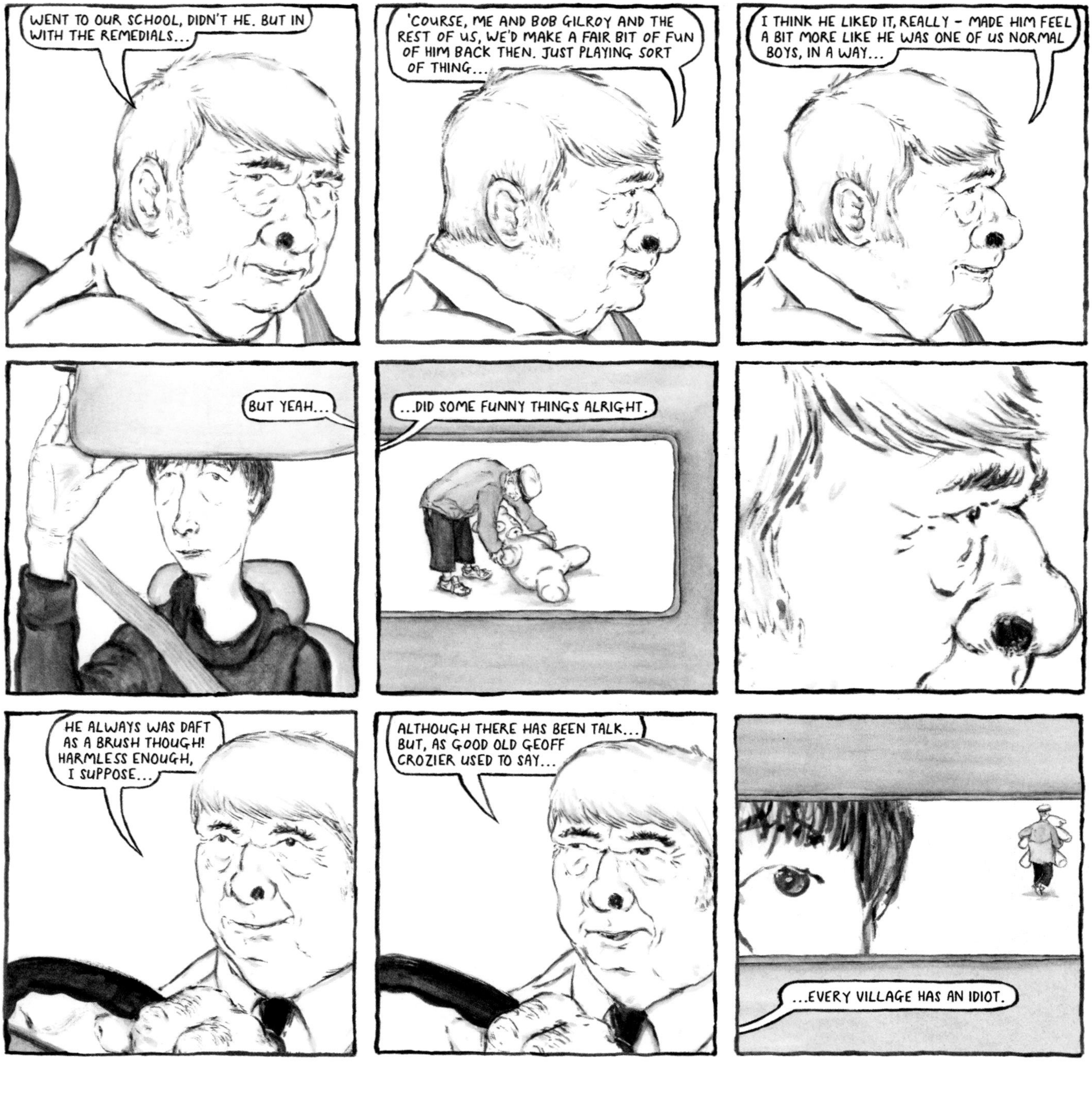
WENT TO OUR SCHOOL, DIDN'T HE. BUT IN WITH THE REMEDIALS...
'COURSE, ME AND BOB GILROY AND THE REST OF US, WE'D MAKE A FAIR BIT OF FUN OF HIM BACK THEN. JUST PLAYING SORT OF THING...
I THINK HE LIKED IT, REALLY - MADE HIM FEEL A BIT MORE LIKE HE WAS ONE OF US NORMAL BOYS, IN A WAY...
BUT YEAH...
...DID SOME FUNNY THINGS ALRIGHT.
HE ALWAYS WAS DAFT AS A BRUSH THOUGH! HARMLESS ENOUGH, I SUPPOSE...
ALTHOUGH THERE HAS BEEN TALK... BUT, AS GOOD OLD GEOFF CROZIER USED TO SAY...
...EVERY VILLAGE HAS AN IDIOT.

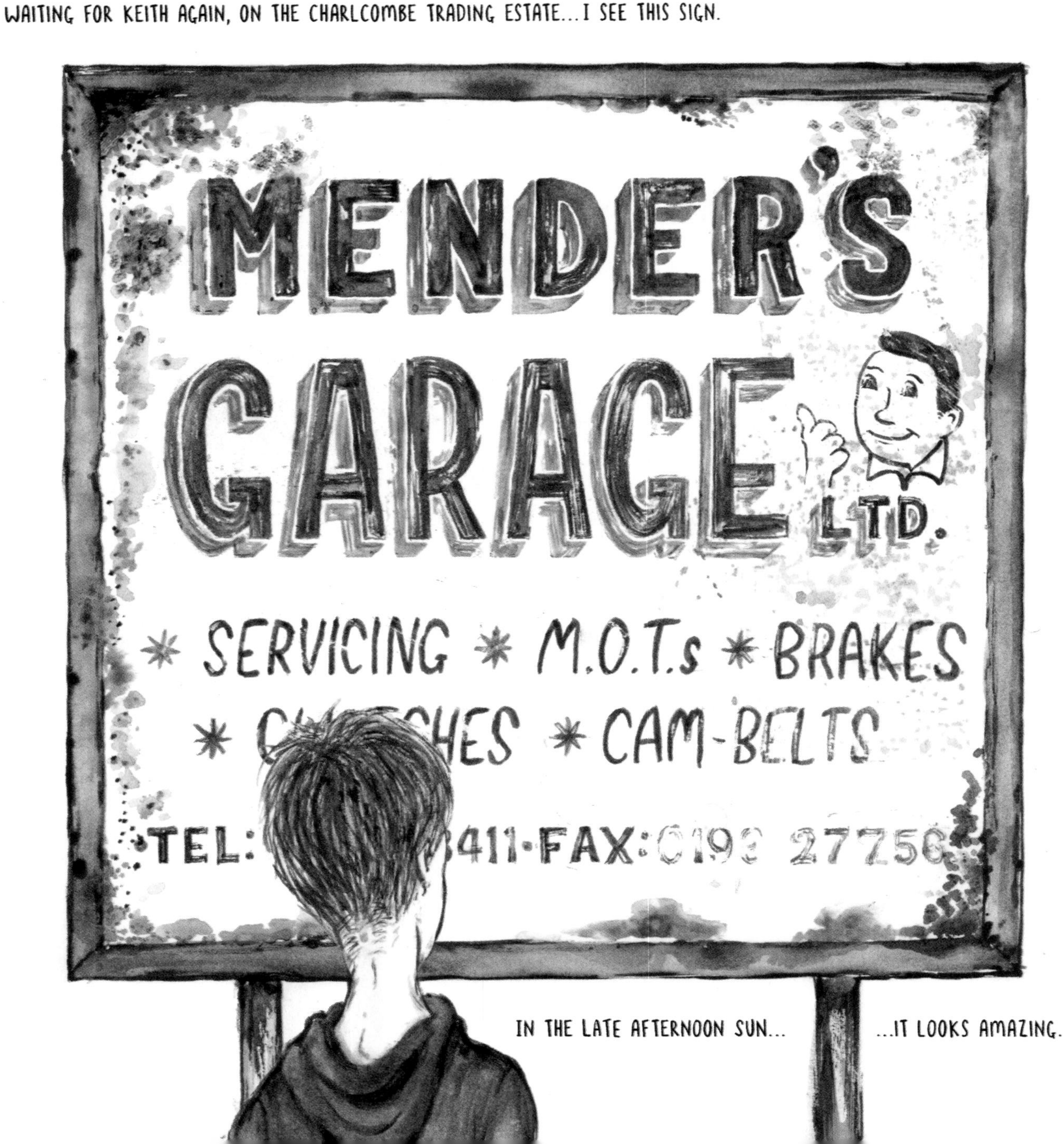
WAITING FOR KEITH AGAIN, ON THE CHARLCOMBE TRADING ESTATE...I SEE THIS SIGN.
MENDER'S GARAGE LTD.
* SERVICING * M.O.T.s * BRAKES
* CAM-BELTS
TEL:
FAX:
IN THE LATE AFTERNOON SUN...
...IT LOOKS AMAZING.

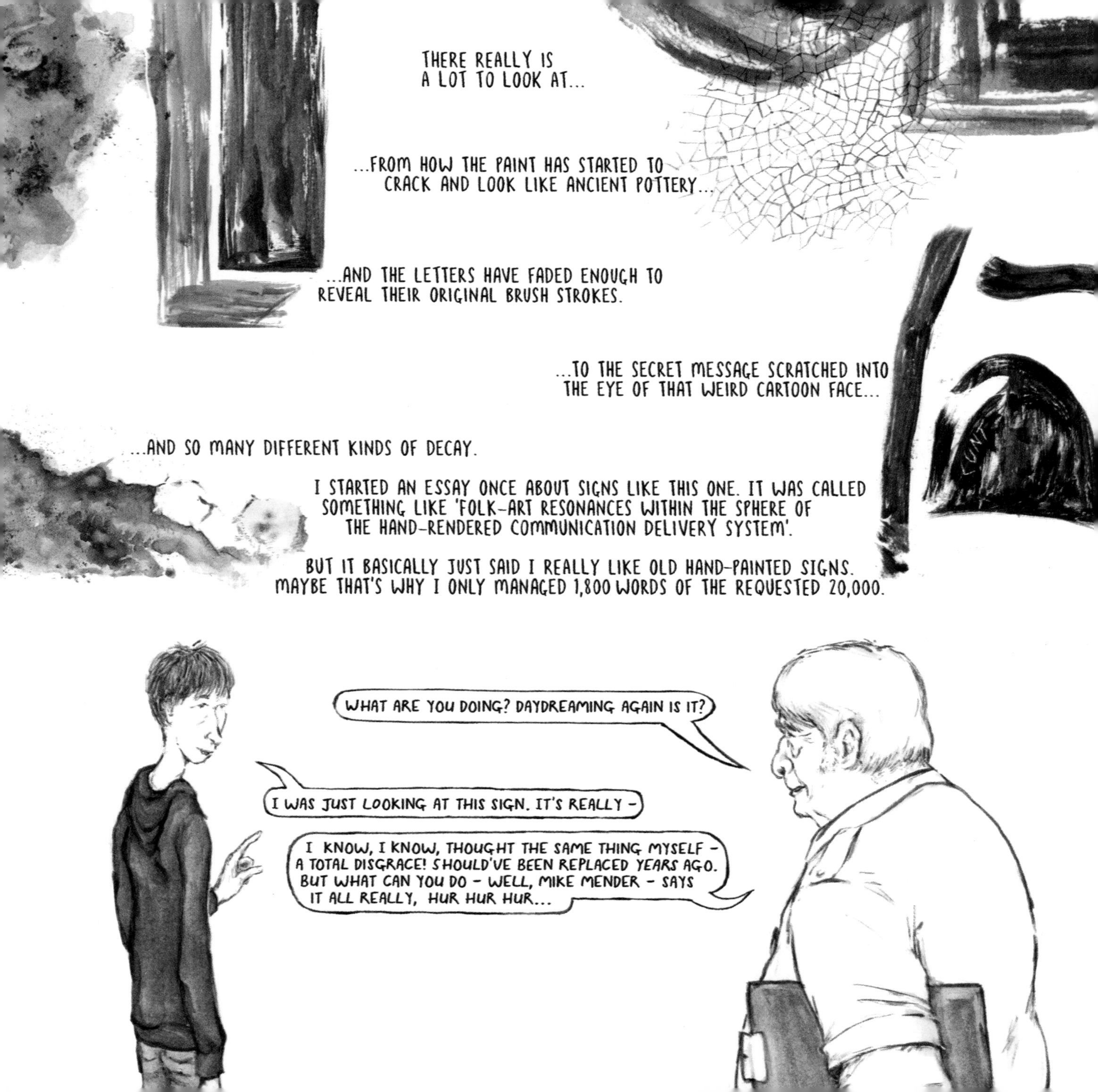
THERE REALLY IS A LOT TO LOOK AT...
...FROM HOW THE PAINT HAS STARTED TO CRACK AND LOOK LIKE ANCIENT POTTERY...
...AND THE LETTERS HAVE FADED ENOUGH TO REVEAL THEIR ORIGINAL BRUSH STROKES.
...TO THE SECRET MESSAGE SCRATCHED INTO THE EYE OF THAT WEIRD CARTOON FACE...
...AND SO MANY DIFFERENT KINDS OF DECAY.
I STARTED AN ESSAY ONCE ABOUT SIGNS LIKE THIS ONE. IT WAS CALLED SOMETHING LIKE 'FOLK-ART RESONANCES WITHIN THE SPHERE OF THE HAND-RENDERED COMMUNICATION DELIVERY SYSTEM'.
BUT IT BASICALLY JUST SAID I REALLY LIKE OLD HAND-PAINTED SIGNS. MAYBE THAT'S WHY I ONLY MANAGED 1,800 WORDS OF THE REQUESTED 20,000.
WHAT ARE YOU DOING? DAYDREAMING AGAIN IS IT?
I WAS JUST LOOKING AT THIS SIGN. IT'S REALLY –
I KNOW, I KNOW, THOUGHT THE SAME THING MYSELF – A TOTAL DISGRACE! SHOULD'VE BEEN REPLACED YEARS AGO. BUT WHAT CAN YOU DO – WELL, MIKE MENDER – SAYS IT ALL REALLY, HUR HUR HUR...

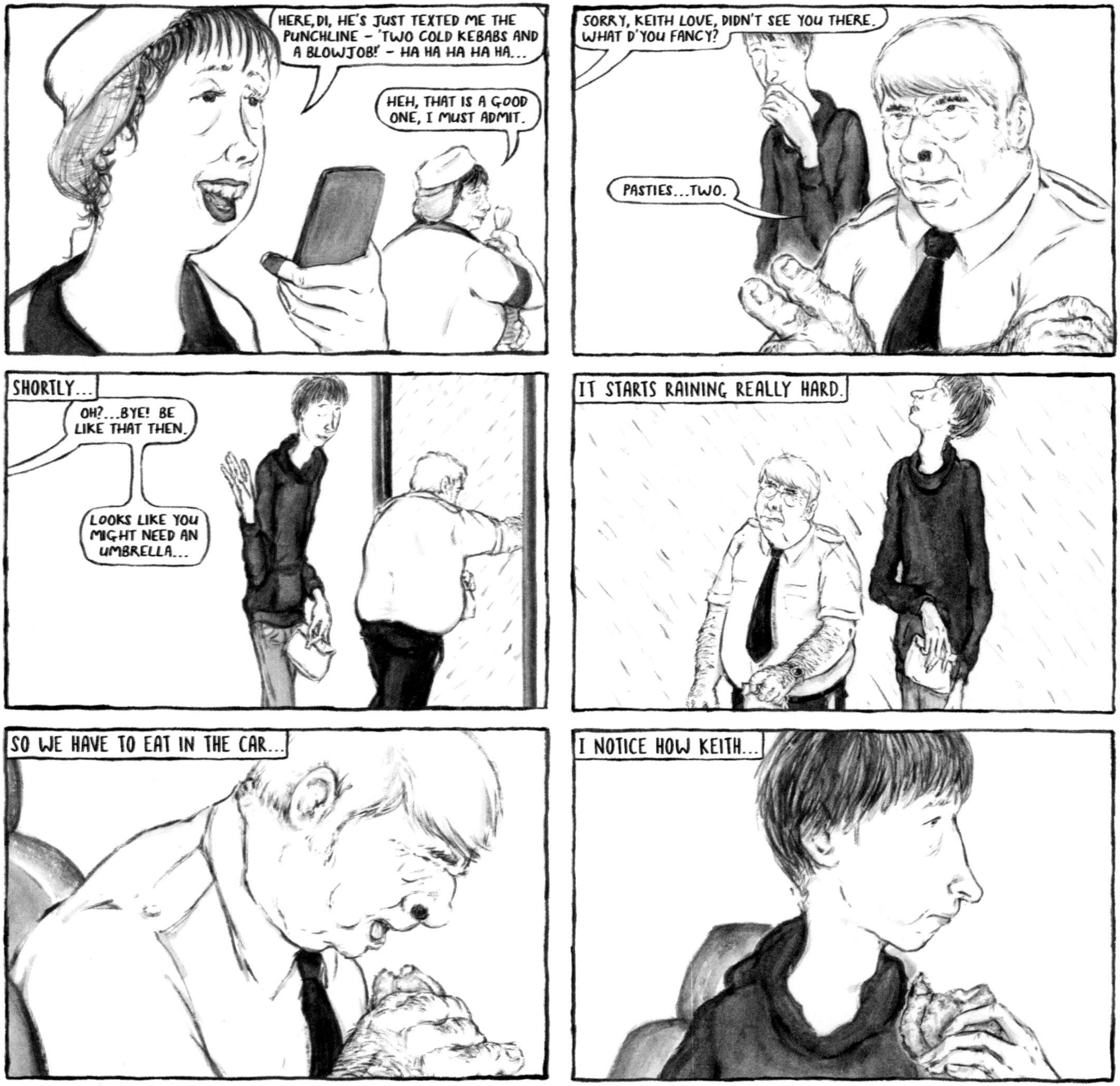
HERE, DI, HE'S JUST TEXTED ME THE PUNCHLINE – 'TWO COLD KEBABS AND A BLOWJOB!' – HA HA HA HA HA...
HEH, THAT IS A GOOD ONE, I MUST ADMIT.
SORRY, KEITH LOVE, DIDN'T SEE YOU THERE. WHAT D'YOU FANCY?
PASTIES...TWO.
SHORTLY...
OH?...BYE! BE LIKE THAT THEN.
LOOKS LIKE YOU MIGHT NEED AN UMBRELLA...
IT STARTS RAINING REALLY HARD.
SO WE HAVE TO EAT IN THE CAR...
I NOTICE HOW KEITH...

...DEFTLY MANOEUVRES HIS PAPER BAG TO CATCH EVERY CRUMB...

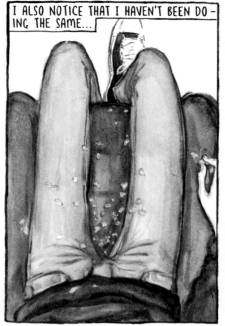

I ALSO NOTICE THAT I HAVEN'T BEEN DO-ING THE SAME...

AS DOES KEITH...

MIND OUT.

GHHZZZZZZZZZ

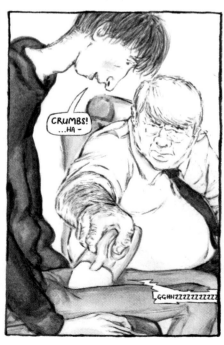

CRUMBS!
...HA -

GGHHZZZZZZZZZZZZ

GHZZ

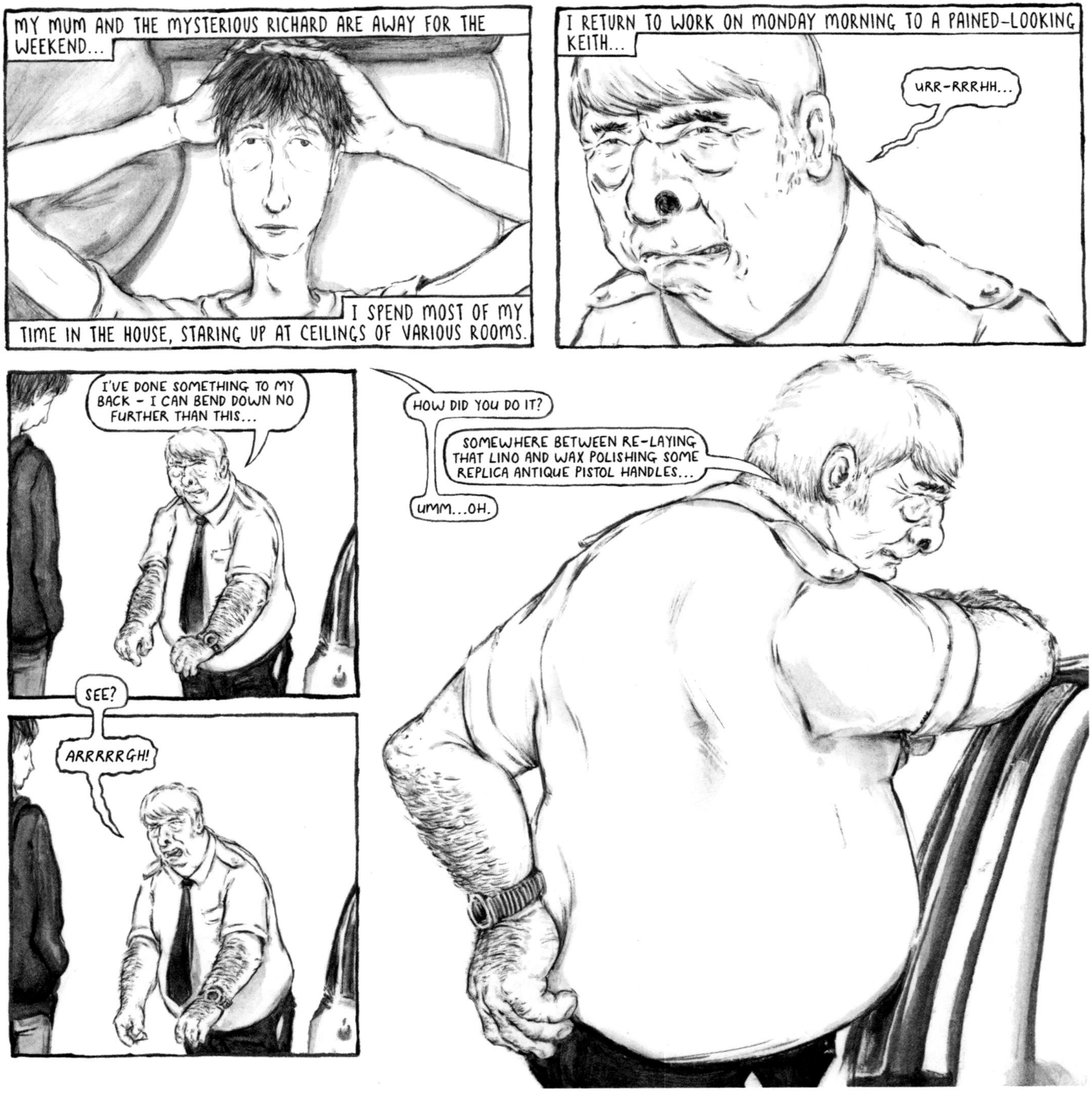

MY MUM AND THE MYSTERIOUS RICHARD ARE AWAY FOR THE WEEKEND...
I SPEND MOST OF MY TIME IN THE HOUSE, STARING UP AT CEILINGS OF VARIOUS ROOMS.
I RETURN TO WORK ON MONDAY MORNING TO A PAINED-LOOKING KEITH...
URR-RRRHH...
I'VE DONE SOMETHING TO MY BACK - I CAN BEND DOWN NO FURTHER THAN THIS...
SEE?
ARRRRRGH!
HOW DID YOU DO IT?
SOMEWHERE BETWEEN RE-LAYING THAT LINO AND WAX POLISHING SOME REPLICA ANTIQUE PISTOL HANDLES...
UMM...OH.

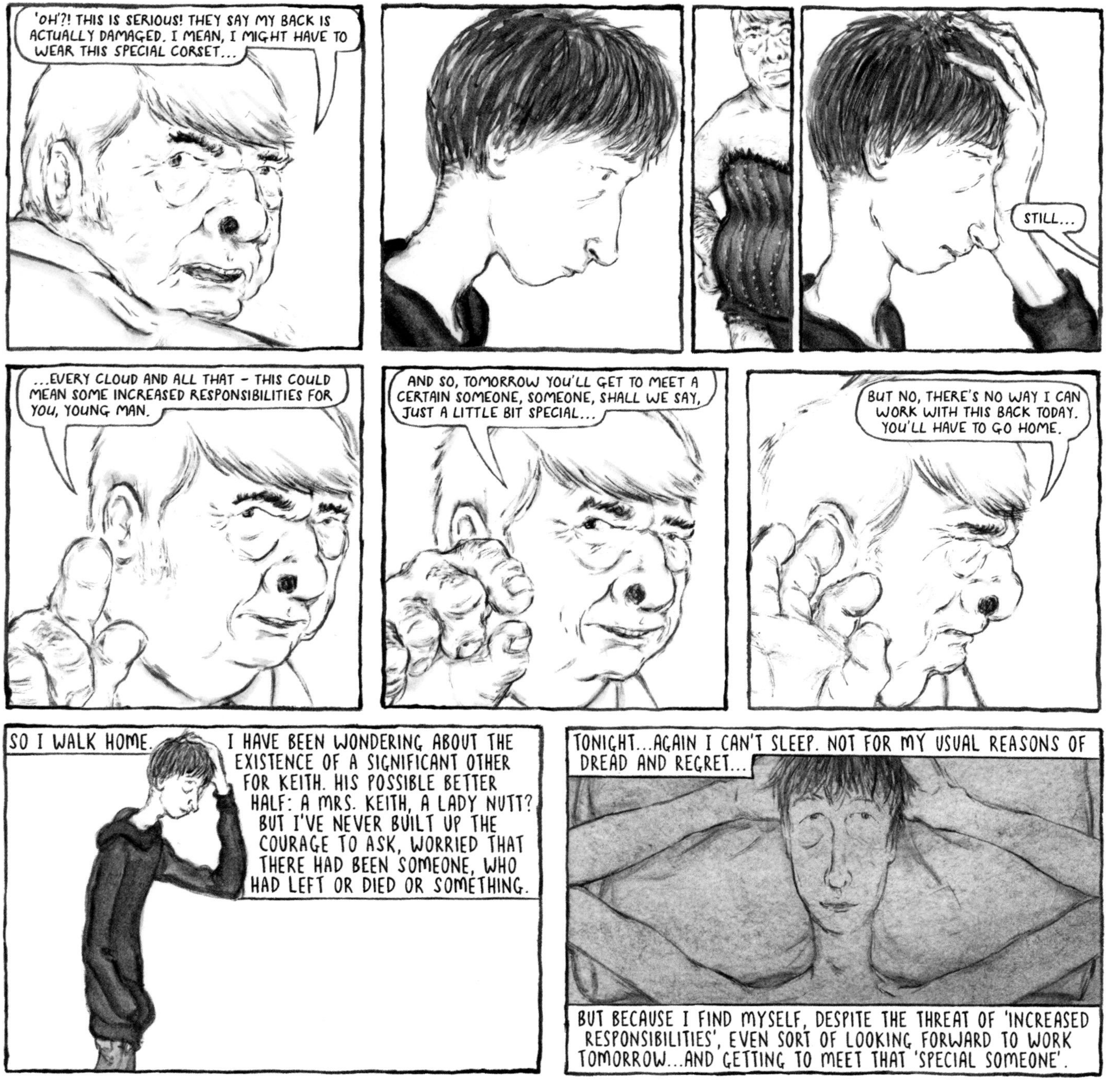
'OH'?! THIS IS SERIOUS! THEY SAY MY BACK IS ACTUALLY DAMAGED. I MEAN, I MIGHT HAVE TO WEAR THIS SPECIAL CORSET...
STILL...
...EVERY CLOUD AND ALL THAT - THIS COULD MEAN SOME INCREASED RESPONSIBILITIES FOR YOU, YOUNG MAN.
AND SO, TOMORROW YOU'LL GET TO MEET A CERTAIN SOMEONE, SOMEONE, SHALL WE SAY, JUST A LITTLE BIT SPECIAL...
BUT NO, THERE'S NO WAY I CAN WORK WITH THIS BACK TODAY. YOU'LL HAVE TO GO HOME.
SO I WALK HOME.
I HAVE BEEN WONDERING ABOUT THE EXISTENCE OF A SIGNIFICANT OTHER FOR KEITH. HIS POSSIBLE BETTER HALF: A MRS. KEITH, A LADY NUTT? BUT I'VE NEVER BUILT UP THE COURAGE TO ASK, WORRIED THAT THERE HAD BEEN SOMEONE, WHO HAD LEFT OR DIED OR SOMETHING.
TONIGHT...AGAIN I CAN'T SLEEP. NOT FOR MY USUAL REASONS OF DREAD AND REGRET...
BUT BECAUSE I FIND MYSELF, DESPITE THE THREAT OF 'INCREASED RESPONSIBILITIES', EVEN SORT OF LOOKING FORWARD TO WORK TOMORROW...AND GETTING TO MEET THAT 'SPECIAL SOMEONE'.

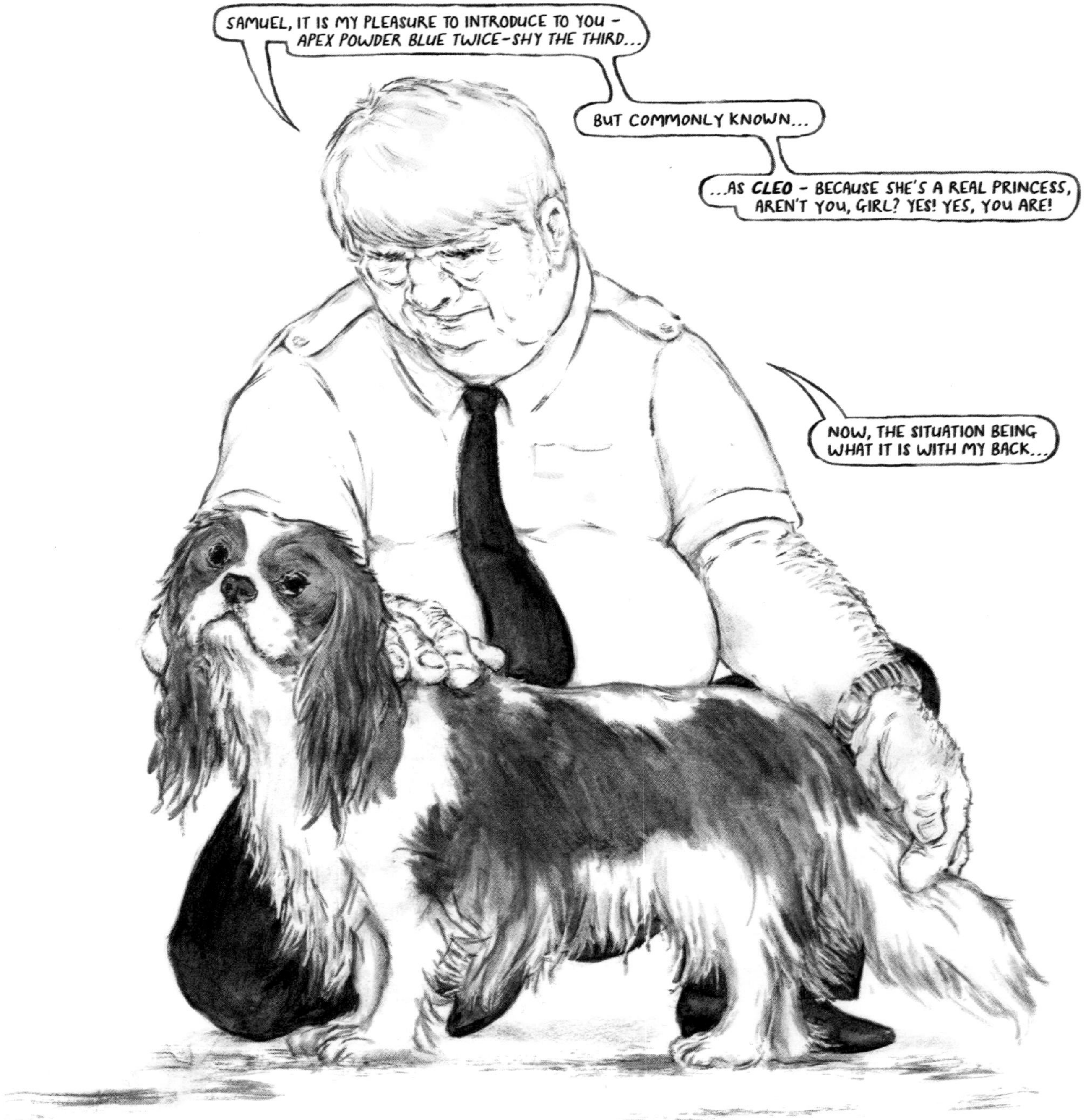
SAMUEL, IT IS MY PLEASURE TO INTRODUCE TO YOU - APEX POWDER BLUE TWICE-SHY THE THIRD...
BUT COMMONLY KNOWN...
...AS **CLEO** - BECAUSE SHE'S A REAL PRINCESS, AREN'T YOU, GIRL? YES! YES, YOU ARE!
NOW, THE SITUATION BEING WHAT IT IS WITH MY BACK...

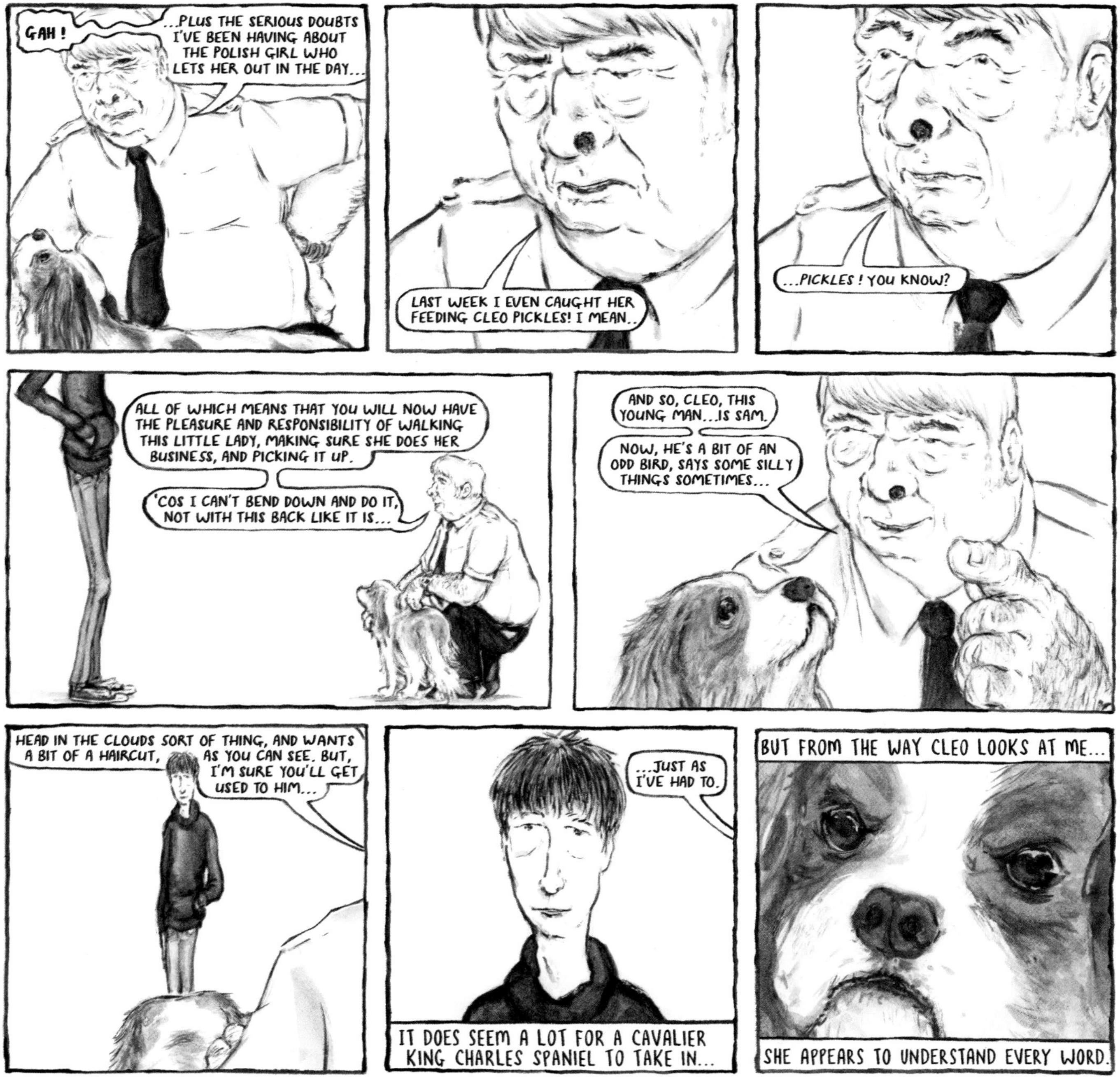
GAH!
...PLUS THE SERIOUS DOUBTS I'VE BEEN HAVING ABOUT THE POLISH GIRL WHO LETS HER OUT IN THE DAY...
LAST WEEK I EVEN CAUGHT HER FEEDING CLEO PICKLES! I MEAN..
...PICKLES! YOU KNOW?
ALL OF WHICH MEANS THAT YOU WILL NOW HAVE THE PLEASURE AND RESPONSIBILITY OF WALKING THIS LITTLE LADY, MAKING SURE SHE DOES HER BUSINESS, AND PICKING IT UP.
'COS I CAN'T BEND DOWN AND DO IT, NOT WITH THIS BACK LIKE IT IS...
AND SO, CLEO, THIS YOUNG MAN...IS SAM.
NOW, HE'S A BIT OF AN ODD BIRD, SAYS SOME SILLY THINGS SOMETIMES...
HEAD IN THE CLOUDS SORT OF THING, AND WANTS A BIT OF A HAIRCUT, AS YOU CAN SEE. BUT, I'M SURE YOU'LL GET USED TO HIM...
...JUST AS I'VE HAD TO.
IT DOES SEEM A LOT FOR A CAVALIER KING CHARLES SPANIEL TO TAKE IN...
BUT FROM THE WAY CLEO LOOKS AT ME...
SHE APPEARS TO UNDERSTAND EVERY WORD.

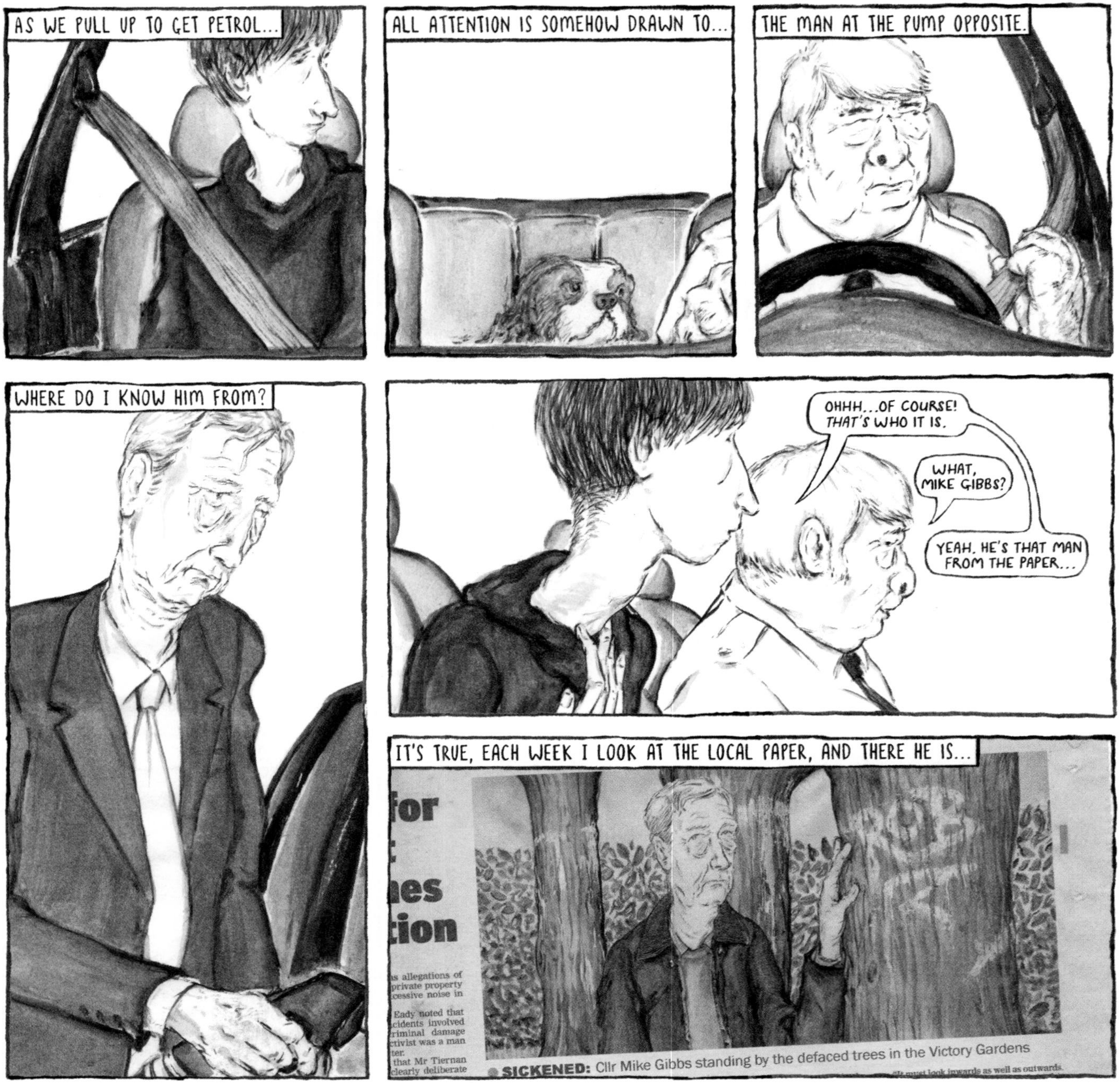
AS WE PULL UP TO GET PETROL...
ALL ATTENTION IS SOMEHOW DRAWN TO...
THE MAN AT THE PUMP OPPOSITE.
WHERE DO I KNOW HIM FROM?
OHHH...OF COURSE! THAT'S WHO IT IS.
WHAT, MIKE GIBBS?
YEAH, HE'S THAT MAN FROM THE PAPER...
IT'S TRUE, EACH WEEK I LOOK AT THE LOCAL PAPER, AND THERE HE IS...
for
es
tion
s allegations of
private property
xcessive noise in
Eady noted that
cidents involved
riminal damage
ctivist was a man
ter.
that Mr Tiernan
clearly deliberate
SICKENED: Cllr Mike Gibbs standing by the defaced trees in the Victory Gardens

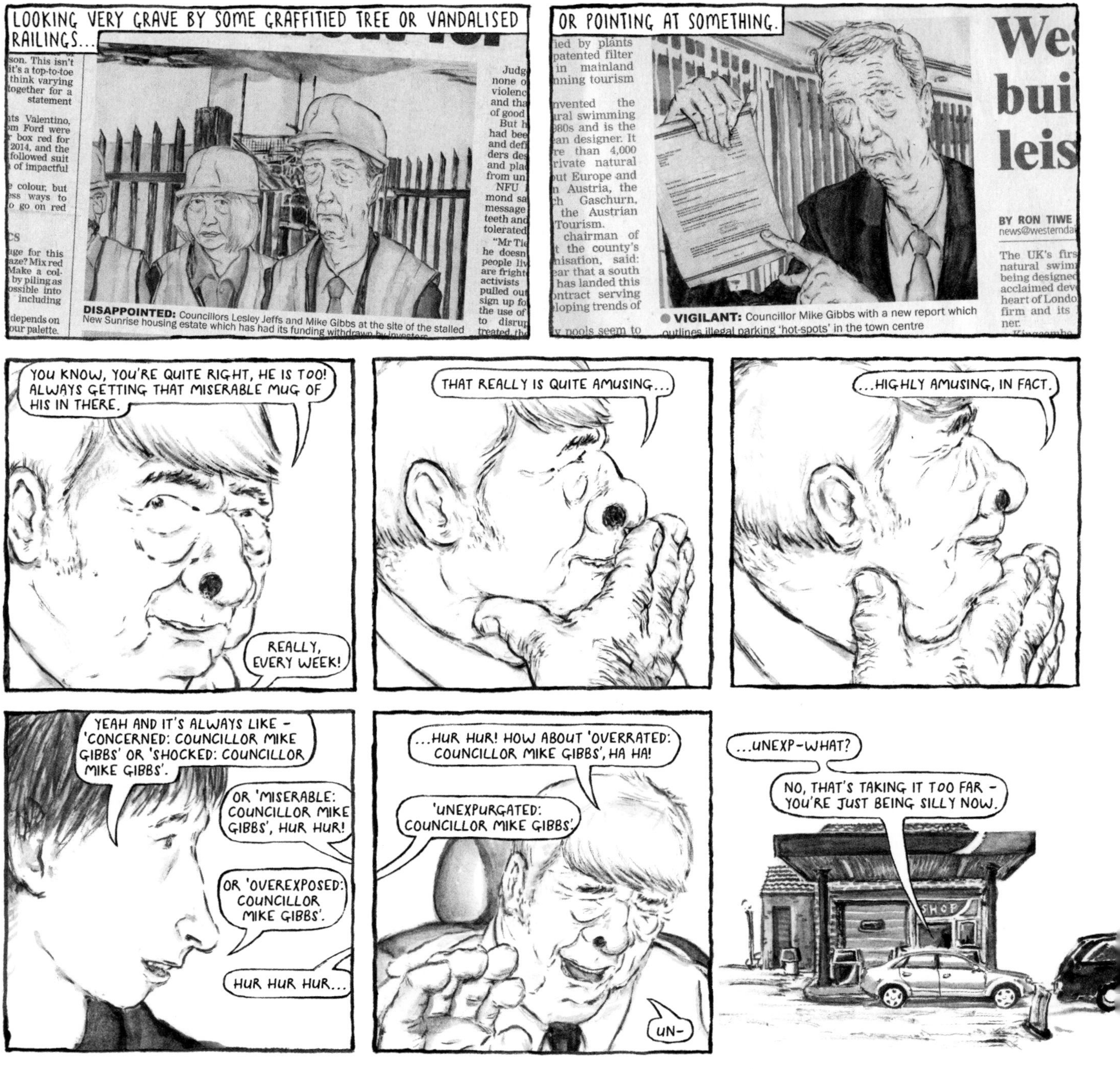
LOOKING VERY GRAVE BY SOME GRAFFITIED TREE OR VANDALISED RAILINGS...
DISAPPOINTED: Councillors Lesley Jeffs and Mike Gibbs at the site of the stalled New Sunrise housing estate which has had its funding withdrawn by investors
OR POINTING AT SOMETHING.
VIGILANT: Councillor Mike Gibbs with a new report which outlines illegal parking 'hot-spots' in the town centre
YOU KNOW, YOU'RE QUITE RIGHT, HE IS TOO! ALWAYS GETTING THAT MISERABLE MUG OF HIS IN THERE.
REALLY, EVERY WEEK!
THAT REALLY IS QUITE AMUSING...
...HIGHLY AMUSING, IN FACT.
YEAH AND IT'S ALWAYS LIKE - 'CONCERNED: COUNCILLOR MIKE GIBBS' OR 'SHOCKED: COUNCILLOR MIKE GIBBS'.
OR 'MISERABLE: COUNCILLOR MIKE GIBBS', HUR HUR!
OR 'OVEREXPOSED: COUNCILLOR MIKE GIBBS'.
HUR HUR HUR...
...HUR HUR! HOW ABOUT 'OVERRATED: COUNCILLOR MIKE GIBBS', HA HA!
'UNEXPURGATED: COUNCILLOR MIKE GIBBS'.
UN-
...UNEXP-WHAT?
NO, THAT'S TAKING IT TOO FAR - YOU'RE JUST BEING SILLY NOW.
SHOP

WALKING TO WORK— — TO MEET KEITH, HIS CAR, AND CLEO.

IN THE USUAL PLACE, UNITS 23-28 OF THE NEW APEX TRADING ESTATE. THINKING ABOUT THIS JOB...

...THERE'S A LOT I LIKE ABOUT IT.

FOR A START, IT'S THE ONLY TIME I'VE EVER MANAGED TO GET NEAR THAT PLACE SELF-HELP BOOKS AND THERAPISTS DESCRIBE...

...A STATE OF NO 'REGRETFUL REFLECTION' NOR 'FEARFUL PROJECTION'.

JUST A FEELING OF BEING TRULY 'IN THE MOMENT'.

AWARE ONLY OF MY MOST IMMEDIATE SURROUNDINGS...

SOMETHING RATTLING DOWN HERE.

(EVENINGS, WEEKENDS, AND MOST OF ALL NIGHTS, ARE ANOTHER MATTER ENTIRELY...)

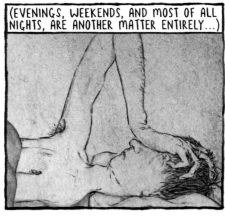

SO, I HAVE MY FORMS TO COPY OUT...

AND SOMETIMES I HAVE TO CARRY BOXES INTO THE CAR...

TWO AT A TIME — I TOLD YOU!

SORRY.

USUALLY THEY ARE EMPTY, SO IT'S PRETTY EASY, REALLY.

BUT MUCH OF MY TIME IS SPENT WAITING, OR LISTENING...

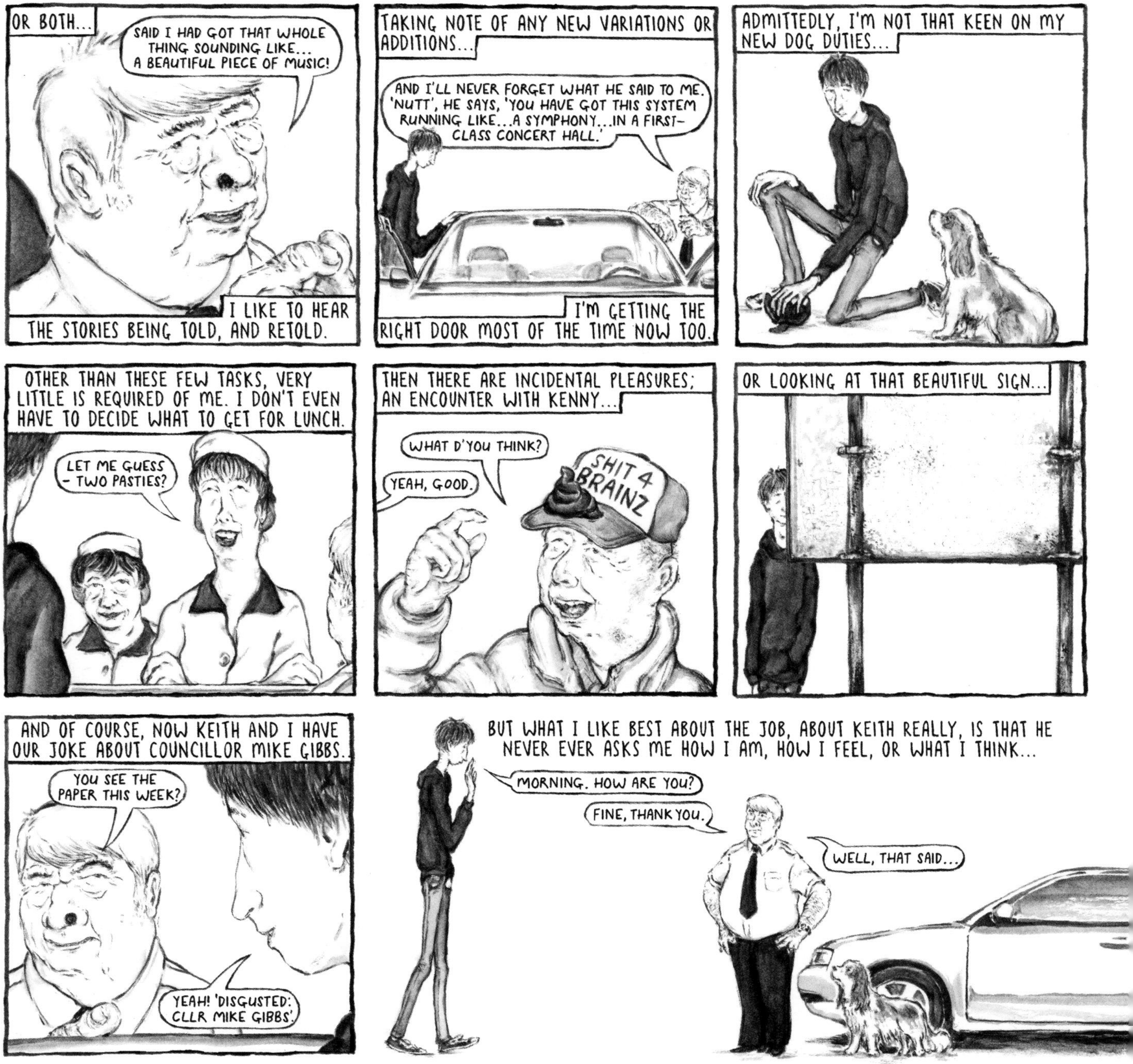
OR BOTH...
SAID I HAD GOT THAT WHOLE THING SOUNDING LIKE... A BEAUTIFUL PIECE OF MUSIC!
I LIKE TO HEAR THE STORIES BEING TOLD, AND RETOLD.
TAKING NOTE OF ANY NEW VARIATIONS OR ADDITIONS...
AND I'LL NEVER FORGET WHAT HE SAID TO ME. 'NUTT', HE SAYS, 'YOU HAVE GOT THIS SYSTEM RUNNING LIKE...A SYMPHONY...IN A FIRST-CLASS CONCERT HALL.'
I'M GETTING THE RIGHT DOOR MOST OF THE TIME NOW TOO.
ADMITTEDLY, I'M NOT THAT KEEN ON MY NEW DOG DUTIES...
OTHER THAN THESE FEW TASKS, VERY LITTLE IS REQUIRED OF ME. I DON'T EVEN HAVE TO DECIDE WHAT TO GET FOR LUNCH.
LET ME GUESS - TWO PASTIES?
THEN THERE ARE INCIDENTAL PLEASURES; AN ENCOUNTER WITH KENNY...
WHAT D'YOU THINK?
YEAH, GOOD.
SHIT 4 BRAINZ
OR LOOKING AT THAT BEAUTIFUL SIGN...
AND OF COURSE, NOW KEITH AND I HAVE OUR JOKE ABOUT COUNCILLOR MIKE GIBBS...
YOU SEE THE PAPER THIS WEEK?
YEAH! 'DISGUSTED: CLLR MIKE GIBBS'.
BUT WHAT I LIKE BEST ABOUT THE JOB, ABOUT KEITH REALLY, IS THAT HE NEVER EVER ASKS ME HOW I AM, HOW I FEEL, OR WHAT I THINK...
MORNING. HOW ARE YOU?
FINE, THANK YOU.
WELL, THAT SAID...

IT ALWAYS HAPPENS; WHENEVER I ALLOW MYSELF TO FEEL LIKE THINGS ARE GOING QUITE WELL...

CONGRATULATIONS, YOUNG MAN...

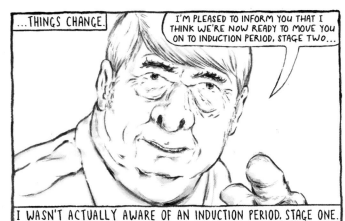

...THINGS CHANGE.

I'M PLEASED TO INFORM YOU THAT I THINK WE'RE NOW READY TO MOVE YOU ON TO INDUCTION PERIOD, STAGE TWO...

I WASN'T ACTUALLY AWARE OF AN INDUCTION PERIOD, STAGE ONE.

THIS WILL MEAN YOU'LL START COMING INTO SOME OF THE UNITS WITH ME NOW...

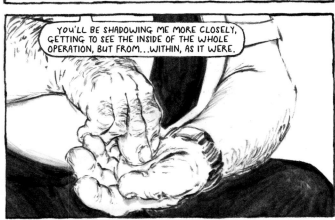

YOU'LL BE SHADOWING ME MORE CLOSELY, GETTING TO SEE THE INSIDE OF THE WHOLE OPERATION, BUT FROM...WITHIN, AS IT WERE.

I HAVE BEEN GETTING SO USED TO A COSY SORT OF CAR-BOUND AGORAPHOBIA, WITH JUST KEITH AND CLEO...

... GETTING TO MEET SOME OF OUR CONTACTS ON THE SHOP FLOOR.

...THAT THE THOUGHT OF MEETING ANY OTHER HUMANS, IN NEW PLACES...

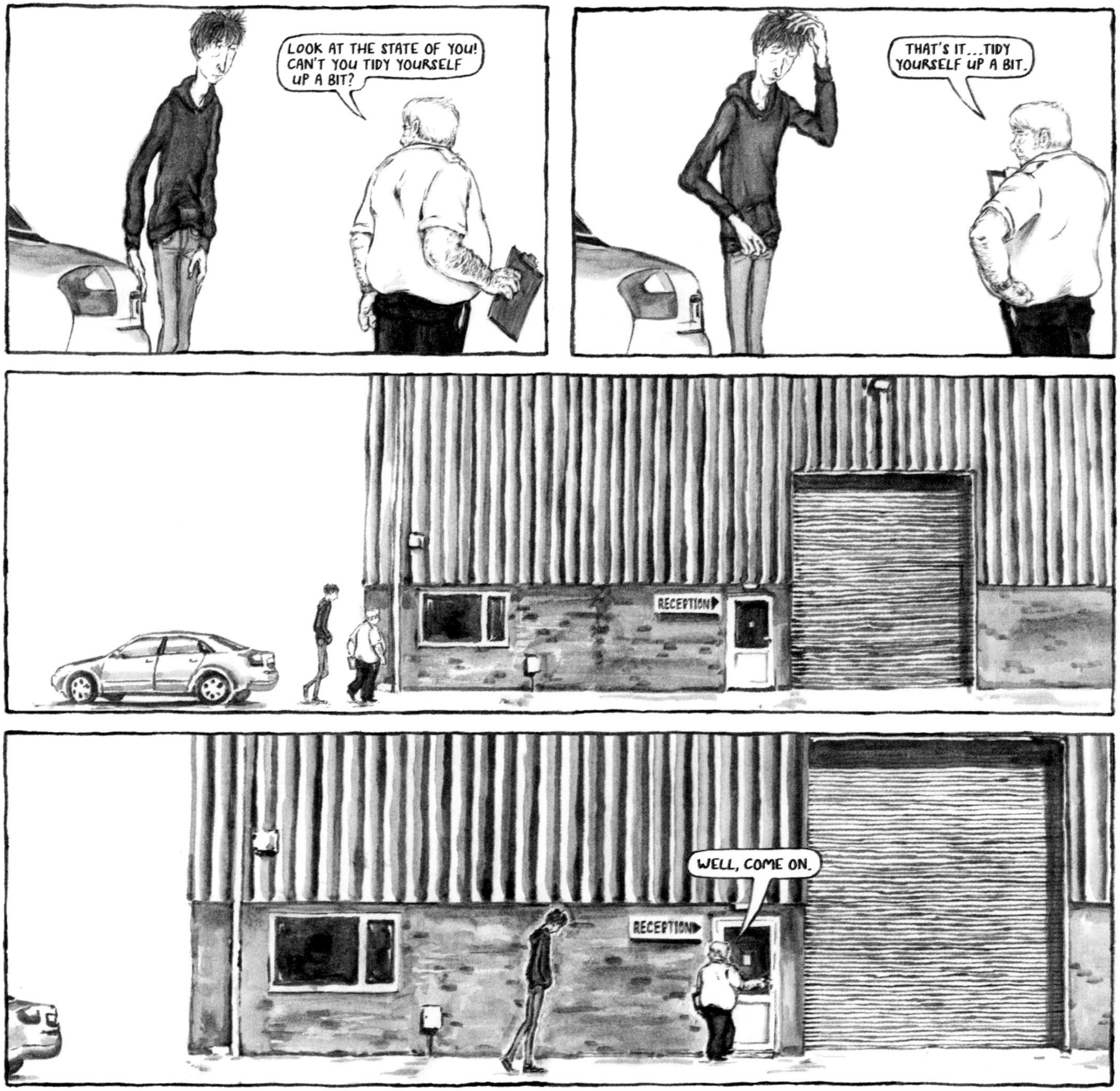
LOOK AT THE STATE OF YOU! CAN'T YOU TIDY YOURSELF UP A BIT?
THAT'S IT...TIDY YOURSELF UP A BIT.
RECEPTION
RECEPTION
WELL, COME ON.

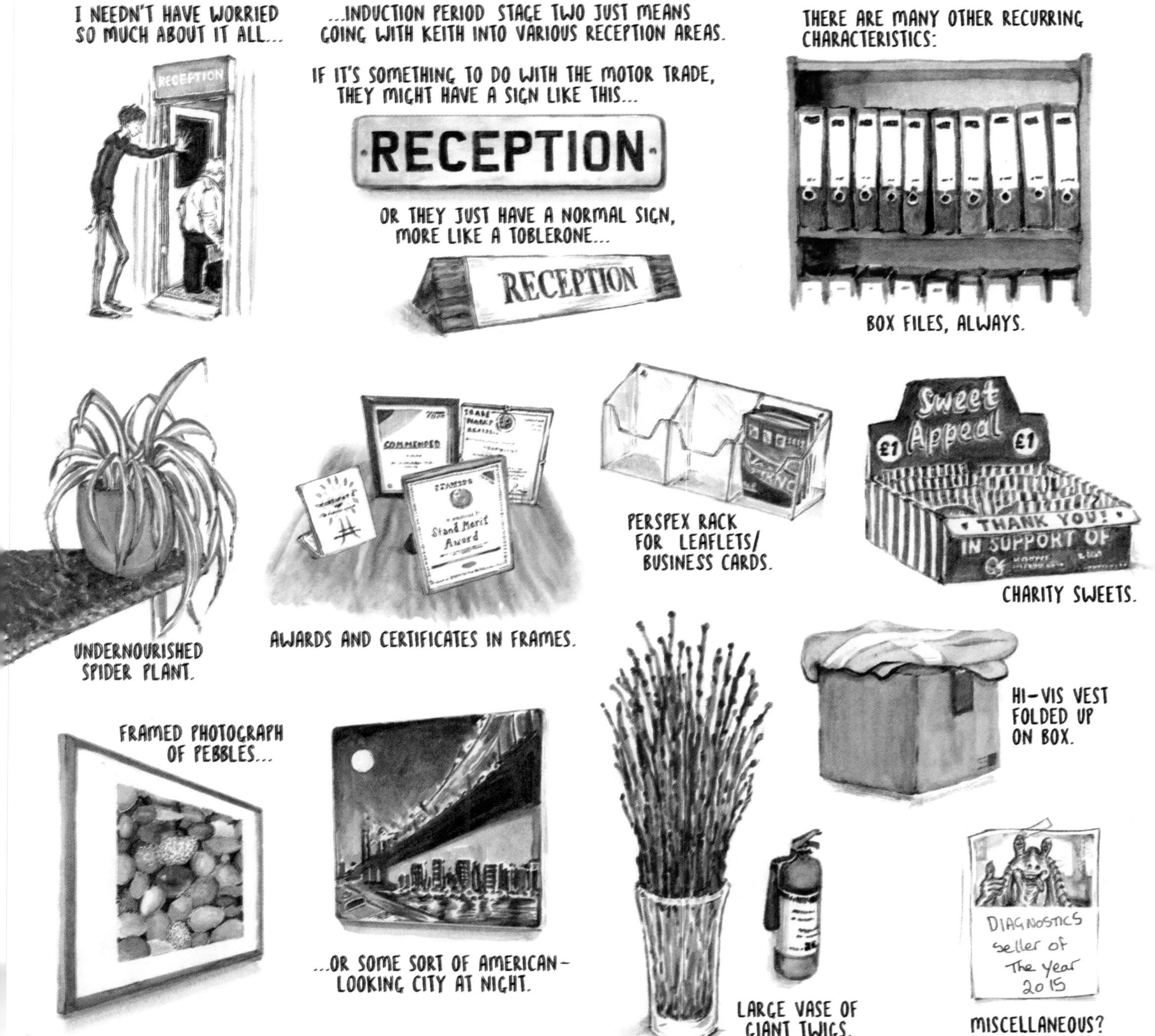
I NEEDN'T HAVE WORRIED SO MUCH ABOUT IT ALL...
RECEPTION
...INDUCTION PERIOD STAGE TWO JUST MEANS GOING WITH KEITH INTO VARIOUS RECEPTION AREAS.
IF IT'S SOMETHING TO DO WITH THE MOTOR TRADE, THEY MIGHT HAVE A SIGN LIKE THIS...
RECEPTION
OR THEY JUST HAVE A NORMAL SIGN, MORE LIKE A TOBLERONE...
RECEPTION
THERE ARE MANY OTHER RECURRING CHARACTERISTICS:
BOX FILES, ALWAYS.
UNDERNOURISHED SPIDER PLANT.
COMMENDED
Stand Merit Award
AWARDS AND CERTIFICATES IN FRAMES.
PERSPEX RACK FOR LEAFLETS/ BUSINESS CARDS.
Sweet Appeal
£1
£1
THANK YOU!
IN SUPPORT OF
CHARITY SWEETS.
FRAMED PHOTOGRAPH OF PEBBLES...
...OR SOME SORT OF AMERICAN-LOOKING CITY AT NIGHT.
LARGE VASE OF GIANT TWIGS.
HI-VIS VEST FOLDED UP ON BOX.
DIAGNOSTICS seller of The year 2015
MISCELLANEOUS?

AND A FEW HAVE A SORT OF GALLERY OF PREVIOUS CHAIRMEN OR MANAGERS...

MORNING, KEITH. CUP OF TEA?

OH...GO ON THEN, YOU'VE TWISTED MY ARM!

(WE ALWAYS AGREE TO TEA.)

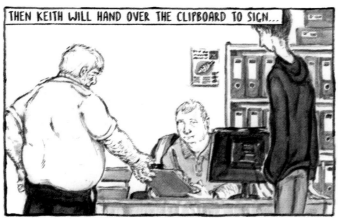

THEN KEITH WILL HAND OVER THE CLIPBOARD TO SIGN...

SOMETIMES WITH A LITTLE FLOURISH...

MADAME...

RECEPTION & TRADE COUNTER

...AND SOMETIMES HE DOESN'T GET IT SIGNED AT ALL.

QUITE OFTEN, IT'S ONE OF KEITH'S FRIENDS RUNNING THE BUSINESS.

SO I WAIT...

...IN RECEPTION.

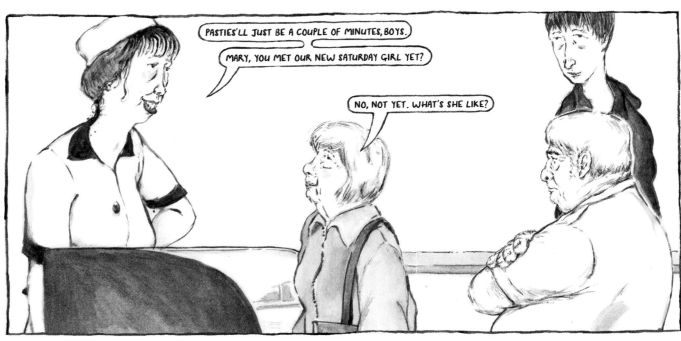

PASTIES'LL JUST BE A COUPLE OF MINUTES, BOYS.
MARY, YOU MET OUR NEW SATURDAY GIRL YET?
NO, NOT YET. WHAT'S SHE LIKE?
FOR ALL KEITH'S TALK OF 'THIN ICE' AND 'STERN WORDS TO BE HAD' WITH HER EMPLOYER...
SHE'S VERY QUIET, BUT - BETWEEN YOU AND ME -
RECKON SHE MIGHT BE A BIT OF A DARK HORSE.
THIS WOMAN CONTINUES TO WORK HERE...
YEAH...YOU CAN JUST IMAGINE FINDING HER OUT THE BACK, TAKING TOPLESS SELFIES WITH A COUPLE OF CHERRY DANISHES...
...APPARENTLY UNCENSORED.
STRATEGICALLY PLACED, IF YOU KNOW WHAT I MEAN! ...AHAHAHAHAHAHAHAHA...

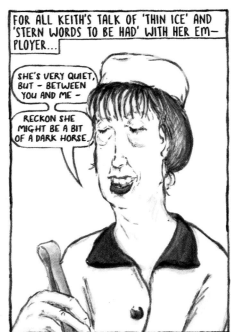

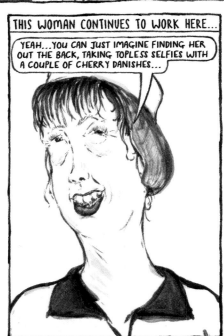

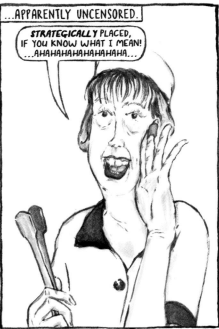

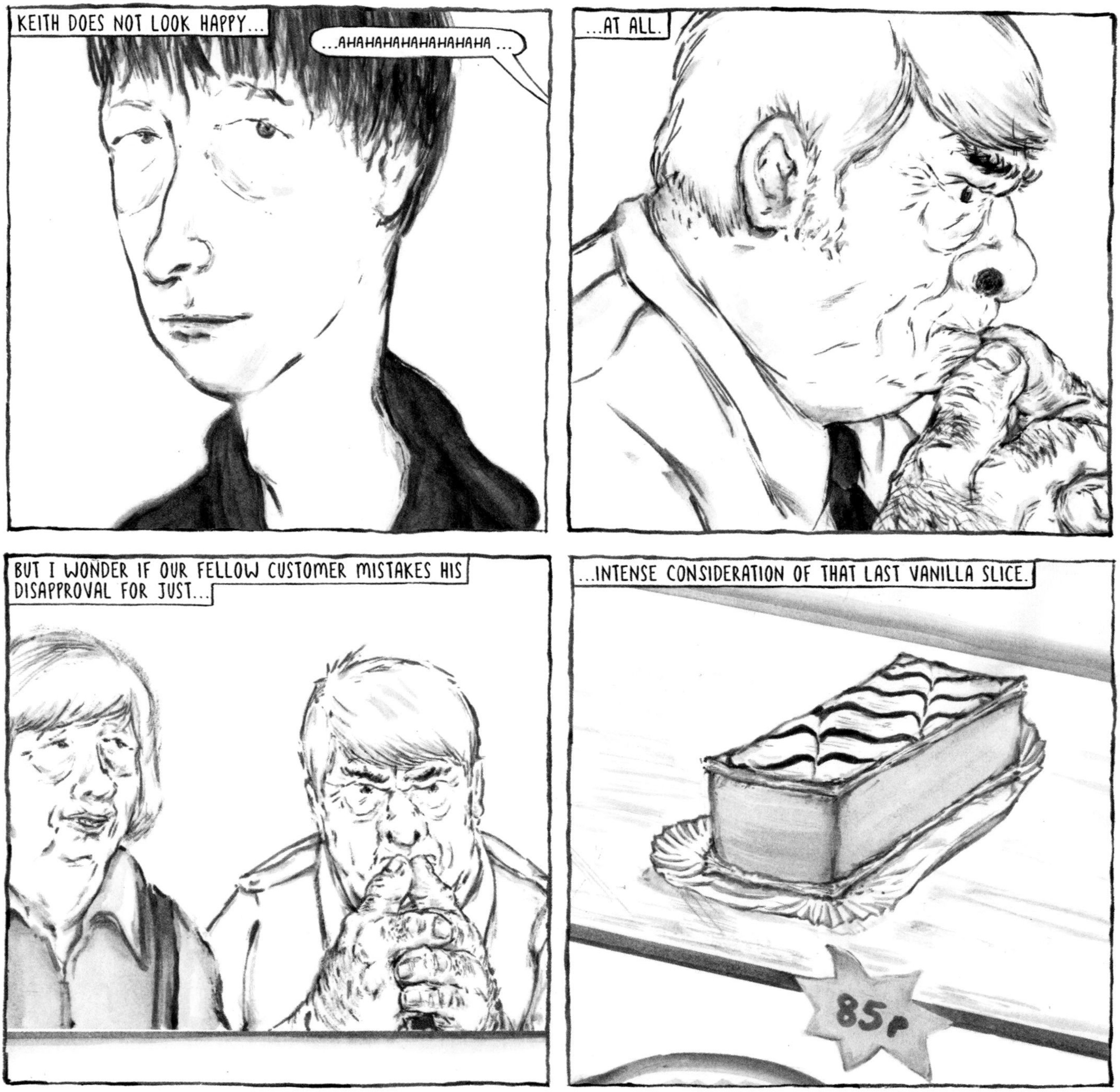
KEITH DOES NOT LOOK HAPPY...
...AHAHAHAHAHAHAHAHA...
...AT ALL.
BUT I WONDER IF OUR FELLOW CUSTOMER MISTAKES HIS DISAPPROVAL FOR JUST...
...INTENSE CONSIDERATION OF THAT LAST VANILLA SLICE.
85p

THERE ARE STILL SOME UNITS I DON'T GO INTO WITH KEITH. OFTEN THE MORE MYSTERIOUS-LOOKING ONES...

SO, MORE CAR TIME. I MUST ADMIT, I AM BEGINNING TO GET A BIT BORED BY NOW.

THAT AND A GROWING CURIOSITY ABOUT KEITH'S LIFE LEAD ME...

...TOWARDS THE GLOVE COMPARTMENT. SEEING WHAT'S BEYOND THE HANDI-VAC...

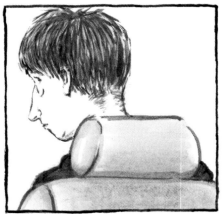

I'M NOT THAT SUPRISED BY THE BOOK...

OUTTHINK YOUR ENEMY
TACTICAL THINKING
THE TELLS OF THE CV
FR AND MIS
BURTON L FLAX

BUT THE CD...

LINE DANCE FEVER...
with
LACHLAN SHIRLEY
COUNTRY
IRISH
SING-A-LONG

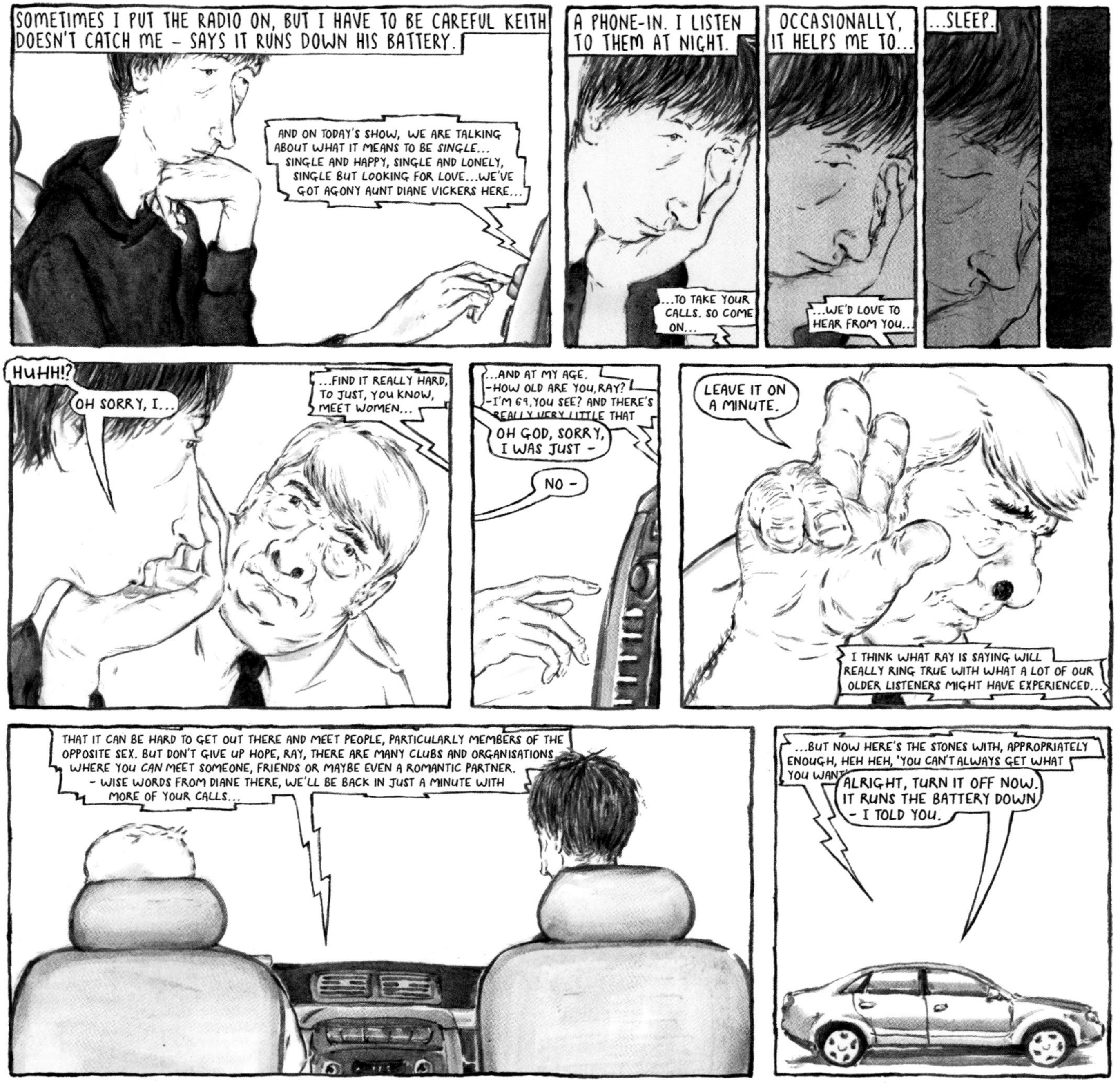
SOMETIMES I PUT THE RADIO ON, BUT I HAVE TO BE CAREFUL KEITH DOESN'T CATCH ME – SAYS IT RUNS DOWN HIS BATTERY.
AND ON TODAY'S SHOW, WE ARE TALKING ABOUT WHAT IT MEANS TO BE *SINGLE*... SINGLE AND HAPPY, SINGLE AND LONELY, SINGLE BUT LOOKING FOR LOVE... WE'VE GOT AGONY AUNT DIANE VICKERS HERE...
A PHONE-IN. I LISTEN TO THEM AT NIGHT.
...TO TAKE YOUR CALLS. SO COME ON...
OCCASIONALLY, IT HELPS ME TO...
...WE'D LOVE TO HEAR FROM YOU...
...SLEEP.
HUHH!?
OH SORRY, I...
...FIND IT REALLY HARD, TO JUST, YOU KNOW, MEET WOMEN...
...AND AT MY AGE. –HOW OLD ARE YOU, RAY? –I'M 69, YOU SEE? AND THERE'S
OH GOD, SORRY, I WAS JUST –
NO –
LEAVE IT ON A MINUTE.
I THINK WHAT RAY IS SAYING WILL REALLY RING TRUE WITH WHAT A LOT OF OUR OLDER LISTENERS MIGHT HAVE EXPERIENCED...
THAT IT CAN BE HARD TO GET OUT THERE AND MEET PEOPLE, PARTICULARLY MEMBERS OF THE OPPOSITE SEX. BUT DON'T GIVE UP HOPE, RAY, THERE ARE MANY CLUBS AND ORGANISATIONS WHERE YOU CAN MEET SOMEONE, FRIENDS OR MAYBE EVEN A ROMANTIC PARTNER. – WISE WORDS FROM DIANE THERE, WE'LL BE BACK IN JUST A MINUTE WITH MORE OF YOUR CALLS...
...BUT NOW HERE'S THE STONES WITH, APPROPRIATELY ENOUGH, HEH HEH, 'YOU CAN'T ALWAYS GET WHAT
ALRIGHT, TURN IT OFF NOW. IT RUNS THE BATTERY DOWN – I TOLD YOU.

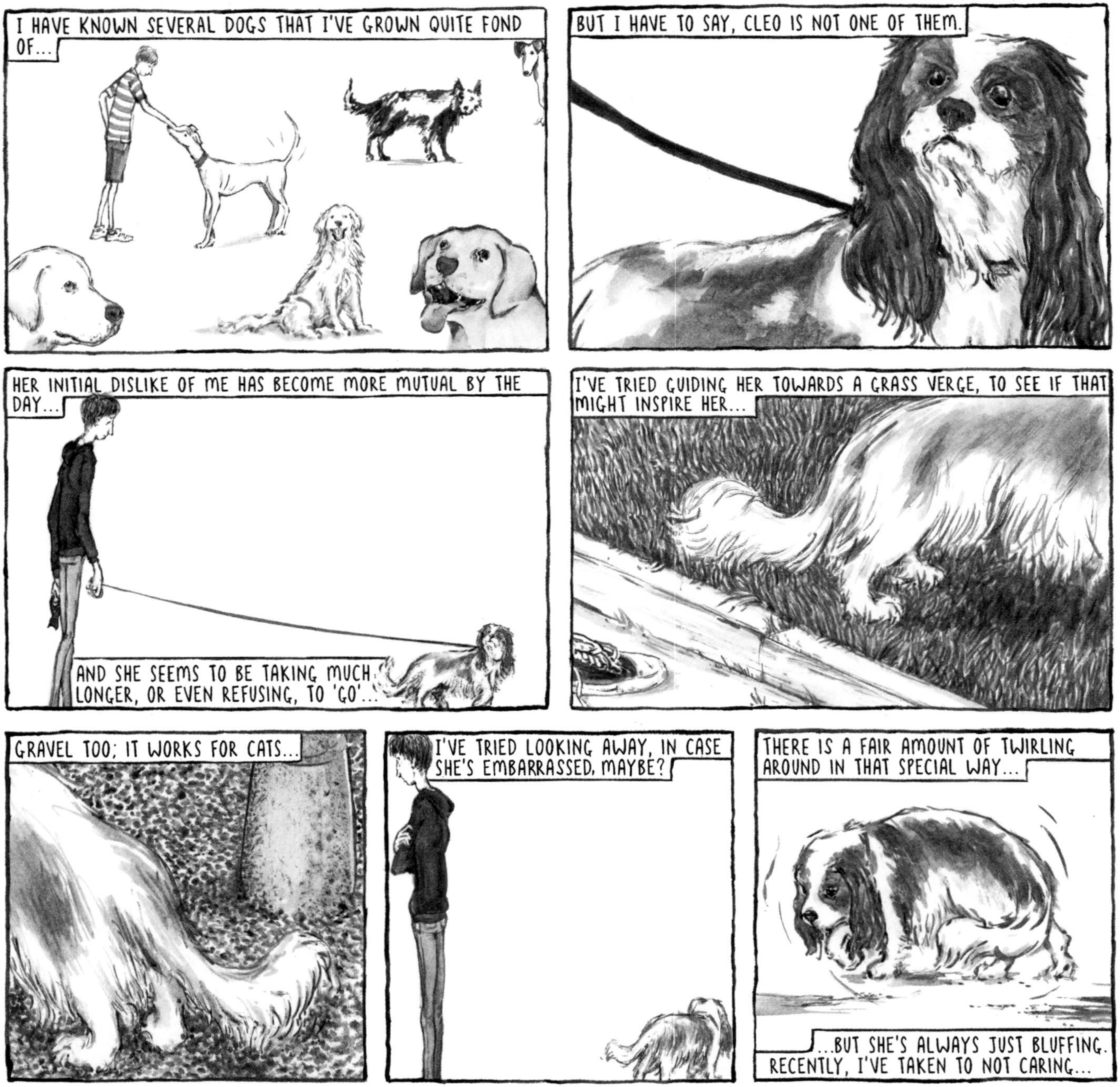
I HAVE KNOWN SEVERAL DOGS THAT I'VE GROWN QUITE FOND OF...
BUT I HAVE TO SAY, CLEO IS NOT ONE OF THEM.
HER INITIAL DISLIKE OF ME HAS BECOME MORE MUTUAL BY THE DAY...
AND SHE SEEMS TO BE TAKING MUCH LONGER, OR EVEN REFUSING, TO 'GO'...
I'VE TRIED GUIDING HER TOWARDS A GRASS VERGE, TO SEE IF THAT MIGHT INSPIRE HER...
GRAVEL TOO; IT WORKS FOR CATS...
I'VE TRIED LOOKING AWAY, IN CASE SHE'S EMBARRASSED, MAYBE?
THERE IS A FAIR AMOUNT OF TWIRLING AROUND IN THAT SPECIAL WAY...
...BUT SHE'S ALWAYS JUST BLUFFING. RECENTLY, I'VE TAKEN TO NOT CARING...

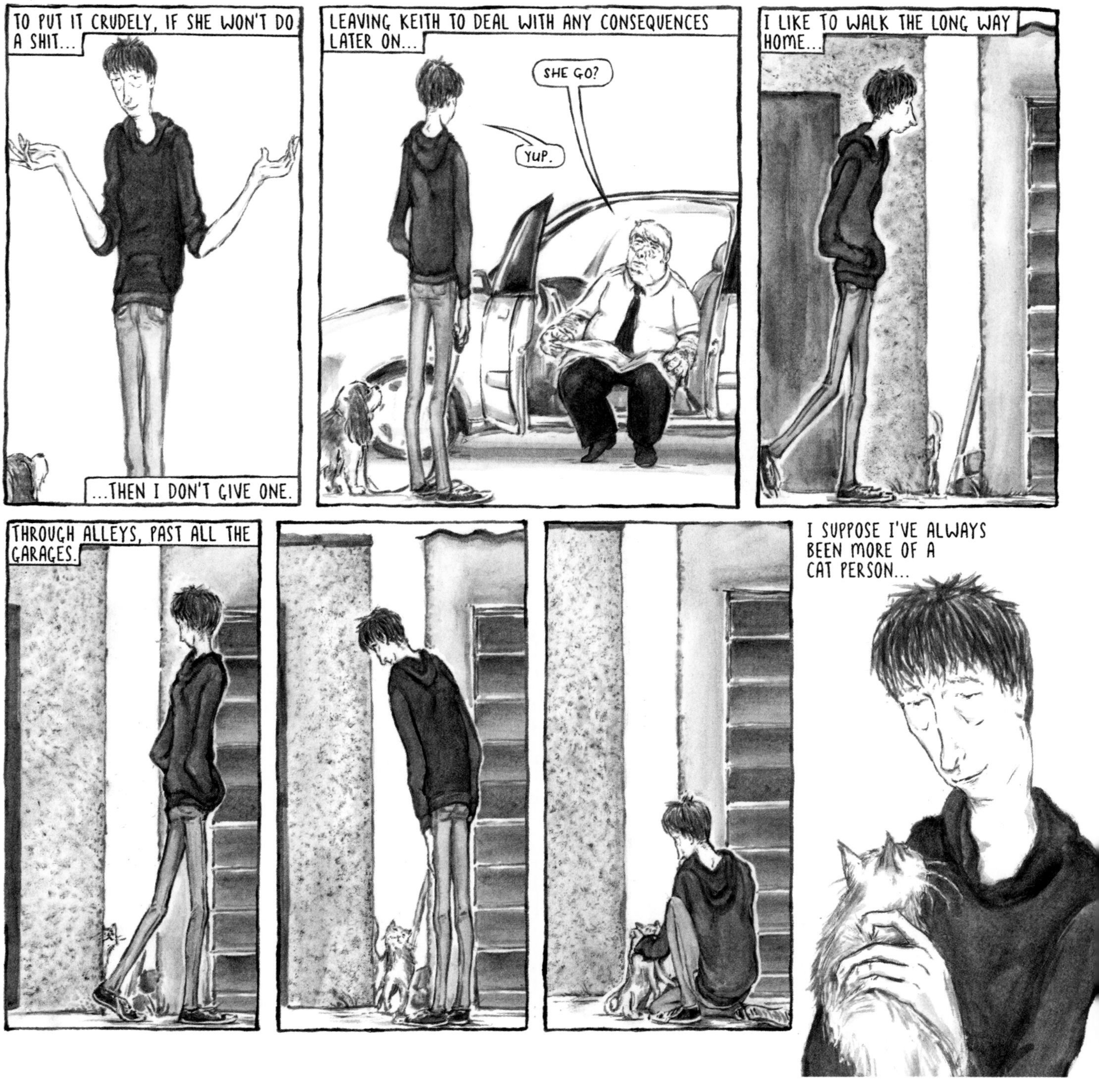
TO PUT IT CRUDELY, IF SHE WON'T DO A SHIT...
...THEN I DON'T GIVE ONE.
LEAVING KEITH TO DEAL WITH ANY CONSEQUENCES LATER ON...
SHE GO?
YUP.
I LIKE TO WALK THE LONG WAY HOME...
THROUGH ALLEYS, PAST ALL THE GARAGES.
I SUPPOSE I'VE ALWAYS BEEN MORE OF A CAT PERSON...

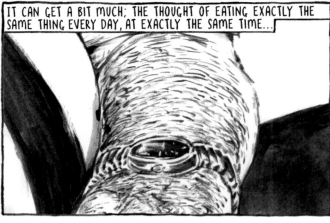

IT CAN GET A BIT MUCH; THE THOUGHT OF EATING EXACTLY THE SAME THING EVERY DAY, AT EXACTLY THE SAME TIME...

THE THOUGHT OF THICK, DRY PASTRY, AND WET MEAT FILLING, AT 1.15 ON THE DOT...

THE ONE TIME I DID SUGGEST NOT HAVING LUNCH THAT DAY, IT DIDN'T GO OVER WELL...

WHAT?!

LOOK AT YOU! YOU ARE STICK-THIN, NO –

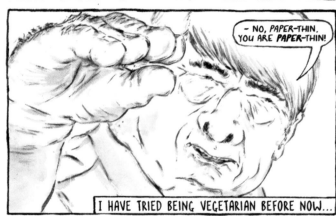

– NO, PAPER-THIN. YOU ARE *PAPER*-THIN!

I HAVE TRIED BEING VEGETARIAN BEFORE NOW...

...BUT LIKE EVERYTHING ELSE I'VE EVER DONE, I DIDN'T KEEP IT UP.

NO, COME ON. WE NEED TO PUT SOME MEAT ON YOU – AN ARMY MARCHES ON ITS STOMACH. YOU'LL HAVE THE SAME AS ME...

SO NOW I JUST HAVE THE SAME THING AS KEITH, HE SEEMS TO LIKE IT THAT WAY.

TWO LARGE PASTIES, PLEASE, DIANE.

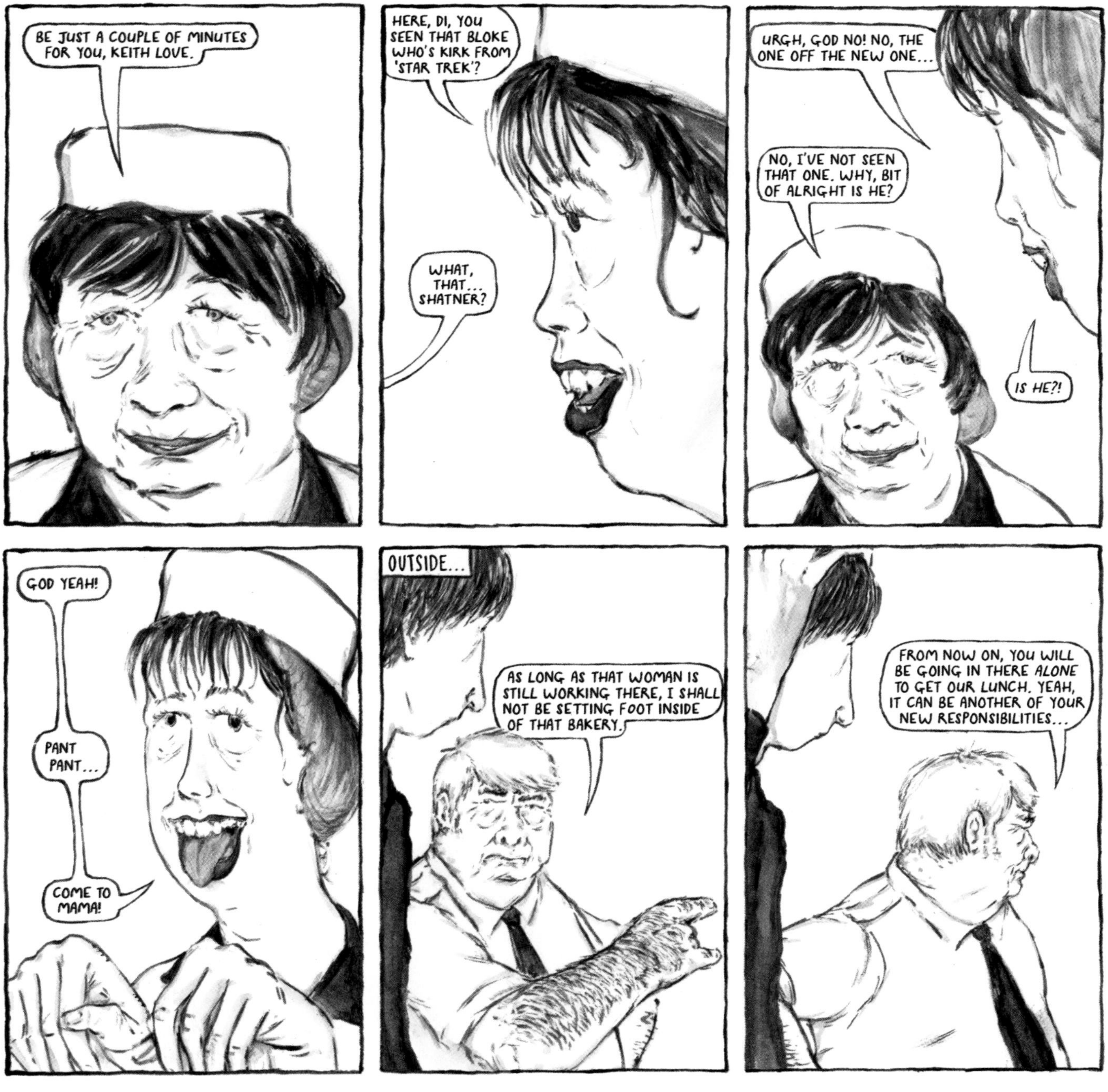
BE JUST A COUPLE OF MINUTES FOR YOU, KEITH LOVE.
HERE, DI, YOU SEEN THAT BLOKE WHO'S KIRK FROM 'STAR TREK'?
WHAT, THAT... SHATNER?
URGH, GOD NO! NO, THE ONE OFF THE NEW ONE...
NO, I'VE NOT SEEN THAT ONE. WHY, BIT OF ALRIGHT IS HE?
IS HE?!
GOD YEAH!
PANT PANT...
COME TO MAMA!
OUTSIDE...
AS LONG AS THAT WOMAN IS STILL WORKING THERE, I SHALL NOT BE SETTING FOOT INSIDE OF THAT BAKERY.
FROM NOW ON, YOU WILL BE GOING IN THERE ALONE TO GET OUR LUNCH. YEAH, IT CAN BE ANOTHER OF YOUR NEW RESPONSIBILITIES...

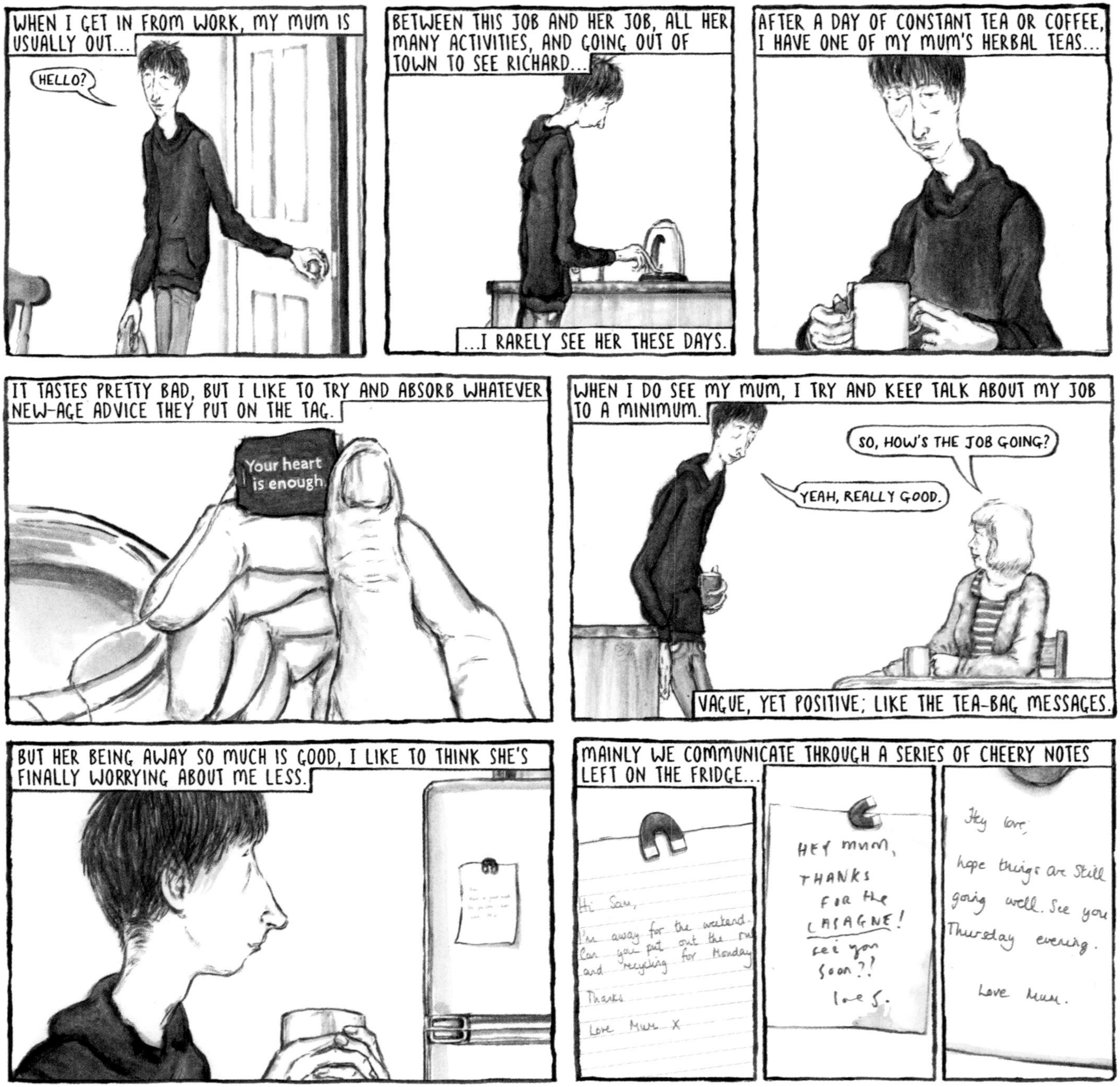
WHEN I GET IN FROM WORK, MY MUM IS USUALLY OUT...
HELLO?
BETWEEN THIS JOB AND HER JOB, ALL HER MANY ACTIVITIES, AND GOING OUT OF TOWN TO SEE RICHARD...
...I RARELY SEE HER THESE DAYS.
AFTER A DAY OF CONSTANT TEA OR COFFEE, I HAVE ONE OF MY MUM'S HERBAL TEAS...
IT TASTES PRETTY BAD, BUT I LIKE TO TRY AND ABSORB WHATEVER NEW-AGE ADVICE THEY PUT ON THE TAG.
Your heart is enough.
WHEN I DO SEE MY MUM, I TRY AND KEEP TALK ABOUT MY JOB TO A MINIMUM.
SO, HOW'S THE JOB GOING?
YEAH, REALLY GOOD.
VAGUE, YET POSITIVE; LIKE THE TEA-BAG MESSAGES.
BUT HER BEING AWAY SO MUCH IS GOOD, I LIKE TO THINK SHE'S FINALLY WORRYING ABOUT ME LESS.
MAINLY WE COMMUNICATE THROUGH A SERIES OF CHEERY NOTES LEFT ON THE FRIDGE...
Hi Sam,
I'm away for the weekend. Can you put out the ru
and recycling for Monday
Thanks
Love Mum x
HEY MUM,
THANKS FOR THE LASAGNE!
SEE YOU SOON?!
love S.
Hey love,
hope things are still going well. See you Thursday evening.
Love Mum.

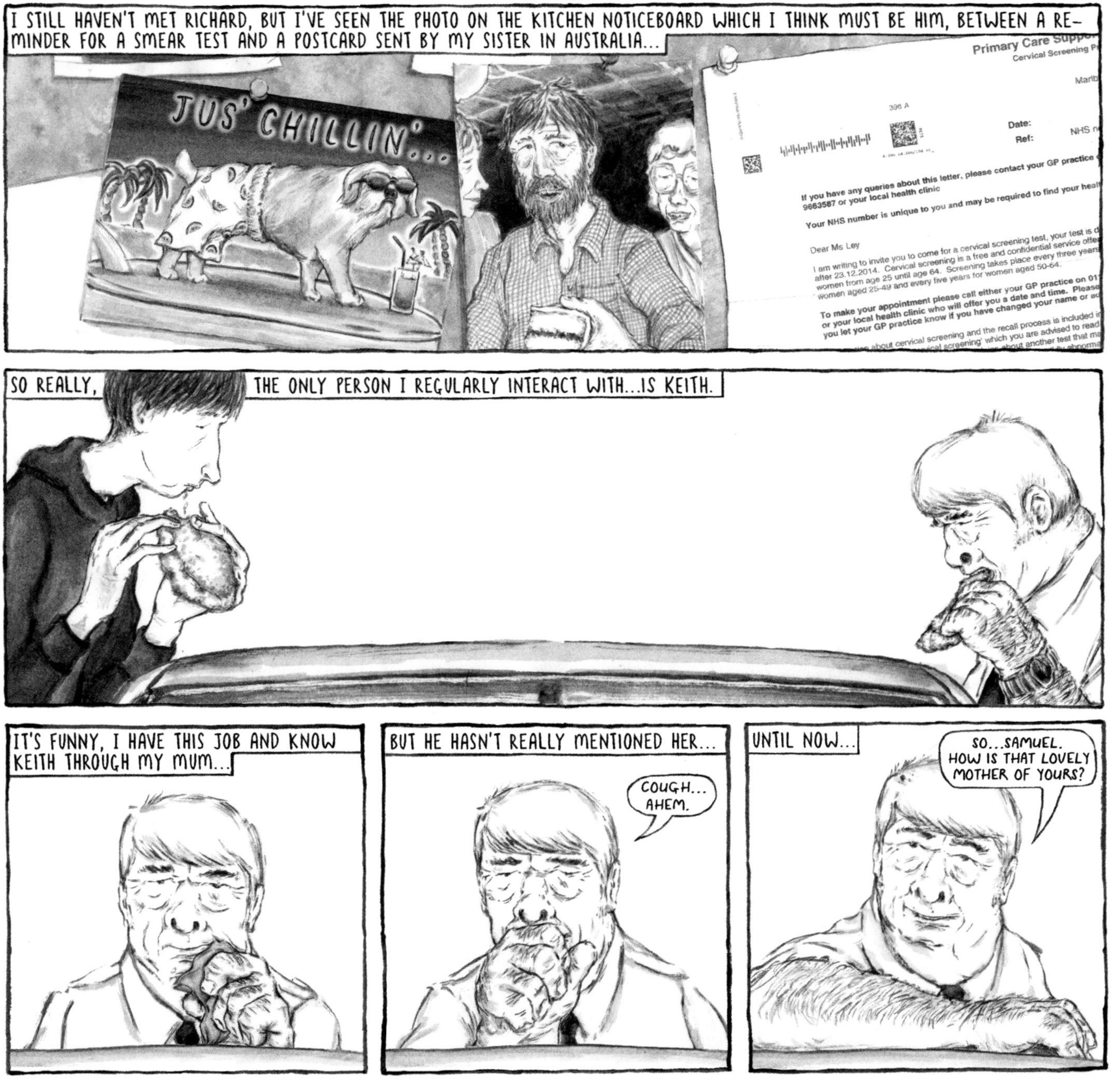
I STILL HAVEN'T MET RICHARD, BUT I'VE SEEN THE PHOTO ON THE KITCHEN NOTICEBOARD WHICH I THINK MUST BE HIM, BETWEEN A REMINDER FOR A SMEAR TEST AND A POSTCARD SENT BY MY SISTER IN AUSTRALIA...
JUS' CHILLIN'...
Dear Ms Ley
SO REALLY, THE ONLY PERSON I REGULARLY INTERACT WITH...IS KEITH.
IT'S FUNNY, I HAVE THIS JOB AND KNOW KEITH THROUGH MY MUM...
BUT HE HASN'T REALLY MENTIONED HER...
COUGH... AHEM.
UNTIL NOW...
SO...SAMUEL. HOW IS THAT LOVELY MOTHER OF YOURS?

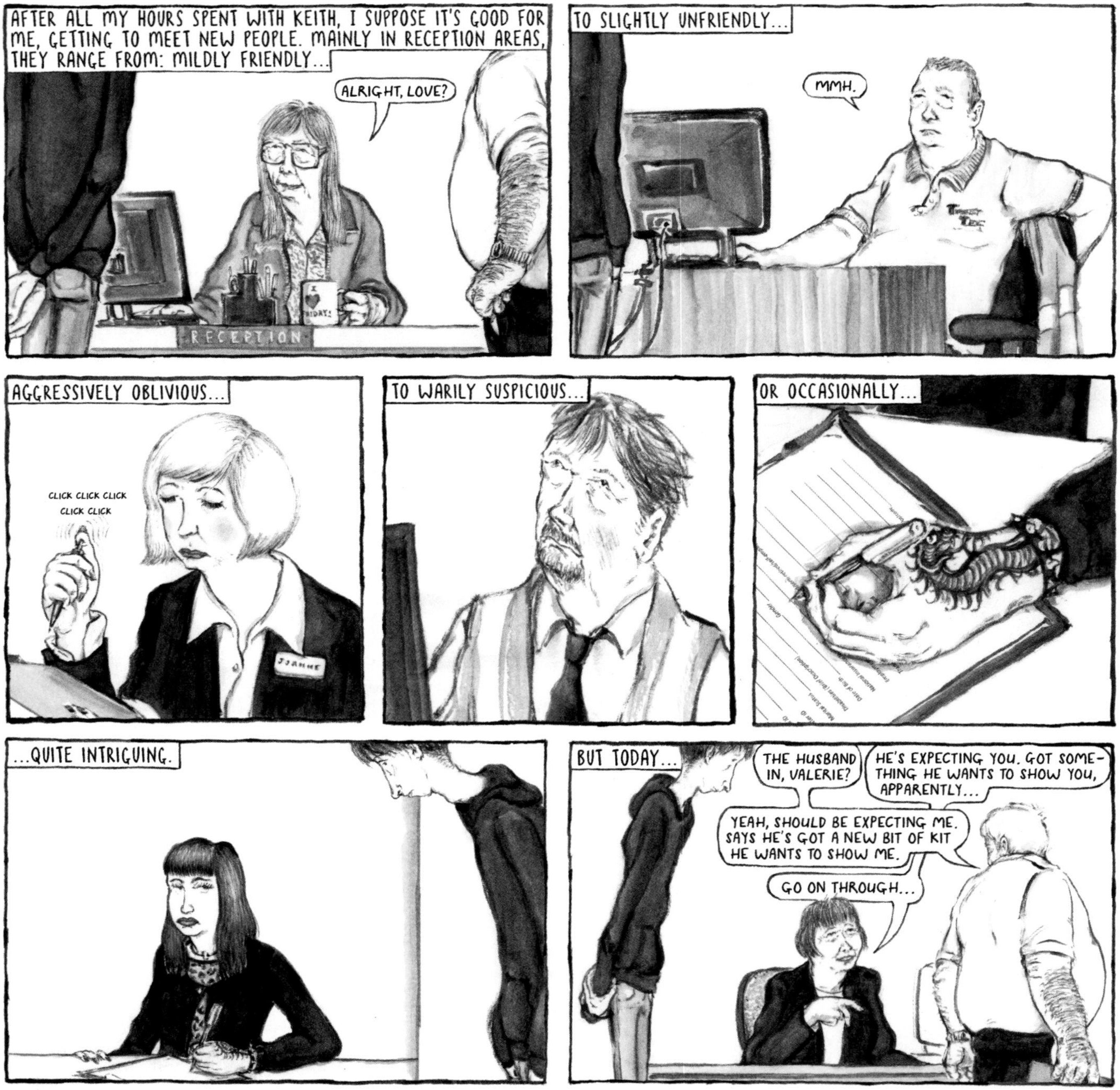
AFTER ALL MY HOURS SPENT WITH KEITH, I SUPPOSE IT'S GOOD FOR ME, GETTING TO MEET NEW PEOPLE. MAINLY IN RECEPTION AREAS, THEY RANGE FROM: MILDLY FRIENDLY...
ALRIGHT, LOVE?
RECEPTION
TO SLIGHTLY UNFRIENDLY...
MMH.
AGGRESSIVELY OBLIVIOUS...
CLICK CLICK CLICK
CLICK CLICK
TO WARILY SUSPICIOUS...
OR OCCASIONALLY...
...QUITE INTRIGUING.
BUT TODAY...
THE HUSBAND IN, VALERIE?
HE'S EXPECTING YOU. GOT SOMETHING HE WANTS TO SHOW YOU, APPARENTLY...
YEAH, SHOULD BE EXPECTING ME. SAYS HE'S GOT A NEW BIT OF KIT HE WANTS TO SHOW ME.
GO ON THROUGH...

HE OFTEN DOES THAT – REPEATS WHAT I'VE JUST TOLD HIM, IN A SLIGHTLY DIFFERENT WAY...

HA! HAHAHA!

NOW, THERE'S A NICE SMILE! WHATS YOUR NAME, YOUNG SWAIN?

SAM.

AND YOU'RE WORKING... FOR KEITH?

UM, YEAH.

WELL, LOVELY TO MEET YOU, SAM.

VAL.

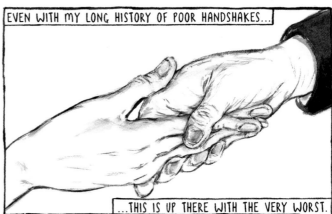

EVEN WITH MY LONG HISTORY OF POOR HANDSHAKES...

...THIS IS UP THERE WITH THE VERY WORST.

YOU MIGHT WANT TO WORK ON THAT HANDSHAKE A LITTLE BIT...

OH GOD, I KNOW, I KNOW... SORRY...

DON'T WORRY ABOUT IT TOO MUCH!

BUT YES, BIT LIKE HOLDING AN EMPTY SOCK.

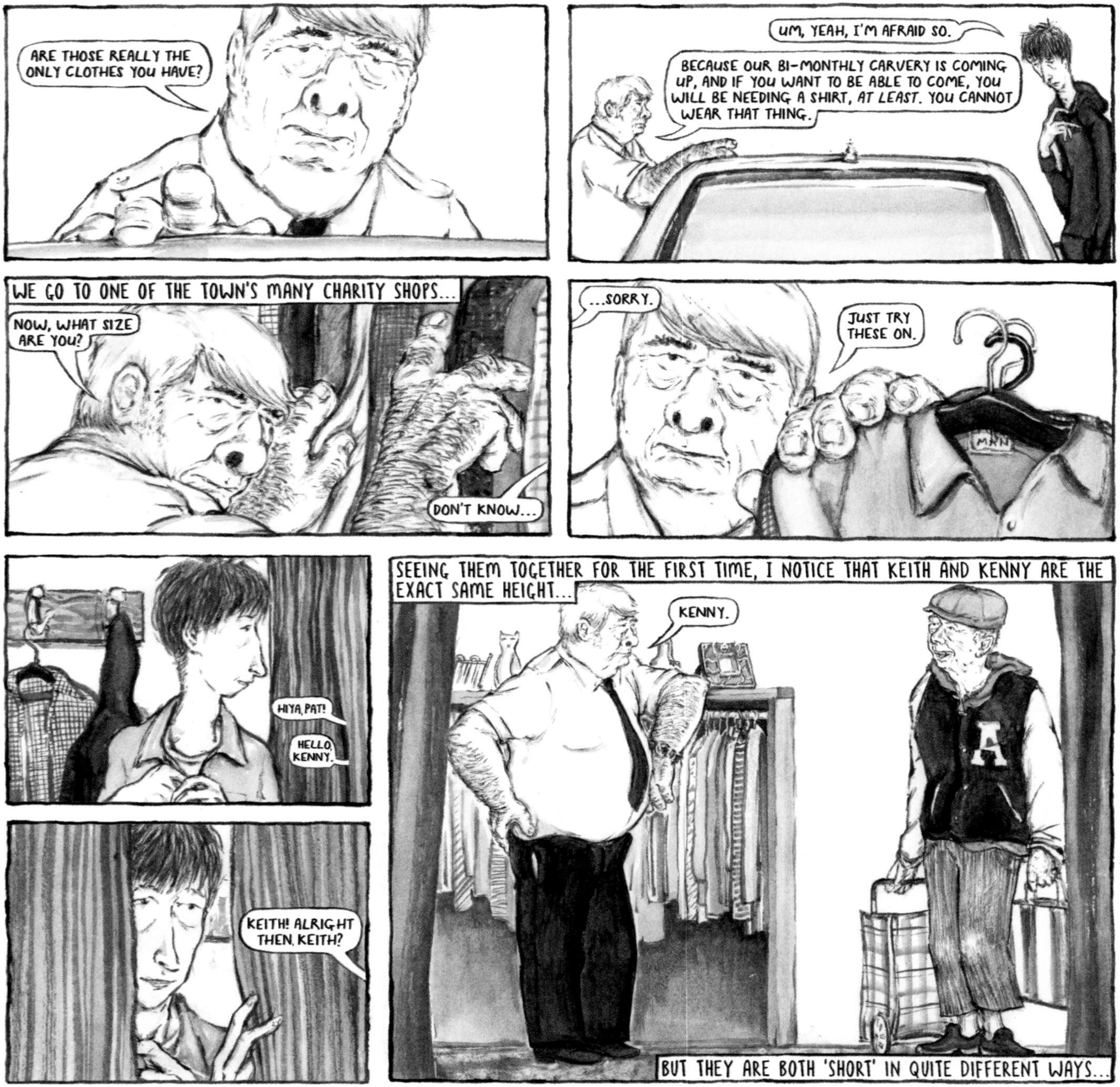

ARE THOSE REALLY THE ONLY CLOTHES YOU HAVE?
UM, YEAH, I'M AFRAID SO.
BECAUSE OUR BI-MONTHLY CARVERY IS COMING UP, AND IF YOU WANT TO BE ABLE TO COME, YOU WILL BE NEEDING A SHIRT, AT LEAST. YOU CANNOT WEAR THAT THING.
WE GO TO ONE OF THE TOWN'S MANY CHARITY SHOPS...
NOW, WHAT SIZE ARE YOU?
DON'T KNOW...
...SORRY.
JUST TRY THESE ON.
M&N
HIYA, PAT!
HELLO, KENNY.
KEITH! ALRIGHT THEN, KEITH?
SEEING THEM TOGETHER FOR THE FIRST TIME, I NOTICE THAT KEITH AND KENNY ARE THE EXACT SAME HEIGHT...
KENNY.
BUT THEY ARE BOTH 'SHORT' IN QUITE DIFFERENT WAYS...

IN HIS NATURAL CHARITY SHOP HABITAT, KENNY MOVES ALMOST LIKE A KID, AGILE AND UNSELFCONSCIOUS...

WHILE KEITH OFTEN LOOKS LIKE HE'S TRYING TO BECOME TALLER...

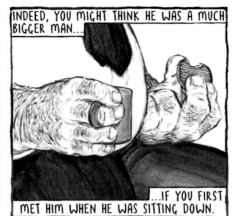

INDEED, YOU MIGHT THINK HE WAS A MUCH BIGGER MAN...

...IF YOU FIRST MET HIM WHEN HE WAS SITTING DOWN.

NO.

TOO SHORT.

CAN'T EVEN TUCK THAT IN!

LOOKS GOOD, THAT DOES.

SO I TRY ON ANOTHER SHIRT...

YEAH, LOOKS EXCELLENT.

...FOR MY UNLIKELY PERSONAL SHOPPERS.

IT'LL DO, I S'POSE, BUT...

...IDEALLY, YOU WANT SOMETHING LIKE THIS.

BUT JUST SMALLER... AND LONGER.

SAM! THIS ONE...?!

LOOK, CAN YOU JUST –

GOD, HE CERTAINLY DOESN'T GET ANY CLEVERER, DOES HE? THAT'S FOR SURE.

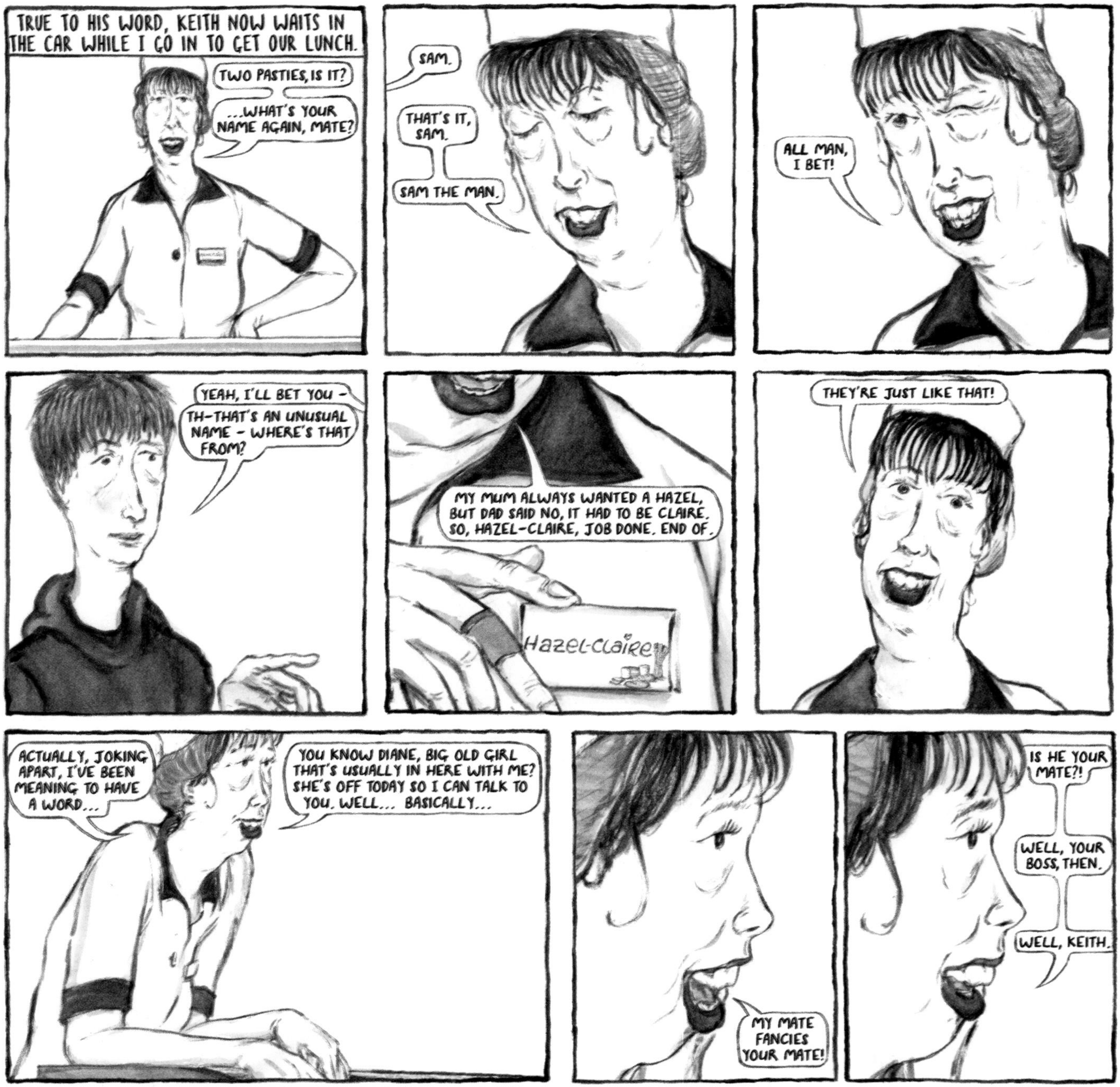

TRUE TO HIS WORD, KEITH NOW WAITS IN THE CAR WHILE I GO IN TO GET OUR LUNCH.
TWO PASTIES, IS IT?
...WHAT'S YOUR NAME AGAIN, MATE?
SAM.
THAT'S IT, SAM.
SAM THE MAN.
ALL MAN, I BET!
YEAH, I'LL BET YOU -
TH-THAT'S AN UNUSUAL NAME - WHERE'S THAT FROM?
MY MUM ALWAYS WANTED A HAZEL, BUT DAD SAID NO, IT HAD TO BE CLAIRE. SO, HAZEL-CLAIRE, JOB DONE. END OF.
Hazel-Claire
THEY'RE JUST LIKE THAT!
ACTUALLY, JOKING APART, I'VE BEEN MEANING TO HAVE A WORD...
YOU KNOW DIANE, BIG OLD GIRL THAT'S USUALLY IN HERE WITH ME? SHE'S OFF TODAY SO I CAN TALK TO YOU. WELL... BASICALLY...
MY MATE FANCIES YOUR MATE!
IS HE YOUR MATE?!
WELL, YOUR BOSS, THEN.
WELL, KEITH.

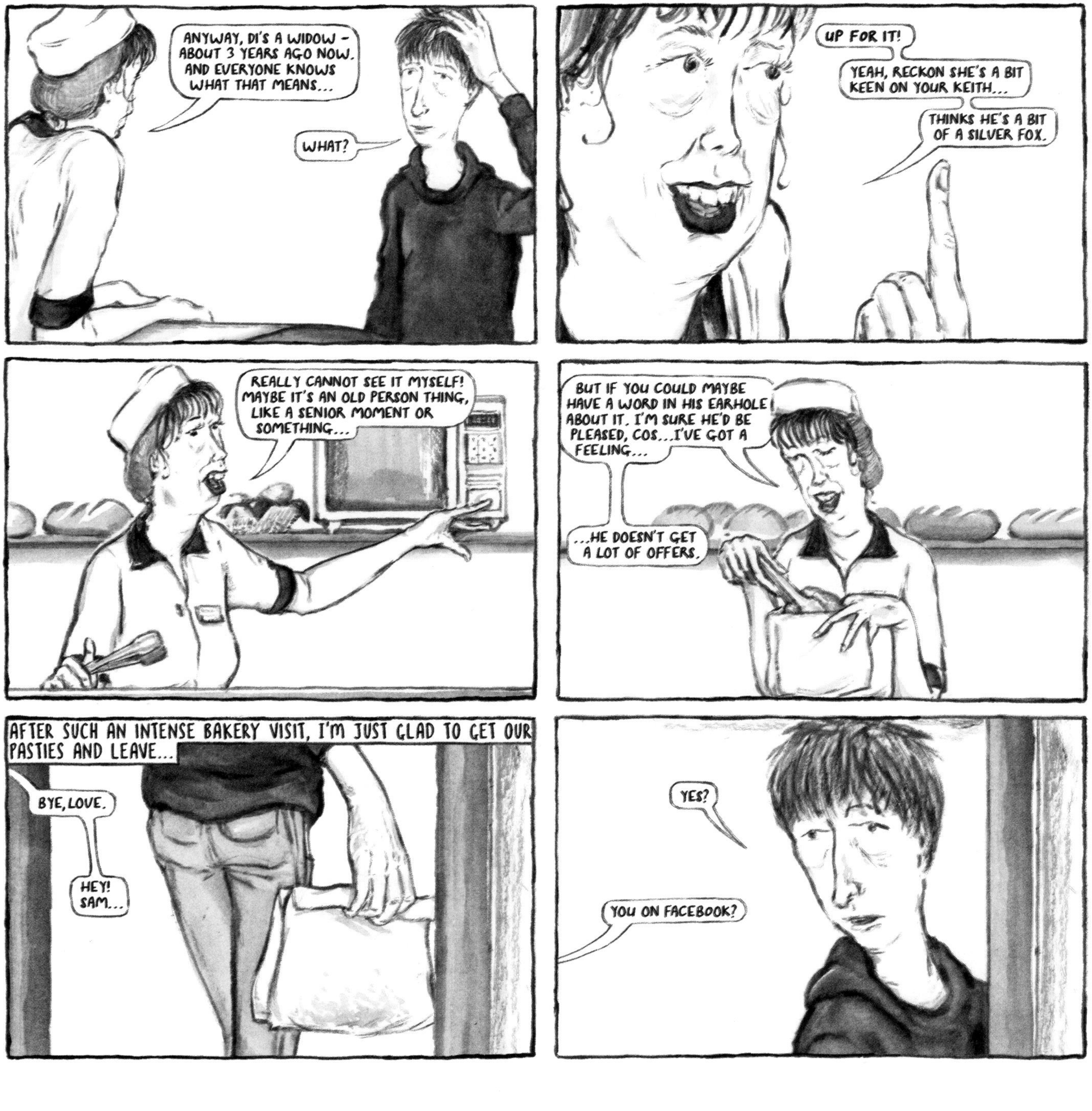
ANYWAY, DI'S A WIDOW - ABOUT 3 YEARS AGO NOW. AND EVERYONE KNOWS WHAT THAT MEANS...
WHAT?
UP FOR IT!
YEAH, RECKON SHE'S A BIT KEEN ON YOUR KEITH...
THINKS HE'S A BIT OF A SILVER FOX.
REALLY CANNOT SEE IT MYSELF! MAYBE IT'S AN OLD PERSON THING, LIKE A SENIOR MOMENT OR SOMETHING...
BUT IF YOU COULD MAYBE HAVE A WORD IN HIS EARHOLE ABOUT IT. I'M SURE HE'D BE PLEASED, COS...I'VE GOT A FEELING...
...HE DOESN'T GET A LOT OF OFFERS.
AFTER SUCH AN INTENSE BAKERY VISIT, I'M JUST GLAD TO GET OUR PASTIES AND LEAVE...
BYE, LOVE.
HEY! SAM...
YES?
YOU ON FACEBOOK?

LUNCHTIME AGAIN...

WHAT'S THAT YOU'VE GOT THERE, THEN?

COCONUT WATER. THEY'VE STARTED DOING IT IN THE BAKERY.

HMM. A TASTE OF THE TROPICS, EH?

YEAH, IT'S LIKE WATER, BUT A BIT NICER. YOU WANT TO TRY SOME?

OOH, NO THANKS! THE FOREIGN STUFF DOES NOT AGREE...

OH, GO ON, THEN. I'LL HAVE A LITTLE TRY.

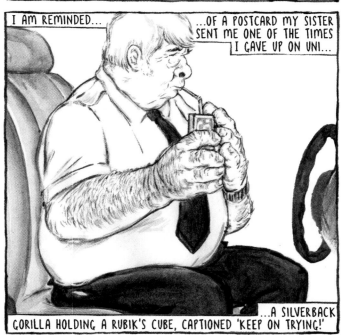

I AM REMINDED...

...OF A POSTCARD MY SISTER SENT ME ONE OF THE TIMES I GAVE UP ON UNI...

...A SILVERBACK GORILLA HOLDING A RUBIK'S CUBE, CAPTIONED 'KEEP ON TRYING!'

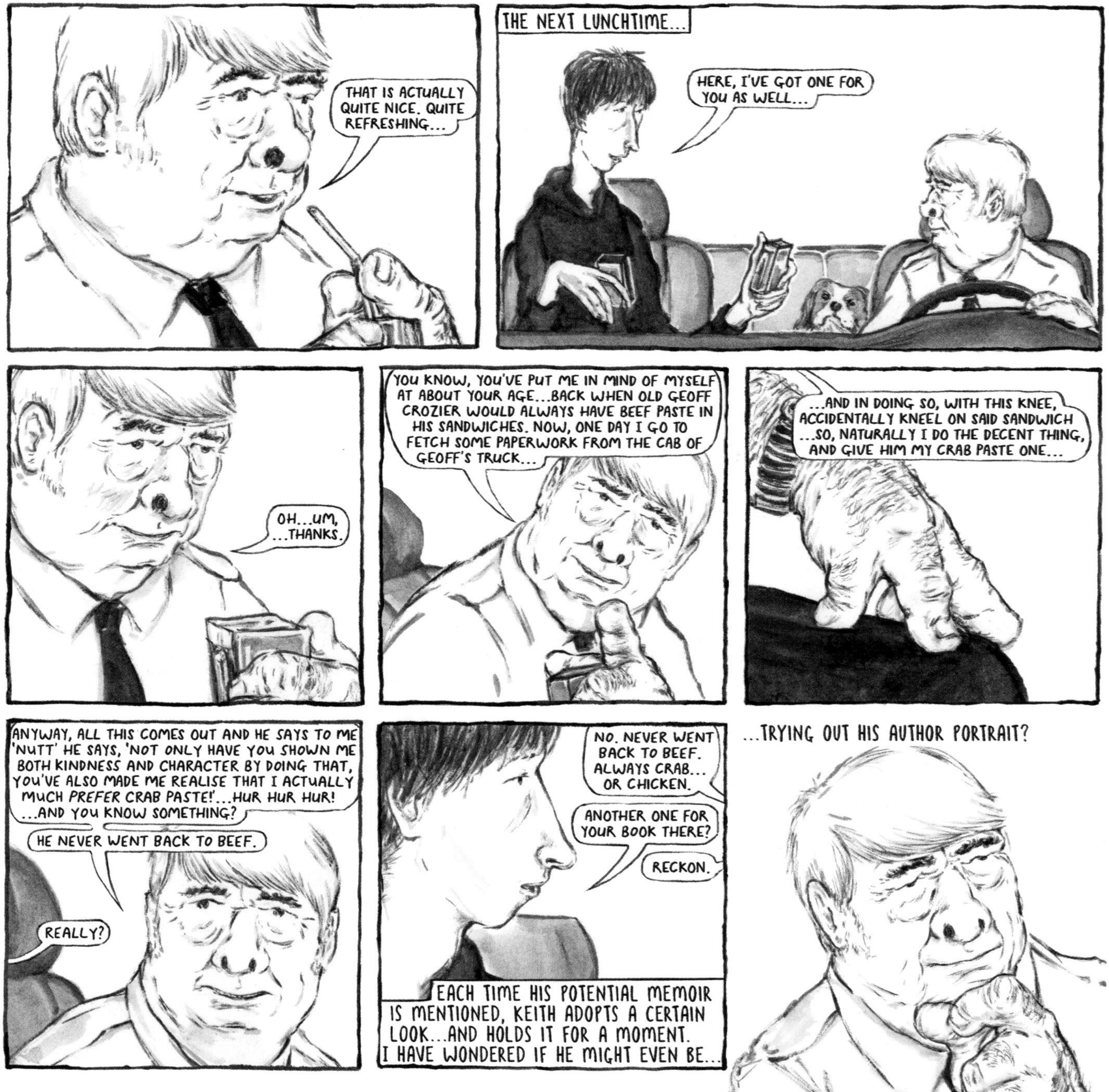
THAT IS ACTUALLY QUITE NICE. QUITE REFRESHING...
THE NEXT LUNCHTIME...
HERE, I'VE GOT ONE FOR YOU AS WELL...
OH...UM, ...THANKS.
YOU KNOW, YOU'VE PUT ME IN MIND OF MYSELF AT ABOUT YOUR AGE...BACK WHEN OLD GEOFF CROZIER WOULD ALWAYS HAVE BEEF PASTE IN HIS SANDWICHES. NOW, ONE DAY I GO TO FETCH SOME PAPERWORK FROM THE CAB OF GEOFF'S TRUCK...
...AND IN DOING SO, WITH THIS KNEE, ACCIDENTALLY KNEEL ON SAID SANDWICH ...SO, NATURALLY I DO THE DECENT THING, AND GIVE HIM MY CRAB PASTE ONE...
ANYWAY, ALL THIS COMES OUT AND HE SAYS TO ME 'NUTT' HE SAYS, 'NOT ONLY HAVE YOU SHOWN ME BOTH KINDNESS AND CHARACTER BY DOING THAT, YOU'VE ALSO MADE ME REALISE THAT I ACTUALLY MUCH *PREFER* CRAB PASTE!'...HUR HUR HUR! ...AND YOU KNOW SOMETHING?
HE NEVER WENT BACK TO BEEF.
REALLY?
NO. NEVER WENT BACK TO BEEF. ALWAYS CRAB... OR CHICKEN.
ANOTHER ONE FOR YOUR BOOK THERE?
RECKON.
EACH TIME HIS POTENTIAL MEMOIR IS MENTIONED, KEITH ADOPTS A CERTAIN LOOK...AND HOLDS IT FOR A MOMENT. I HAVE WONDERED IF HE MIGHT EVEN BE...
...TRYING OUT HIS AUTHOR PORTRAIT?

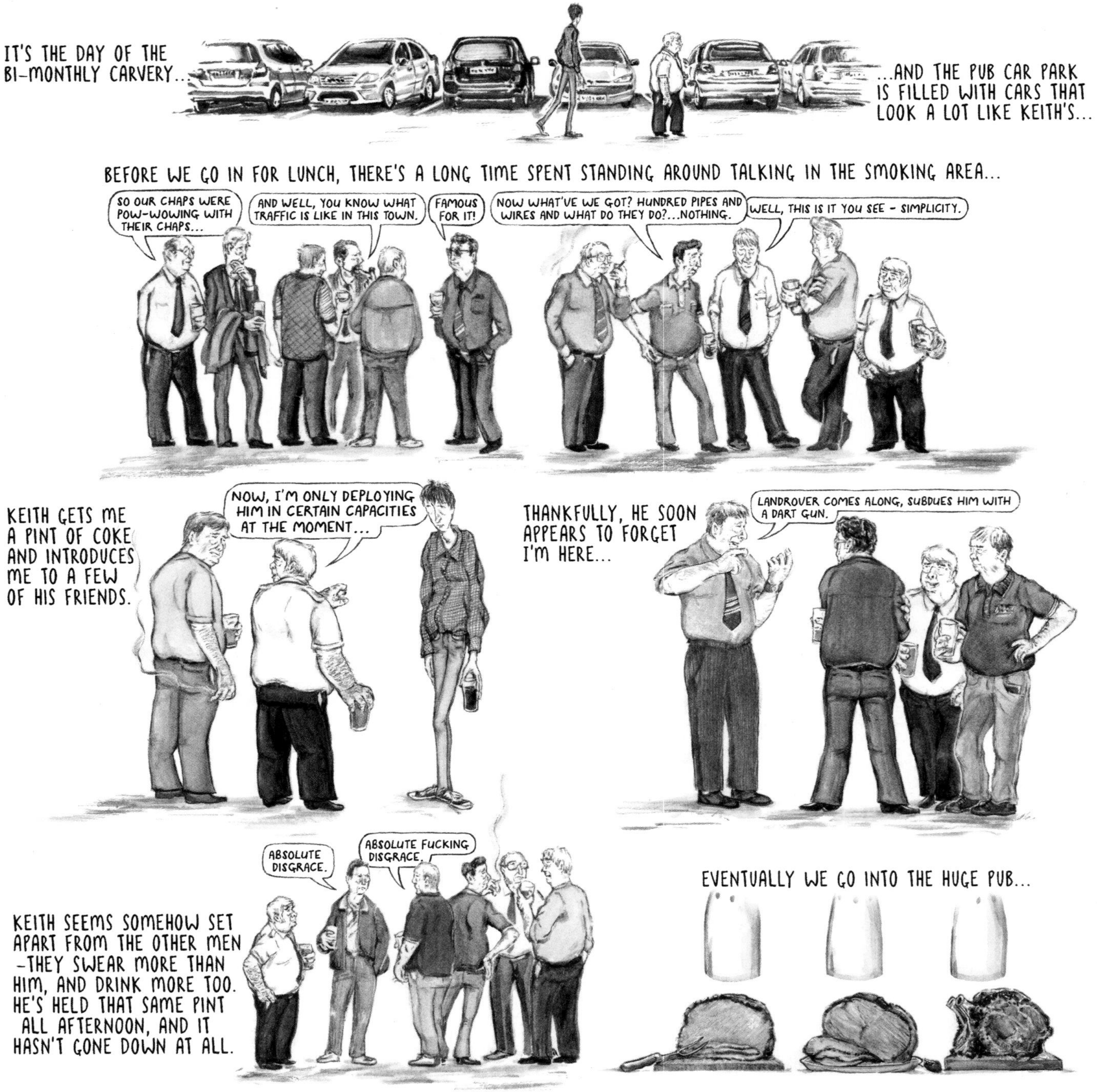
IT'S THE DAY OF THE BI-MONTHLY CARVERY...
...AND THE PUB CAR PARK IS FILLED WITH CARS THAT LOOK A LOT LIKE KEITH'S...
BEFORE WE GO IN FOR LUNCH, THERE'S A LONG TIME SPENT STANDING AROUND TALKING IN THE SMOKING AREA...
SO OUR CHAPS WERE POW-WOWING WITH THEIR CHAPS...
AND WELL, YOU KNOW WHAT TRAFFIC IS LIKE IN THIS TOWN.
FAMOUS FOR IT!
NOW WHAT'VE WE GOT? HUNDRED PIPES AND WIRES AND WHAT DO THEY DO?...NOTHING.
WELL, THIS IS IT YOU SEE - SIMPLICITY.
KEITH GETS ME A PINT OF COKE AND INTRODUCES ME TO A FEW OF HIS FRIENDS.
NOW, I'M ONLY DEPLOYING HIM IN CERTAIN CAPACITIES AT THE MOMENT...
THANKFULLY, HE SOON APPEARS TO FORGET I'M HERE...
LANDROVER COMES ALONG, SUBDUES HIM WITH A DART GUN.
KEITH SEEMS SOMEHOW SET APART FROM THE OTHER MEN -THEY SWEAR MORE THAN HIM, AND DRINK MORE TOO. HE'S HELD THAT SAME PINT ALL AFTERNOON, AND IT HASN'T GONE DOWN AT ALL.
ABSOLUTE DISGRACE.
ABSOLUTE FUCKING DISGRACE.
EVENTUALLY WE GO INTO THE HUGE PUB...

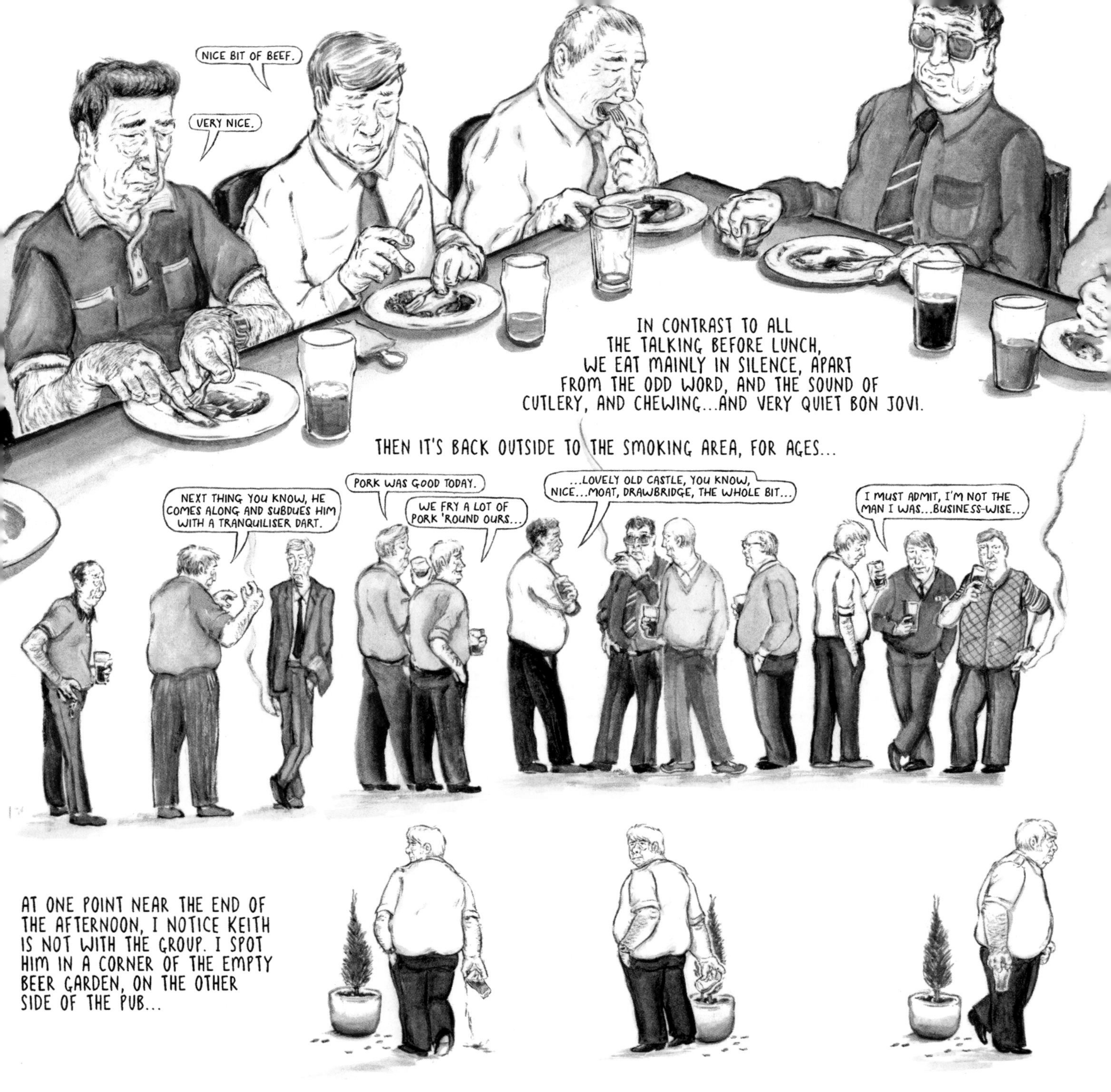
NICE BIT OF BEEF.
VERY NICE.
IN CONTRAST TO ALL THE TALKING BEFORE LUNCH, WE EAT MAINLY IN SILENCE, APART FROM THE ODD WORD, AND THE SOUND OF CUTLERY, AND CHEWING...AND VERY QUIET BON JOVI.
THEN IT'S BACK OUTSIDE TO THE SMOKING AREA, FOR AGES...
NEXT THING YOU KNOW, HE COMES ALONG AND SUBDUES HIM WITH A TRANQUILISER DART.
PORK WAS GOOD TODAY.
WE FRY A LOT OF PORK 'ROUND OURS...
...LOVELY OLD CASTLE, YOU KNOW, NICE...MOAT, DRAWBRIDGE, THE WHOLE BIT...
I MUST ADMIT, I'M NOT THE MAN I WAS...BUSINESS-WISE...
AT ONE POINT NEAR THE END OF THE AFTERNOON, I NOTICE KEITH IS NOT WITH THE GROUP. I SPOT HIM IN A CORNER OF THE EMPTY BEER GARDEN, ON THE OTHER SIDE OF THE PUB...

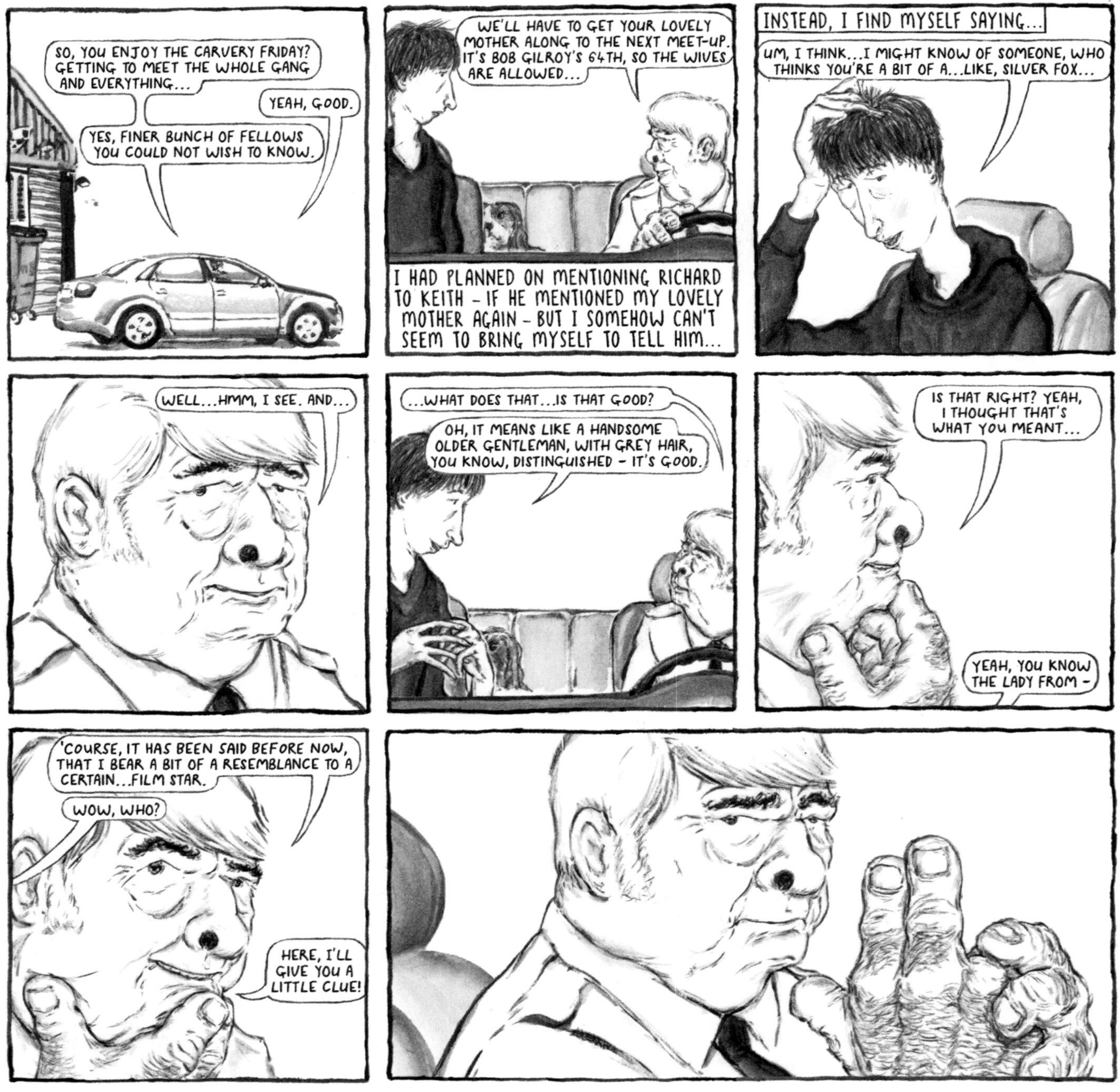

SO, YOU ENJOY THE CARVERY FRIDAY? GETTING TO MEET THE WHOLE GANG AND EVERYTHING...
YEAH, GOOD.
YES, FINER BUNCH OF FELLOWS YOU COULD NOT WISH TO KNOW.
WE'LL HAVE TO GET YOUR LOVELY MOTHER ALONG TO THE NEXT MEET-UP. IT'S BOB GILROY'S 64TH, SO THE WIVES ARE ALLOWED...
I HAD PLANNED ON MENTIONING RICHARD TO KEITH – IF HE MENTIONED MY LOVELY MOTHER AGAIN – BUT I SOMEHOW CAN'T SEEM TO BRING MYSELF TO TELL HIM...
INSTEAD, I FIND MYSELF SAYING...
UM, I THINK...I MIGHT KNOW OF SOMEONE, WHO THINKS YOU'RE A BIT OF A...LIKE, SILVER FOX...
WELL...HMM, I SEE. AND...
...WHAT DOES THAT...IS THAT GOOD?
OH, IT MEANS LIKE A HANDSOME OLDER GENTLEMAN, WITH GREY HAIR, YOU KNOW, DISTINGUISHED – IT'S GOOD.
IS THAT RIGHT? YEAH, I THOUGHT THAT'S WHAT YOU MEANT...
YEAH, YOU KNOW THE LADY FROM –
'COURSE, IT HAS BEEN SAID BEFORE NOW, THAT I BEAR A BIT OF A RESEMBLANCE TO A CERTAIN...FILM STAR.
WOW, WHO?
HERE, I'LL GIVE YOU A LITTLE CLUE!

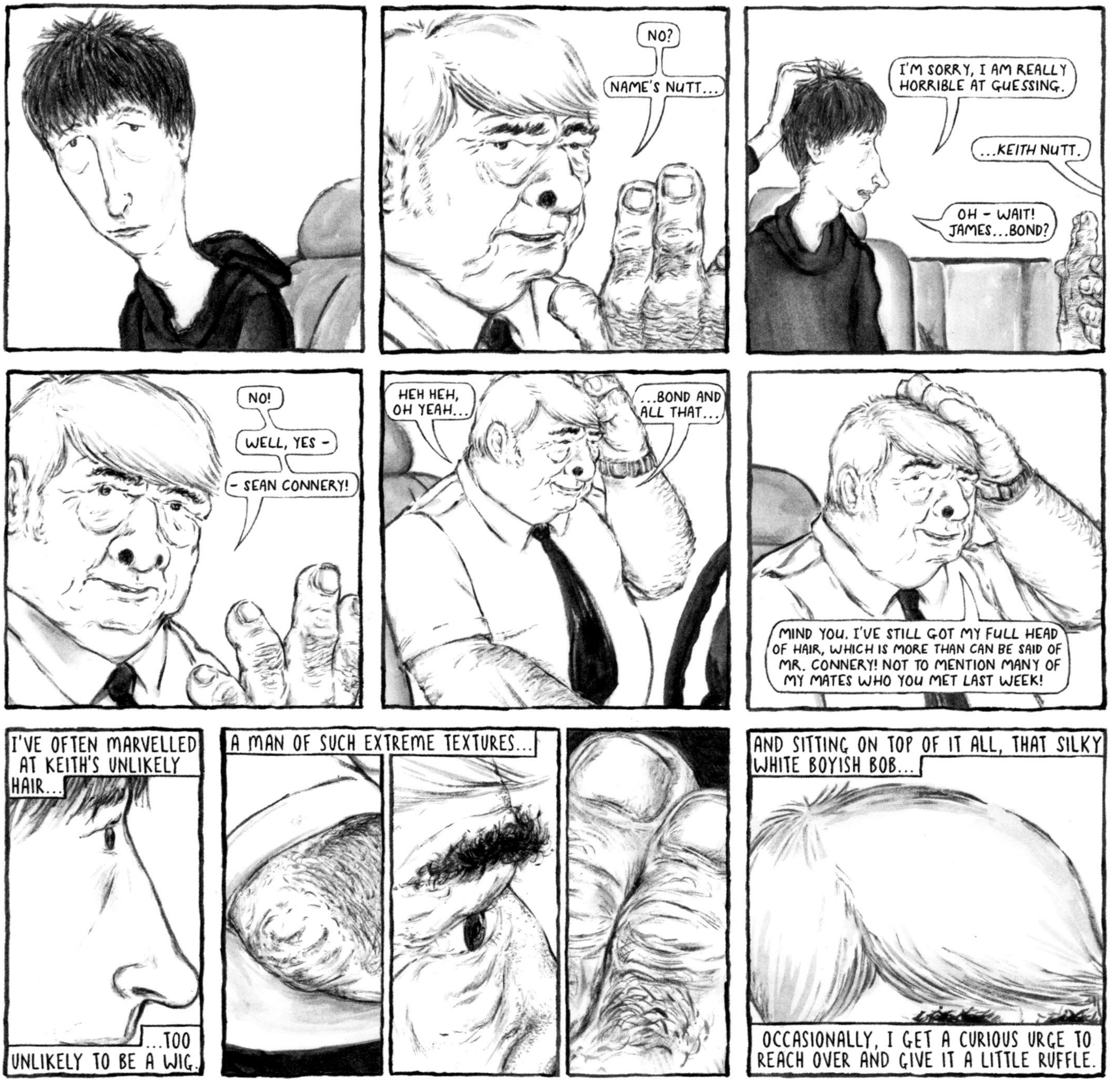
NO?
NAME'S NUTT...
I'M SORRY, I AM REALLY HORRIBLE AT GUESSING.
...KEITH NUTT.
OH - WAIT! JAMES...BOND?
NO!
WELL, YES -
- SEAN CONNERY!
HEH HEH, OH YEAH...
...BOND AND ALL THAT...
MIND YOU. I'VE STILL GOT MY FULL HEAD OF HAIR, WHICH IS MORE THAN CAN BE SAID OF MR. CONNERY! NOT TO MENTION MANY OF MY MATES WHO YOU MET LAST WEEK!
I'VE OFTEN MARVELLED AT KEITH'S UNLIKELY HAIR...
...TOO UNLIKELY TO BE A WIG.
A MAN OF SUCH EXTREME TEXTURES...
AND SITTING ON TOP OF IT ALL, THAT SILKY WHITE BOYISH BOB...
OCCASIONALLY, I GET A CURIOUS URGE TO REACH OVER AND GIVE IT A LITTLE RUFFLE.

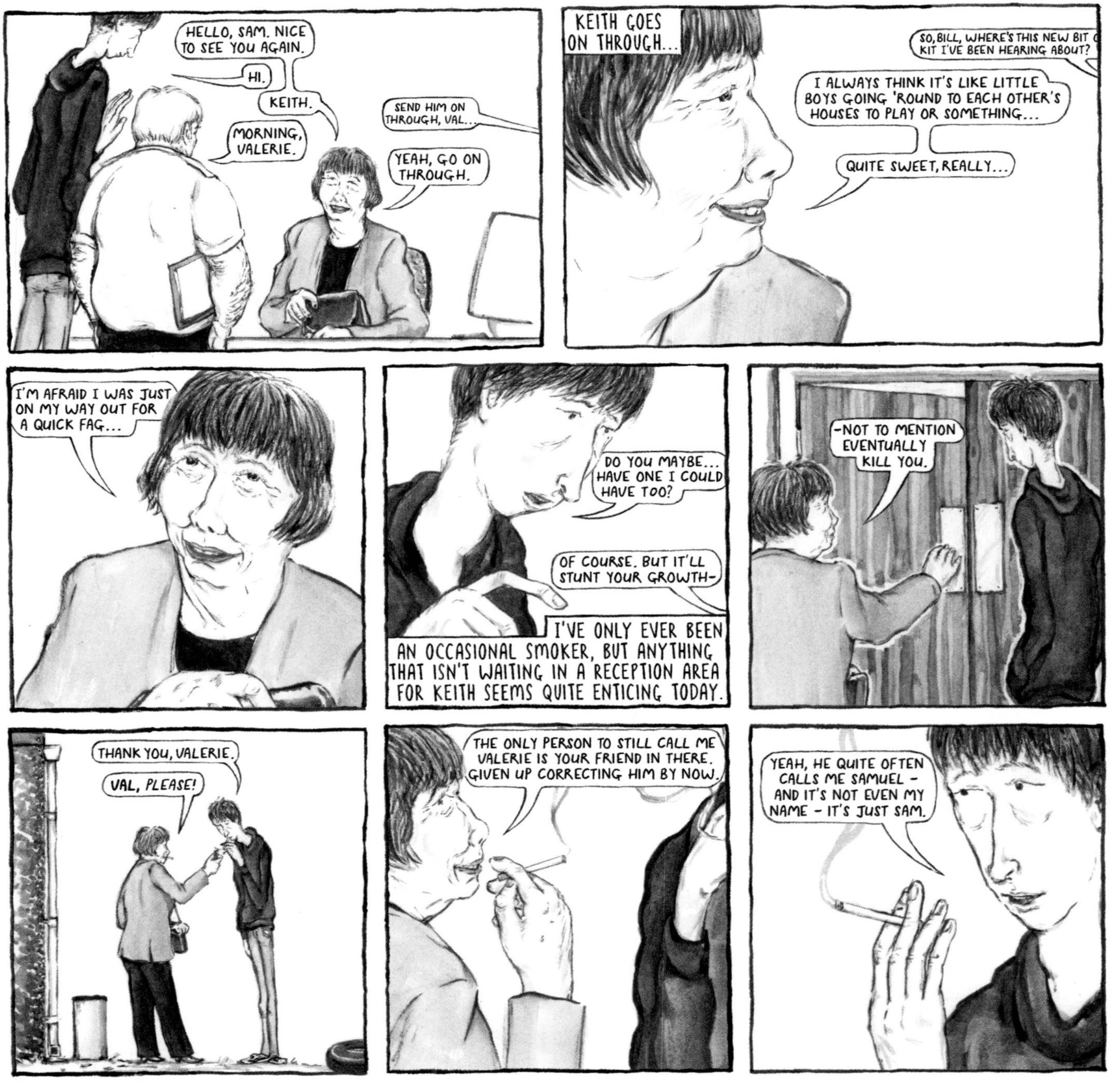
HELLO, SAM. NICE TO SEE YOU AGAIN.
HI.
KEITH.
MORNING, VALERIE.
SEND HIM ON THROUGH, VAL...
YEAH, GO ON THROUGH.
KEITH GOES ON THROUGH...
SO, BILL, WHERE'S THIS NEW BIT OF KIT I'VE BEEN HEARING ABOUT?
I ALWAYS THINK IT'S LIKE LITTLE BOYS GOING 'ROUND TO EACH OTHER'S HOUSES TO PLAY OR SOMETHING...
QUITE SWEET, REALLY...
I'M AFRAID I WAS JUST ON MY WAY OUT FOR A QUICK FAG...
DO YOU MAYBE... HAVE ONE I COULD HAVE TOO?
OF COURSE. BUT IT'LL STUNT YOUR GROWTH-
I'VE ONLY EVER BEEN AN OCCASIONAL SMOKER, BUT ANYTHING THAT ISN'T WAITING IN A RECEPTION AREA FOR KEITH SEEMS QUITE ENTICING TODAY.
-NOT TO MENTION EVENTUALLY KILL YOU.
THANK YOU, VALERIE.
VAL, PLEASE!
THE ONLY PERSON TO STILL CALL ME VALERIE IS YOUR FRIEND IN THERE. GIVEN UP CORRECTING HIM BY NOW.
YEAH, HE QUITE OFTEN CALLS ME SAMUEL - AND IT'S NOT EVEN MY NAME - IT'S JUST SAM.

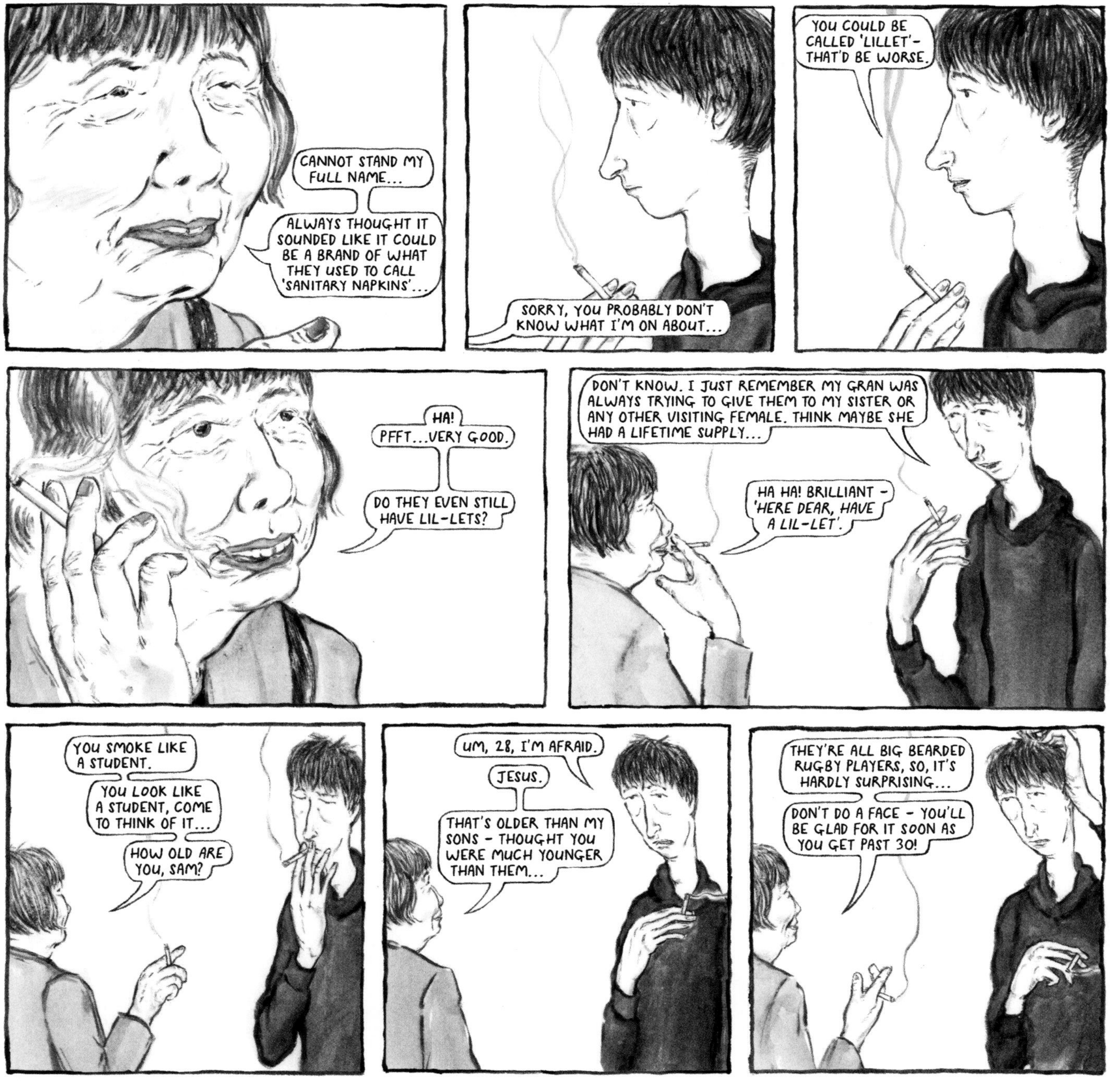
CANNOT STAND MY FULL NAME...
ALWAYS THOUGHT IT SOUNDED LIKE IT COULD BE A BRAND OF WHAT THEY USED TO CALL 'SANITARY NAPKINS'...
SORRY, YOU PROBABLY DON'T KNOW WHAT I'M ON ABOUT...
YOU COULD BE CALLED 'LILLET'- THAT'D BE WORSE.
HA!
PFFT...VERY GOOD.
DO THEY EVEN STILL HAVE LIL-LETS?
DON'T KNOW. I JUST REMEMBER MY GRAN WAS ALWAYS TRYING TO GIVE THEM TO MY SISTER OR ANY OTHER VISITING FEMALE. THINK MAYBE SHE HAD A LIFETIME SUPPLY...
HA HA! BRILLIANT - 'HERE DEAR, HAVE A LIL-LET'.
YOU SMOKE LIKE A STUDENT.
YOU LOOK LIKE A STUDENT, COME TO THINK OF IT...
HOW OLD ARE YOU, SAM?
UM, 28, I'M AFRAID.
JESUS.
THAT'S OLDER THAN MY SONS - THOUGHT YOU WERE MUCH YOUNGER THAN THEM...
THEY'RE ALL BIG BEARDED RUGBY PLAYERS, SO, IT'S HARDLY SURPRISING...
DON'T DO A FACE - YOU'LL BE GLAD FOR IT SOON AS YOU GET PAST 30!

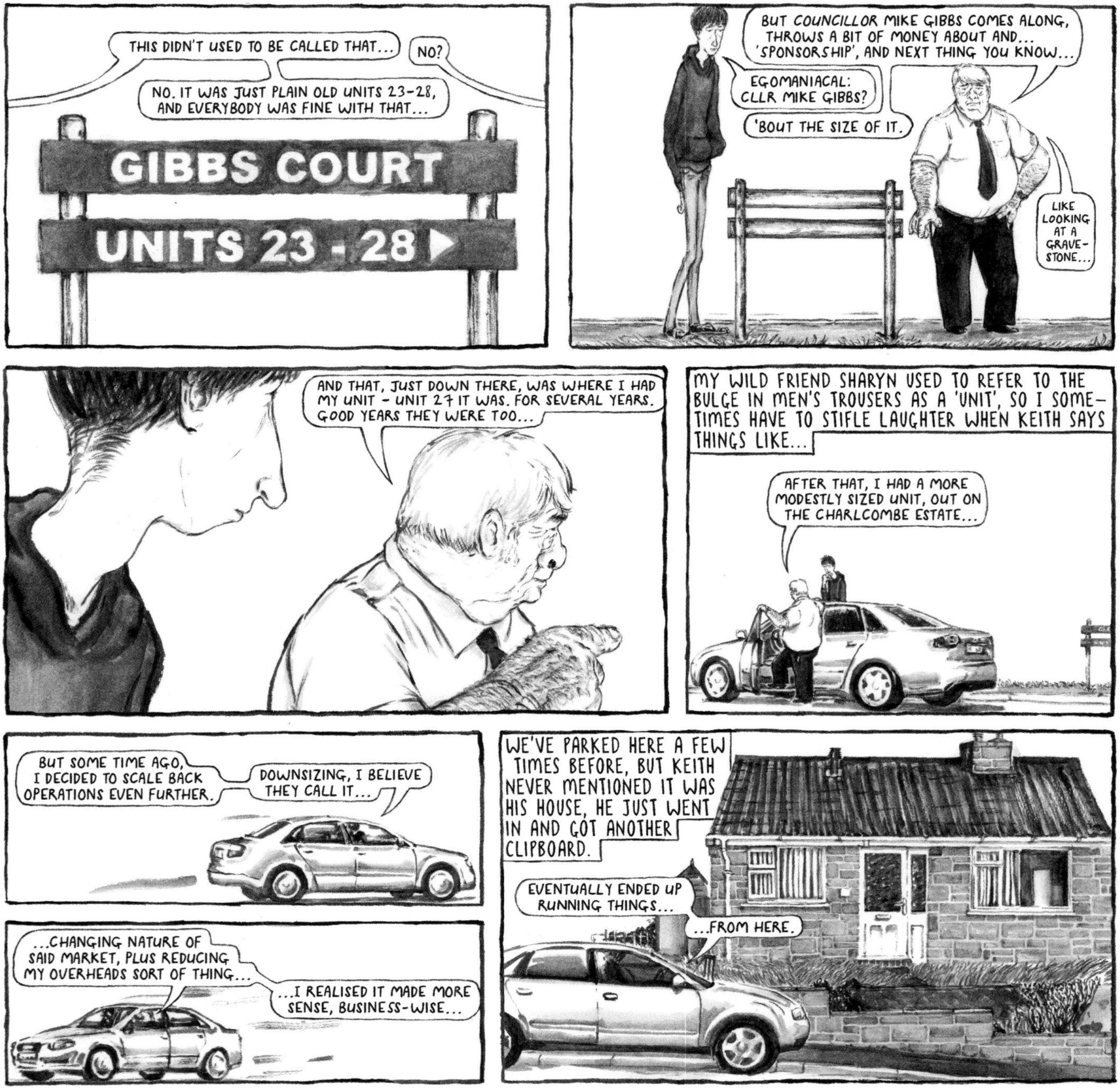
THIS DIDN'T USED TO BE CALLED THAT...
NO?
NO. IT WAS JUST PLAIN OLD UNITS 23-28, AND EVERYBODY WAS FINE WITH THAT...
GIBBS COURT
UNITS 23 - 28
BUT COUNCILLOR MIKE GIBBS COMES ALONG, THROWS A BIT OF MONEY ABOUT AND... 'SPONSORSHIP', AND NEXT THING YOU KNOW...
EGOMANIACAL: CLLR MIKE GIBBS?
'BOUT THE SIZE OF IT.
LIKE LOOKING AT A GRAVE-STONE...
AND THAT, JUST DOWN THERE, WAS WHERE I HAD MY UNIT - UNIT 27 IT WAS. FOR SEVERAL YEARS. GOOD YEARS THEY WERE TOO...
MY WILD FRIEND SHARYN USED TO REFER TO THE BULGE IN MEN'S TROUSERS AS A 'UNIT', SO I SOME-TIMES HAVE TO STIFLE LAUGHTER WHEN KEITH SAYS THINGS LIKE...
AFTER THAT, I HAD A MORE MODESTLY SIZED UNIT, OUT ON THE CHARLCOMBE ESTATE...
BUT SOME TIME AGO, I DECIDED TO SCALE BACK OPERATIONS EVEN FURTHER.
DOWNSIZING, I BELIEVE THEY CALL IT...
...CHANGING NATURE OF SAID MARKET, PLUS REDUCING MY OVERHEADS SORT OF THING...
...I REALISED IT MADE MORE SENSE, BUSINESS-WISE...
WE'VE PARKED HERE A FEW TIMES BEFORE, BUT KEITH NEVER MENTIONED IT WAS HIS HOUSE, HE JUST WENT IN AND GOT ANOTHER CLIPBOARD.
EVENTUALLY ENDED UP RUNNING THINGS...
...FROM HERE.

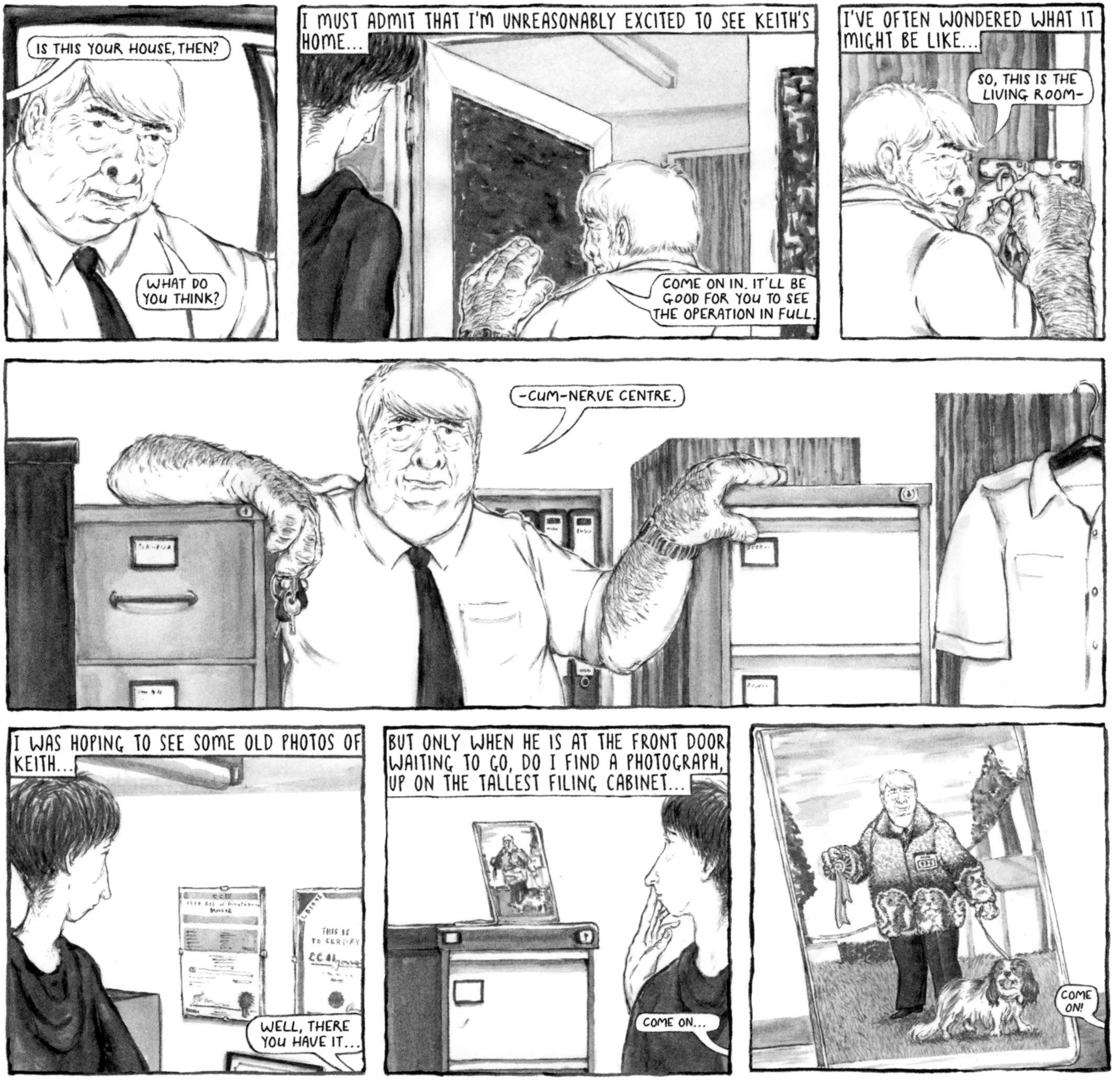
IS THIS YOUR HOUSE, THEN?
WHAT DO YOU THINK?
I MUST ADMIT THAT I'M UNREASONABLY EXCITED TO SEE KEITH'S HOME...
COME ON IN. IT'LL BE GOOD FOR YOU TO SEE THE OPERATION IN FULL.
I'VE OFTEN WONDERED WHAT IT MIGHT BE LIKE...
SO, THIS IS THE LIVING ROOM-
-CUM-NERVE CENTRE.
I WAS HOPING TO SEE SOME OLD PHOTOS OF KEITH...
WELL, THERE YOU HAVE IT...
BUT ONLY WHEN HE IS AT THE FRONT DOOR WAITING TO GO, DO I FIND A PHOTOGRAPH, UP ON THE TALLEST FILING CABINET...
COME ON...
COME ON!

AGAIN, I CAN'T SLEEP...

IN AN ATTEMPT TO CALM MY OVERHEATING MIND, I BEGIN MAKING A MENTAL LIST OF THINGS THAT LOOK LIKE KEITH. THOUGH I FAIL TO SEE THE SEAN CONNERY COMPARISON, I HAVE NOTICED HE HAS STARTED TO RESEMBLE OTHER THINGS, OR, MAYBE, THEY'VE STARTED TO RESEMBLE HIM...

PEOPLE ALWAYS SAY THAT THING ABOUT DOGS AND THEIR OWNERS, AND IT STARTED WITH THAT...

THEN THAT TORTOISE ON A TUPPERWARE MY MUM AND I SAW ON 'BRITAIN'S RANDIEST REPTILE'...

A JUSTIN BIEBER CD SINGLE IN SUE RYDER...

ALSO SEEN IN MANY CHARITY SHOPS, VARIOUS LPS BY MALE COUNTRY SINGERS...

DAVE DUDLEY
15 TRUCKIN' CLASSICS
T. HALL

ANOTHER POSTCARD FROM MY SISTER IN AUSTRALIA...

MONDAY AGAIN

THE UNBAKED COB LOAVES BEHIND HAZEL-CLAIRE IN THE BAKERY...

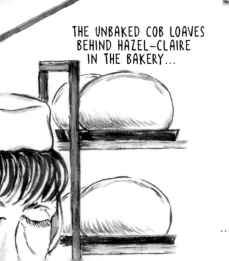

KEITH CROSSING THE STREET AT THE SAME TIME...

...AS A WOMAN COMING FROM PILATES CLASS.

THE TIME HE POINTED IN AT THE BUTCHER'S WINDOW, SAYING...

TONIGHT, I SHALL BE DINING...

...ON THOSE.

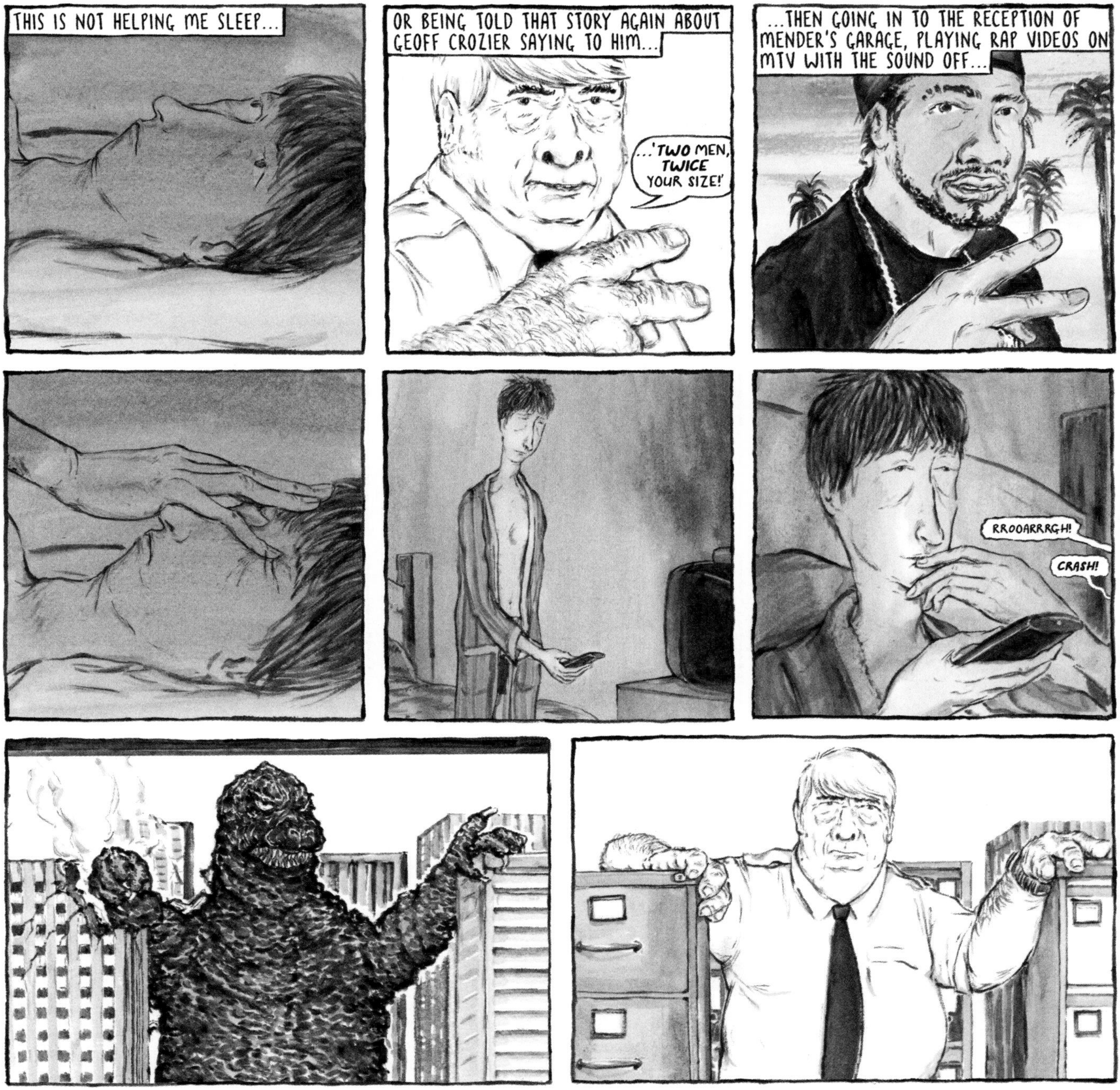
THIS IS NOT HELPING ME SLEEP...
OR BEING TOLD THAT STORY AGAIN ABOUT GEOFF CROZIER SAYING TO HIM...
...'TWO MEN, TWICE YOUR SIZE!'
...THEN GOING IN TO THE RECEPTION OF MENDER'S GARAGE, PLAYING RAP VIDEOS ON MTV WITH THE SOUND OFF...
RROOARRRGH!
CRASH!

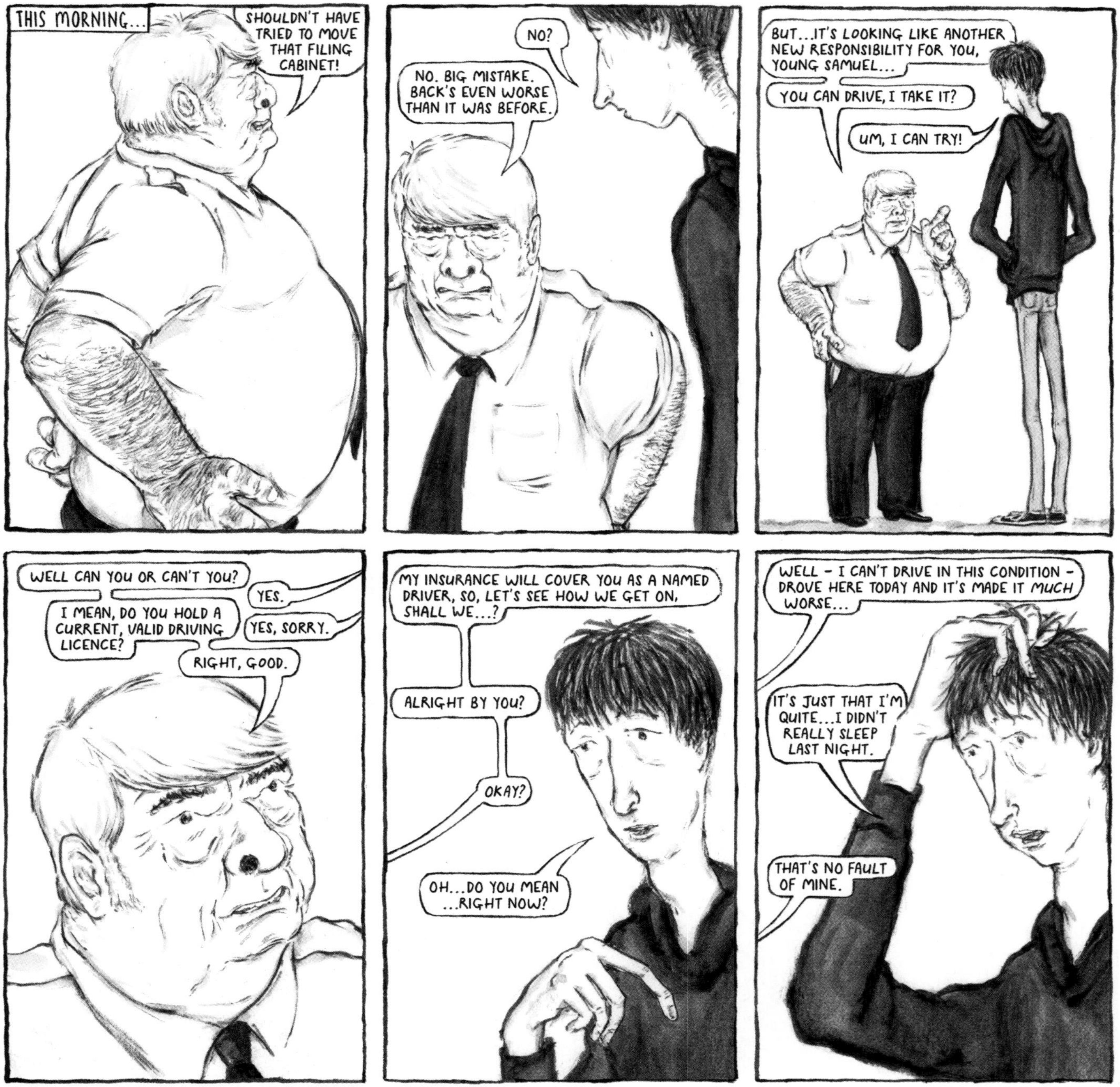
THIS MORNING...
SHOULDN'T HAVE TRIED TO MOVE THAT FILING CABINET!
NO?
NO. BIG MISTAKE. BACK'S EVEN WORSE THAN IT WAS BEFORE.
BUT...IT'S LOOKING LIKE ANOTHER NEW RESPONSIBILITY FOR YOU, YOUNG SAMUEL...
YOU CAN DRIVE, I TAKE IT?
UM, I CAN TRY!
WELL CAN YOU OR CAN'T YOU?
YES.
I MEAN, DO YOU HOLD A CURRENT, VALID DRIVING LICENCE?
YES, SORRY.
RIGHT, GOOD.
MY INSURANCE WILL COVER YOU AS A NAMED DRIVER, SO, LET'S SEE HOW WE GET ON, SHALL WE...?
ALRIGHT BY YOU?
OKAY?
OH...DO YOU MEAN ...RIGHT NOW?
WELL - I CAN'T DRIVE IN THIS CONDITION - DROVE HERE TODAY AND IT'S MADE IT MUCH WORSE...
IT'S JUST THAT I'M QUITE...I DIDN'T REALLY SLEEP LAST NIGHT.
THAT'S NO FAULT OF MINE.

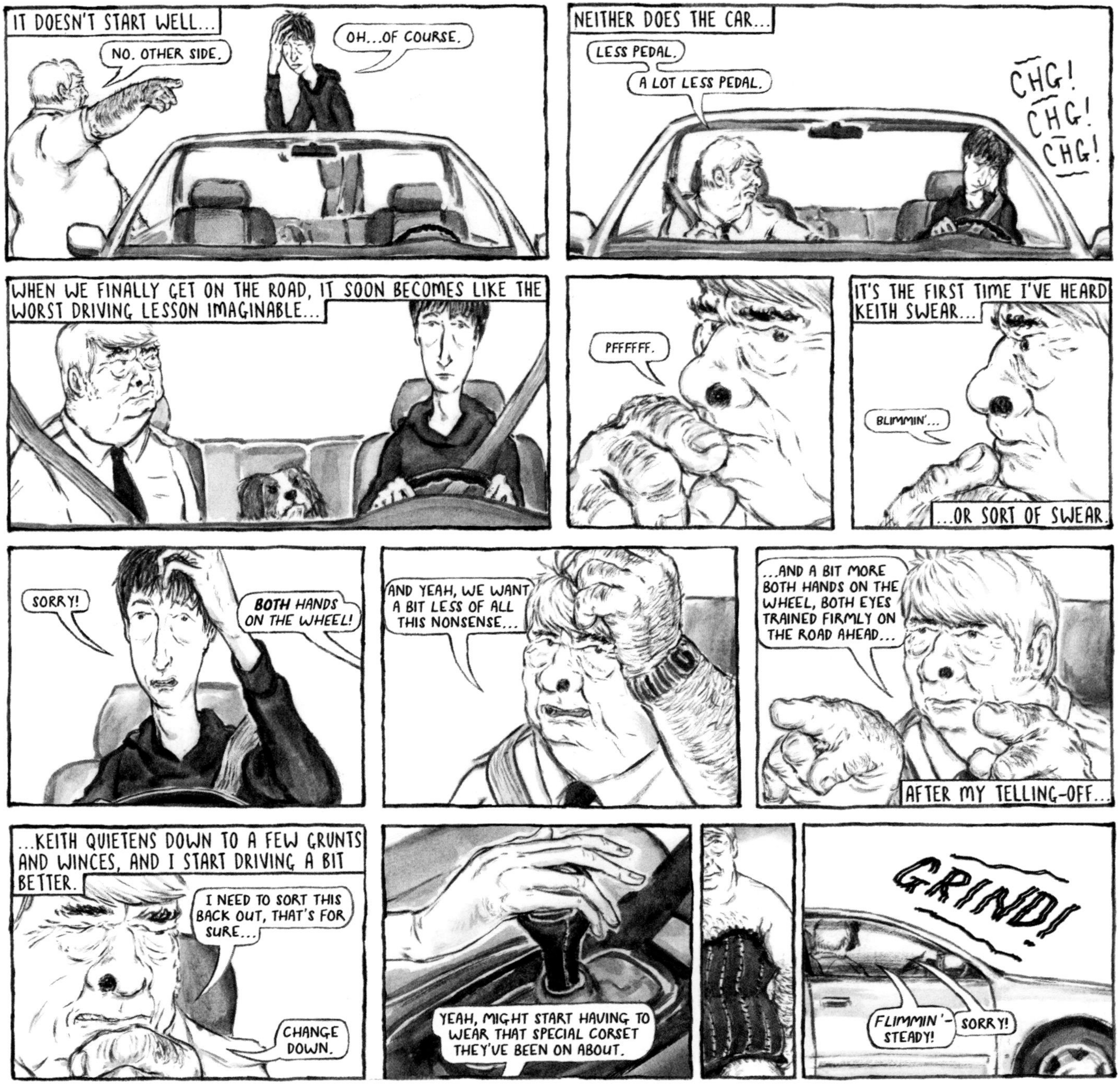
IT DOESN'T START WELL...
NO. OTHER SIDE.
OH...OF COURSE.
NEITHER DOES THE CAR...
LESS PEDAL.
A LOT LESS PEDAL.
CHG! CHG! CHG!
WHEN WE FINALLY GET ON THE ROAD, IT SOON BECOMES LIKE THE WORST DRIVING LESSON IMAGINABLE...
PFFFFFF.
IT'S THE FIRST TIME I'VE HEARD KEITH SWEAR...
BLIMMIN'...
...OR SORT OF SWEAR.
SORRY!
BOTH HANDS ON THE WHEEL!
AND YEAH, WE WANT A BIT LESS OF ALL THIS NONSENSE...
...AND A BIT MORE BOTH HANDS ON THE WHEEL, BOTH EYES TRAINED FIRMLY ON THE ROAD AHEAD...
AFTER MY TELLING-OFF...
...KEITH QUIETENS DOWN TO A FEW GRUNTS AND WINCES, AND I START DRIVING A BIT BETTER.
I NEED TO SORT THIS BACK OUT, THAT'S FOR SURE...
CHANGE DOWN.
YEAH, MIGHT START HAVING TO WEAR THAT SPECIAL CORSET THEY'VE BEEN ON ABOUT.
GRIND!
FLIMMIN'- STEADY!
SORRY!

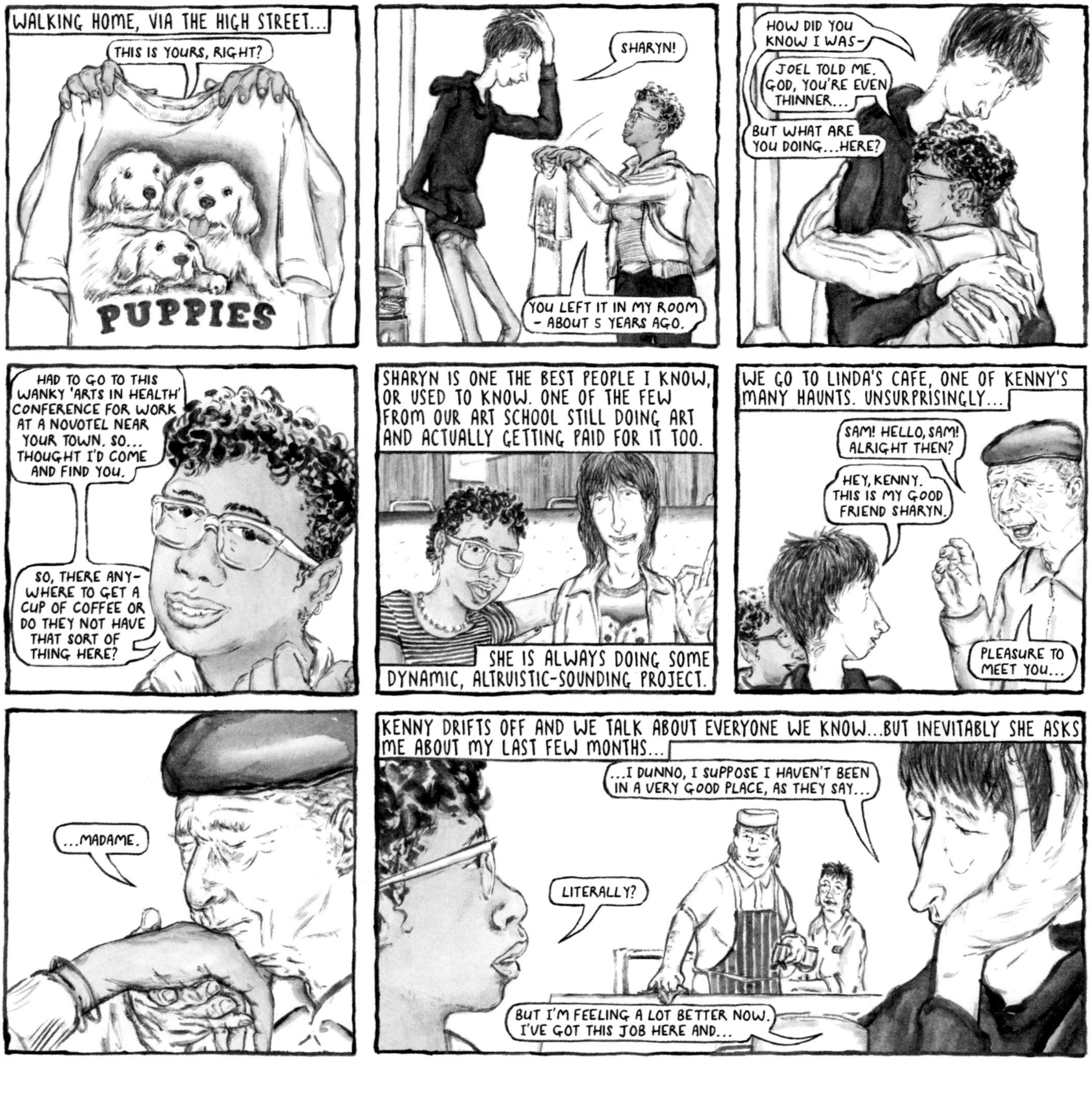
WALKING HOME, VIA THE HIGH STREET...
THIS IS YOURS, RIGHT?
PUPPIES
SHARYN!
YOU LEFT IT IN MY ROOM - ABOUT 5 YEARS AGO.
HOW DID YOU KNOW I WAS-
JOEL TOLD ME. GOD, YOU'RE EVEN THINNER...
BUT WHAT ARE YOU DOING...HERE?
HAD TO GO TO THIS WANKY 'ARTS IN HEALTH' CONFERENCE FOR WORK AT A NOVOTEL NEAR YOUR TOWN. SO... THOUGHT I'D COME AND FIND YOU.
SO, THERE ANYWHERE TO GET A CUP OF COFFEE OR DO THEY NOT HAVE THAT SORT OF THING HERE?
SHARYN IS ONE THE BEST PEOPLE I KNOW, OR USED TO KNOW. ONE OF THE FEW FROM OUR ART SCHOOL STILL DOING ART AND ACTUALLY GETTING PAID FOR IT TOO.
SHE IS ALWAYS DOING SOME DYNAMIC, ALTRUISTIC-SOUNDING PROJECT.
WE GO TO LINDA'S CAFE, ONE OF KENNY'S MANY HAUNTS. UNSURPRISINGLY...
SAM! HELLO, SAM! ALRIGHT THEN?
HEY, KENNY. THIS IS MY GOOD FRIEND SHARYN.
PLEASURE TO MEET YOU...
...MADAME.
KENNY DRIFTS OFF AND WE TALK ABOUT EVERYONE WE KNOW...BUT INEVITABLY SHE ASKS ME ABOUT MY LAST FEW MONTHS...
...I DUNNO, I SUPPOSE I HAVEN'T BEEN IN A VERY GOOD PLACE, AS THEY SAY...
LITERALLY?
BUT I'M FEELING A LOT BETTER NOW. I'VE GOT THIS JOB HERE AND...

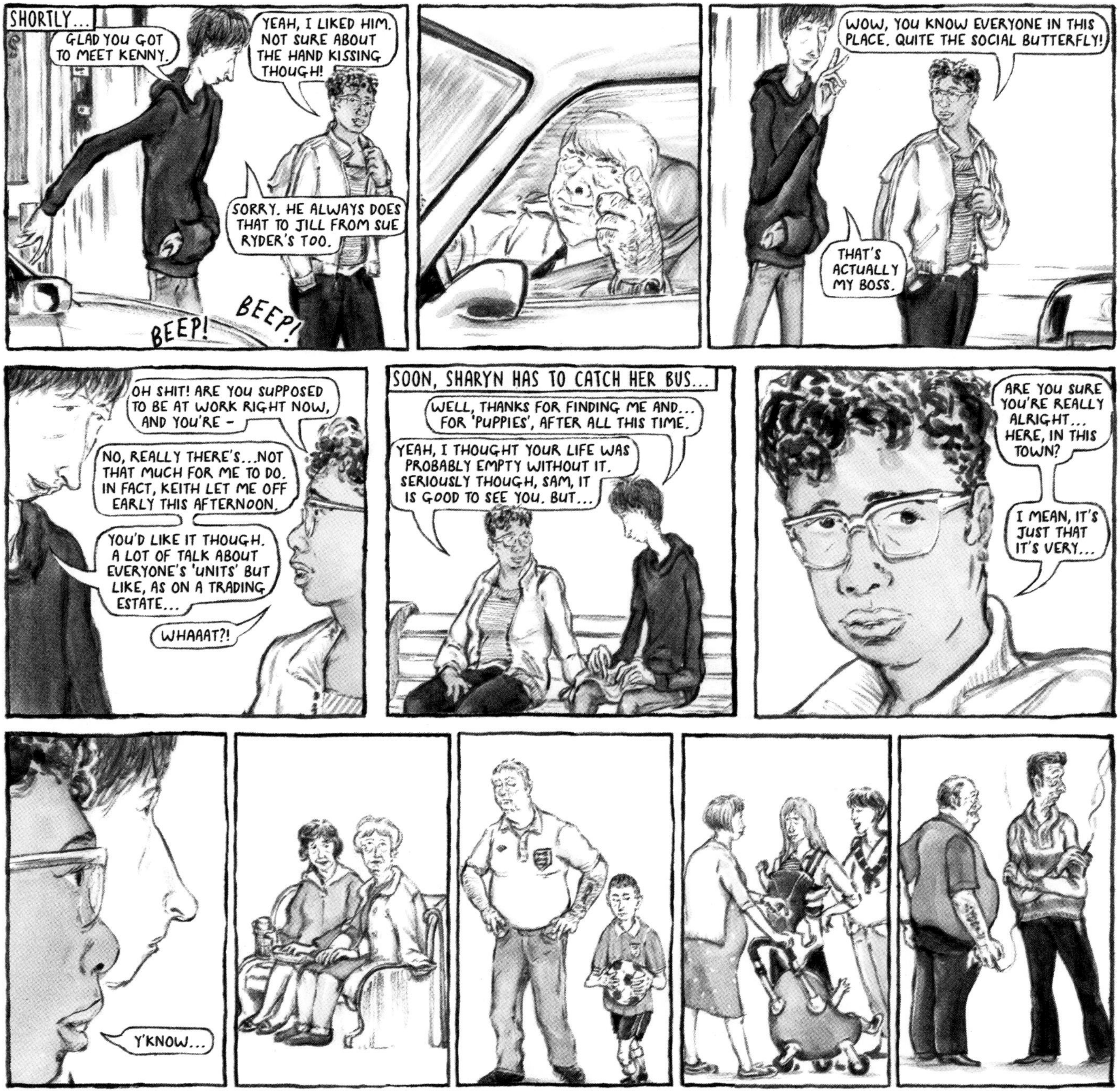
SHORTLY...
GLAD YOU GOT TO MEET KENNY.
YEAH, I LIKED HIM. NOT SURE ABOUT THE HAND KISSING THOUGH!
SORRY. HE ALWAYS DOES THAT TO JILL FROM SUE RYDER'S TOO.
BEEP!
BEEP!
WOW, YOU KNOW EVERYONE IN THIS PLACE. QUITE THE SOCIAL BUTTERFLY!
THAT'S ACTUALLY MY BOSS.
OH SHIT! ARE YOU SUPPOSED TO BE AT WORK RIGHT NOW, AND YOU'RE –
NO, REALLY THERE'S...NOT THAT MUCH FOR ME TO DO. IN FACT, KEITH LET ME OFF EARLY THIS AFTERNOON.
YOU'D LIKE IT THOUGH. A LOT OF TALK ABOUT EVERYONE'S 'UNITS' BUT LIKE, AS ON A TRADING ESTATE...
WHAAAT?!
SOON, SHARYN HAS TO CATCH HER BUS...
WELL, THANKS FOR FINDING ME AND... FOR 'PUPPIES', AFTER ALL THIS TIME.
YEAH, I THOUGHT YOUR LIFE WAS PROBABLY EMPTY WITHOUT IT. SERIOUSLY THOUGH, SAM, IT IS GOOD TO SEE YOU. BUT...
ARE YOU SURE YOU'RE REALLY ALRIGHT... HERE, IN THIS TOWN?
I MEAN, IT'S JUST THAT IT'S VERY...
Y'KNOW...

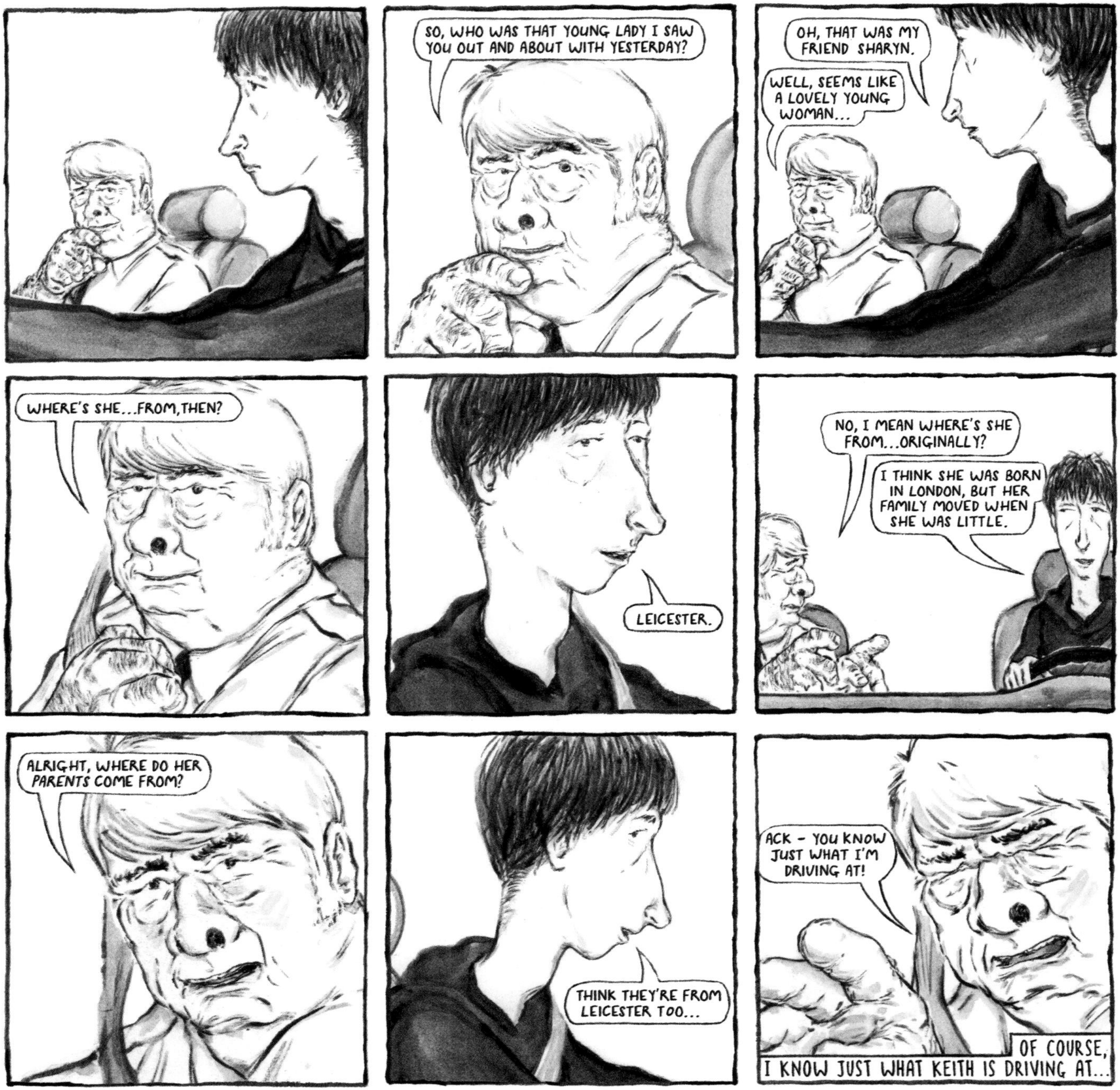
SO, WHO WAS THAT YOUNG LADY I SAW YOU OUT AND ABOUT WITH YESTERDAY?
OH, THAT WAS MY FRIEND SHARYN.
WELL, SEEMS LIKE A LOVELY YOUNG WOMAN...
WHERE'S SHE...FROM, THEN?
LEICESTER.
NO, I MEAN WHERE'S SHE FROM...ORIGINALLY?
I THINK SHE WAS BORN IN LONDON, BUT HER FAMILY MOVED WHEN SHE WAS LITTLE.
ALRIGHT, WHERE DO HER PARENTS COME FROM?
THINK THEY'RE FROM LEICESTER TOO...
ACK - YOU KNOW JUST WHAT I'M DRIVING AT!
OF COURSE, I KNOW JUST WHAT KEITH IS DRIVING AT...

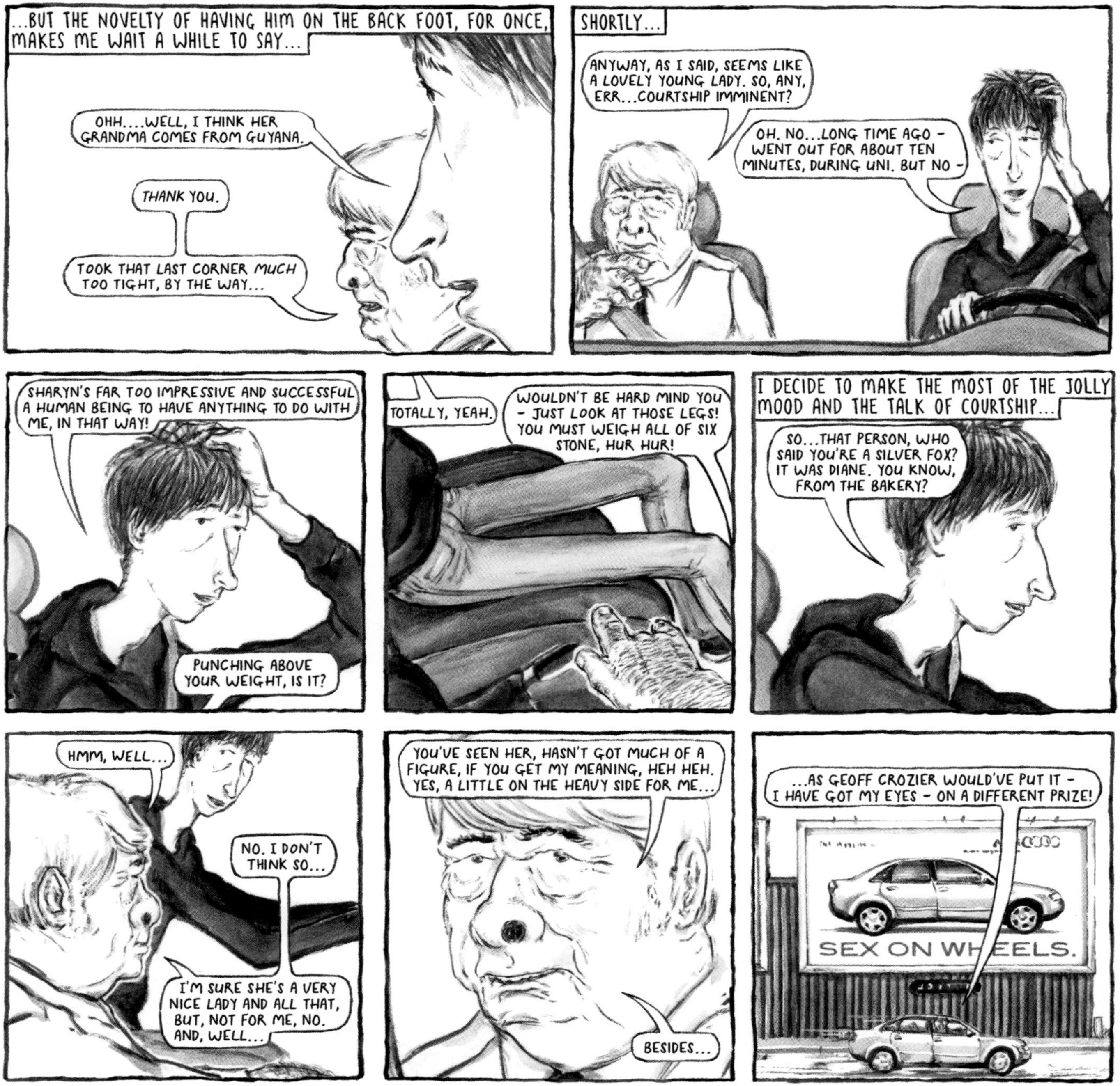
...BUT THE NOVELTY OF HAVING HIM ON THE BACK FOOT, FOR ONCE, MAKES ME WAIT A WHILE TO SAY...
OHH....WELL, I THINK HER GRANDMA COMES FROM GUYANA.
THANK YOU.
TOOK THAT LAST CORNER *MUCH* TOO TIGHT, BY THE WAY...
SHORTLY...
ANYWAY, AS I SAID, SEEMS LIKE A LOVELY YOUNG LADY. SO, ANY, ERR...COURTSHIP IMMINENT?
OH. NO...LONG TIME AGO - WENT OUT FOR ABOUT TEN MINUTES, DURING UNI. BUT NO -
SHARYN'S FAR TOO IMPRESSIVE AND SUCCESSFUL A HUMAN BEING TO HAVE ANYTHING TO DO WITH ME, IN THAT WAY!
PUNCHING ABOVE YOUR WEIGHT, IS IT?
TOTALLY, YEAH.
WOULDN'T BE HARD MIND YOU - JUST LOOK AT THOSE LEGS! YOU MUST WEIGH ALL OF SIX STONE, HUR HUR!
I DECIDE TO MAKE THE MOST OF THE JOLLY MOOD AND THE TALK OF COURTSHIP...
SO...THAT PERSON, WHO SAID YOU'RE A SILVER FOX? IT WAS DIANE. YOU KNOW, FROM THE BAKERY?
HMM, WELL...
NO. I DON'T THINK SO...
I'M SURE SHE'S A VERY NICE LADY AND ALL THAT, BUT, NOT FOR ME, NO. AND, WELL...
YOU'VE SEEN HER, HASN'T GOT MUCH OF A FIGURE, IF YOU GET MY MEANING, HEH HEH. YES, A LITTLE ON THE HEAVY SIDE FOR ME...
BESIDES...
...AS GEOFF CROZIER WOULD'VE PUT IT - I HAVE GOT MY EYES - ON A DIFFERENT PRIZE!
SEX ON WHEELS.

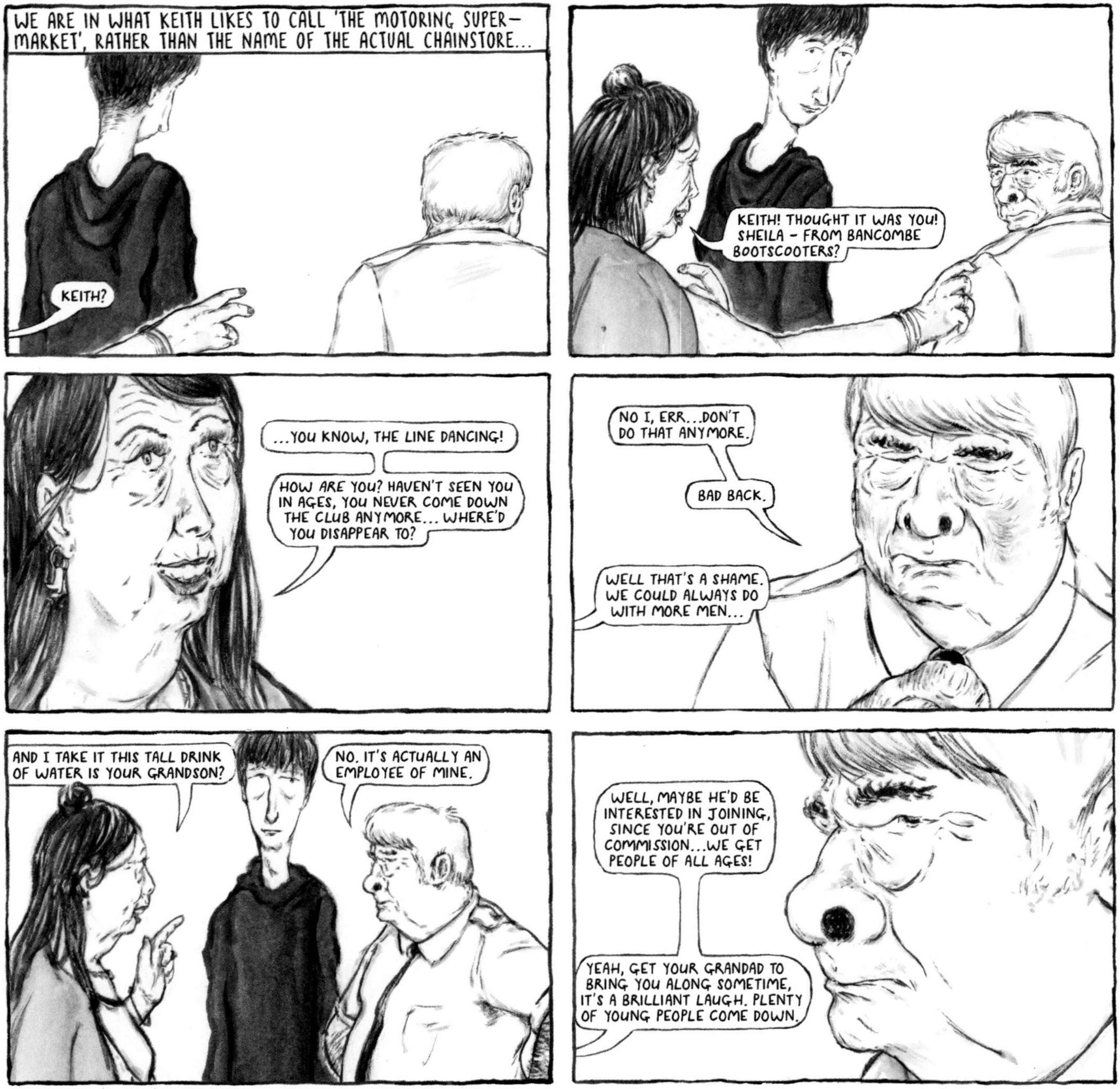
WE ARE IN WHAT KEITH LIKES TO CALL 'THE MOTORING SUPER-MARKET', RATHER THAN THE NAME OF THE ACTUAL CHAINSTORE...
KEITH?
KEITH! THOUGHT IT WAS YOU! SHEILA - FROM BANCOMBE BOOTSCOOTERS?
...YOU KNOW, THE LINE DANCING!
HOW ARE YOU? HAVEN'T SEEN YOU IN AGES, YOU NEVER COME DOWN THE CLUB ANYMORE... WHERE'D YOU DISAPPEAR TO?
NO I, ERR...DON'T DO THAT ANYMORE.
BAD BACK.
WELL THAT'S A SHAME. WE COULD ALWAYS DO WITH MORE MEN...
AND I TAKE IT THIS TALL DRINK OF WATER IS YOUR GRANDSON?
NO. IT'S ACTUALLY AN EMPLOYEE OF MINE.
WELL, MAYBE HE'D BE INTERESTED IN JOINING, SINCE YOU'RE OUT OF COMMISSION...WE GET PEOPLE OF ALL AGES!
YEAH, GET YOUR GRANDAD TO BRING YOU ALONG SOMETIME, IT'S A BRILLIANT LAUGH. PLENTY OF YOUNG PEOPLE COME DOWN.

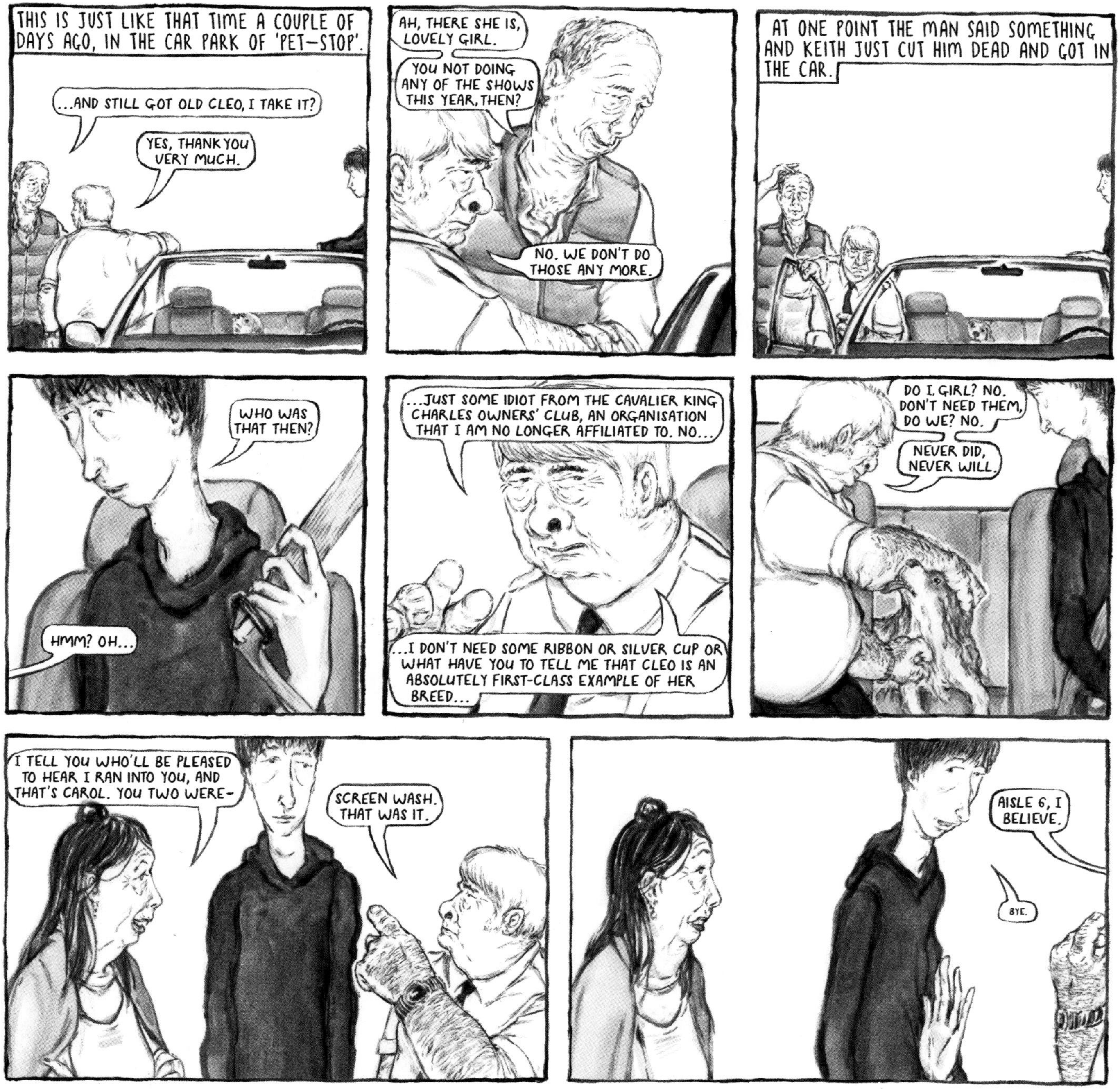
THIS IS JUST LIKE THAT TIME A COUPLE OF DAYS AGO, IN THE CAR PARK OF 'PET-STOP'.
...AND STILL GOT OLD CLEO, I TAKE IT?
YES, THANK YOU VERY MUCH.
AH, THERE SHE IS, LOVELY GIRL.
YOU NOT DOING ANY OF THE SHOWS THIS YEAR, THEN?
NO. WE DON'T DO THOSE ANY MORE.
AT ONE POINT THE MAN SAID SOMETHING AND KEITH JUST CUT HIM DEAD AND GOT IN THE CAR.
WHO WAS THAT THEN?
HMM? OH...
...JUST SOME IDIOT FROM THE CAVALIER KING CHARLES OWNERS' CLUB, AN ORGANISATION THAT I AM NO LONGER AFFILIATED TO. NO...
...I DON'T NEED SOME RIBBON OR SILVER CUP OR WHAT HAVE YOU TO TELL ME THAT CLEO IS AN ABSOLUTELY FIRST-CLASS EXAMPLE OF HER BREED...
DO I, GIRL? NO. DON'T NEED THEM, DO WE? NO.
NEVER DID, NEVER WILL.
I TELL YOU WHO'LL BE PLEASED TO HEAR I RAN INTO YOU, AND THAT'S CAROL. YOU TWO WERE-
SCREEN WASH. THAT WAS IT.
AISLE 6, I BELIEVE.
BYE.

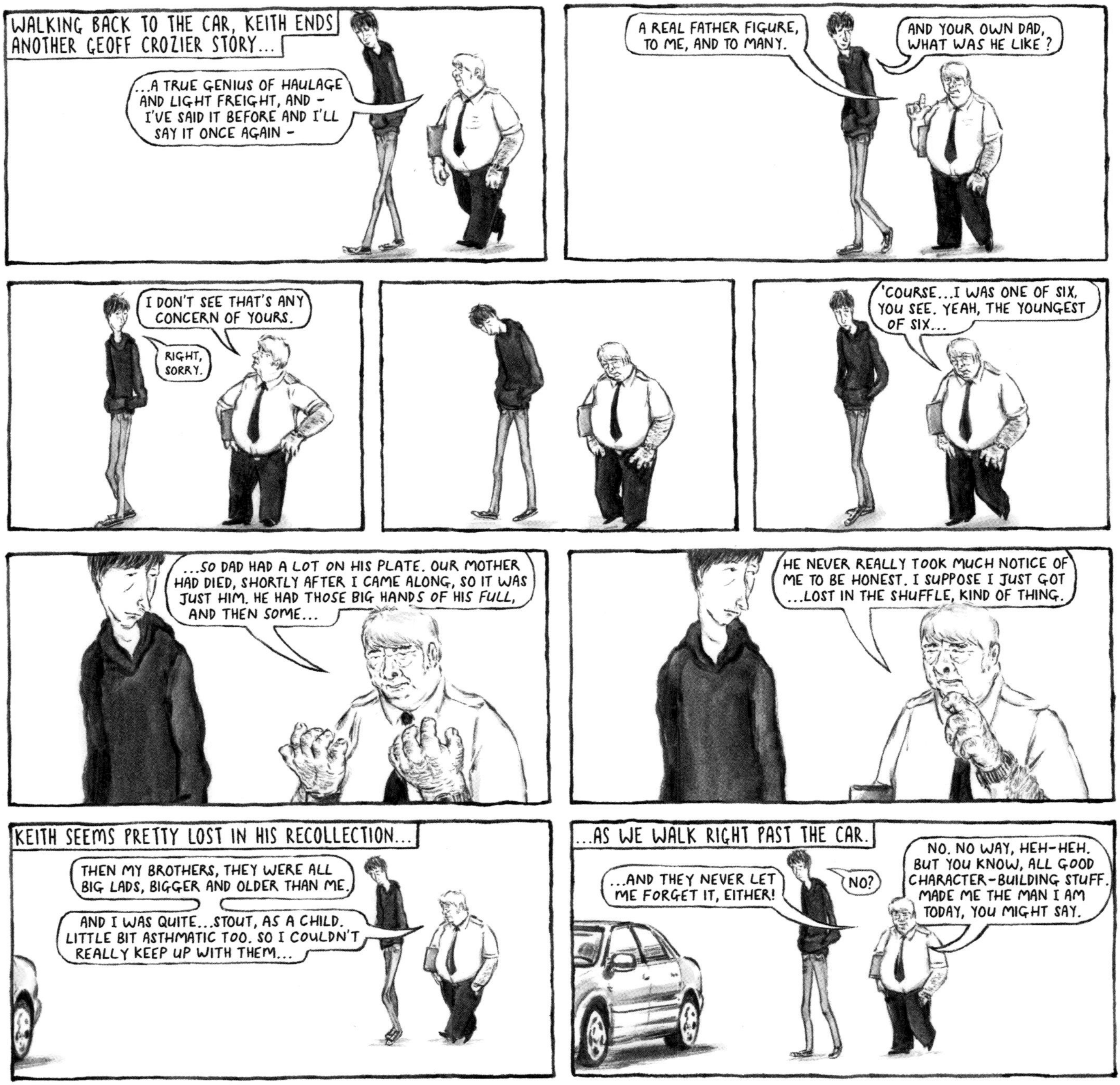
WALKING BACK TO THE CAR, KEITH ENDS ANOTHER GEOFF CROZIER STORY...
...A TRUE GENIUS OF HAULAGE AND LIGHT FREIGHT, AND - I'VE SAID IT BEFORE AND I'LL SAY IT ONCE AGAIN -
A REAL FATHER FIGURE, TO ME, AND TO MANY.
AND YOUR OWN DAD, WHAT WAS HE LIKE?
I DON'T SEE THAT'S ANY CONCERN OF YOURS.
RIGHT, SORRY.
'COURSE...I WAS ONE OF SIX, YOU SEE. YEAH, THE YOUNGEST OF SIX...
...SO DAD HAD A LOT ON HIS PLATE. OUR MOTHER HAD DIED, SHORTLY AFTER I CAME ALONG, SO IT WAS JUST HIM. HE HAD THOSE BIG HANDS OF HIS FULL, AND THEN SOME...
HE NEVER REALLY TOOK MUCH NOTICE OF ME TO BE HONEST. I SUPPOSE I JUST GOT ...LOST IN THE SHUFFLE, KIND OF THING.
KEITH SEEMS PRETTY LOST IN HIS RECOLLECTION...
THEN MY BROTHERS, THEY WERE ALL BIG LADS, BIGGER AND OLDER THAN ME.
AND I WAS QUITE...STOUT, AS A CHILD. LITTLE BIT ASTHMATIC TOO. SO I COULDN'T REALLY KEEP UP WITH THEM...
...AS WE WALK RIGHT PAST THE CAR.
...AND THEY NEVER LET ME FORGET IT, EITHER!
NO?
NO. NO WAY, HEH-HEH. BUT YOU KNOW, ALL GOOD CHARACTER-BUILDING STUFF. MADE ME THE MAN I AM TODAY, YOU MIGHT SAY.

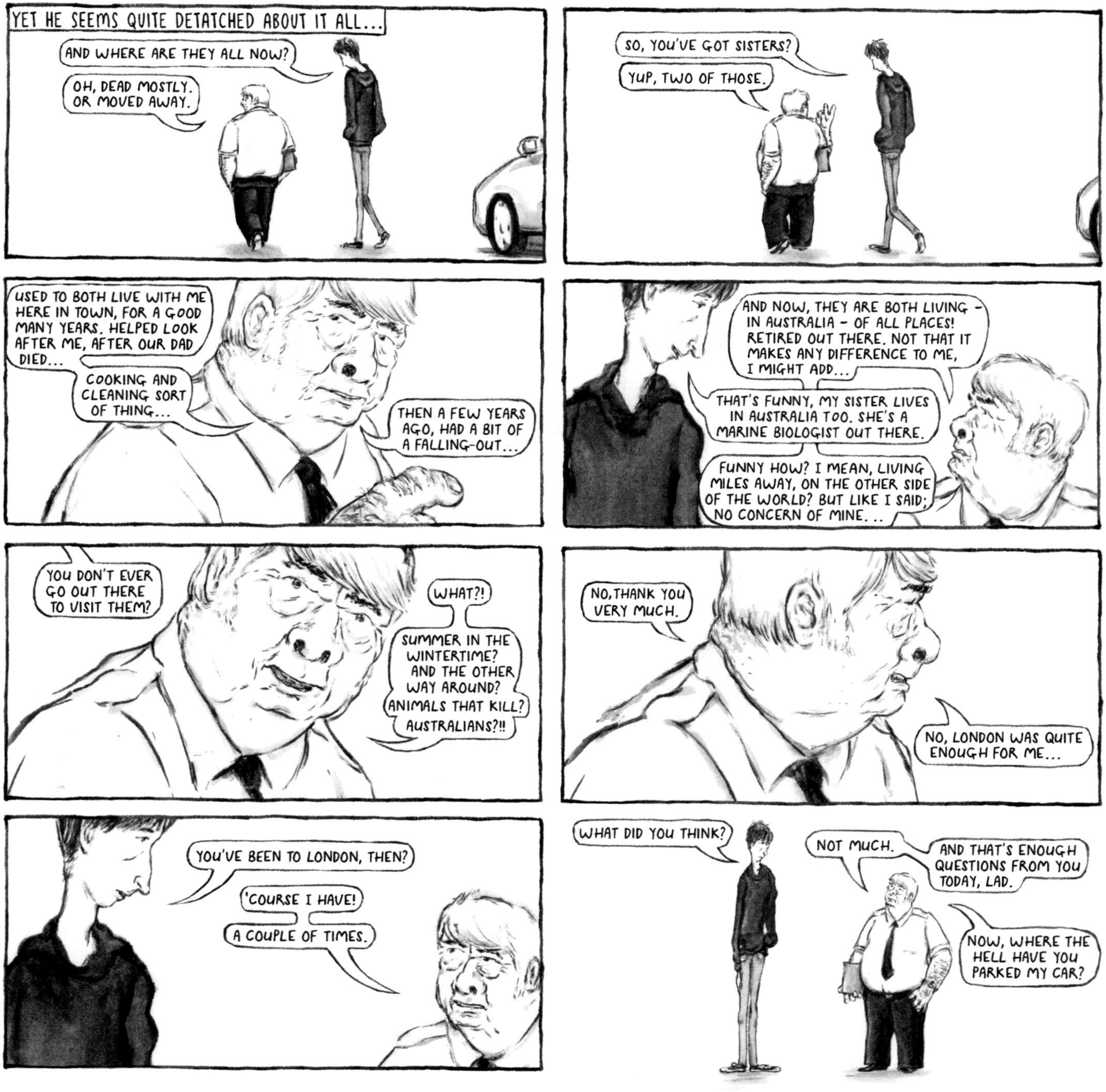
YET HE SEEMS QUITE DETATCHED ABOUT IT ALL...
AND WHERE ARE THEY ALL NOW?
OH, DEAD MOSTLY. OR MOVED AWAY.
SO, YOU'VE GOT SISTERS?
YUP, TWO OF THOSE.
USED TO BOTH LIVE WITH ME HERE IN TOWN, FOR A GOOD MANY YEARS. HELPED LOOK AFTER ME, AFTER OUR DAD DIED...
COOKING AND CLEANING SORT OF THING...
THEN A FEW YEARS AGO, HAD A BIT OF A FALLING-OUT...
AND NOW, THEY ARE BOTH LIVING - IN AUSTRALIA - OF ALL PLACES! RETIRED OUT THERE. NOT THAT IT MAKES ANY DIFFERENCE TO ME, I MIGHT ADD...
THAT'S FUNNY, MY SISTER LIVES IN AUSTRALIA TOO. SHE'S A MARINE BIOLOGIST OUT THERE.
FUNNY HOW? I MEAN, LIVING MILES AWAY, ON THE OTHER SIDE OF THE WORLD? BUT LIKE I SAID; NO CONCERN OF MINE...
YOU DON'T EVER GO OUT THERE TO VISIT THEM?
WHAT?!
SUMMER IN THE WINTERTIME? AND THE OTHER WAY AROUND? ANIMALS THAT KILL? AUSTRALIANS?!!
NO, THANK YOU VERY MUCH.
NO, LONDON WAS QUITE ENOUGH FOR ME...
YOU'VE BEEN TO LONDON, THEN?
'COURSE I HAVE!
A COUPLE OF TIMES.
WHAT DID YOU THINK?
NOT MUCH.
AND THAT'S ENOUGH QUESTIONS FROM YOU TODAY, LAD.
NOW, WHERE THE HELL HAVE YOU PARKED MY CAR?

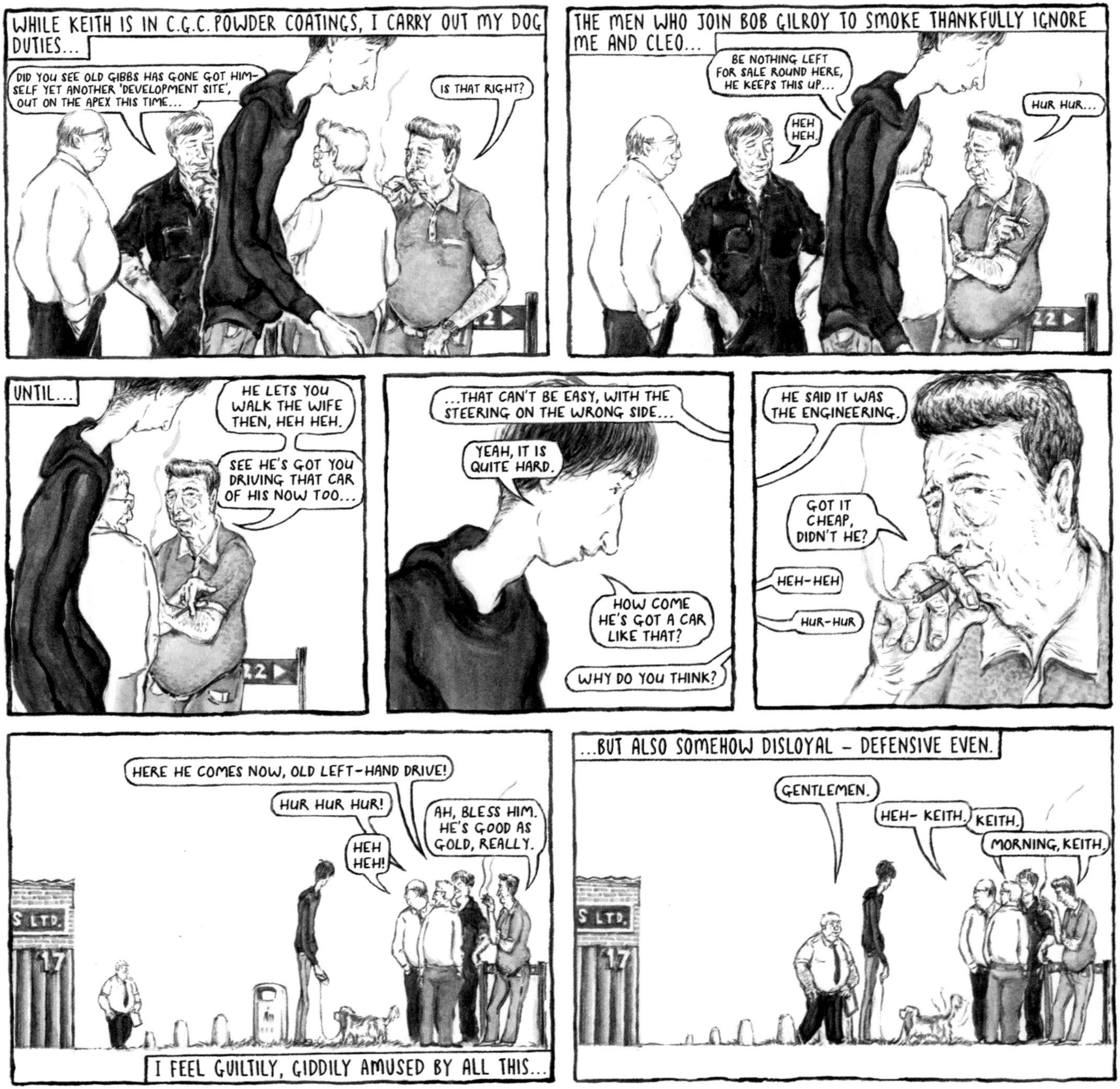

WHILE KEITH IS IN C.G.C. POWDER COATINGS, I CARRY OUT MY DOG DUTIES...
DID YOU SEE OLD GIBBS HAS GONE GOT HIMSELF YET ANOTHER 'DEVELOPMENT SITE', OUT ON THE APEX THIS TIME...
IS THAT RIGHT?
22
THE MEN WHO JOIN BOB GILROY TO SMOKE THANKFULLY IGNORE ME AND CLEO...
BE NOTHING LEFT FOR SALE ROUND HERE, HE KEEPS THIS UP...
HEH HEH.
HUR HUR...
22
UNTIL...
HE LETS YOU WALK THE WIFE THEN, HEH HEH.
SEE HE'S GOT YOU DRIVING THAT CAR OF HIS NOW TOO...
22
...THAT CAN'T BE EASY, WITH THE STEERING ON THE WRONG SIDE...
YEAH, IT IS QUITE HARD.
HOW COME HE'S GOT A CAR LIKE THAT?
WHY DO YOU THINK?
HE SAID IT WAS THE ENGINEERING.
GOT IT CHEAP, DIDN'T HE?
HEH-HEH
HUR-HUR
HERE HE COMES NOW, OLD LEFT-HAND DRIVE!
HUR HUR HUR!
HEH HEH!
AH, BLESS HIM. HE'S GOOD AS GOLD, REALLY.
S LTD.
17
I FEEL GUILTILY, GIDDILY AMUSED BY ALL THIS...
...BUT ALSO SOMEHOW DISLOYAL – DEFENSIVE EVEN.
GENTLEMEN.
HEH- KEITH.
KEITH.
MORNING, KEITH.
S LTD.
17

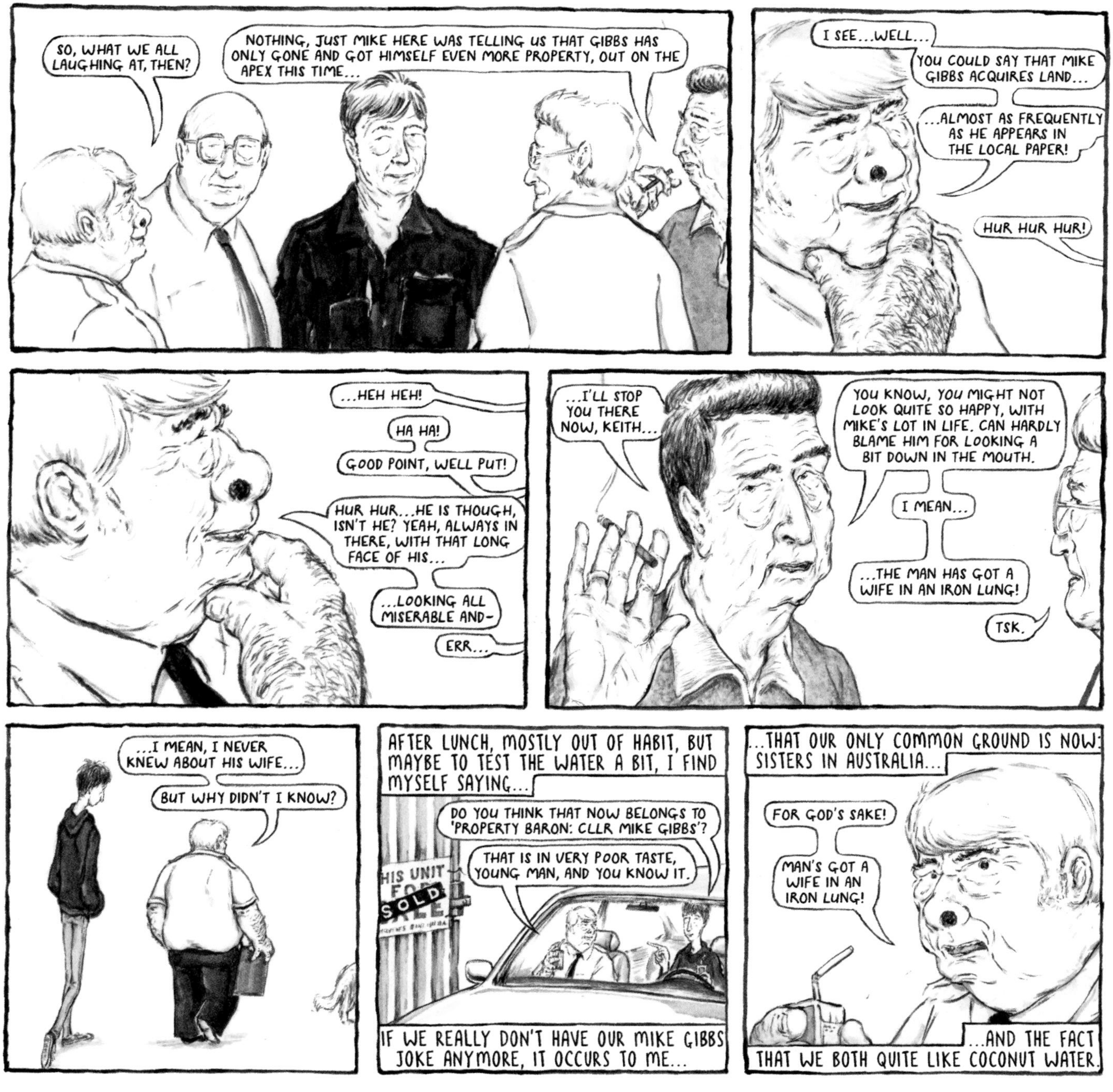
SO, WHAT WE ALL LAUGHING AT, THEN?
NOTHING, JUST MIKE HERE WAS TELLING US THAT GIBBS HAS ONLY GONE AND GOT HIMSELF EVEN MORE PROPERTY, OUT ON THE APEX THIS TIME...
I SEE...WELL...
YOU COULD SAY THAT MIKE GIBBS ACQUIRES LAND...
...ALMOST AS FREQUENTLY AS HE APPEARS IN THE LOCAL PAPER!
HUR HUR HUR!
...HEH HEH!
HA HA!
GOOD POINT, WELL PUT!
HUR HUR...HE IS THOUGH, ISN'T HE? YEAH, ALWAYS IN THERE, WITH THAT LONG FACE OF HIS...
...LOOKING ALL MISERABLE AND-
ERR...
...I'LL STOP YOU THERE NOW, KEITH...
YOU KNOW, YOU MIGHT NOT LOOK QUITE SO HAPPY, WITH MIKE'S LOT IN LIFE. CAN HARDLY BLAME HIM FOR LOOKING A BIT DOWN IN THE MOUTH.
I MEAN...
...THE MAN HAS GOT A WIFE IN AN IRON LUNG!
TSK.
...I MEAN, I NEVER KNEW ABOUT HIS WIFE...
BUT WHY DIDN'T I KNOW?
AFTER LUNCH, MOSTLY OUT OF HABIT, BUT MAYBE TO TEST THE WATER A BIT, I FIND MYSELF SAYING...
DO YOU THINK THAT NOW BELONGS TO 'PROPERTY BARON: CLLR MIKE GIBBS'?
THAT IS IN VERY POOR TASTE, YOUNG MAN, AND YOU KNOW IT.
HIS UNIT FOR SALE
SOLD
IF WE REALLY DON'T HAVE OUR MIKE GIBBS JOKE ANYMORE, IT OCCURS TO ME...
...THAT OUR ONLY COMMON GROUND IS NOW: SISTERS IN AUSTRALIA...
FOR GOD'S SAKE!
MAN'S GOT A WIFE IN AN IRON LUNG!
...AND THE FACT THAT WE BOTH QUITE LIKE COCONUT WATER.

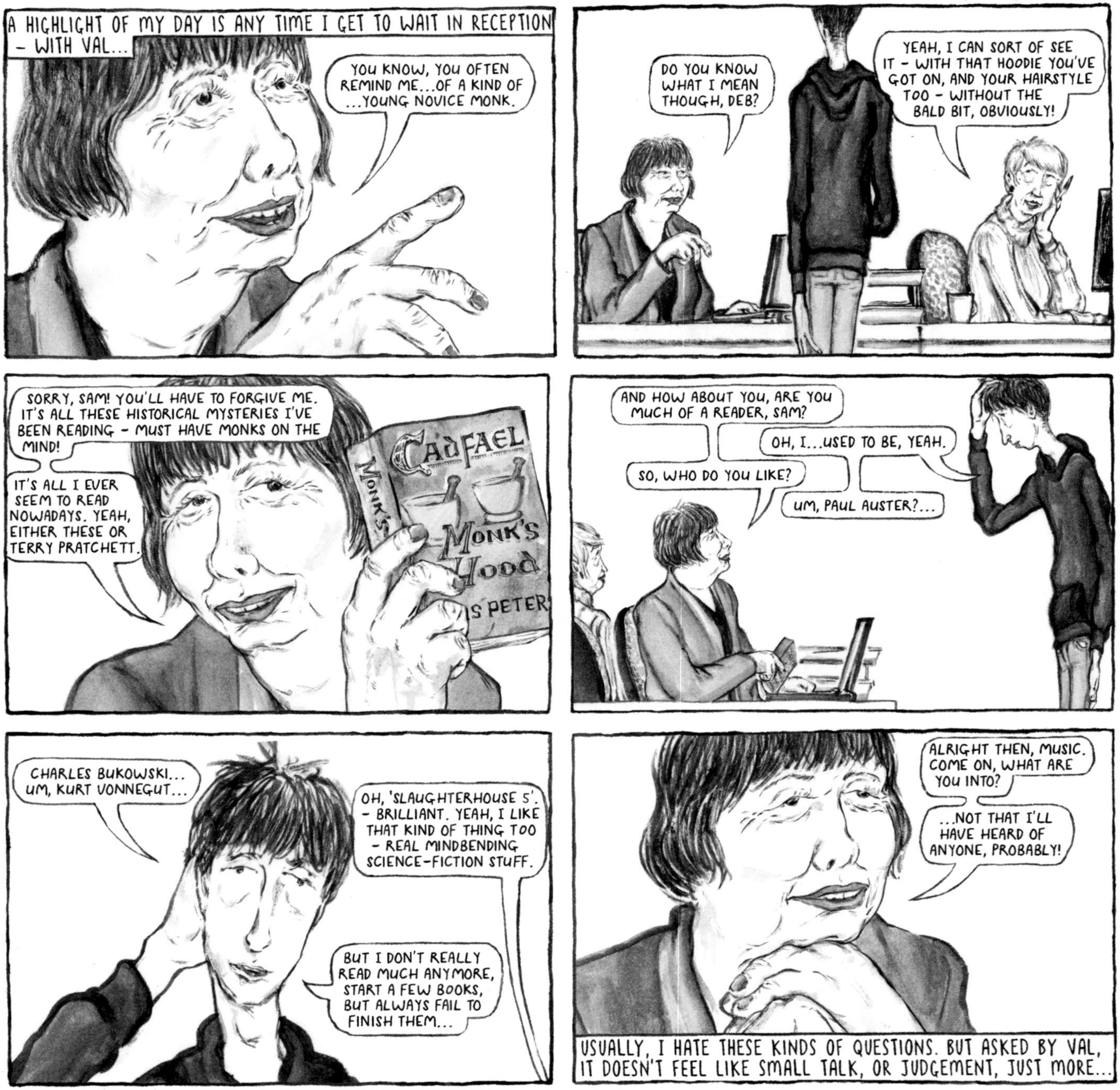
A HIGHLIGHT OF MY DAY IS ANY TIME I GET TO WAIT IN RECEPTION – WITH VAL...
YOU KNOW, YOU OFTEN REMIND ME...OF A KIND OF ...YOUNG NOVICE MONK.
DO YOU KNOW WHAT I MEAN THOUGH, DEB?
YEAH, I CAN SORT OF SEE IT – WITH THAT HOODIE YOU'VE GOT ON, AND YOUR HAIRSTYLE TOO – WITHOUT THE BALD BIT, OBVIOUSLY!
SORRY, SAM! YOU'LL HAVE TO FORGIVE ME. IT'S ALL THESE HISTORICAL MYSTERIES I'VE BEEN READING – MUST HAVE MONKS ON THE MIND!
IT'S ALL I EVER SEEM TO READ NOWADAYS. YEAH, EITHER THESE OR TERRY PRATCHETT.
CADFAEL
MONK'S HOOD
AND HOW ABOUT YOU, ARE YOU MUCH OF A READER, SAM?
OH, I...USED TO BE, YEAH.
SO, WHO DO YOU LIKE?
UM, PAUL AUSTER?...
CHARLES BUKOWSKI... UM, KURT VONNEGUT...
OH, 'SLAUGHTERHOUSE 5'. – BRILLIANT. YEAH, I LIKE THAT KIND OF THING TOO – REAL MINDBENDING SCIENCE-FICTION STUFF.
BUT I DON'T REALLY READ MUCH ANYMORE, START A FEW BOOKS, BUT ALWAYS FAIL TO FINISH THEM...
ALRIGHT THEN, MUSIC. COME ON, WHAT ARE YOU INTO?
...NOT THAT I'LL HAVE HEARD OF ANYONE, PROBABLY!
USUALLY, I HATE THESE KINDS OF QUESTIONS. BUT ASKED BY VAL, IT DOESN'T FEEL LIKE SMALL TALK, OR JUDGEMENT, JUST MORE...

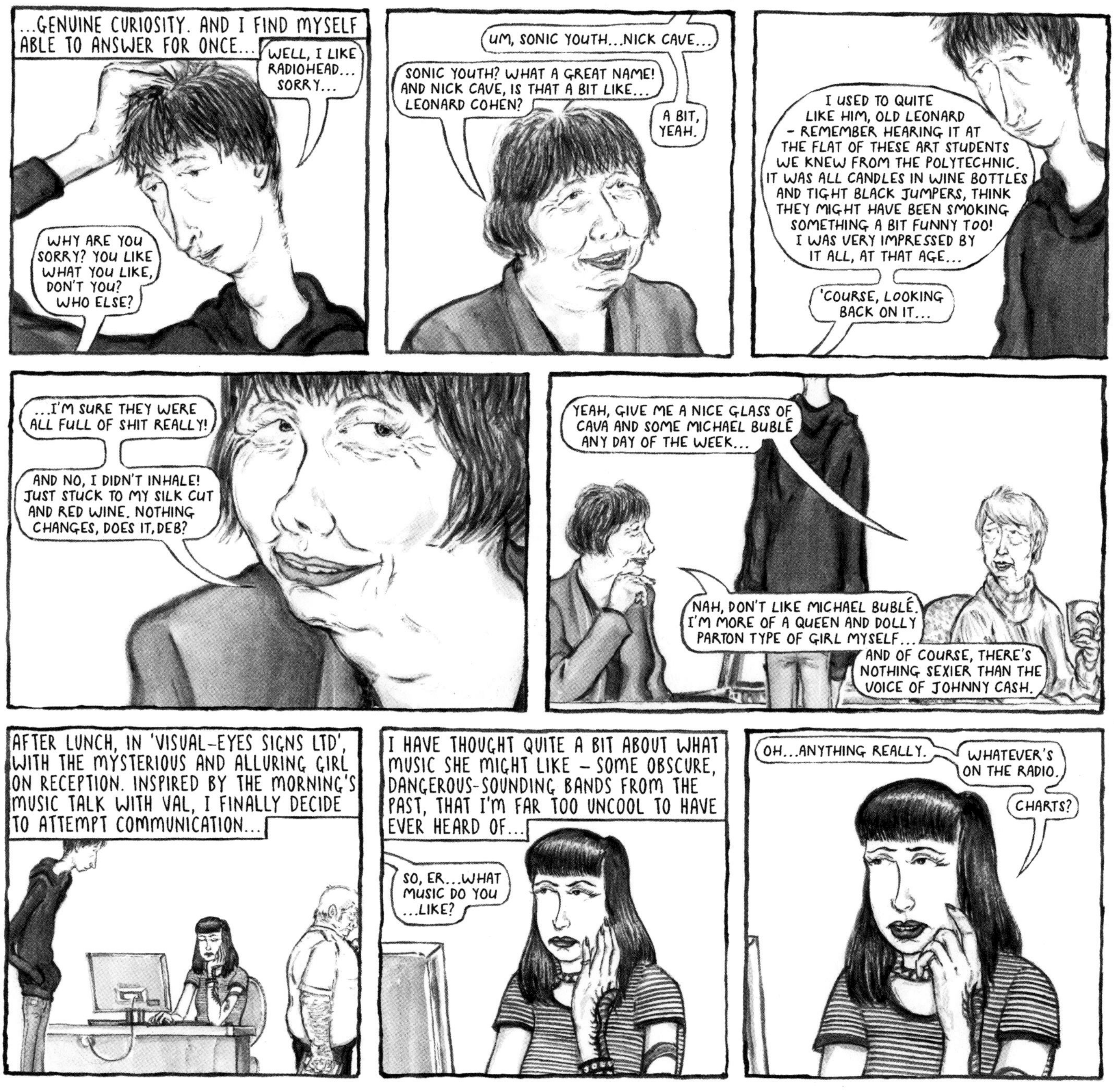
...GENUINE CURIOSITY. AND I FIND MYSELF ABLE TO ANSWER FOR ONCE...
WELL, I LIKE RADIOHEAD... SORRY...
WHY ARE YOU SORRY? YOU LIKE WHAT YOU LIKE, DON'T YOU? WHO ELSE?
UM, SONIC YOUTH...NICK CAVE...
SONIC YOUTH? WHAT A GREAT NAME! AND NICK CAVE, IS THAT A BIT LIKE... LEONARD COHEN?
A BIT, YEAH.
I USED TO QUITE LIKE HIM, OLD LEONARD - REMEMBER HEARING IT AT THE FLAT OF THESE ART STUDENTS WE KNEW FROM THE POLYTECHNIC. IT WAS ALL CANDLES IN WINE BOTTLES AND TIGHT BLACK JUMPERS, THINK THEY MIGHT HAVE BEEN SMOKING SOMETHING A BIT FUNNY TOO! I WAS VERY IMPRESSED BY IT ALL, AT THAT AGE...
'COURSE, LOOKING BACK ON IT...
...I'M SURE THEY WERE ALL FULL OF SHIT REALLY!
AND NO, I DIDN'T INHALE! JUST STUCK TO MY SILK CUT AND RED WINE. NOTHING CHANGES, DOES IT, DEB?
YEAH, GIVE ME A NICE GLASS OF CAVA AND SOME MICHAEL BUBLÉ ANY DAY OF THE WEEK...
NAH, DON'T LIKE MICHAEL BUBLÉ. I'M MORE OF A QUEEN AND DOLLY PARTON TYPE OF GIRL MYSELF...
AND OF COURSE, THERE'S NOTHING SEXIER THAN THE VOICE OF JOHNNY CASH.
AFTER LUNCH, IN 'VISUAL-EYES SIGNS LTD', WITH THE MYSTERIOUS AND ALLURING GIRL ON RECEPTION. INSPIRED BY THE MORNING'S MUSIC TALK WITH VAL, I FINALLY DECIDE TO ATTEMPT COMMUNICATION...
I HAVE THOUGHT QUITE A BIT ABOUT WHAT MUSIC SHE MIGHT LIKE - SOME OBSCURE, DANGEROUS-SOUNDING BANDS FROM THE PAST, THAT I'M FAR TOO UNCOOL TO HAVE EVER HEARD OF...
SO, ER...WHAT MUSIC DO YOU ...LIKE?
OH...ANYTHING REALLY.
WHATEVER'S ON THE RADIO.
CHARTS?

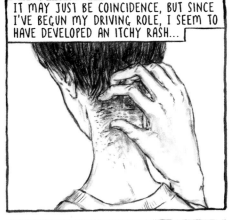

IT MAY JUST BE COINCIDENCE, BUT SINCE I'VE BEGUN MY DRIVING ROLE, I SEEM TO HAVE DEVELOPED AN ITCHY RASH...

ANOTHER EFFECT OF THE DRIVING IS THAT I NOTICE I'M LOOKING FORWARD TO WEEK-ENDS MORE.

WITH MUM AND RICHARD IN FRANCE FOR 2 WEEKS, I WRITE A LONG LIST OF MY PLANS FOR TODAY, TO MAKE CONSTRUCTIVE USE OF THIS PRECIOUS TIME OFF ALONE.

I RESOLVE...TO READ AT LEAST ONE OF MY SEVERAL LIBRARY BOOKS.

...TO WRITE SHARYN AN ACTUAL LETTER, ON PAPER.

...TO NOT GO ON THE INTERNET AT ALL.

...TO NOT THINK ABOUT THE PAST TOO MUCH.

BUT I END UP GOING THROUGH A DRAWER IN MY OLD ROOM, FINDING THE MANY VIDEO GAME DEVICES OF MY YOUTH...

...THEN USING MY ADMITTEDLY MEAGRE WAGES TO GO AND BUY BATTERIES FOR THEM.

-BIKE RIDE?!

I SHOULD AT LEAST TRY AND DO ONE THING ON MY LIST.

BUT THE ONLY BIKE I CAN FIND WITH 2 SERVICEABLE TYRES IS MY SISTER'S BMX FROM WHEN SHE WAS 12...

DESPITE HAVING BEEN WITH HIM ALL WEEK, I STILL FIND MYSELF BIKING TOWARDS KEITH'S ROAD. I HADN'T NOTICED...

LEFTHAM DRIVE

...HOW IT SOUNDS LIKE HIS FRIENDS' SECRET NAME FOR HIM.

AND THERE HE IS, IN THE LIVING ROOM-CUM-NERVE CENTRE, JUST ...STANDING.

I WATCH HIM THERE FOR A GOOD WHILE, AND HE BARELY MOVES.

I SUPPOSE I TOO HAVE DONE MY FAIR SHARE OF JUST STANDING IN THE MIDDLE OF A ROOM, DOING NOTHING...

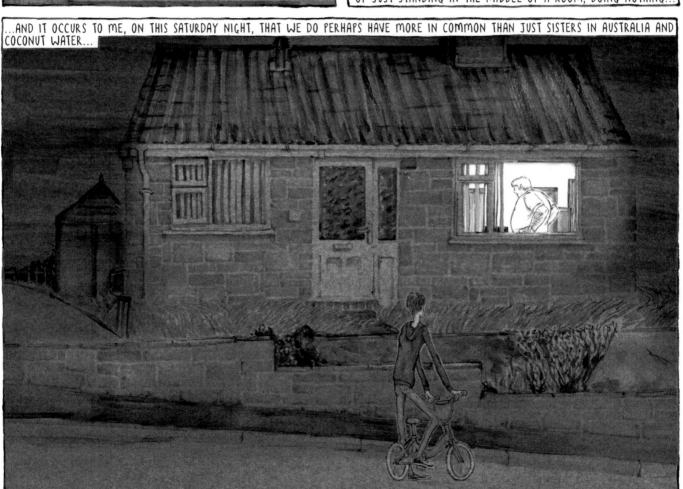

...AND IT OCCURS TO ME, ON THIS SATURDAY NIGHT, THAT WE DO PERHAPS HAVE MORE IN COMMON THAN JUST SISTERS IN AUSTRALIA AND COCONUT WATER...

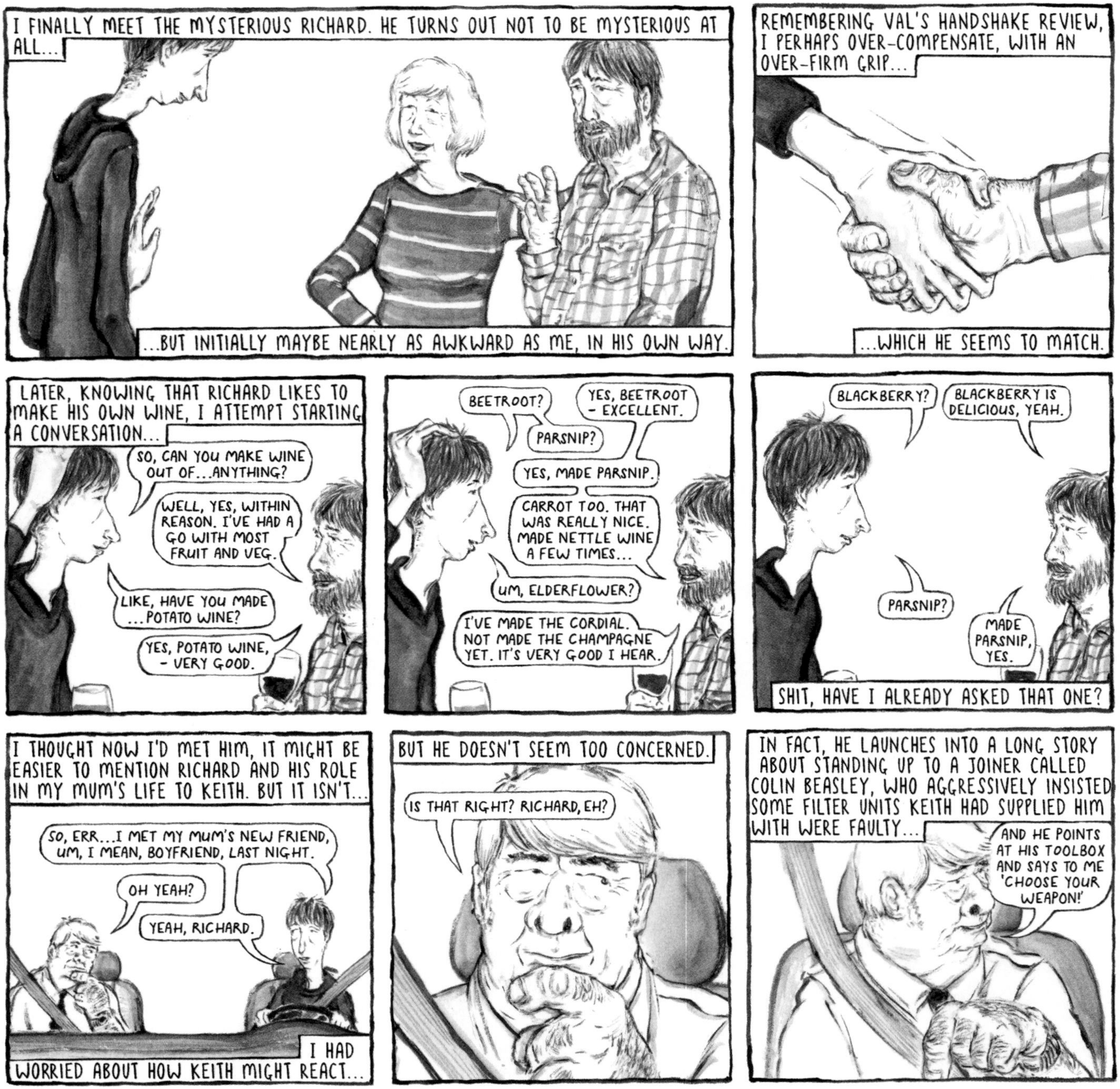

I FINALLY MEET THE MYSTERIOUS RICHARD. HE TURNS OUT NOT TO BE MYSTERIOUS AT ALL...
...BUT INITIALLY MAYBE NEARLY AS AWKWARD AS ME, IN HIS OWN WAY.
REMEMBERING VAL'S HANDSHAKE REVIEW, I PERHAPS OVER-COMPENSATE, WITH AN OVER-FIRM GRIP...
...WHICH HE SEEMS TO MATCH.
LATER, KNOWING THAT RICHARD LIKES TO MAKE HIS OWN WINE, I ATTEMPT STARTING A CONVERSATION...
SO, CAN YOU MAKE WINE OUT OF...ANYTHING?
WELL, YES, WITHIN REASON. I'VE HAD A GO WITH MOST FRUIT AND VEG.
LIKE, HAVE YOU MADE ...POTATO WINE?
YES, POTATO WINE, - VERY GOOD.
BEETROOT?
YES, BEETROOT - EXCELLENT.
PARSNIP?
YES, MADE PARSNIP.
CARROT TOO. THAT WAS REALLY NICE. MADE NETTLE WINE A FEW TIMES...
UM, ELDERFLOWER?
I'VE MADE THE CORDIAL. NOT MADE THE CHAMPAGNE YET. IT'S VERY GOOD I HEAR.
BLACKBERRY?
BLACKBERRY IS DELICIOUS, YEAH.
PARSNIP?
MADE PARSNIP, YES.
SHIT, HAVE I ALREADY ASKED THAT ONE?
I THOUGHT NOW I'D MET HIM, IT MIGHT BE EASIER TO MENTION RICHARD AND HIS ROLE IN MY MUM'S LIFE TO KEITH. BUT IT ISN'T...
SO, ERR...I MET MY MUM'S NEW FRIEND, UM, I MEAN, BOYFRIEND, LAST NIGHT.
OH YEAH?
YEAH, RICHARD.
I HAD WORRIED ABOUT HOW KEITH MIGHT REACT...
BUT HE DOESN'T SEEM TOO CONCERNED.
IS THAT RIGHT? RICHARD, EH?
IN FACT, HE LAUNCHES INTO A LONG STORY ABOUT STANDING UP TO A JOINER CALLED COLIN BEASLEY, WHO AGGRESSIVELY INSISTED SOME FILTER UNITS KEITH HAD SUPPLIED HIM WITH WERE FAULTY...
AND HE POINTS AT HIS TOOLBOX AND SAYS TO ME 'CHOOSE YOUR WEAPON!'

WOW, WHAT'D YOU DO?

I JUST STOOD THERE WITH MY ARMS FOLDED. CALM AS A CUCUMBER.

SO YEAH, I DO LIKE A BIT OF A CHALLENGE.

IS HE TALKING ABOUT MY MUM? IF SHE IS INDEED 'THE PRIZE' KEITH HAS HIS EYES ON. HE NEVER SEEMS VERY PROACTIVE IN TRYING TO SEE HER, OR EVEN ASKING AFTER HER. I WONDER ABOUT HIS PREVIOUS ROMANTIC CAMPAIGNS, WHEN THE WOMAN FROM LINEDANCING MENTIONED 'CAROL', OR WHATEVER THAT DOG CLUB MAN HAD SAID?

6-8 →

SCREEN WASH!

25 OF

AND WAS IT KEITH THEY WERE TALKING ABOUT AT THAT LAST BI-MONTHLY CARVERY?

WELL, DON''T FORGET, HE HAS MISSED HIS MOMENT BEFORE, OLD ROMEO...

YEAH, SPENT TOO LONG SITTING ON HIS HANDS!

NO NO NO...MAYBE HE'S JUST WAITING FOR HIS TIME ...TO STRIKE! HUR HUR...

HA HA!

MUCH LIKE... THE COBRA!

HUR HUR!

YEAH, THAT WAS COLIN BEASLEY - A RIGHT NUTJOB, AS THEY LIKE TO SAY NOWADAYS.

HA HA! 'NUT-JOB' THAT'S—

AH - NOW I'LL STOP YOU THERE, YOUNG MAN. DON'T THINK THAT THERE ISN'T A JOKE ABOUT MY NAME THAT I'VE NOT HEARD MANY TIMES BEFORE. I'VE HAD THEM ALL, AND THEN SOME!

YEAH...NUTJOB... NUTCASE...HARD NUT TO CRACK...

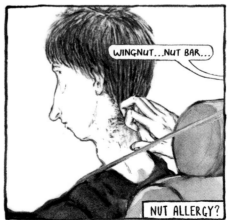

WINGNUT...NUT BAR...

NUT ALLERGY?

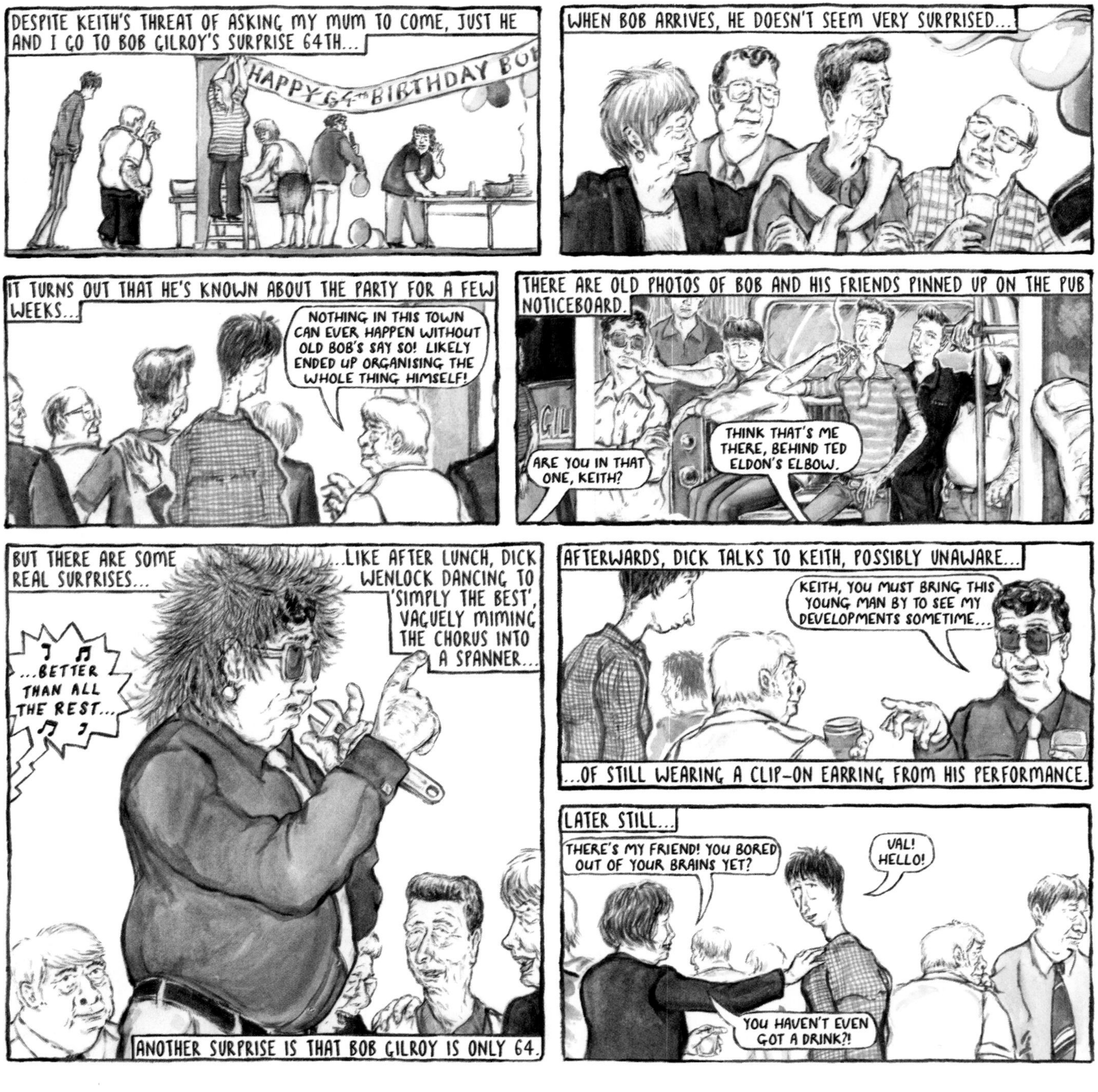
DESPITE KEITH'S THREAT OF ASKING MY MUM TO COME, JUST HE AND I GO TO BOB GILROY'S SURPRISE 64TH...
HAPPY 64TH BIRTHDAY BO
WHEN BOB ARRIVES, HE DOESN'T SEEM VERY SURPRISED...
IT TURNS OUT THAT HE'S KNOWN ABOUT THE PARTY FOR A FEW WEEKS...
NOTHING IN THIS TOWN CAN EVER HAPPEN WITHOUT OLD BOB'S SAY SO! LIKELY ENDED UP ORGANISING THE WHOLE THING HIMSELF!
THERE ARE OLD PHOTOS OF BOB AND HIS FRIENDS PINNED UP ON THE PUB NOTICEBOARD.
ARE YOU IN THAT ONE, KEITH?
THINK THAT'S ME THERE, BEHIND TED ELDON'S ELBOW.
BUT THERE ARE SOME REAL SURPRISES...
...LIKE AFTER LUNCH, DICK WENLOCK DANCING TO 'SIMPLY THE BEST', VAGUELY MIMING THE CHORUS INTO A SPANNER...
...BETTER THAN ALL THE REST...
ANOTHER SURPRISE IS THAT BOB GILROY IS ONLY 64.
AFTERWARDS, DICK TALKS TO KEITH, POSSIBLY UNAWARE...
KEITH, YOU MUST BRING THIS YOUNG MAN BY TO SEE MY DEVELOPMENTS SOMETIME...
...OF STILL WEARING A CLIP-ON EARRING FROM HIS PERFORMANCE.
LATER STILL...
THERE'S MY FRIEND! YOU BORED OUT OF YOUR BRAINS YET?
VAL! HELLO!
YOU HAVEN'T EVEN GOT A DRINK?!

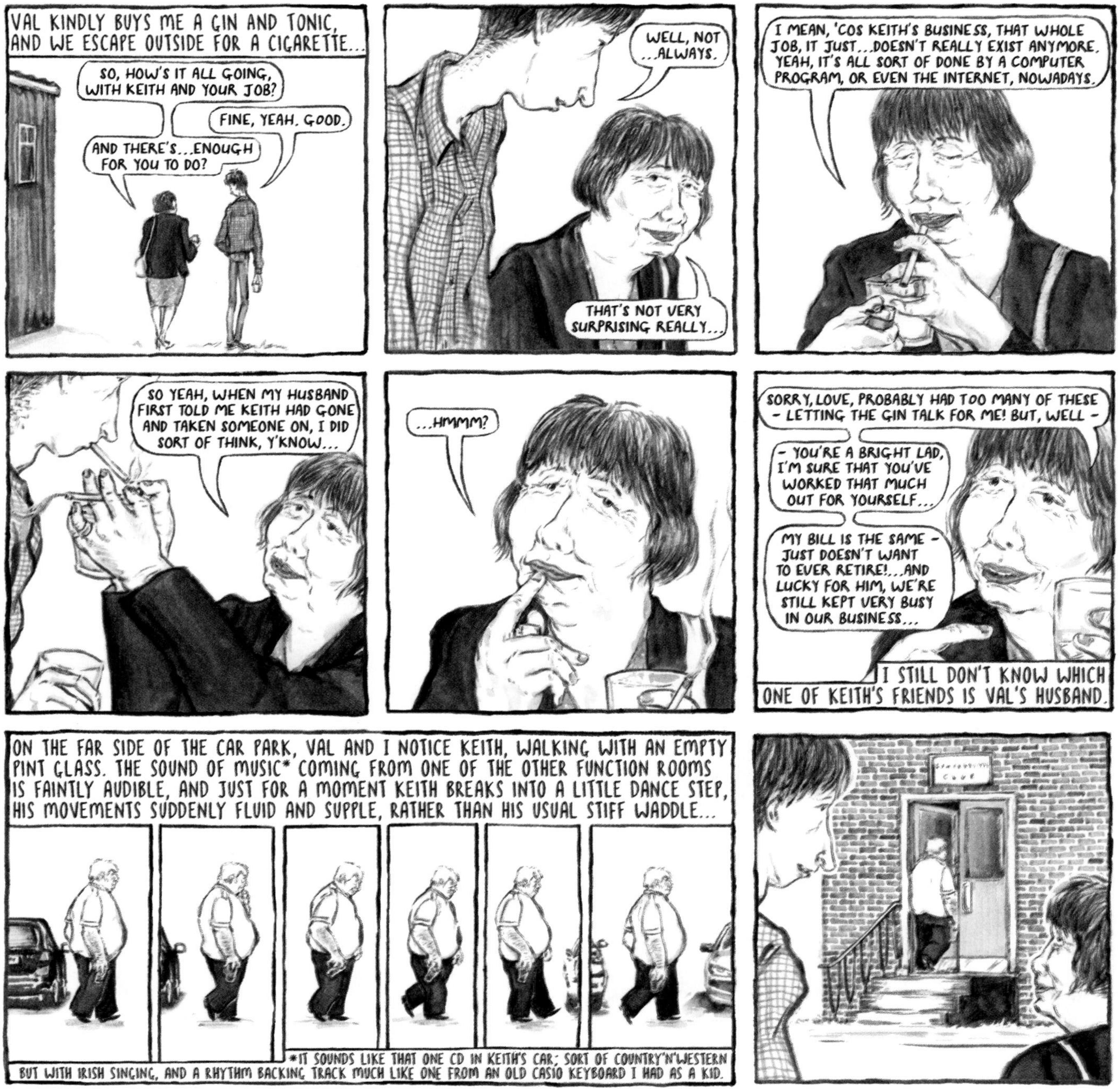
VAL KINDLY BUYS ME A GIN AND TONIC, AND WE ESCAPE OUTSIDE FOR A CIGARETTE...
SO, HOW'S IT ALL GOING, WITH KEITH AND YOUR JOB?
FINE, YEAH. GOOD.
AND THERE'S...ENOUGH FOR YOU TO DO?
WELL, NOT ...ALWAYS.
THAT'S NOT VERY SURPRISING REALLY...
I MEAN, 'COS KEITH'S BUSINESS, THAT WHOLE JOB, IT JUST...DOESN'T REALLY EXIST ANYMORE. YEAH, IT'S ALL SORT OF DONE BY A COMPUTER PROGRAM, OR EVEN THE INTERNET, NOWADAYS.
SO YEAH, WHEN MY HUSBAND FIRST TOLD ME KEITH HAD GONE AND TAKEN SOMEONE ON, I DID SORT OF THINK, Y'KNOW...
...HMMM?
SORRY, LOVE, PROBABLY HAD TOO MANY OF THESE - LETTING THE GIN TALK FOR ME! BUT, WELL -
- YOU'RE A BRIGHT LAD, I'M SURE THAT YOU'VE WORKED THAT MUCH OUT FOR YOURSELF...
MY BILL IS THE SAME - JUST DOESN'T WANT TO EVER RETIRE!...AND LUCKY FOR HIM, WE'RE STILL KEPT VERY BUSY IN OUR BUSINESS...
I STILL DON'T KNOW WHICH ONE OF KEITH'S FRIENDS IS VAL'S HUSBAND.
ON THE FAR SIDE OF THE CAR PARK, VAL AND I NOTICE KEITH, WALKING WITH AN EMPTY PINT GLASS. THE SOUND OF MUSIC* COMING FROM ONE OF THE OTHER FUNCTION ROOMS IS FAINTLY AUDIBLE, AND JUST FOR A MOMENT KEITH BREAKS INTO A LITTLE DANCE STEP, HIS MOVEMENTS SUDDENLY FLUID AND SUPPLE, RATHER THAN HIS USUAL STIFF WADDLE...
*IT SOUNDS LIKE THAT ONE CD IN KEITH'S CAR; SORT OF COUNTRY'N'WESTERN BUT WITH IRISH SINGING, AND A RHYTHM BACKING TRACK MUCH LIKE ONE FROM AN OLD CASIO KEYBOARD I HAD AS A KID.

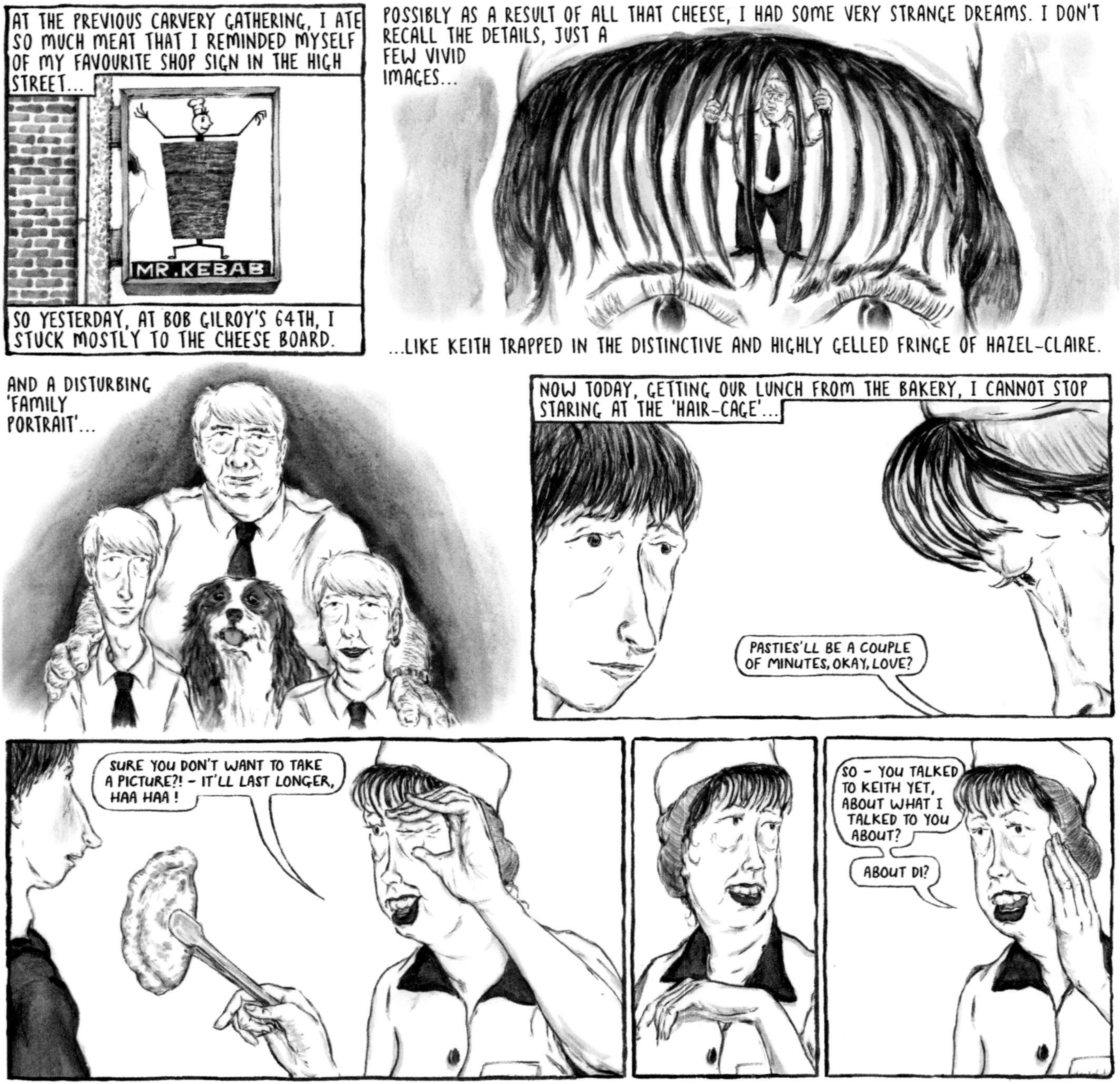
AT THE PREVIOUS CARVERY GATHERING, I ATE SO MUCH MEAT THAT I REMINDED MYSELF OF MY FAVOURITE SHOP SIGN IN THE HIGH STREET...
MR.KEBAB
SO YESTERDAY, AT BOB GILROY'S 64TH, I STUCK MOSTLY TO THE CHEESE BOARD.
POSSIBLY AS A RESULT OF ALL THAT CHEESE, I HAD SOME VERY STRANGE DREAMS. I DON'T RECALL THE DETAILS, JUST A FEW VIVID IMAGES...
...LIKE KEITH TRAPPED IN THE DISTINCTIVE AND HIGHLY GELLED FRINGE OF HAZEL-CLAIRE.
AND A DISTURBING 'FAMILY PORTRAIT'...
NOW TODAY, GETTING OUR LUNCH FROM THE BAKERY, I CANNOT STOP STARING AT THE 'HAIR-CAGE'...
PASTIES'LL BE A COUPLE OF MINUTES, OKAY, LOVE?
SURE YOU DON'T WANT TO TAKE A PICTURE?! – IT'LL LAST LONGER, HAA HAA !
SO – YOU TALKED TO KEITH YET, ABOUT WHAT I TALKED TO YOU ABOUT?
ABOUT DI?

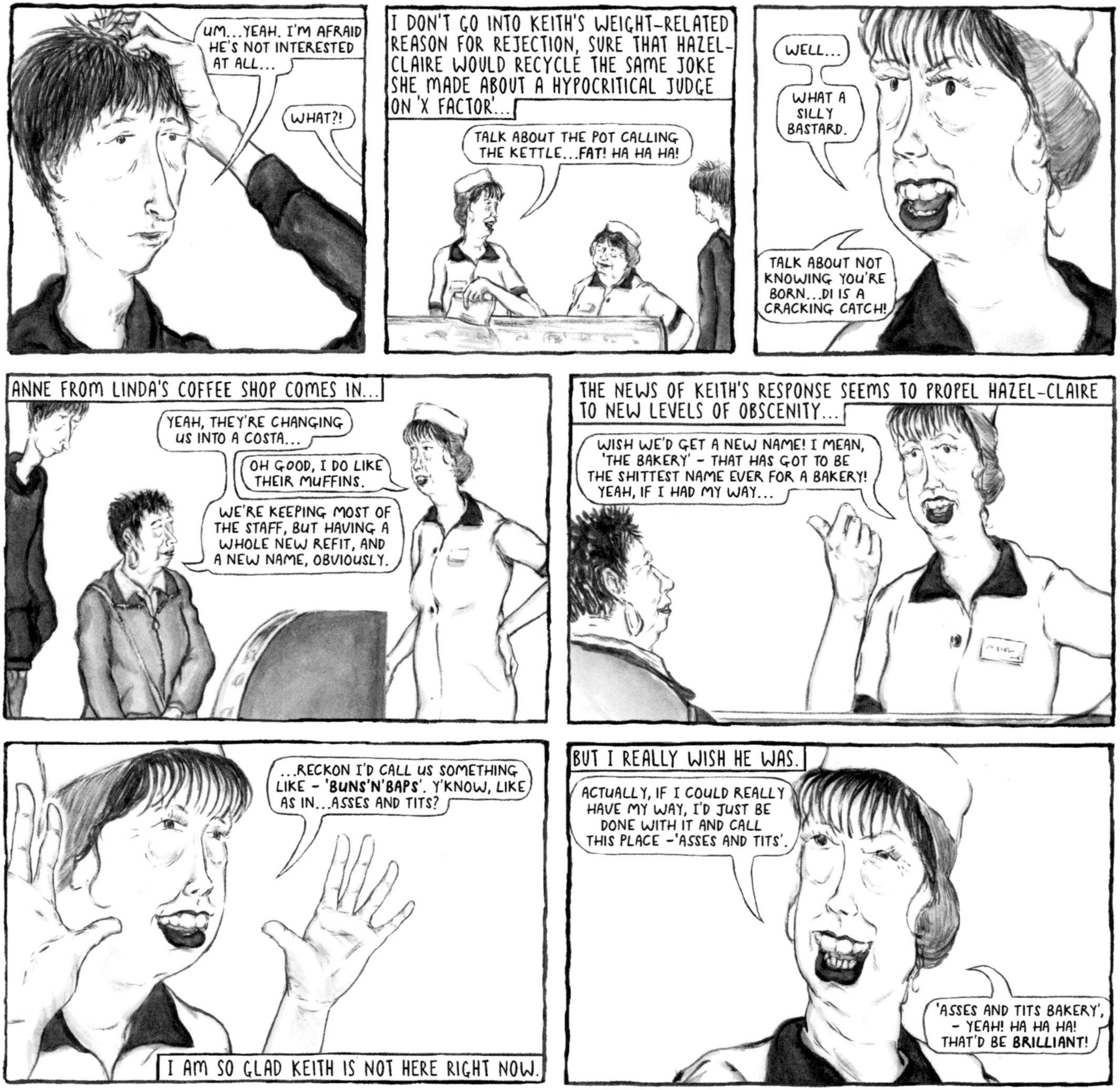
UM...YEAH. I'M AFRAID HE'S NOT INTERESTED AT ALL...
WHAT?!
I DON'T GO INTO KEITH'S WEIGHT-RELATED REASON FOR REJECTION, SURE THAT HAZEL-CLAIRE WOULD RECYCLE THE SAME JOKE SHE MADE ABOUT A HYPOCRITICAL JUDGE ON 'X FACTOR'...
TALK ABOUT THE POT CALLING THE KETTLE...FAT! HA HA HA!
WELL...
WHAT A SILLY BASTARD.
TALK ABOUT NOT KNOWING YOU'RE BORN...DI IS A CRACKING CATCH!
ANNE FROM LINDA'S COFFEE SHOP COMES IN...
YEAH, THEY'RE CHANGING US INTO A COSTA...
OH GOOD, I DO LIKE THEIR MUFFINS.
WE'RE KEEPING MOST OF THE STAFF, BUT HAVING A WHOLE NEW REFIT, AND A NEW NAME, OBVIOUSLY.
THE NEWS OF KEITH'S RESPONSE SEEMS TO PROPEL HAZEL-CLAIRE TO NEW LEVELS OF OBSCENITY...
WISH WE'D GET A NEW NAME! I MEAN, 'THE BAKERY' - THAT HAS GOT TO BE THE SHITTEST NAME EVER FOR A BAKERY! YEAH, IF I HAD MY WAY...
...RECKON I'D CALL US SOMETHING LIKE - '**BUNS'N'BAPS**'. Y'KNOW, LIKE AS IN...ASSES AND TITS?
I AM SO GLAD KEITH IS NOT HERE RIGHT NOW.
BUT I REALLY WISH HE WAS.
ACTUALLY, IF I COULD REALLY HAVE MY WAY, I'D JUST BE DONE WITH IT AND CALL THIS PLACE -'ASSES AND TITS'.
'ASSES AND TITS BAKERY', - YEAH! HA HA HA! THAT'D BE **BRILLIANT**!

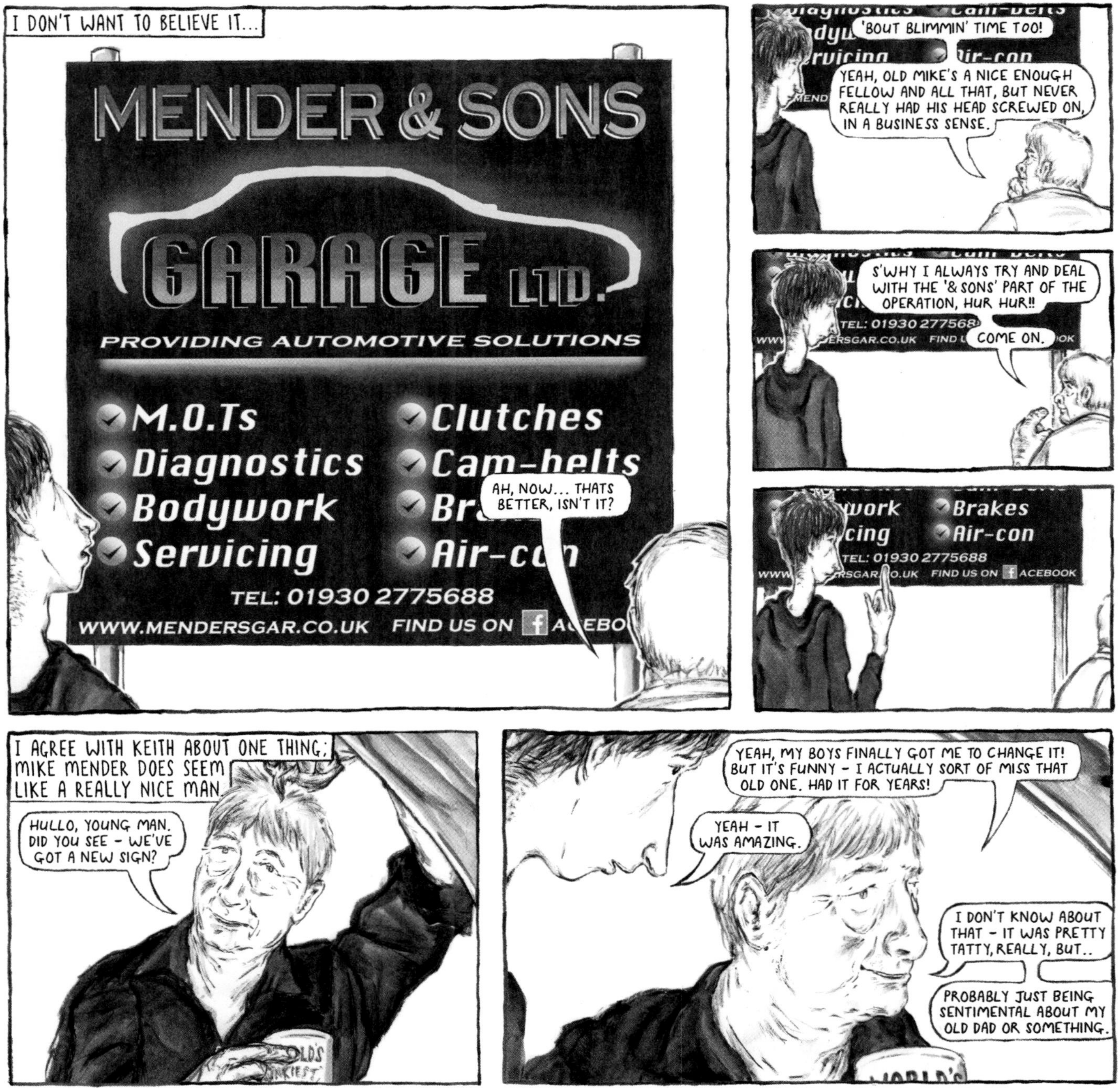
I DON'T WANT TO BELIEVE IT...
MENDER & SONS
GARAGE LTD.
PROVIDING AUTOMOTIVE SOLUTIONS
M.O.Ts
Clutches
Diagnostics
Cam-belts
Bodywork
Servicing
Air-con
TEL: 01930 2775688
WWW.MENDERSGAR.CO.UK FIND US ON FACEBOOK
AH, NOW... THATS BETTER, ISN'T IT?
'BOUT BLIMMIN' TIME TOO!
YEAH, OLD MIKE'S A NICE ENOUGH FELLOW AND ALL THAT, BUT NEVER REALLY HAD HIS HEAD SCREWED ON, IN A BUSINESS SENSE.
S'WHY I ALWAYS TRY AND DEAL WITH THE '& SONS' PART OF THE OPERATION, HUR HUR!!
COME ON.
Brakes
Air-con
TEL: 01930 2775688
FIND US ON FACEBOOK
I AGREE WITH KEITH ABOUT ONE THING; MIKE MENDER DOES SEEM LIKE A REALLY NICE MAN.
HULLO, YOUNG MAN. DID YOU SEE - WE'VE GOT A NEW SIGN?
YEAH, MY BOYS FINALLY GOT ME TO CHANGE IT! BUT IT'S FUNNY - I ACTUALLY SORT OF MISS THAT OLD ONE. HAD IT FOR YEARS!
YEAH - IT WAS AMAZING.
I DON'T KNOW ABOUT THAT - IT WAS PRETTY TATTY, REALLY, BUT..
PROBABLY JUST BEING SENTIMENTAL ABOUT MY OLD DAD OR SOMETHING.

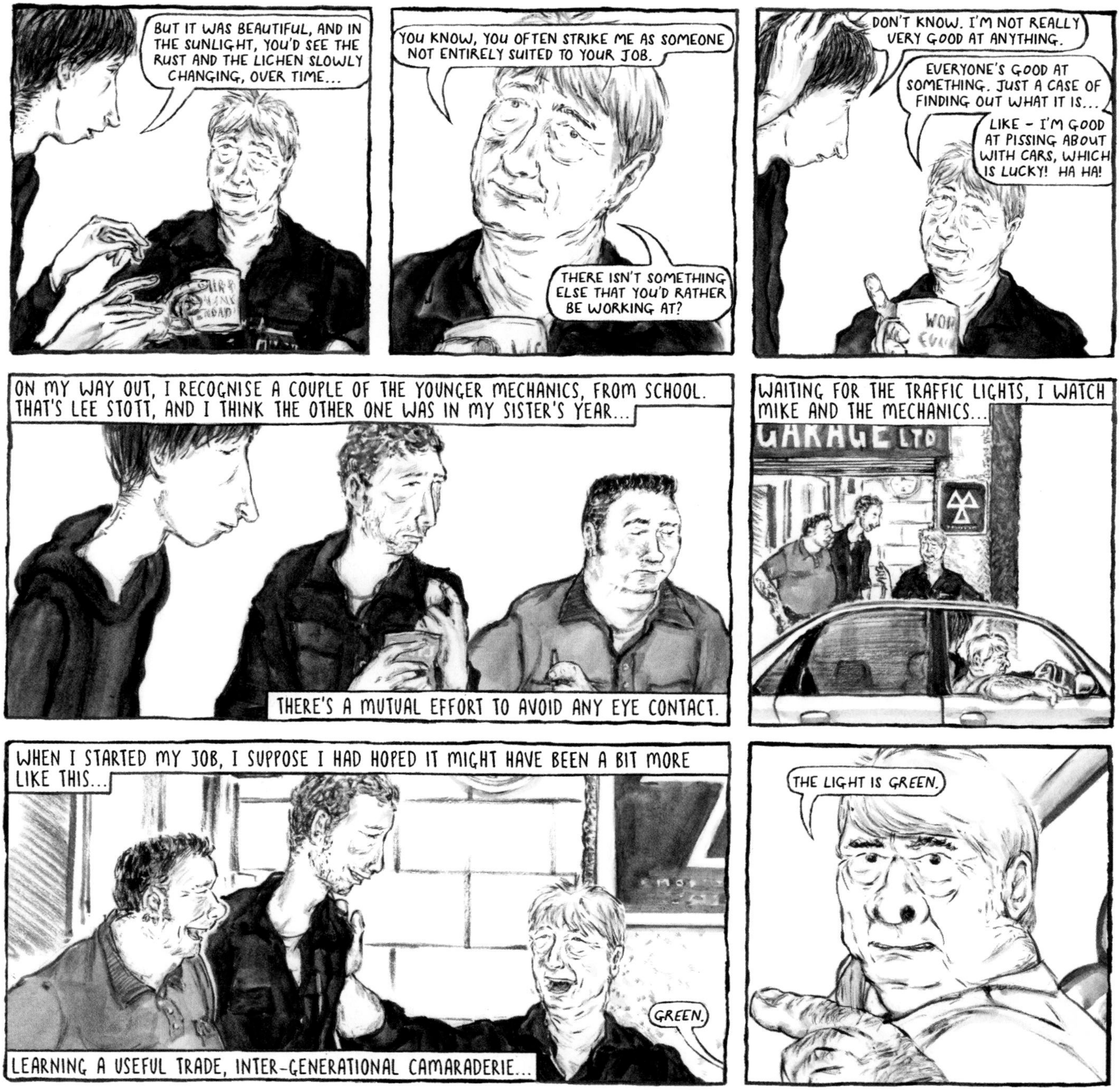

BUT IT WAS BEAUTIFUL, AND IN THE SUNLIGHT, YOU'D SEE THE RUST AND THE LICHEN SLOWLY CHANGING, OVER TIME...
YOU KNOW, YOU OFTEN STRIKE ME AS SOMEONE NOT ENTIRELY SUITED TO YOUR JOB.
THERE ISN'T SOMETHING ELSE THAT YOU'D RATHER BE WORKING AT?
DON'T KNOW. I'M NOT REALLY VERY GOOD AT ANYTHING.
EVERYONE'S GOOD AT SOMETHING. JUST A CASE OF FINDING OUT WHAT IT IS...
LIKE - I'M GOOD AT PISSING ABOUT WITH CARS, WHICH IS LUCKY! HA HA!
ON MY WAY OUT, I RECOGNISE A COUPLE OF THE YOUNGER MECHANICS, FROM SCHOOL. THAT'S LEE STOTT, AND I THINK THE OTHER ONE WAS IN MY SISTER'S YEAR...
THERE'S A MUTUAL EFFORT TO AVOID ANY EYE CONTACT.
WAITING FOR THE TRAFFIC LIGHTS, I WATCH MIKE AND THE MECHANICS...
GARAGE LTD
WHEN I STARTED MY JOB, I SUPPOSE I HAD HOPED IT MIGHT HAVE BEEN A BIT MORE LIKE THIS...
GREEN.
LEARNING A USEFUL TRADE, INTER-GENERATIONAL CAMARADERIE...
THE LIGHT IS GREEN.

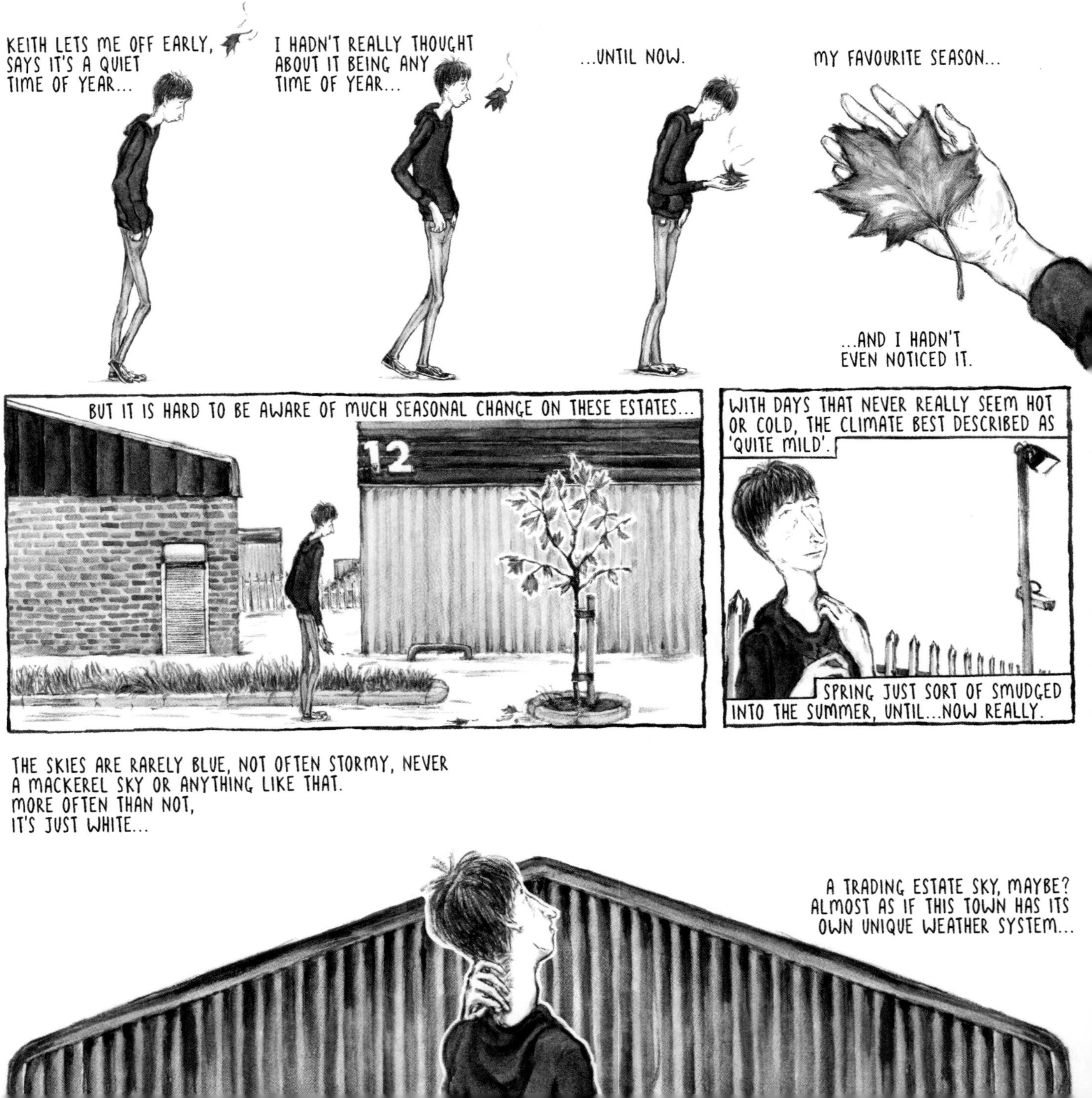
KEITH LETS ME OFF EARLY, SAYS IT'S A QUIET TIME OF YEAR...
I HADN'T REALLY THOUGHT ABOUT IT BEING ANY TIME OF YEAR...
...UNTIL NOW.
MY FAVOURITE SEASON...
...AND I HADN'T EVEN NOTICED IT.
BUT IT IS HARD TO BE AWARE OF MUCH SEASONAL CHANGE ON THESE ESTATES...
12
WITH DAYS THAT NEVER REALLY SEEM HOT OR COLD, THE CLIMATE BEST DESCRIBED AS 'QUITE MILD'.
SPRING JUST SORT OF SMUDGED INTO THE SUMMER, UNTIL...NOW REALLY.
THE SKIES ARE RARELY BLUE, NOT OFTEN STORMY, NEVER A MACKEREL SKY OR ANYTHING LIKE THAT. MORE OFTEN THAN NOT, IT'S JUST WHITE...
A TRADING ESTATE SKY, MAYBE? ALMOST AS IF THIS TOWN HAS ITS OWN UNIQUE WEATHER SYSTEM...

THIS TOWN, GROWING UP HERE, I NEVER GAVE IT MUCH THOUGHT AT ALL. BEYOND LEAVING IT AS SOON AS I COULD...

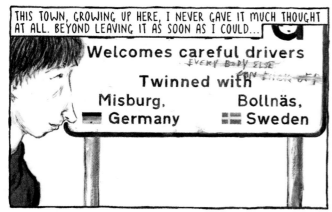

Welcomes careful drivers

Twinned with

Misburg, Germany

Bollnäs, Sweden

AND I NEVER REALLY NOTICED ANY OF THESE OLDER MEN BEFORE; PEOPLE LIKE KEITH AND HIS FRIENDS...

IT MIGHT JUST BE THAT THING WHEN YOUR MUM GETS A NEW CAR AND SUDDENLY EVERY OTHER CAR YOU SEE IS A NISSAN MICRA, BUT EVER SINCE I STARTED WORKING FOR KEITH...

I SEE THEM EVERYWHERE...THESE MEN. A WHOLE TOWN OF MEN.

A TOWN OF FATHERS, GRANDFATHERS, GODFATHERS, UNCLES, COUNCILLORS, GARAGE OWNERS, NEWSAGENTS, ESTATE AGENTS, POSSIBLE FREEMASONS, KEY JANGLERS AND COINSHAKERS, TYRE KICKERS, MILITARY MEMORABILIASTS, CARD CARRIERS, AND WEARERS OF VERY STRONG AFTERSHAVE...THEY'VE ALMOST BECOME CELEBRITIES TO ME.

PERHAPS I HAVE BEEN DOING THIS JOB A BIT TOO LONG?

I MEAN, IF KEITH'S JOB BARELY EXISTS, THEN MY JOB?

BUT I SUPPOSE IT'S QUITE FITTING REALLY...

...AS I OFTEN FEEL THAT WAY MYSELF.

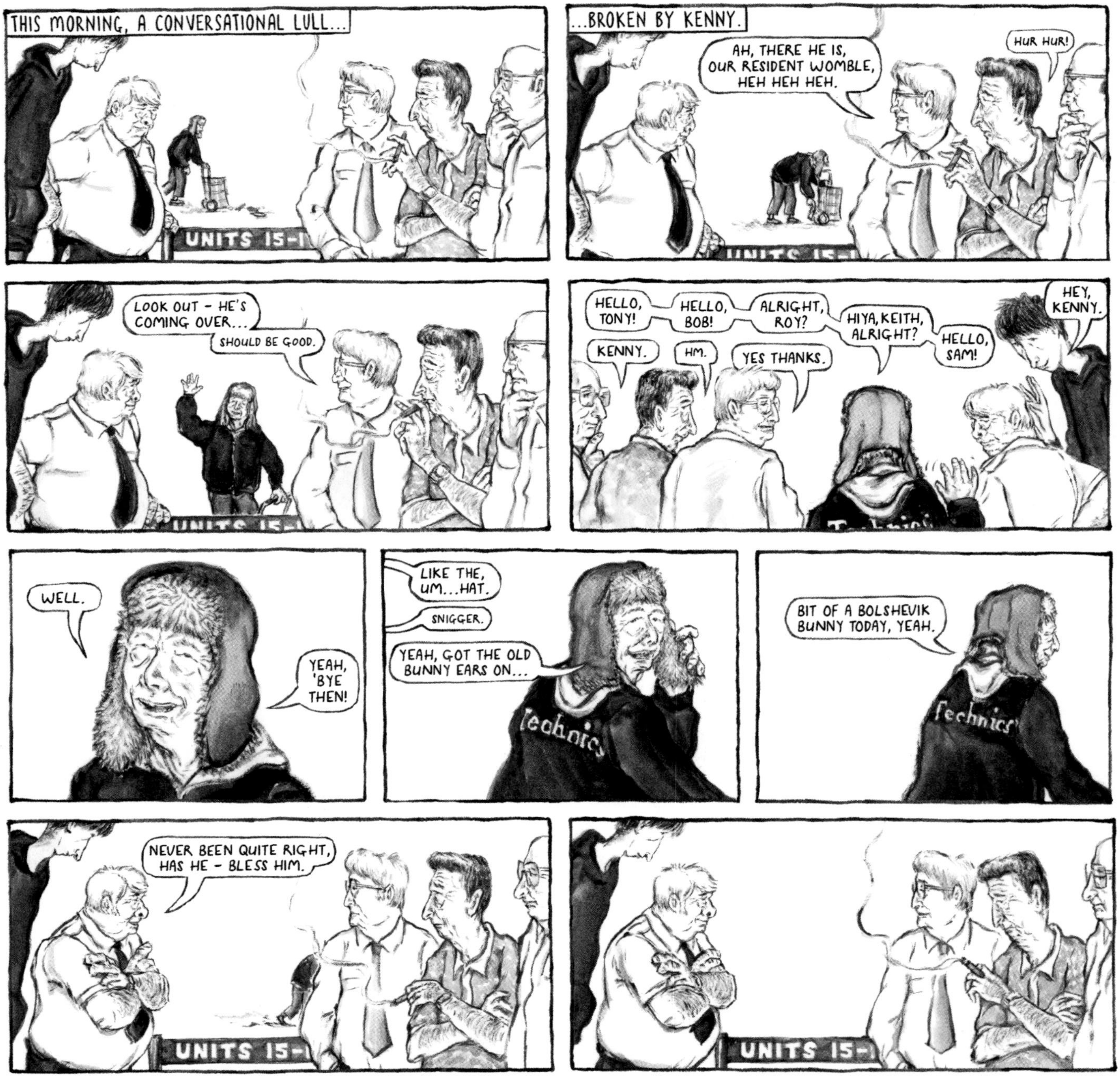
THIS MORNING, A CONVERSATIONAL LULL...
UNITS 15-1
...BROKEN BY KENNY.
AH, THERE HE IS, OUR RESIDENT WOMBLE, HEH HEH HEH.
HUR HUR!
LOOK OUT - HE'S COMING OVER...
SHOULD BE GOOD.
HELLO, TONY!
HELLO, BOB!
ALRIGHT, ROY?
HIYA, KEITH, ALRIGHT?
HELLO, SAM!
HEY, KENNY.
KENNY.
HM.
YES THANKS.
WELL.
YEAH, 'BYE THEN!
LIKE THE, UM...HAT.
SNIGGER.
YEAH, GOT THE OLD BUNNY EARS ON...
Technics
BIT OF A BOLSHEVIK BUNNY TODAY, YEAH.
Technics
NEVER BEEN QUITE RIGHT, HAS HE - BLESS HIM.
UNITS 15-1
UNITS 15-1

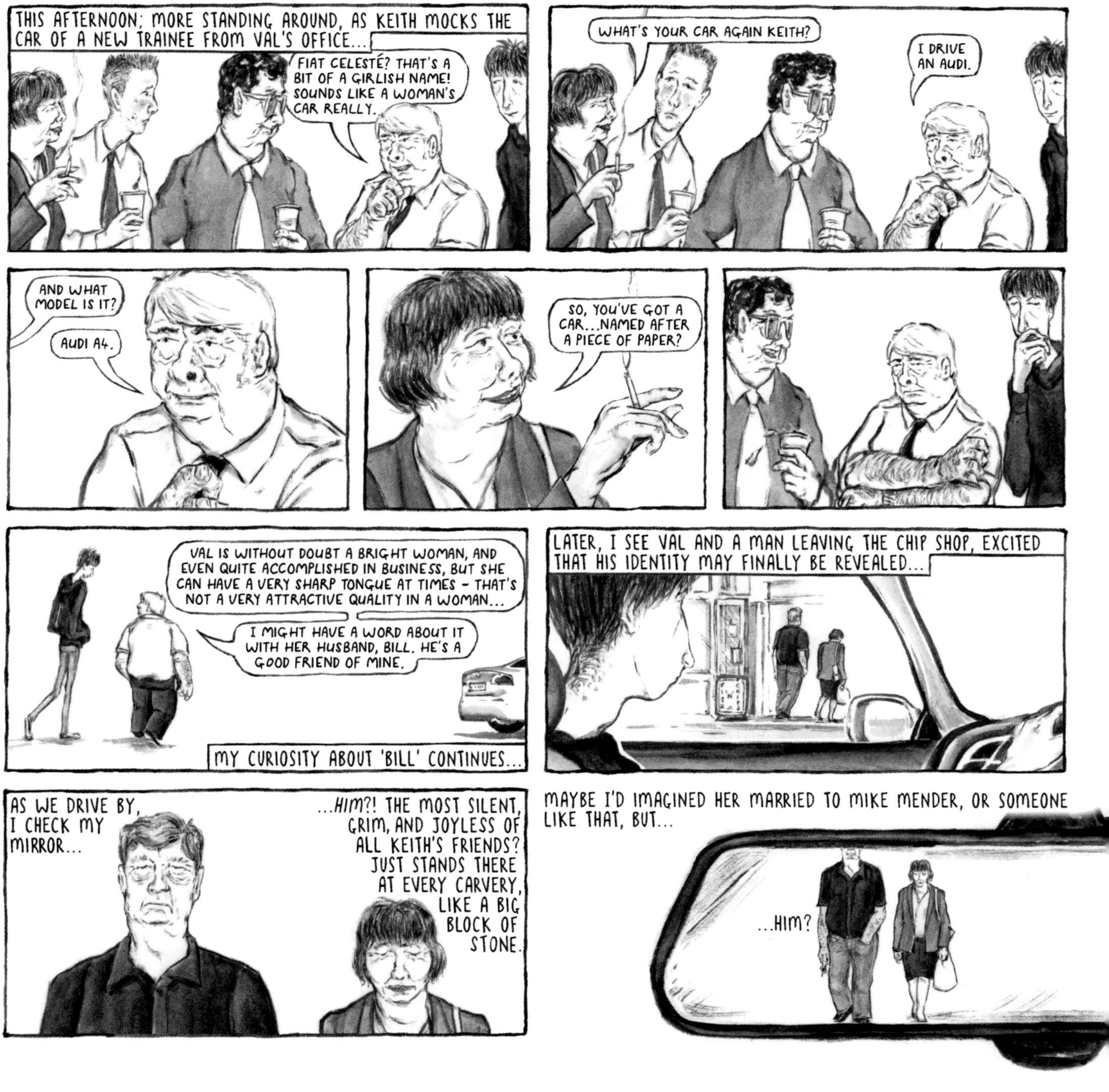

THIS AFTERNOON; MORE STANDING AROUND, AS KEITH MOCKS THE CAR OF A NEW TRAINEE FROM VAL'S OFFICE...
FIAT CELESTÉ? THAT'S A BIT OF A GIRLISH NAME! SOUNDS LIKE A WOMAN'S CAR REALLY.
WHAT'S YOUR CAR AGAIN KEITH?
I DRIVE AN AUDI.
AND WHAT MODEL IS IT?
AUDI A4.
SO, YOU'VE GOT A CAR...NAMED AFTER A PIECE OF PAPER?
VAL IS WITHOUT DOUBT A BRIGHT WOMAN, AND EVEN QUITE ACCOMPLISHED IN BUSINESS, BUT SHE CAN HAVE A VERY SHARP TONGUE AT TIMES - THAT'S NOT A VERY ATTRACTIVE QUALITY IN A WOMAN...
I MIGHT HAVE A WORD ABOUT IT WITH HER HUSBAND, BILL. HE'S A GOOD FRIEND OF MINE.
MY CURIOSITY ABOUT 'BILL' CONTINUES...
LATER, I SEE VAL AND A MAN LEAVING THE CHIP SHOP, EXCITED THAT HIS IDENTITY MAY FINALLY BE REVEALED...
AS WE DRIVE BY, I CHECK MY MIRROR...
...HIM?! THE MOST SILENT, GRIM, AND JOYLESS OF ALL KEITH'S FRIENDS? JUST STANDS THERE AT EVERY CARVERY, LIKE A BIG BLOCK OF STONE.
MAYBE I'D IMAGINED HER MARRIED TO MIKE MENDER, OR SOMEONE LIKE THAT, BUT...
...HIM?

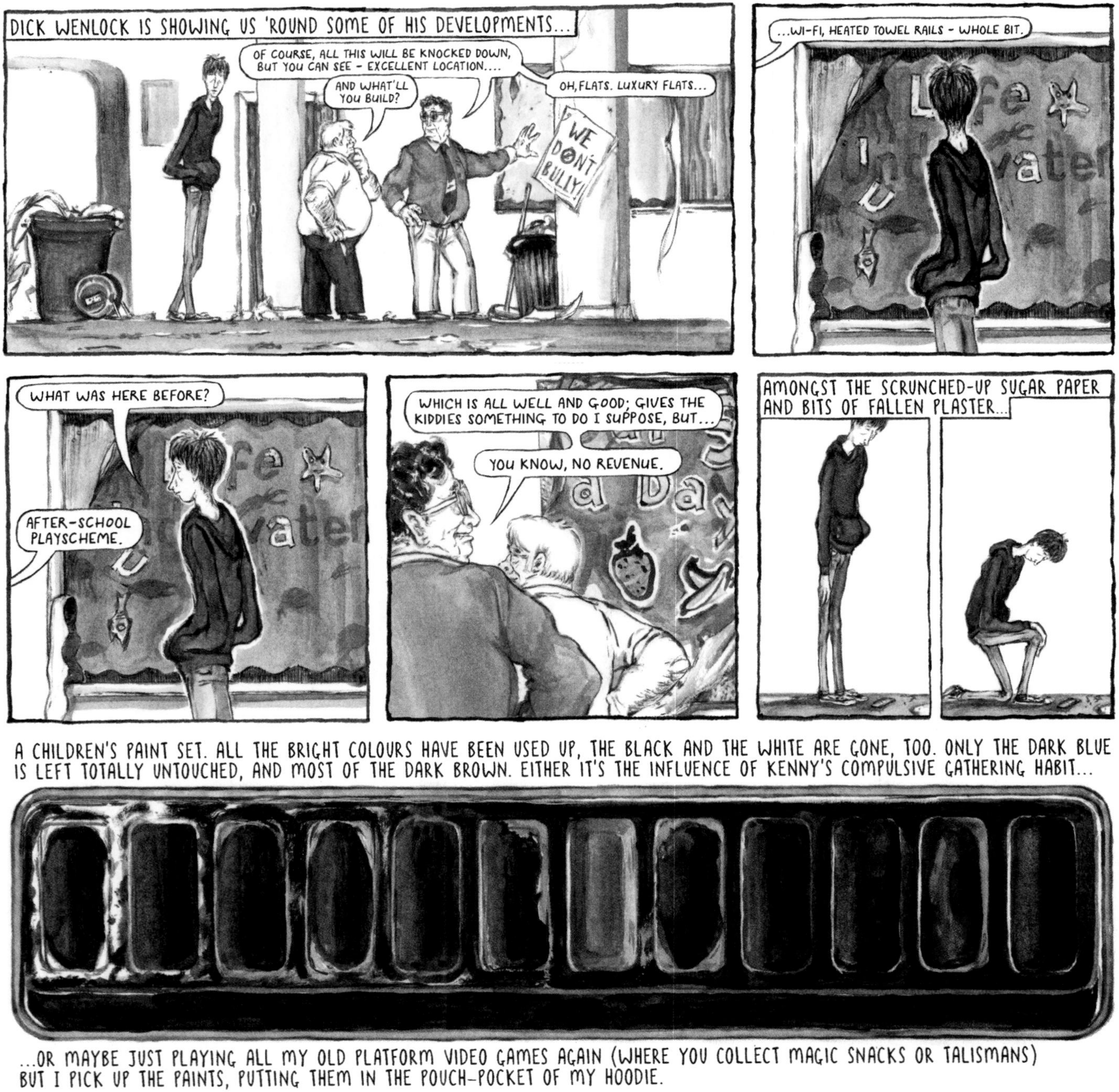
DICK WENLOCK IS SHOWING US 'ROUND SOME OF HIS DEVELOPMENTS...
OF COURSE, ALL THIS WILL BE KNOCKED DOWN, BUT YOU CAN SEE - EXCELLENT LOCATION....
AND WHAT'LL YOU BUILD?
OH, FLATS. LUXURY FLATS...
WE DON'T BULLY!
...WI-FI, HEATED TOWEL RAILS - WHOLE BIT.
WHAT WAS HERE BEFORE?
AFTER-SCHOOL PLAYSCHEME.
WHICH IS ALL WELL AND GOOD; GIVES THE KIDDIES SOMETHING TO DO I SUPPOSE, BUT...
YOU KNOW, NO REVENUE.
AMONGST THE SCRUNCHED-UP SUGAR PAPER AND BITS OF FALLEN PLASTER...
A CHILDREN'S PAINT SET. ALL THE BRIGHT COLOURS HAVE BEEN USED UP, THE BLACK AND THE WHITE ARE GONE, TOO. ONLY THE DARK BLUE IS LEFT TOTALLY UNTOUCHED, AND MOST OF THE DARK BROWN. EITHER IT'S THE INFLUENCE OF KENNY'S COMPULSIVE GATHERING HABIT...
...OR MAYBE JUST PLAYING ALL MY OLD PLATFORM VIDEO GAMES AGAIN (WHERE YOU COLLECT MAGIC SNACKS OR TALISMANS) BUT I PICK UP THE PAINTS, PUTTING THEM IN THE POUCH-POCKET OF MY HOODIE.

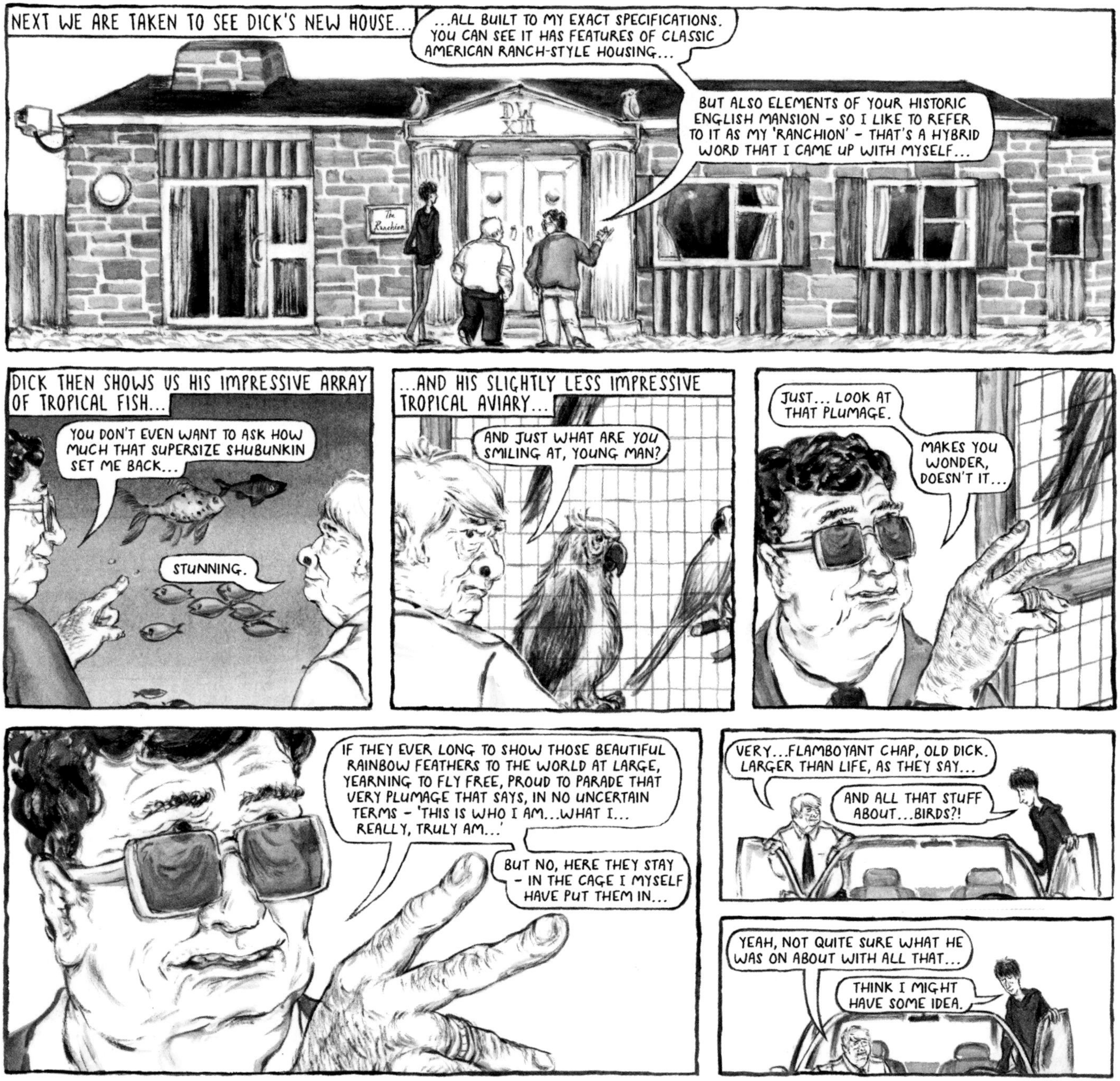

NEXT WE ARE TAKEN TO SEE DICK'S NEW HOUSE...
...ALL BUILT TO MY EXACT SPECIFICATIONS. YOU CAN SEE IT HAS FEATURES OF CLASSIC AMERICAN RANCH-STYLE HOUSING...
BUT ALSO ELEMENTS OF YOUR HISTORIC ENGLISH MANSION – SO I LIKE TO REFER TO IT AS MY 'RANCHION' – THAT'S A HYBRID WORD THAT I CAME UP WITH MYSELF...
DICK THEN SHOWS US HIS IMPRESSIVE ARRAY OF TROPICAL FISH...
YOU DON'T EVEN WANT TO ASK HOW MUCH THAT SUPERSIZE SHUBUNKIN SET ME BACK...
STUNNING.
...AND HIS SLIGHTLY LESS IMPRESSIVE TROPICAL AVIARY...
AND JUST WHAT ARE YOU SMILING AT, YOUNG MAN?
JUST... LOOK AT THAT PLUMAGE.
MAKES YOU WONDER, DOESN'T IT...
IF THEY EVER LONG TO SHOW THOSE BEAUTIFUL RAINBOW FEATHERS TO THE WORLD AT LARGE, YEARNING TO FLY FREE, PROUD TO PARADE THAT VERY PLUMAGE THAT SAYS, IN NO UNCERTAIN TERMS – 'THIS IS WHO I AM...WHAT I... REALLY, TRULY AM...'
BUT NO, HERE THEY STAY – IN THE CAGE I MYSELF HAVE PUT THEM IN...
VERY...FLAMBOYANT CHAP, OLD DICK. LARGER THAN LIFE, AS THEY SAY...
AND ALL THAT STUFF ABOUT...BIRDS?!
YEAH, NOT QUITE SURE WHAT HE WAS ON ABOUT WITH ALL THAT...
THINK I MIGHT HAVE SOME IDEA.

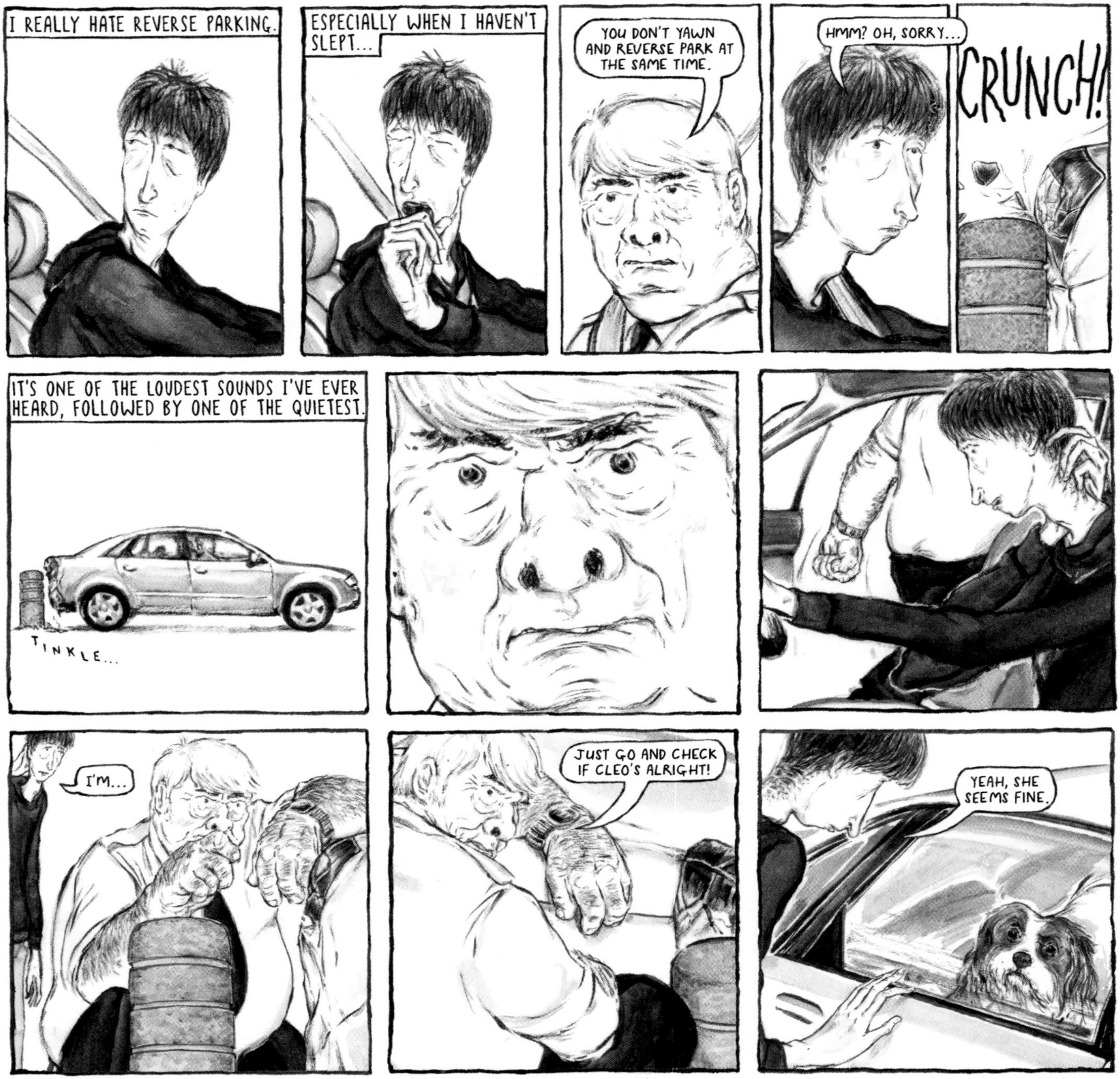
I REALLY HATE REVERSE PARKING.
ESPECIALLY WHEN I HAVEN'T SLEPT...
YOU DON'T YAWN AND REVERSE PARK AT THE SAME TIME.
HMM? OH, SORRY...
CRUNCH!
IT'S ONE OF THE LOUDEST SOUNDS I'VE EVER HEARD, FOLLOWED BY ONE OF THE QUIETEST.
TINKLE...
I'M...
JUST GO AND CHECK IF CLEO'S ALRIGHT!
YEAH, SHE SEEMS FINE.

EVENTUALLY...

OF COURSE, ANY REPAIR COSTS WILL BE COMING STRAIGHT OUT OF YOUR WAGES.

OF COURSE, SORRY.

...WE GO INTO MARCHANT LOGISTICS AS INTENDED...

...WHERE KEITH SEEMS LIKE HE MIGHT HAVE BEGUN TO FORGIVE ME?

THIS ONE HERE - JUST TOOK OUT MY TAILLIGHT, AND A GOOD PORTION OF THE BACK BUMPER... YEAH, TYPICAL YOUNG MAN'S ACCIDENT, NO REAL HARM DONE. ALTHOUGH - MIGHT WANT TO DOUBLE CHECK YOUR BOLLARD.

BUT OUTSIDE...

COME ON, KEYS.

THERE IS NO WAY YOU'RE GETTING BACK IN THAT DRIVER'S SEAT. BAD BACK REGARDLESS...

THIS AFTERNOON IN TANGENT LOGISTICS...

YEAH, CLASSIC YOUNG MAN'S ACCIDENT - A REAL YOUNG MAN'S MISTAKE.

WELL, IT'S HOW YOU LEARN.

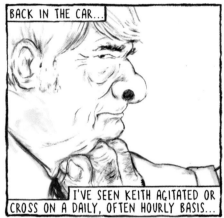
BACK IN THE CAR...

I'VE SEEN KEITH AGITATED OR CROSS ON A DAILY, OFTEN HOURLY BASIS...

BUT NEVER QUITE LIKE THIS...

LOOK, I REALLY AM SO SORRY. I JUST...

...HAVEN'T BEEN SLEEPING VERY MUCH LATELY AND- AWWWH...

...DIDDUMS.

I...WAS DISTRACTED-

DON'T GO PUTTING THIS ON ME!

I'M NOT, I'M NOT! I'M... I'M JUSTREALLYFUCKING...

...SORRY, OKAY?

TEN MINUTES OF ICY SILENCE LATER...

YOU WILL BE PLEASED TO KNOW -

- I'VE THOUGHT THE BETTER OF TELLING YOUR POOR MOTHER ABOUT ALL OF THIS, INCLUDING THAT...

...LANGUAGE YOU USED.

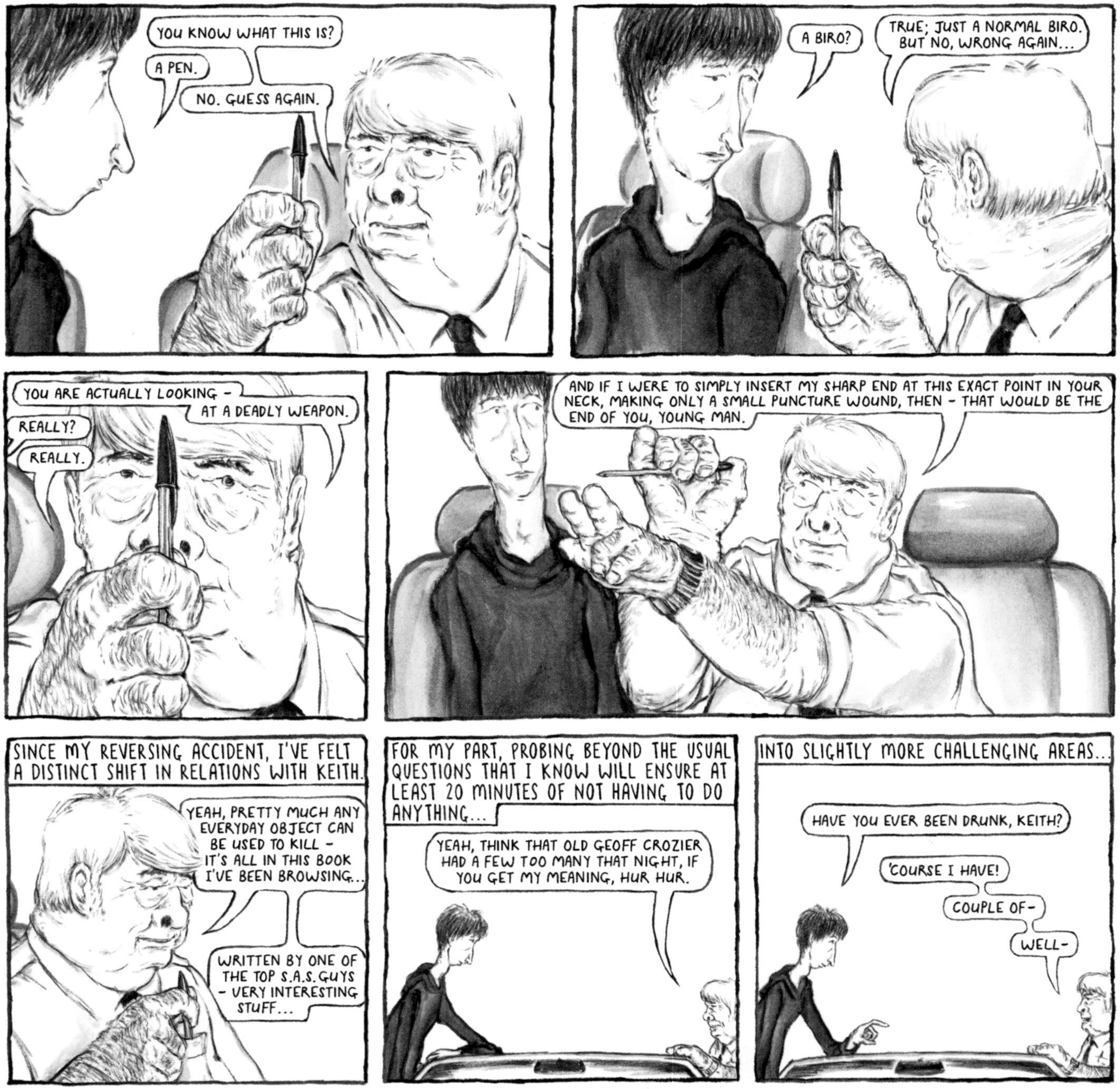
YOU KNOW WHAT THIS IS?
A PEN.
NO. GUESS AGAIN.
A BIRO?
TRUE; JUST A NORMAL BIRO. BUT NO, WRONG AGAIN...
YOU ARE ACTUALLY LOOKING -
AT A DEADLY WEAPON.
REALLY?
REALLY.
AND IF I WERE TO SIMPLY INSERT MY SHARP END AT THIS EXACT POINT IN YOUR NECK, MAKING ONLY A SMALL PUNCTURE WOUND, THEN - THAT WOULD BE THE END OF YOU, YOUNG MAN.
SINCE MY REVERSING ACCIDENT, I'VE FELT A DISTINCT SHIFT IN RELATIONS WITH KEITH.
YEAH, PRETTY MUCH ANY EVERYDAY OBJECT CAN BE USED TO KILL - IT'S ALL IN THIS BOOK I'VE BEEN BROWSING...
WRITTEN BY ONE OF THE TOP S.A.S. GUYS - VERY INTERESTING STUFF...
FOR MY PART, PROBING BEYOND THE USUAL QUESTIONS THAT I KNOW WILL ENSURE AT LEAST 20 MINUTES OF NOT HAVING TO DO ANYTHING...
YEAH, THINK THAT OLD GEOFF CROZIER HAD A FEW TOO MANY THAT NIGHT, IF YOU GET MY MEANING, HUR HUR.
INTO SLIGHTLY MORE CHALLENGING AREAS...
HAVE YOU EVER BEEN DRUNK, KEITH?
'COURSE I HAVE!
COUPLE OF-
WELL-

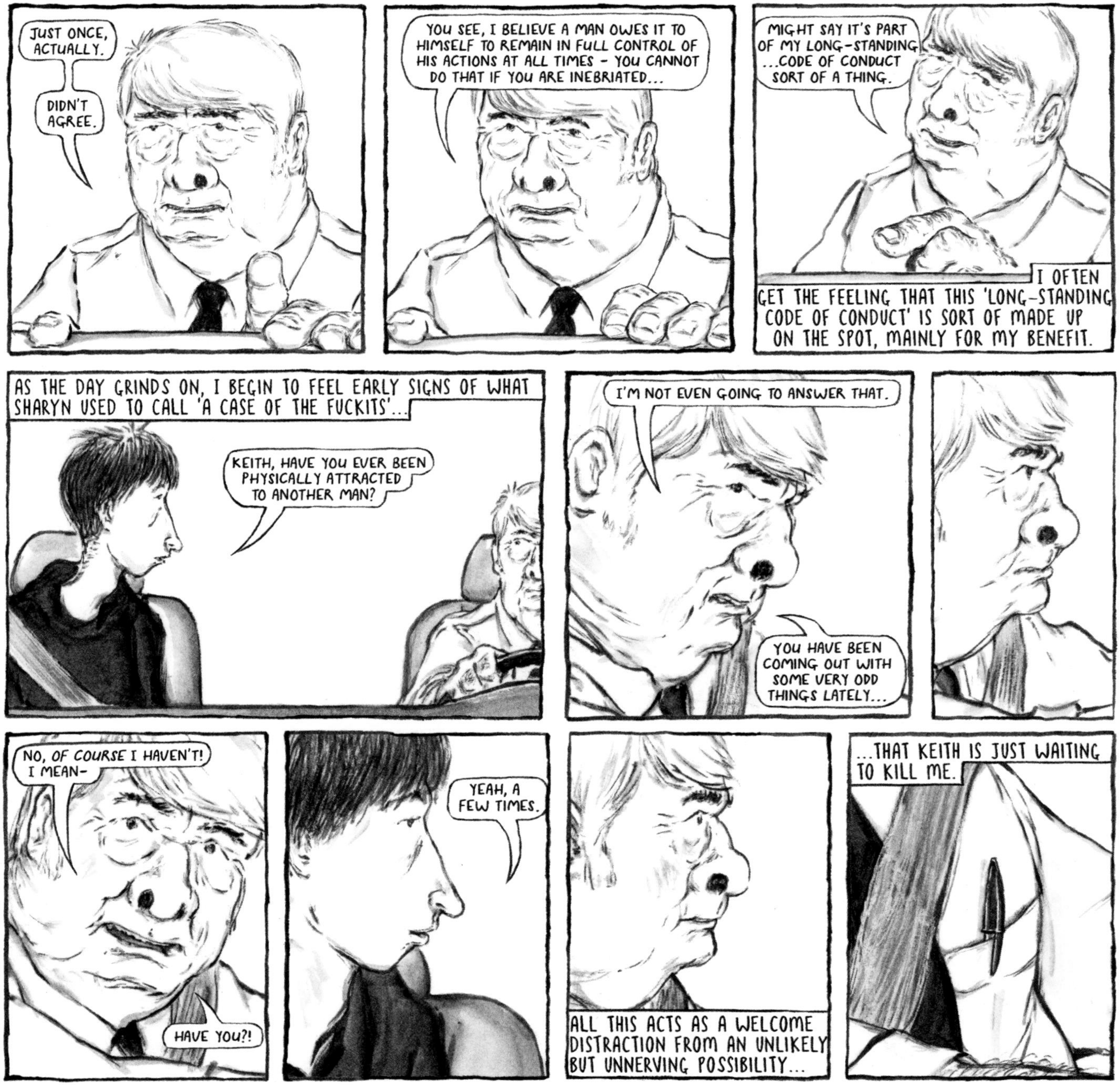
JUST ONCE, ACTUALLY.
DIDN'T AGREE.
YOU SEE, I BELIEVE A MAN OWES IT TO HIMSELF TO REMAIN IN FULL CONTROL OF HIS ACTIONS AT ALL TIMES - YOU CANNOT DO THAT IF YOU ARE INEBRIATED...
MIGHT SAY IT'S PART OF MY LONG-STANDING ...CODE OF CONDUCT SORT OF A THING.
I OFTEN GET THE FEELING THAT THIS 'LONG-STANDING CODE OF CONDUCT' IS SORT OF MADE UP ON THE SPOT, MAINLY FOR MY BENEFIT.
AS THE DAY GRINDS ON, I BEGIN TO FEEL EARLY SIGNS OF WHAT SHARYN USED TO CALL 'A CASE OF THE FUCKITS'...
KEITH, HAVE YOU EVER BEEN PHYSICALLY ATTRACTED TO ANOTHER MAN?
I'M NOT EVEN GOING TO ANSWER THAT.
YOU HAVE BEEN COMING OUT WITH SOME VERY ODD THINGS LATELY...
NO, OF COURSE I HAVEN'T! I MEAN-
HAVE YOU?!
YEAH, A FEW TIMES.
ALL THIS ACTS AS A WELCOME DISTRACTION FROM AN UNLIKELY BUT UNNERVING POSSIBILITY...
...THAT KEITH IS JUST WAITING TO KILL ME.

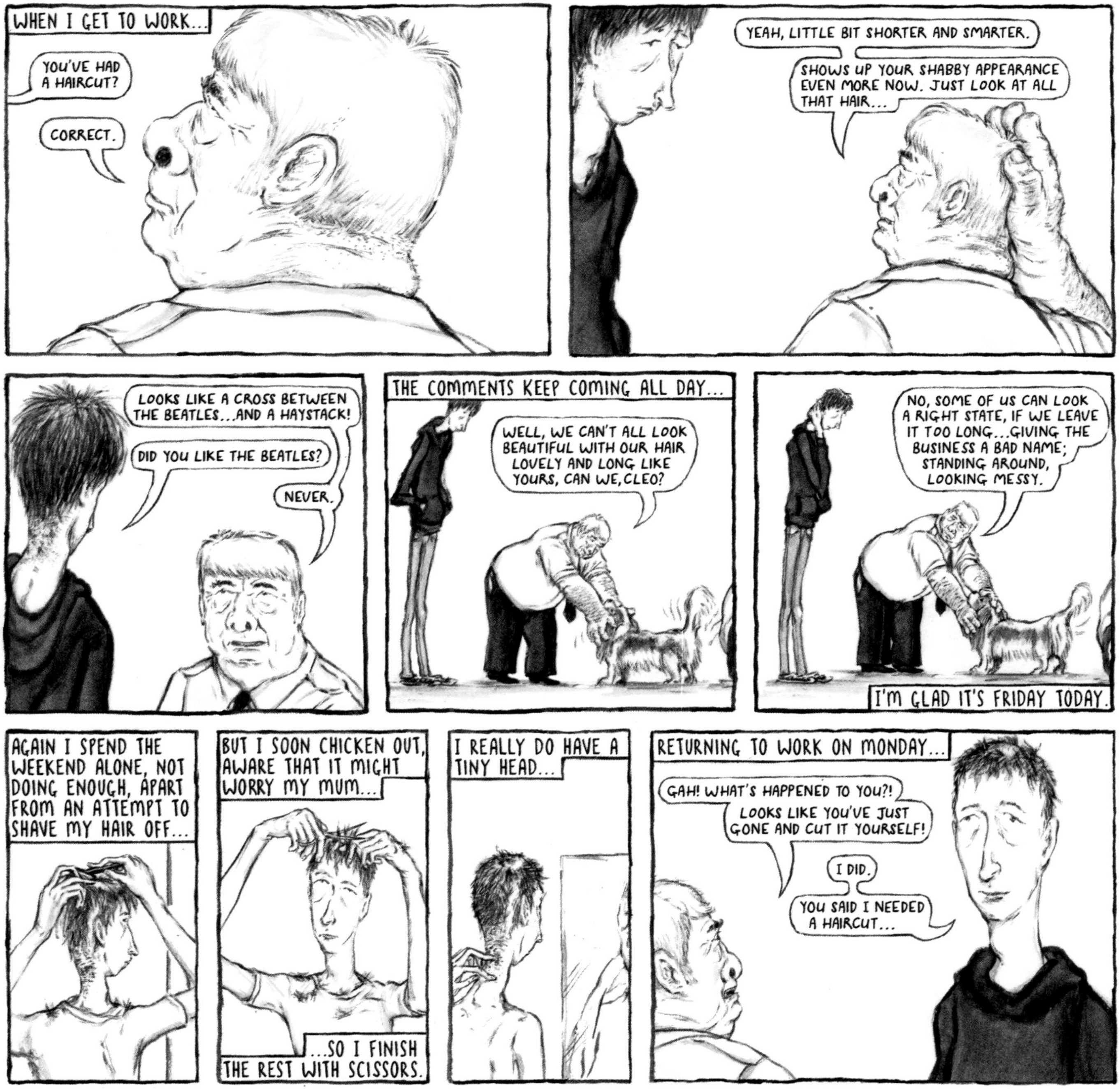
WHEN I GET TO WORK...
YOU'VE HAD A HAIRCUT?
CORRECT.
YEAH, LITTLE BIT SHORTER AND SMARTER.
SHOWS UP YOUR SHABBY APPEARANCE EVEN MORE NOW. JUST LOOK AT ALL THAT HAIR...
LOOKS LIKE A CROSS BETWEEN THE BEATLES...AND A HAYSTACK!
DID YOU LIKE THE BEATLES?
NEVER.
THE COMMENTS KEEP COMING ALL DAY...
WELL, WE CAN'T ALL LOOK BEAUTIFUL WITH OUR HAIR LOVELY AND LONG LIKE YOURS, CAN WE, CLEO?
NO, SOME OF US CAN LOOK A RIGHT STATE, IF WE LEAVE IT TOO LONG...GIVING THE BUSINESS A BAD NAME; STANDING AROUND, LOOKING MESSY.
I'M GLAD IT'S FRIDAY TODAY.
AGAIN I SPEND THE WEEKEND ALONE, NOT DOING ENOUGH, APART FROM AN ATTEMPT TO SHAVE MY HAIR OFF...
BUT I SOON CHICKEN OUT, AWARE THAT IT MIGHT WORRY MY MUM...
...SO I FINISH THE REST WITH SCISSORS.
I REALLY DO HAVE A TINY HEAD...
RETURNING TO WORK ON MONDAY...
GAH! WHAT'S HAPPENED TO YOU?!
LOOKS LIKE YOU'VE JUST GONE AND CUT IT YOURSELF!
I DID.
YOU SAID I NEEDED A HAIRCUT...

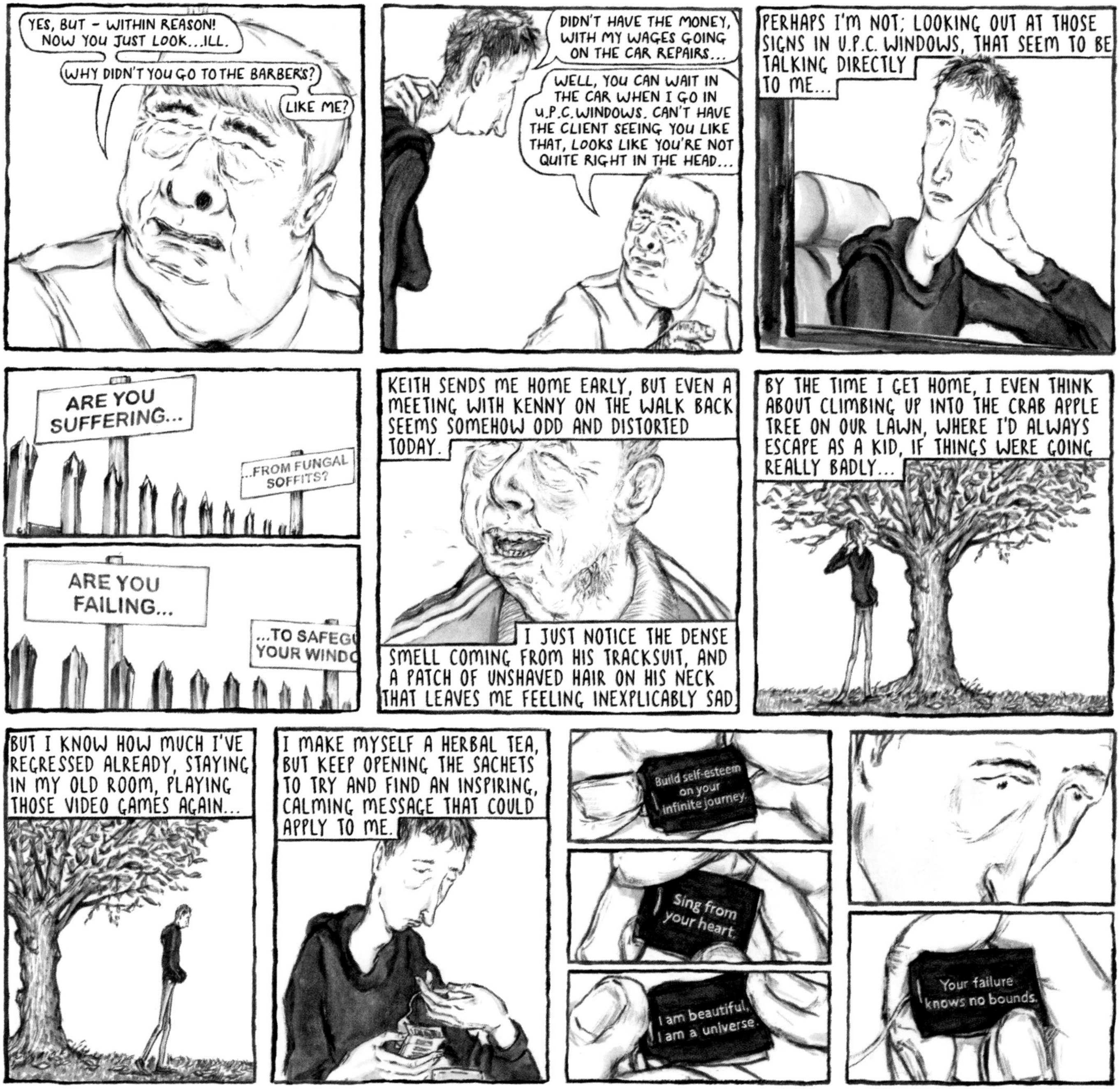
YES, BUT - WITHIN REASON! NOW YOU JUST LOOK...ILL.
WHY DIDN'T YOU GO TO THE BARBER'S?
LIKE ME?
DIDN'T HAVE THE MONEY, WITH MY WAGES GOING ON THE CAR REPAIRS...
WELL, YOU CAN WAIT IN THE CAR WHEN I GO IN U.P.C. WINDOWS. CAN'T HAVE THE CLIENT SEEING YOU LIKE THAT, LOOKS LIKE YOU'RE NOT QUITE RIGHT IN THE HEAD...
PERHAPS I'M NOT; LOOKING OUT AT THOSE SIGNS IN U.P.C. WINDOWS, THAT SEEM TO BE TALKING DIRECTLY TO ME...
ARE YOU SUFFERING...
...FROM FUNGAL SOFFITS?
ARE YOU FAILING...
...TO SAFEGU
YOUR WINDO
KEITH SENDS ME HOME EARLY, BUT EVEN A MEETING WITH KENNY ON THE WALK BACK SEEMS SOMEHOW ODD AND DISTORTED TODAY.
I JUST NOTICE THE DENSE SMELL COMING FROM HIS TRACKSUIT, AND A PATCH OF UNSHAVED HAIR ON HIS NECK THAT LEAVES ME FEELING INEXPLICABLY SAD.
BY THE TIME I GET HOME, I EVEN THINK ABOUT CLIMBING UP INTO THE CRAB APPLE TREE ON OUR LAWN, WHERE I'D ALWAYS ESCAPE AS A KID, IF THINGS WERE GOING REALLY BADLY...
BUT I KNOW HOW MUCH I'VE REGRESSED ALREADY, STAYING IN MY OLD ROOM, PLAYING THOSE VIDEO GAMES AGAIN...
I MAKE MYSELF A HERBAL TEA, BUT KEEP OPENING THE SACHETS TO TRY AND FIND AN INSPIRING, CALMING MESSAGE THAT COULD APPLY TO ME.
Build self-esteem on your infinite journey.
Sing from your heart.
I am beautiful, I am a universe.
Your failure knows no bounds.

AGAIN, KEITH HAS TOLD ME TO STAY IN THE CAR WHILE HE GOES INTO GILROY'S SCRAP-YARD...

FEELING A CURIOUS MIX OF ANXIETY AND BOREDOM...

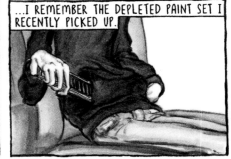

...I REMEMBER THE DEPLETED PAINT SET I RECENTLY PICKED UP.

USING THE PUFFER BRUSH KEITH KEEPS FOR THE CAR'S 'TRICKY CREVICES', AND THE TOP FROM MY BOTTLE OF WATER, I BEGIN TO PAINT ON THE BACK OF A B38 FORM...

I DON'T KNOW WHY BUT...

...I DO A PORTRAIT OF KEITH. I'VE NEVER BEEN ANY GOOD AT LIKENESSES, BUT IT LOOKS JUST LIKE HIM. MAYBE IT'S ALL THESE MONTHS OF SEEING HIM NEARLY EVERY DAY? AND I DON'T EVEN FEEL THE STRESS I OFTEN GET WHEN I TRY DRAWING. IN FACT, IT'S THE BEST I'VE FELT IN DAYS...

KEITH EVENTUALLY RETURNS...

ERR, WHAT HAVE YOU BEEN DOING TO THAT PAPERWORK?!

I SEE. VERY CLEVER.

AND I SUPPOSE THAT'S SUPPOSED TO BE ME, IS IT?

YUP.

I SEE.

ALWAYS KNEW IT WAS A GAMBLE, TAKING YOU ON...

AND I'M NOT A GAMBLING MAN — NEVER HAVE BEEN. BUT I...

I'M SORRY TO SAY, THAT THIS ONE GAMBLE HAS NOT PAID OFF, IN ANY WAY, SHAPE, OR FORM...

I SUPPOSE I WAS JUST...TRYING TO HELP YOU. OFFERING EMPLOYMENT, YES, BUT MORE IMPORTANTLY GUIDANCE. JUST AS OTHERS HAVE DONE FOR ME, AT A CERTAIN AGE — NAMELY, MR. GEOFF CROZIER...

...PROVIDING YOU WITH A FATHER FIGURE OF SORTS.

I'VE NEVER HEARD HIM TALK QUITE LIKE THIS...

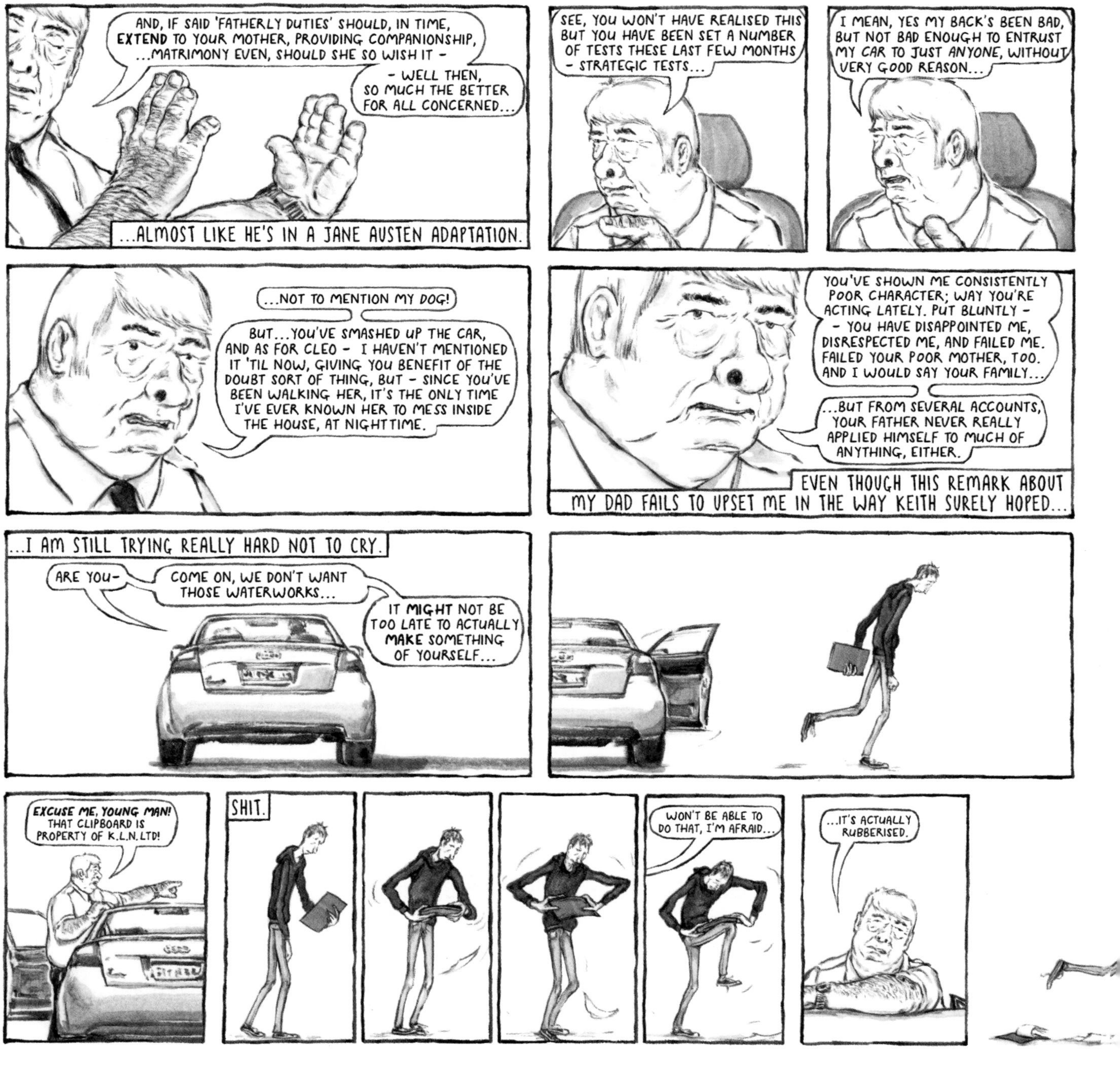
AND, IF SAID 'FATHERLY DUTIES' SHOULD, IN TIME, **EXTEND** TO YOUR MOTHER, PROVIDING COMPANIONSHIP, ...MATRIMONY EVEN, SHOULD SHE SO WISH IT -
- WELL THEN, SO MUCH THE BETTER FOR ALL CONCERNED...
...ALMOST LIKE HE'S IN A JANE AUSTEN ADAPTATION.
SEE, YOU WON'T HAVE REALISED THIS BUT YOU HAVE BEEN SET A NUMBER OF TESTS THESE LAST FEW MONTHS - STRATEGIC TESTS...
I MEAN, YES MY BACK'S BEEN BAD, BUT NOT BAD ENOUGH TO ENTRUST MY CAR TO JUST *ANYONE*, WITHOUT VERY GOOD REASON...
BUT...YOU'VE SMASHED UP THE CAR, AND AS FOR CLEO - I HAVEN'T MENTIONED IT 'TIL NOW, GIVING YOU BENEFIT OF THE DOUBT SORT OF THING, BUT - SINCE YOU'VE BEEN WALKING HER, IT'S THE ONLY TIME I'VE EVER KNOWN HER TO MESS INSIDE THE HOUSE, AT NIGHTTIME.
...NOT TO MENTION MY *DOG*!
YOU'VE SHOWN ME CONSISTENTLY POOR CHARACTER; WAY YOU'RE ACTING LATELY. PUT BLUNTLY -
- YOU HAVE DISAPPOINTED ME, DISRESPECTED ME, AND FAILED ME. FAILED YOUR POOR MOTHER, TOO. AND I WOULD SAY YOUR FAMILY...
...BUT FROM SEVERAL ACCOUNTS, YOUR FATHER NEVER REALLY APPLIED HIMSELF TO MUCH OF ANYTHING, EITHER.
EVEN THOUGH THIS REMARK ABOUT MY DAD FAILS TO UPSET ME IN THE WAY KEITH SURELY HOPED...
...I AM STILL TRYING REALLY HARD NOT TO CRY.
ARE YOU-
COME ON, WE DON'T WANT THOSE WATERWORKS...
IT **MIGHT** NOT BE TOO LATE TO ACTUALLY **MAKE** SOMETHING OF YOURSELF...
EXCUSE ME, YOUNG MAN! THAT CLIPBOARD IS PROPERTY OF K.L.N. LTD!
SHIT.
WON'T BE ABLE TO DO THAT, I'M AFRAID...
...IT'S ACTUALLY RUBBERISED.

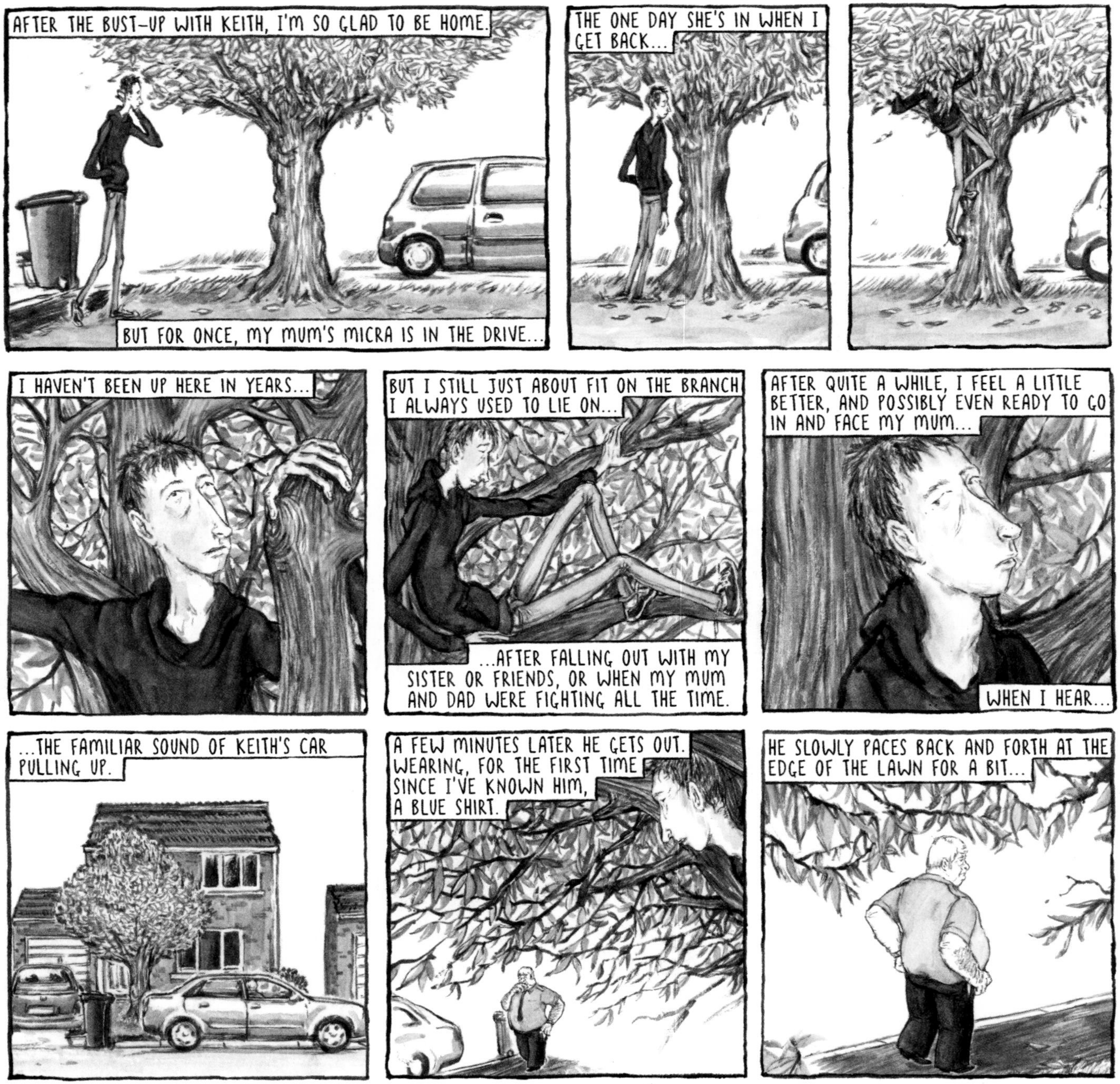
AFTER THE BUST-UP WITH KEITH, I'M SO GLAD TO BE HOME.
BUT FOR ONCE, MY MUM'S MICRA IS IN THE DRIVE...
THE ONE DAY SHE'S IN WHEN I GET BACK...
I HAVEN'T BEEN UP HERE IN YEARS...
BUT I STILL JUST ABOUT FIT ON THE BRANCH I ALWAYS USED TO LIE ON...
...AFTER FALLING OUT WITH MY SISTER OR FRIENDS, OR WHEN MY MUM AND DAD WERE FIGHTING ALL THE TIME.
AFTER QUITE A WHILE, I FEEL A LITTLE BETTER, AND POSSIBLY EVEN READY TO GO IN AND FACE MY MUM...
WHEN I HEAR...
...THE FAMILIAR SOUND OF KEITH'S CAR PULLING UP.
A FEW MINUTES LATER HE GETS OUT. WEARING, FOR THE FIRST TIME SINCE I'VE KNOWN HIM, A BLUE SHIRT.
HE SLOWLY PACES BACK AND FORTH AT THE EDGE OF THE LAWN FOR A BIT...

I HEAR THE FRONT DOOR OPEN...

HELLO, CAN I HELP—

OH. HELLO, KEITH! ARE YOU LOOKING FOR SAM? HE DOESN'T SEEM TO BE BACK YET.

NO, UM, IT WAS ACTUALLY YOU I WAS HOPING TO HAVE A WORD WITH, MARIE.

WELL, WOULD YOU LIKE TO COME IN, HAVE A CUP OF—

NO, I'LL SAY MY PIECE HERE, IF YOU DON'T MIND, WHILE I'VE GOT IT...SET OUT IN MY MIND.

AS KEITH CONTINUES, IT'S HARD TO CATCH EVERYTHING HE'S SAYING...

...HAD BEEN HOPING FOR A MORE APPROPRIATE MOMENT...

BUT SAMUEL'S RECENT BEHAVIOUR, ...SORT OF FORCED MY HAND A BIT, SO TO SPEAK...

CARDS ON THE TABLE, SORT OF THING...

...SOMETHING OF A FATHER FIGURE...

...MIGHT EXTEND... ...COMPANIONSHIP.

BUT KEITH, HE'S 28 YEARS OLD, NOT A BOY ANYMORE.

HE'S TALKING EVEN QUIETER NOW, AND MAINLY TO THE LAWN...

NO, I – HOW WAS I GOING TO PUT IT...?

...HAD HIS UPS AND DOWNS, BUT HE'S DONE PRETTY WELL REALLY, GROWING UP WITHOUT HIS DAD...

WELL...

AND AS FOR ME...

I'M SURE SAM HAS MENTIONED THAT I ALREADY HAVE A PARTNER, RICHARD.

YES, I KNOW ABOUT ALL THAT!

BUT YOU HAVE TO ADMIT, THAT THIS WOULD MAKE MUCH MORE SENSE, GIVEN THE...

I CAN'T HEAR ALL THAT MY MUM SAYS EITHER, BUT I KNOW HER TONE. THE SAME ONE WE'D GET AS KIDS IF SOMETHING WAS DISAPPOINTING OR SAD.

... THINK YOU MIGHT HAVE GONE AND GOT THE WRONG IDEA SOMEHOW...

I TRY TO EDGE FURTHER ALONG MY BRANCH TO HEAR BETTER...

WAY I LOOK AT IT IS – THERE'S CLEO AND MYSELF, AND THEN YOU AND—

CRACK!

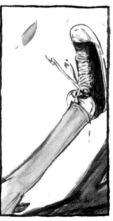

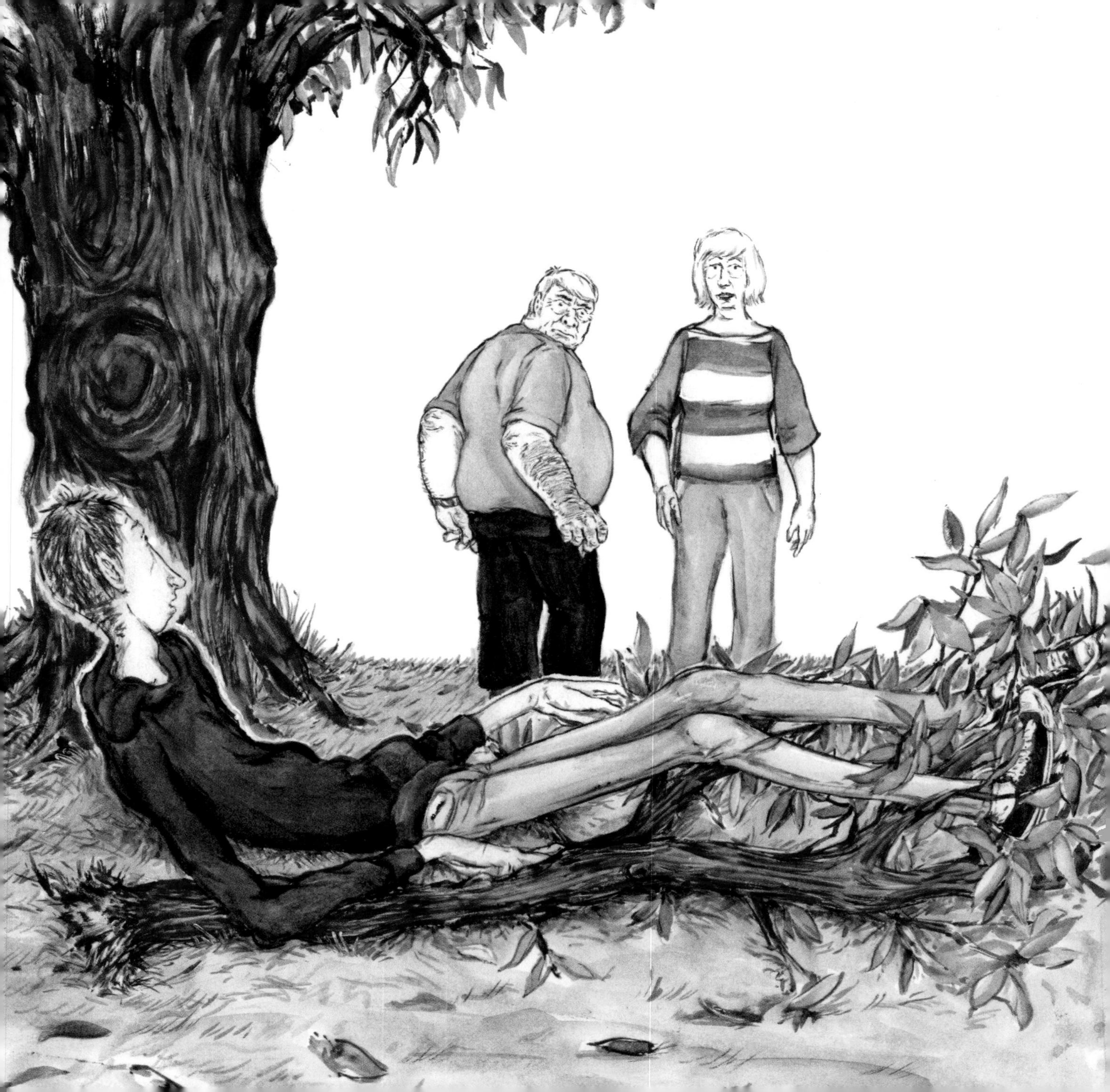

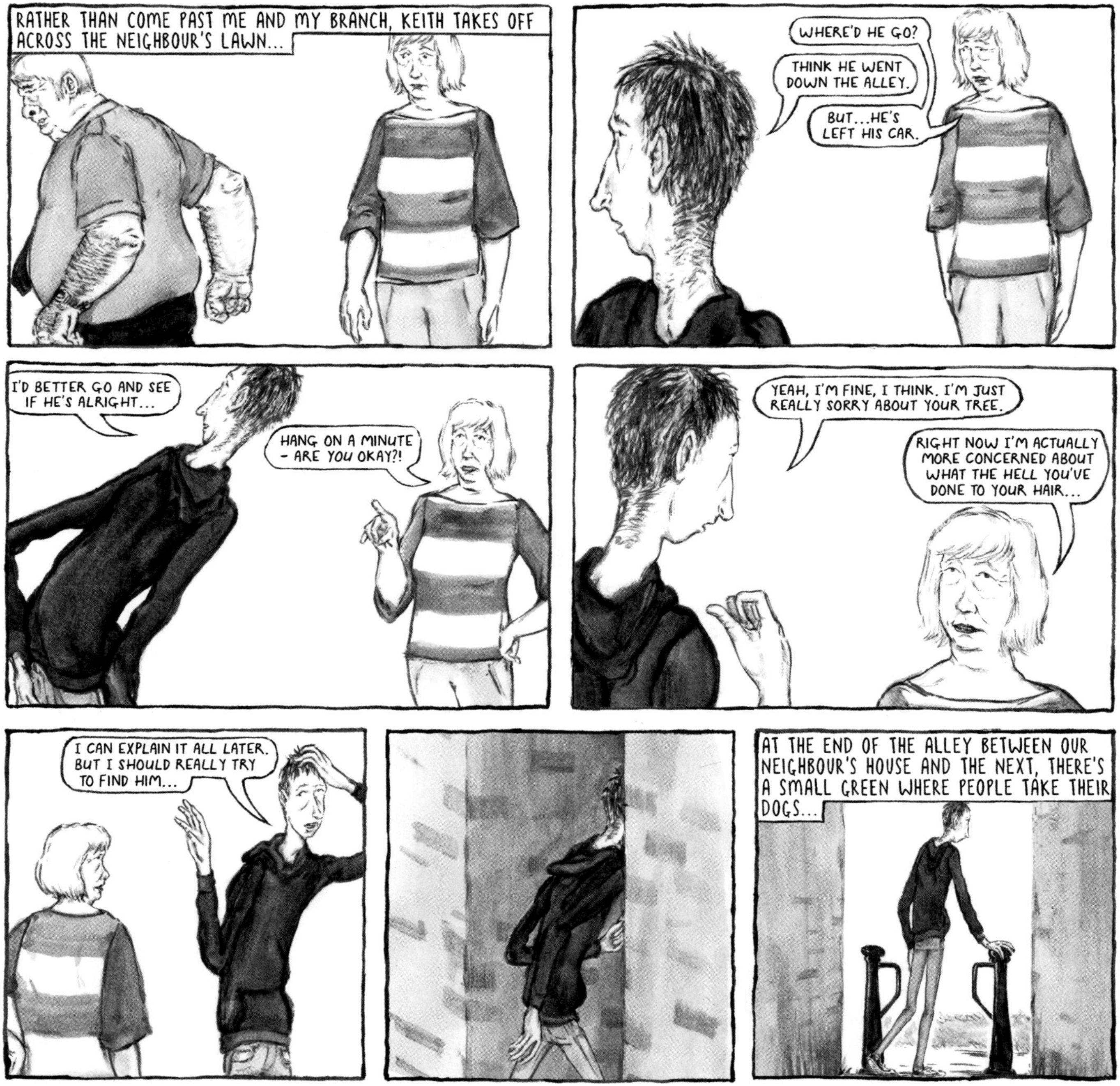
RATHER THAN COME PAST ME AND MY BRANCH, KEITH TAKES OFF ACROSS THE NEIGHBOUR'S LAWN...
WHERE'D HE GO?
THINK HE WENT DOWN THE ALLEY.
BUT...HE'S LEFT HIS CAR.
I'D BETTER GO AND SEE IF HE'S ALRIGHT...
HANG ON A MINUTE - ARE YOU OKAY?!
YEAH, I'M FINE, I THINK. I'M JUST REALLY SORRY ABOUT YOUR TREE.
RIGHT NOW I'M ACTUALLY MORE CONCERNED ABOUT WHAT THE HELL YOU'VE DONE TO YOUR HAIR...
I CAN EXPLAIN IT ALL LATER. BUT I SHOULD REALLY TRY TO FIND HIM...
AT THE END OF THE ALLEY BETWEEN OUR NEIGHBOUR'S HOUSE AND THE NEXT, THERE'S A SMALL GREEN WHERE PEOPLE TAKE THEIR DOGS...

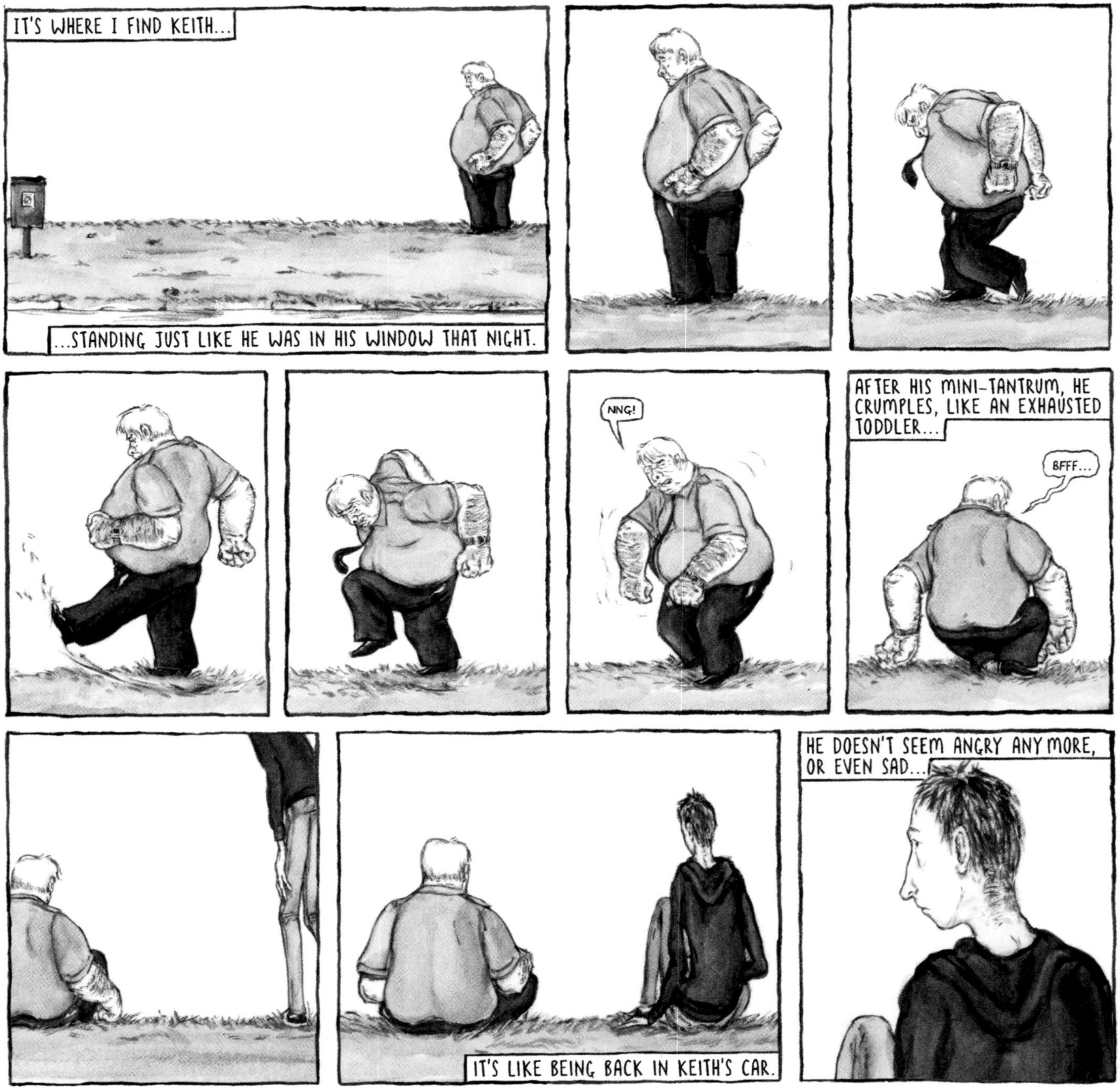

IT'S WHERE I FIND KEITH...
...STANDING JUST LIKE HE WAS IN HIS WINDOW THAT NIGHT.
NNG!
AFTER HIS MINI-TANTRUM, HE CRUMPLES, LIKE AN EXHAUSTED TODDLER...
BFFF...
IT'S LIKE BEING BACK IN KEITH'S CAR.
HE DOESN'T SEEM ANGRY ANY MORE, OR EVEN SAD...

...JUST A BIT CONFUSED.

YOU HAVE A PLAN AND...

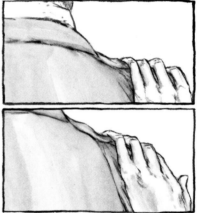

WHEN I GET BACK TO THE HOUSE, KEITH'S CAR IS STILL THERE...

A FEW HOURS LATER, MY MUM NOTICES IT HAS GONE.

TWO WEEKS LATER...

OVER THESE LAST COUPLE OF WEEKS, I SEE A BIT MORE OF MY MUM. SHE EVEN TIDIES UP MY D.I.Y. HAIRCUT...

LOOKING A BIT BETTER.

I ALSO CALL SHARYN, THE FIRST PERSON I'VE PHONED IN MONTHS.

UM, HELLO?

WOW – YOU'VE CALLED ME?! THAT IS SO WEIRD, I WAS ACTUALLY ABOUT TO CALL YOU! WE'RE DOING THIS PROJECT WITH ASYLUM SEEKERS, MAKING SIGNS WITH THEM, ABOUT THEIR STATUS AND STORIES, AND I THOUGHT OF YOU – 'COS IT'S HAND-PAINTED SIGNS – YOU LOVE THAT SHIT!

YEAH, SOUNDS COOL.

AND I CAN PAY YOU, WE'VE GOT FUNDING FOR THE WHOLE THING...

YEAH, SEEMS LIKE ANYTHING 'HAND RENDERED' IS BACK IN NOW; IT'S LIKE ARTISANAL OR WHATEVER...SORRY, I HAVEN'T EVEN ASKED HOW YOU ARE – STILL DOING THAT MYSTERIOUS JOB IN YOUR HOMETOWN?

NO, I'M, UH...NOT DOING THAT ANYMORE.

WELL THEN – YOU HAVE TO COME AND WORK ON THIS THING...THERE'S LOADS OF STUFF TO DO THAT I KNOW YOU'LL BE REALLY GOOD AT. I MEAN, WHAT ELSE ARE YOU GOING TO DO?!

AFTER LOSING A NIGHT'S SLEEP OVER IT, I TEXT SHARYN TO SAY A PROVISIONAL YES. MOSTLY BECAUSE I CAN'T THINK OF ANY-THING ELSE TO DO...

...urse totally terrified! but ive been thinking about it - Yes, think i'd like to come and do it...THANKYOU so much S!

Congratulations! You've actually made a decision! ;) Seriously tho' its gotta be better than working for that old dude in your weird town. Amiright?

And you can stay at mine the whole time, we've got a spare ...Julie is off

I HAVEN'T SEEN THAT OLD DUDE AT ALL SINCE HIS EXIT ON THE GREEN THAT DAY.

I DID RIDE PAST HIS HOUSE LAST WEEK; HIS CAR WAS THERE, BUT ALL THE LIGHTS WERE OFF...

...WHICH JUST MADE ME WORRY MORE.

A FEW DAYS LATER, I GO TO SAY GOODBYE TO VAL, HOPING YET DREADING THAT I'LL SEE KEITH ON HIS ROUNDS. BUT ENCOUNTER ONLY KENNY.

HEY, KENNY, I'M LEAVING TOWN IN A FEW DAYS. I'VE GOT THIS NEW JOB...

OH YEAH, BRILLIANT!

SHORTLY...

WELL, BYE, KENNY.

YEAH, BYE THEN. SEE YOU AGAIN!

HE SAYS GOODBYE TO ME JUST LIKE HE ALWAYS DOES; AS IF WE'LL RUN INTO EACH OTHER IN A FEW DAYS' TIME.

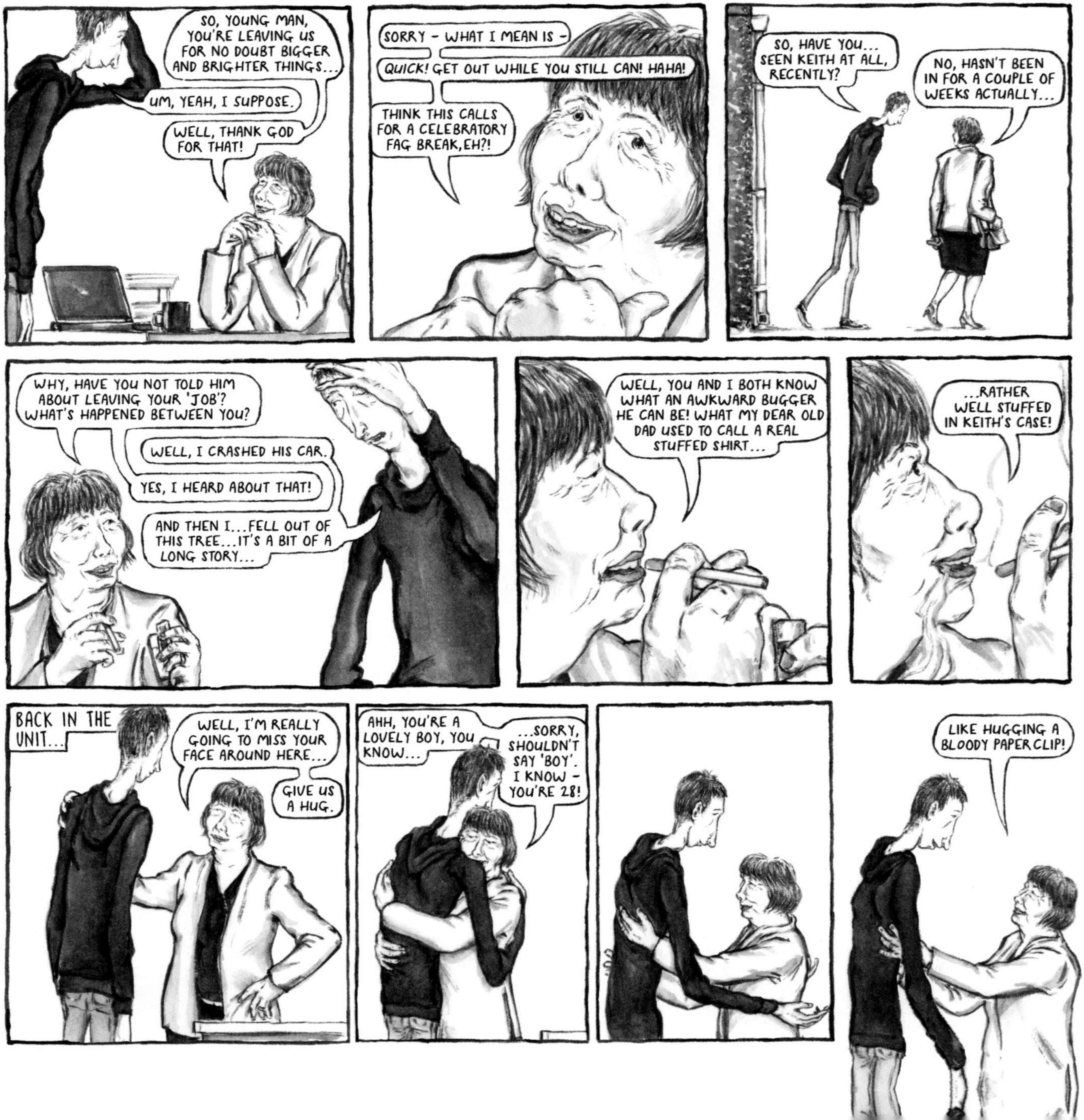
SO, YOUNG MAN, YOU'RE LEAVING US FOR NO DOUBT BIGGER AND BRIGHTER THINGS...
UM, YEAH, I SUPPOSE.
WELL, THANK GOD FOR THAT!
SORRY - WHAT I MEAN IS -
QUICK! GET OUT WHILE YOU STILL CAN! HAHA!
THINK THIS CALLS FOR A CELEBRATORY FAG BREAK, EH?!
SO, HAVE YOU... SEEN KEITH AT ALL, RECENTLY?
NO, HASN'T BEEN IN FOR A COUPLE OF WEEKS ACTUALLY...
WHY, HAVE YOU NOT TOLD HIM ABOUT LEAVING YOUR 'JOB'? WHAT'S HAPPENED BETWEEN YOU?
WELL, I CRASHED HIS CAR.
YES, I HEARD ABOUT THAT!
AND THEN I...FELL OUT OF THIS TREE...IT'S A BIT OF A LONG STORY...
WELL, YOU AND I BOTH KNOW WHAT AN AWKWARD BUGGER HE CAN BE! WHAT MY DEAR OLD DAD USED TO CALL A REAL STUFFED SHIRT...
...RATHER WELL STUFFED IN KEITH'S CASE!
BACK IN THE UNIT...
WELL, I'M REALLY GOING TO MISS YOUR FACE AROUND HERE...
GIVE US A HUG.
AHH, YOU'RE A LOVELY BOY, YOU KNOW...
...SORRY, SHOULDN'T SAY 'BOY'. I KNOW - YOU'RE 28!
LIKE HUGGING A BLOODY PAPERCLIP!

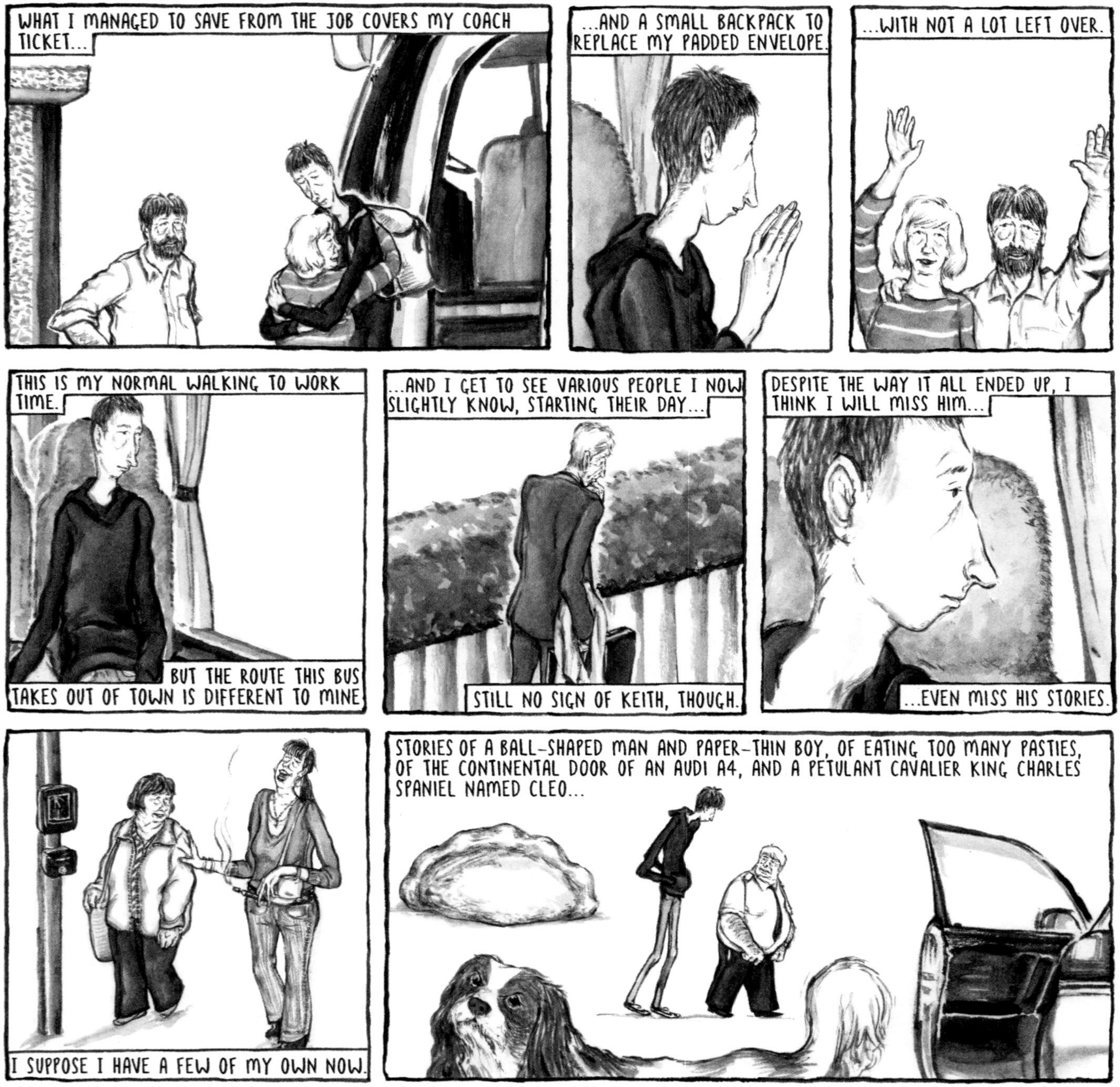
WHAT I MANAGED TO SAVE FROM THE JOB COVERS MY COACH TICKET...
...AND A SMALL BACKPACK TO REPLACE MY PADDED ENVELOPE.
...WITH NOT A LOT LEFT OVER.
THIS IS MY NORMAL WALKING TO WORK TIME.
BUT THE ROUTE THIS BUS TAKES OUT OF TOWN IS DIFFERENT TO MINE
...AND I GET TO SEE VARIOUS PEOPLE I NOW SLIGHTLY KNOW, STARTING THEIR DAY...
STILL NO SIGN OF KEITH, THOUGH.
DESPITE THE WAY IT ALL ENDED UP, I THINK I WILL MISS HIM...
...EVEN MISS HIS STORIES.
I SUPPOSE I HAVE A FEW OF MY OWN NOW.
STORIES OF A BALL-SHAPED MAN AND PAPER-THIN BOY, OF EATING TOO MANY PASTIES, OF THE CONTINENTAL DOOR OF AN AUDI A4, AND A PETULANT CAVALIER KING CHARLES SPANIEL NAMED CLEO...

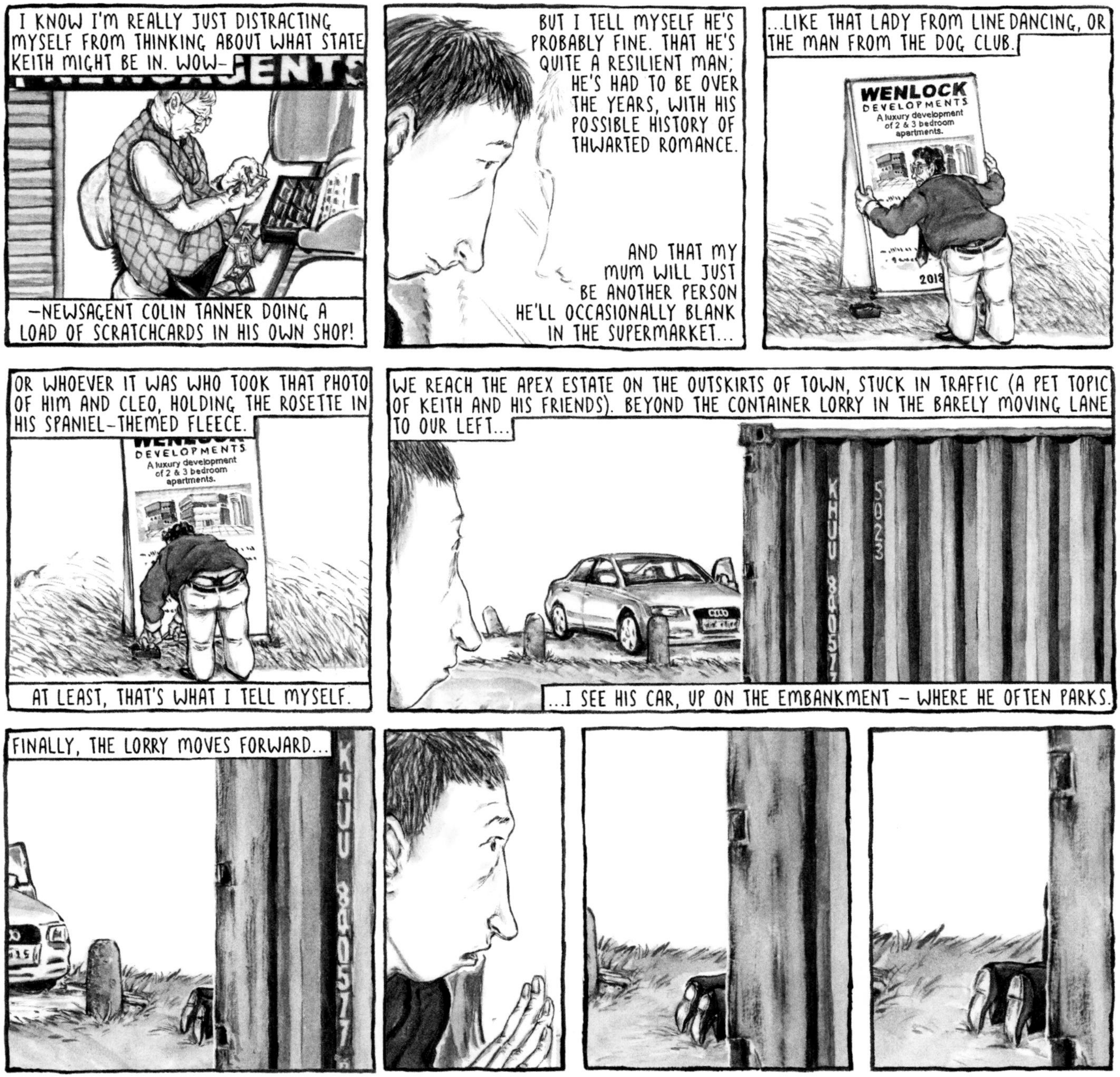
I KNOW I'M REALLY JUST DISTRACTING MYSELF FROM THINKING ABOUT WHAT STATE KEITH MIGHT BE IN. WOW—
—NEWSAGENT COLIN TANNER DOING A LOAD OF SCRATCHCARDS IN HIS OWN SHOP!
BUT I TELL MYSELF HE'S PROBABLY FINE. THAT HE'S QUITE A RESILIENT MAN; HE'S HAD TO BE OVER THE YEARS, WITH HIS POSSIBLE HISTORY OF THWARTED ROMANCE.
AND THAT MY MUM WILL JUST BE ANOTHER PERSON HE'LL OCCASIONALLY BLANK IN THE SUPERMARKET...
...LIKE THAT LADY FROM LINE DANCING, OR THE MAN FROM THE DOG CLUB.
WENLOCK
DEVELOPMENTS
A luxury development of 2 & 3 bedroom apartments.
2018
OR WHOEVER IT WAS WHO TOOK THAT PHOTO OF HIM AND CLEO, HOLDING THE ROSETTE IN HIS SPANIEL-THEMED FLEECE.
DEVELOPMENTS
A luxury development of 2 & 3 bedroom apartments.
AT LEAST, THAT'S WHAT I TELL MYSELF.
WE REACH THE APEX ESTATE ON THE OUTSKIRTS OF TOWN, STUCK IN TRAFFIC (A PET TOPIC OF KEITH AND HIS FRIENDS). BEYOND THE CONTAINER LORRY IN THE BARELY MOVING LANE TO OUR LEFT...
KHUU 880577
5023
...I SEE HIS CAR, UP ON THE EMBANKMENT — WHERE HE OFTEN PARKS.
FINALLY, THE LORRY MOVES FORWARD...
KHUU 880577

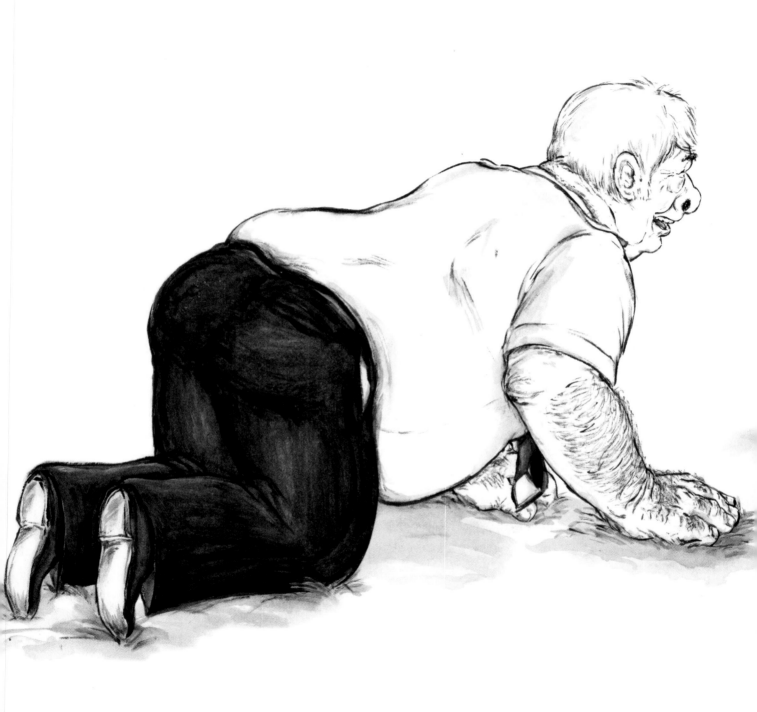

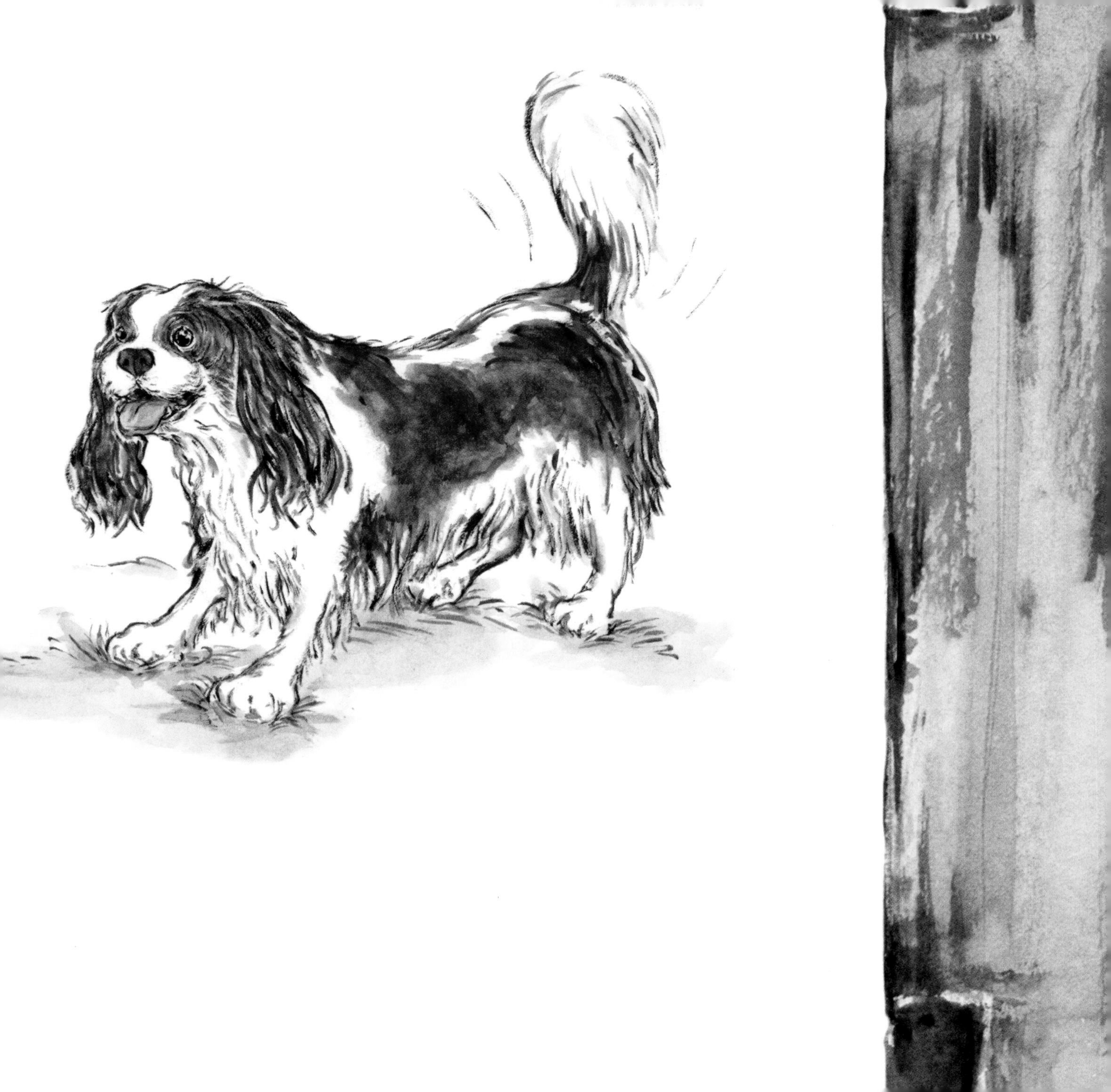

THE END.

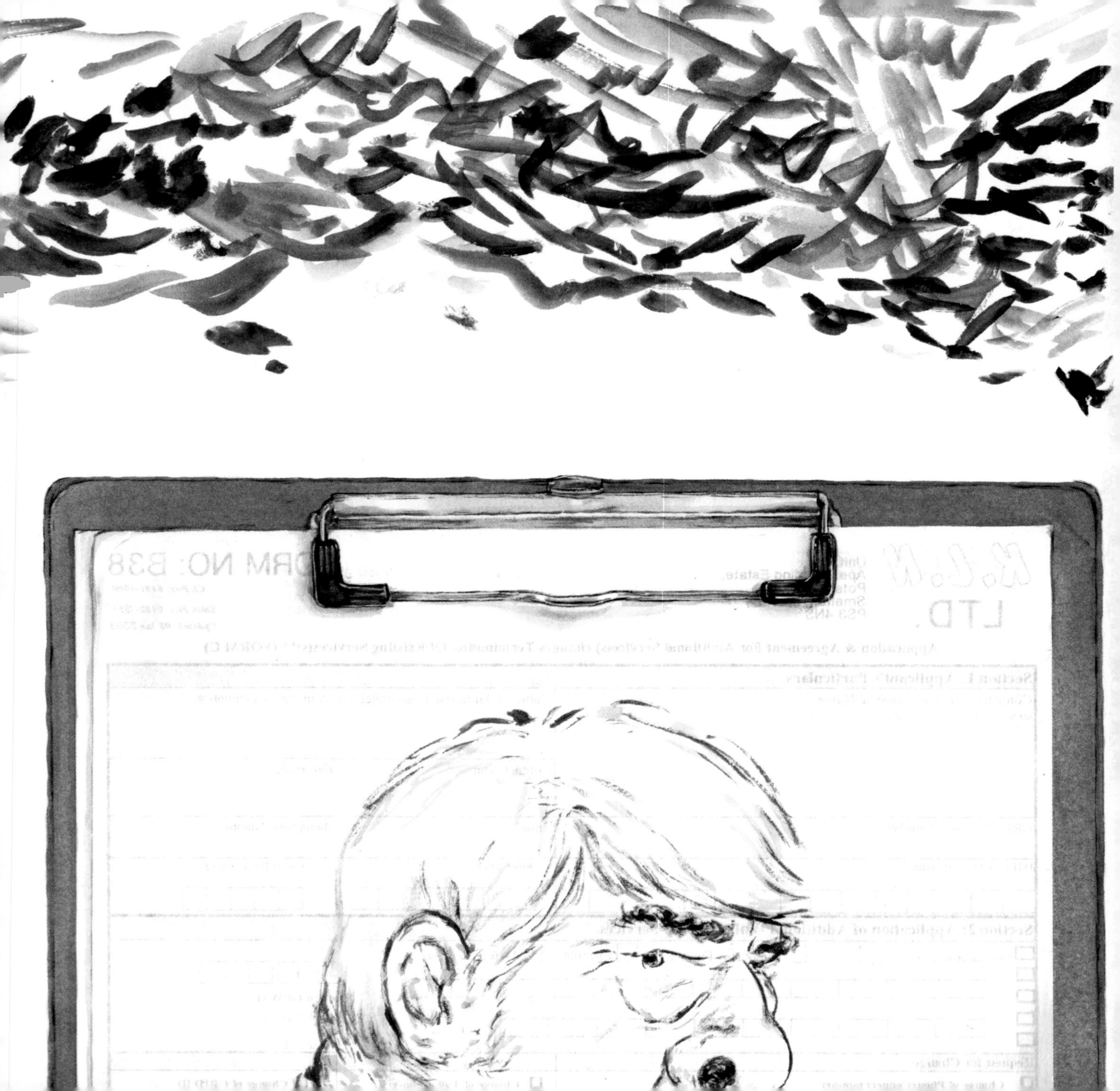